# MYTHS
# OF THE
# ANCIENT
# GREEKS

# MYTHS
# OF THE
# ANCIENT
# GREEKS

## RICHARD P. MARTIN

ILLUSTRATIONS BY PATRICK HUNT

NEW AMERICAN LIBRARY

New American Library
Published by New American Library, a division of
Penguin Putnam Inc., 375 Hudson Street,
New York, New York 10014, U.S.A.
Penguin Books Ltd, 80 Strand,
London WC2R 0RL, England
Penguin Books Australia Ltd, 250 Camberwell Road
Camberwell, Victoria 3124, Australia
Penguin Books Canada Ltd, 10 Alcorn Avenue,
Toronto, Ontario, Canada M4V 3B2
Penguin Books (N.Z.) Ltd, Cnr Rosedale and Airborne Roads,
Albany, Auckland 1310, New Zealand

Penguin Books Ltd, Registered Offices:
Harmondsworth, Middlesex, England

First published by New American Library, a division of Penguin Putnam Inc.

First Printing, April 2003
10 9 8 7 6 5 4 3 2 1

 REGISTERED TRADEMARK—MARCA REGISTRADA

LIBRARY OF CONGRESS CATALOGING IN PUBLICATION DATA:

Myths of the ancient Greeks / Richard P. Martin, [editor]; illustrations by Patrick Hunt.
   p.  cm.
   Includes bibliographical references and index.
   ISBN 0-451-20685-1 (alk. paper)
   1. Mythology, Greek. I. Martin, Richard P.

  BL783.M98   2003
  398.2'0938'01—dc21        2002070270

Set in Garamond #3
Designed by Ginger Legato
Printed in the United States of America

*For Tom and Catherine,*
*who liked stories*

# CONTENTS

# The Beginnings: Gods and Creatures

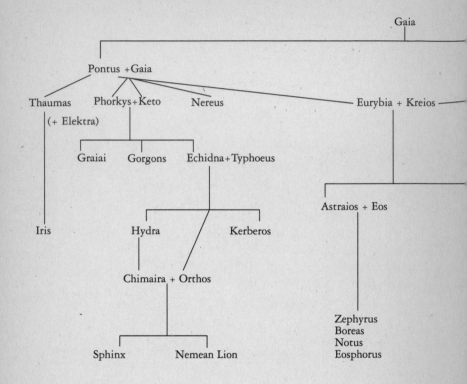

Gaia

Pontus +Gaia

Thaumas    Phorkys+Keto    Nereus    Eurybia + Kreios

(+ Elektra)

Graiai    Gorgons    Echidna+Typhoeus

Astraios + Eos

Iris

Hydra    Kerberos

Chimaira + Orthos

Zephyrus
Boreas
Notus
Eosphorus

Sphinx    Nemean Lion

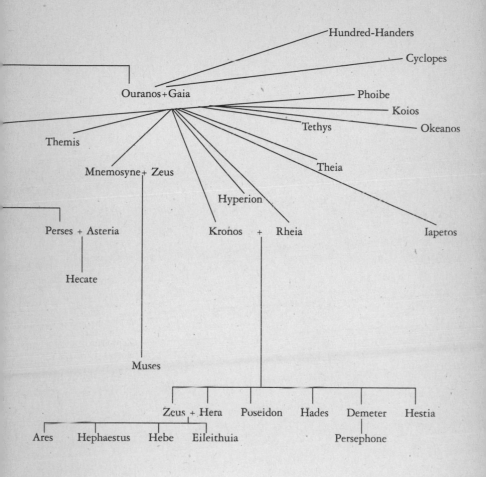

# OFFSPRING OF IAPETOS THE TITAN

Iapetos (son of Ouranos

Prometheus
+?

Deukalion +

Doros

Aiolos

Five daughters + Hermes

Nymphs      Satyrs      Kouretes

Perieres

Sisyphus                     Kretheus          Salmoneus
    +Merope                      +Tyro

Glaukos              Aison              ( * = by Poseidon)
  + Eurynome

                                         *Pelias      * Neleus +Chloris

*Bellerophon              Jason                        Nestor

and Gaia) + Klymene

Epimetheus
+ Pandora

Pyrrha (+ Zeus)

Hellen

Xuthus
+ Kreousa

Minyas

Achaios          Ion

Athamas          Deion+Diomede
+Nephele

Philonis

Phrixos      Helle

Philammon (by Apollo)      Autolykos (by Hermes)

Thamyris          Antikleia + Laertes

Odysseus

# Descendants of Atlas, Greek and Trojan

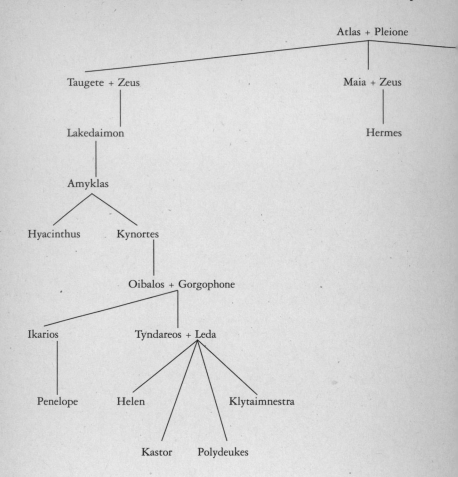

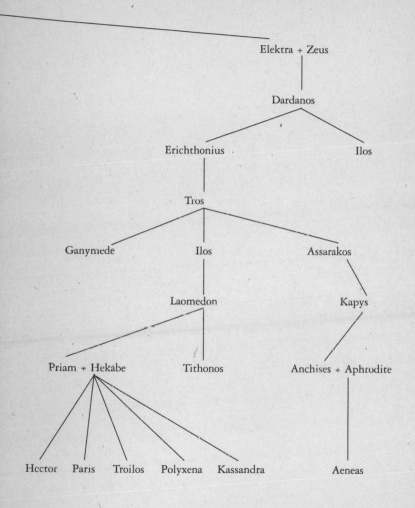

Elektra + Zeus

Dardanos

Erichthonius      Ilos

Tros

Ganymede      Ilos      Assarakos

Laomedon      Kapys

Priam + Hekabe      Tithonos      Anchises + Aphrodite

Hector   Paris   Troilos   Polyxena   Kassandra      Aeneas

# WARRIORS, KINGS, AND HEROINES FROM ZEUS

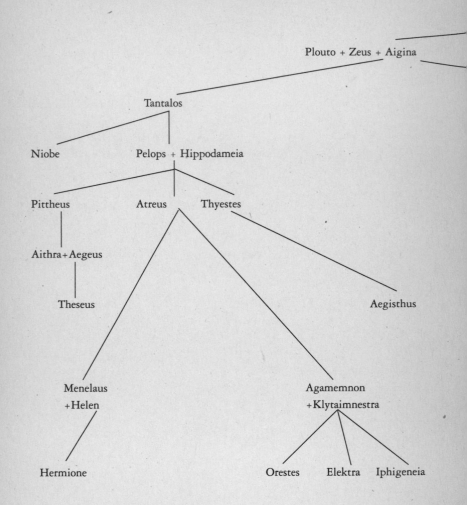

Plouto + Zeus + Aigina

Tantalos

Niobe

Pelops + Hippodameia

Pittheus

Atreus   Thyestes

Aithra+Aegeus

Theseus

Aegisthus

Menelaus
+Helen

Agamemnon
+Klytaimnestra

Hermione

Orestes   Elektra   Iphigeneia

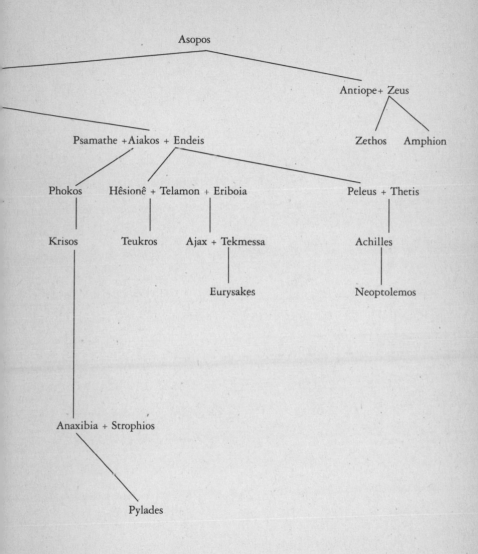

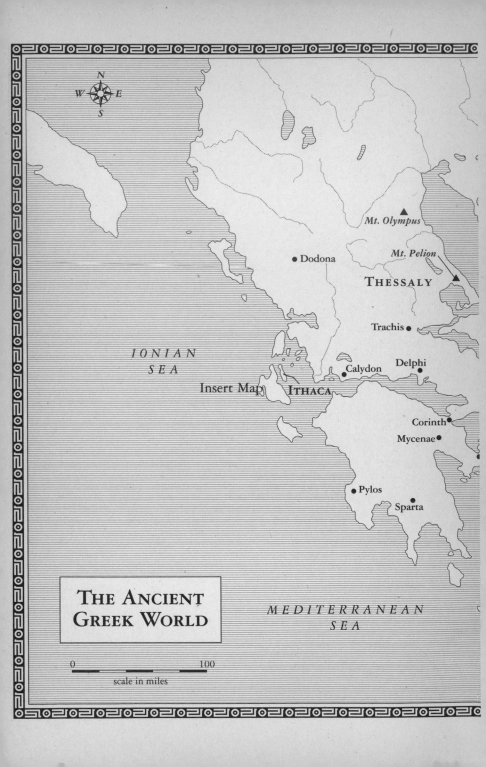

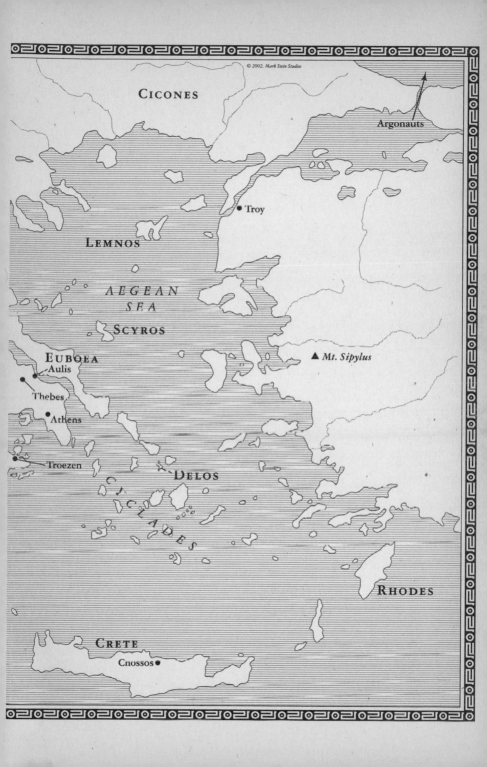

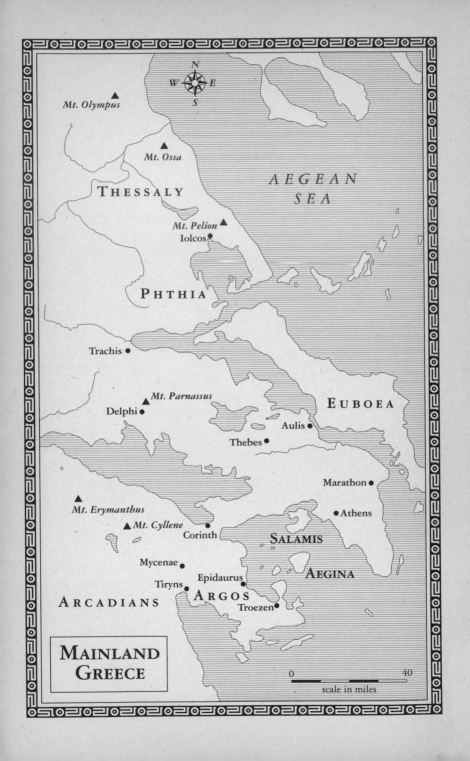

Mt. Olympus

Mt. Ossa

THESSALY

*AEGEAN
SEA*

Mt. Pelion
Iolcos

PHTHIA

Trachis

Mt. Parnassus
Delphi

EUBOEA

Aulis
Thebes

Marathon

Mt. Erymanthus

Mt. Cyllene
Corinth

Athens

SALAMIS

Mycenae

AEGINA

Tiryns
Epidaurus

ARCADIANS

ARGOS

Troezen

MAINLAND
GREECE

0                    40
scale in miles

# INTRODUCTION

MYTHS ARE STORIES THAT CON-
tinue to engage the imagina-
tion of a society over a long period of
time. The stories you are about to read were
told more than two thousand years ago by
Greeks who lived in communities all around the
Mediterranean Sea and beyond, from what is today
southern France to the eastern shore of the Black Sea,
from the northern Balkans to North Africa. They reflect
the thoughts of a complex civilization and at the same time
allow us to enter the vibrant private spaces of an archaic culture.
Long before they were written down, myths from Greek-speaking
lands were passed from one generation to the next by word of mouth.
Later, they were recorded in a bewildering number of epic and lyric
poems, tragedies, comedies, histories, scholarly compilations, travel
books, philosophical dialogues, and scientific works of all sorts, from
the eighth century B.C. until Constantinople fell to the Ottoman
Turks in 1453 A.D. Although some entire works made their way down
to our time, painstakingly copied and recopied in manuscripts until
the age of printing, many of these ancient writings are today lost. We
have what survived in papyrus fragments or literary quotations. Already by the third century B.C. the Romans had discovered this rich
body of stories and had begun to exploit it in creating their own art
and literature. By 100 B.C., when the Roman empire had expanded to

include most of the Greek-speaking world, the classic myths had become a part of basic schooling. Through Latin sources—especially the works of the poet Ovid—the tales found their way into later European culture, where they became so deeply embedded in art, literature, and thought that, to this day, no one in the West who is unfamiliar with Greek myths can seriously claim to be an educated person.

At the same time, there is the risk that the myths become *too* familiar to us. The Greek gods and goddesses have been taken over for less than divine objects, providing labels and images for everything from rockets to sneakers to cement. Jellyfish, software programs, moths, and Jupiter's moons bear names from myths. Cartoons and children's books have spread awareness of the stories, but at the cost of distorting and trivializing them. Meanwhile, self-help and assertiveness-training books appropriate myths for their own ends, urging us to follow our quests, find inner heroes and goddesses, mimic Artemis in the boardroom or Herakles in the gym. Tales that once unified a whole culture, enabling it to reflect on major public concerns, have largely turned into private icons, ripped from their social, religious, and artistic roots.

A book that presents these tales to the twenty-first century must do more than make the stories known to those encountering them for the first time. It must also defamiliarize the tales for those who already know the gist of them. Classical scholarship for the past two hundred years has increasingly uncovered the contexts for Greek myths. Thousands of books and articles have explored the intricate web of meaning that binds these narratives to their society and to one another. Thus, even people who recall the basic stories might not be aware of the latest thinking on how the stories fit within ancient Greek culture. My headnotes, the sections introducing each "book," include the interpretive work of scholars, while not overwhelming the down-to-earth retelling that follows. I hope that the combined method makes myth more familiar and yet keeps it at one remove—enough to remind the reader that the ancient Greeks were never quite like us.

## WHERE DID GREEK MYTHS COME FROM?

There are two types of answers to this question: practical and speculative. Both should be kept in mind.

Practically speaking, myths derive from writings in ancient Greek (or Latin writings based on Greek sources). The major surviving works include:

•The *Iliad* and *Odyssey* (roughly 700 B.C.). These two epics attributed to the poet Homer tell the story of the siege of Troy and the return home of one of the heroes. They contain some flashbacks to prior mythic events, but only allude to and do not dramatize many stories recorded elsewhere (for example, the judgment of Paris, the building of the Trojan Horse, or the death of Achilles).

•The *Theogony.* Attributed to the poet Hesiod, who was thought to be contemporary with Homer, this composition in dactylic hexameter is our earliest and most dramatic rendering of events from the beginning of the world up through the marriages of Zeus. Additional details on some myths (e.g., Pandora, the Five Ages) are provided by the *Works and Days*, a composition based on traditional wisdom and agricultural lore attributed to the same poet. The (now fragmentary) *Catalogue of Women,* said to be by Hesiod, tells of love affairs between mortals and gods.

•The *Homeric Hymns* (seventh–sixth centuries B.C.). A collection of narrative poems in epic style, praising the Greek gods. Five of these (to Demeter, Apollo, Hermes, Aphrodite, and Dionysus) provide the earliest continuous stories of the major episodes concerning the divinities.

•Pindar (518–438 B.C.). A composer of many types of lyric songs for choral performance, he is best known for victory odes in praise of winners at the great athletic games, men and boys whom the poet compared to traditional heroes of the distant past. These *epinikia* are dense with mythic allusions, and many times they provide narrative variants found in no other source.

•The tragedians. The three most celebrated Athenian writers of tragic plays, already famous by the end of their own era, were Aeschylus (525–456 B.C.), Sophocles (496–406 B.C.), and Euripides (485–406 B.C.). From their surviving dramatic productions, though a fraction of their total output, we have learned many valuable details about myths, especially the stories of events surrounding the Trojan War and the siege of Thebes.

•Herodotus (mid-fifth century B.C.). The "father of history" in his long narrative about the war between Greeks and Persians includes a number of myths and legends heard from local informants as he traveled through Greek and foreign lands. While he is skeptical about many of these stories, Herodotus does treat as plausible historical fact a number of narratives we would identify as myth.

•Callimachus (third century B.C.). A scholar-poet from Alexandria, Egypt, he composed highly polished verses filled with allusions to myth and legend. Of these, six hymns in Homeric style survive intact. They are valuable for their stories of Zeus, Artemis, Apollo, Athena, Demeter, and the sacred island Delos. Hundreds of fragments from papyrus scrolls that once contained copies of his poetry give us further scraps of information about gods and heroes.

•Apollonius of Rhodes (third century B.C.). Another Alexandrian poet, he composed the epic *Argonautica* in four books (5,835 hexameter lines). It tells the story of Jason and his quest for the Golden Fleece. The poem had a great influence on later writers, such as Virgil, and still survives in its entirety.

•"Apollodorus." The original scholar with this name lived from about 180 to 120 B.C. and wrote historical chronicles and an account of Greek religion. The surviving *Library* that goes under his name is a long summary of mythic stories from other sources, many of which did not survive in their original form. The book was probably composed in the first or second century A.D. and attributed to the earlier scholar.

•Plutarch (50–120 A.D.). A Greek philosopher and antiquarian writer best known for his series of twenty-three "parallel lives" comparing the careers of famous Greeks and Romans. His "biography" of Theseus is a valuable compendium of ancient traditions about the Athenian hero.

•Pausanias (mid-second century A.D.). Greek travel writer whose *Description of Greece* preserves many myths connected with the shrines and sanctuaries he visited.

•Virgil (70–19 B.C.). Roman poet whose brooding and sensitive epic, the *Aeneid,* drew on the whole range of Greek literature in narrating the story of the Trojan hero who fled to Italy and established the beginnings of Rome.

•Ovid (43 B.C.–17 A.D.). A prolific Roman poet, his intricate and brilliant *Metamorphoses*—an epic poem in fifteen books—tells those mythic stories that revolve around supernatural changes in form. This poem became the single most influential narrative about myth in Western literature. His sources included many Greek works now completely lost.

In addition to these literary sources, we have to take into account an enormously valuable artistic tradition that transmitted Greek myths: ancient vase painting. Thousands of these artistic works survive. They illustrate episodes from mythic stories that are otherwise known, and many times present other versions that have not survived in writing. (One famous example, a vase now in the Vatican Museum, shows Jason emerging from the mouth of the dragon that guarded the Fleece. In this book, see pages 130 and 176.)

All this may seem like a large amount of material. Yet if the evidence of other traditional cultures is a guide, there were most likely hundreds of other stories in circulation that have not come down to us in any form. Storytelling has always been primarily an oral art, so it is likely that many early narratives tied to the specific occasions of archaic Greek life vanished when people no longer practiced or understood the ritual events connected to the stories. Furthermore, villagers in one locale in the days before writing became generally used might have had a stock of tales completely different from those living less than fifty miles away. After the eighth century B.C., there began a trend toward privileging the particular myths and institutions that all the Greeks held in common. This process, called "Panhellenization" by scholars, slowly began to erase or override local variations in religious cults, song making, and other cultural forms. The myths we read today have been reshaped in this way for millennia, varied, shifted, and elaborated to serve different audiences and goals.

This brings us to the second type of answer to the question of myth origins. This involves speculation based on comparisons with the small-scale cultures that we can still explore in remote parts of the world today. Myths may come down to us in art and literature, but they seem to have developed in more general social performances. In other words, myth functions as a sort of communication system, a way of making meaningful statements and assertions within a group that knows the stories. In this connection, it is important to realize that the Greek word *muthos* (the basis of our English word) originally referred to an act of speaking. Translators of early Greek texts usually employ the English terms "word" or "story" when *muthos* occurs. Within our earliest complete texts, however—the Homeric epics—*muthos* has a quite specific range of meaning: it refers to the sorts of speech-acts that demand action or command respect. When Agamemnon gives orders to the troops, or old Nestor recalls his youth (to teach younger heroes how to act), the poet describes the speech as a *muthos*. Usually, men make such speeches. Among Homeric women characters, only the laments they make are regularly so named.

We can imagine that such acts had to rely both on a depiction of the past and on references to glorious ancestors or origins. Gradually, such assertions came to be recognized as a different kind of speech unlike everyday stories. One could never prove or disprove a *muthos*, precisely because a tale of this type referred to the distant past. Until the use of writing became widespread in Greek lands, well after 800 B.C., it was impossible for anyone to check "facts." Historical reality was simply what was remembered and talked about. Not by accident, the ancient Greek word for "truth" (*alêtheia*) is a compound word meaning, literally, "not-forgotten-ness." (Compare the name for the River of Forgetfulness, *Lêthê*).

Nor is it by chance that the older meaning of *muthos* as "authoritative speech" began to change, even within Greek culture, to mean something closer to "lie" or "fiction" exactly at the period when the Greeks started using alphabetic writing, which they borrowed from the Phoenicians. Once such stories began to be written down, anyone could compare multiple versions of what used to pass for the single truth. By the sixth century B.C., it was being discovered that the versions never matched up. As happens in an oral culture, the old stories varied widely from region to region, even from one family to another. Thus, Greek thinkers and writers in the more modern, literate culture that evolved began to criticize the "myths." It was possible to interpret the stories within Homeric poetry as allegories. We know that at least one man, Theagenes of Rhegium (a Greek city in southern Italy), used this method in teaching that the clash between Hephaestus and the river Scamander in the *Iliad* was really just a way of describing a cosmic war of physical elements: fire versus water. By the next century, enlightened intellectuals were dismantling all the "myths." Their use of the term and their way of talking about the old tales hardly differs from the attitude of scholars all the way through the nineteenth century. Prodicus of Ceos, a contemporary of Socrates in the latter half of the fifth century B.C., went so far as to say that Demeter and Dionysus arose from the thinking of "primitive" people who worshiped as gods the substances that were most beneficial in their lives: bread and wine.

To try to push back beyond the centuries in which Greek myths were recorded, elaborated, and analyzed involves asking much larger questions, to which there are no satisfactory answers. Why *these* particular heroes and tales? What was the influence of stories from other cultures, either from contemporary Near Eastern neighbors or from ancient pre-Greek peoples, on Greek myth? How did myths fit into religion, and where did Greek rituals come from? What deeper meanings do these myths have?

## STUDYING GREEK MYTHS

As scholars attempted to solve these mysteries, a number of methods were developed, starting in the eighteenth century. As we have seen, the roots of myth analysis extend much earlier, back to the Greeks themselves. More modern critics of myth had the advantage of using comparative material from other cultures to try to unlock the secrets of ancient tales. At the same time, they had the disadvantage of distance. More often than not, the scholars of the last few centuries unwittingly imposed their own views of religion and society on archaic Greece. Nevertheless, much valuable work has been done to clarify the meanings of myth. Here are some of the leading ways of understanding the material, in their historical contexts.

### MYTH AND RITUAL

When the modern science of anthropology was developing in the second half of the nineteenth century, British explorers and soldiers were expanding the empire and reporting on the customs and beliefs of distant lands. One scholar especially made use of this flood of new data to approach Greek myth in a fresh way. James George Frazer (1854–1941), the first person in the world to hold a university chair in social anthropology, was the son of a well-off Glasgow merchant family. He studied classical literature at Glasgow University and later at Trinity College, Cambridge, and edited Pausanias, Apollodorus, and the *Fasti* of Ovid. Interested especially in the obscure rites and customs described by these ancient writers, in 1890 Frazer published in two volumes *The Golden Bough: A Study in Comparative Religion.* In it he set out to answer two questions about a custom described in ancient sources: why was the priest at Nemi in Italy obliged to kill his predecessor and why, before doing so, did he have to pluck a branch of the sacred grove there (which Frazer speculated was the "golden bough" mentioned in Virgil's *Aeneid*)? Frazer's answer, which he expanded and elaborated over the next twenty-five years, was that the priest represented an original sacred king, who had to be killed and revived (in the form of a new priest) each year to make sure that the crops would grow. By 1915, Frazer had moved from this problem in ancient Roman religion to shaping a general theory about how human thought developed. For him, myths and rituals attached to them were what gave birth to religion and even science. By assuming that all humans underwent the same stages of development, he tried to use the new data about distant "exotic" tribes to reconstruct stages in Greek and Roman intellectual evolution.

Despite many criticisms by later anthropologists, Frazer's work on myth and ritual had a vast influence. Even beyond technical scholarship, it inspired creative writers such as T. S. Eliot (who cites Frazer as a source for his poem *The Waste Land*), Yeats and Joyce, Lawrence and Conrad. Ironically, the scholars whose work made Frazer popular among students of Greek myth relied primarily on the bolder, earlier views that Frazer himself later gave up. Between 1900 and 1915, a close-knit group of Classicists at Cambridge University began to use Frazer's method to reconsider the main monuments of Greek culture, the classical art and literature that was widely held to be the ideal of taste and civilized culture.

The informal "Cambridge school" of interpreters centered around a remarkable woman from Yorkshire, Jane Ellen Harrison (1850–1928)—known to some as Bloody Jane, since she sometimes carried to an extreme Frazer's view that Greek myth arose from misunderstood rituals of the most primitive type. (She seems to have been convinced, for instance, that the ecstatic female followers of Dionysus really did tear apart animals with their bare hands. When the philosopher Bertrand Russell promised to buy Harrison a bull if she and her devotees would demonstrate how this could be done, Harrison declined.) In *Prolegomena to the Study of Greek Religion* (1903) and *Themis* (1912), Harrison focused on the importance of darker "chthonic" rites within Greek religion and also argued that myth and ritual coexisted in Greece, as mutually dependent ways of expressing religious feeling. Some of her major insights have lasted the test of time. In recent years, increasingly sophisticated applications of the method, controlled by better anthropology, have been able to suggest intriguing connections. At the same time, scholars have come to see that myth can often represent, in a dramatic, thrilling way, and project into the past, what are actually very ordinary everyday customs. It does not take real madness and the killing of cows to produce the tale of the Bacchae.

### PSYCHOLOGICAL APPROACHES

Sigmund Freud (1856–1939) and Carl Gustav Jung (1875–1961) began the study of myths from the standpoint of psychology. Both had European classical educations and could quote passages in Greek and Latin from memory. Naturally, in their studies on the human mind, both men turned first to the world of Greek mythology for analogies and examples. Freud, the son of a Jewish wool merchant, spent most of his life in Vienna, where he began work as a neurologist and later practiced and wrote about the revolutionary treatment method he termed "psychoanalysis." In *The Interpretation of Dreams* (1899), Freud argued that what we see in our sleeping hours are psychologically necessary means of wish fulfillment. It was in this connection that Freud made his first public statement of what he came to call the "Oedipus complex" (see Book 8: The Saga of Thebes).

The similarity between myths and dreams has often been noticed. Australian aboriginal peoples make the connection directly when they talk of the "Dreamtime" as the distant foundation period when their sacred ancestors lived and their sacred stories took shape. The major gain that Freudian psychology offers for the study of myth lies in the detailed analogy drawn between myth and dream as *processes*. It seems that myths and dreams have several common characteristics. In both, various elements can be unconsciously welded into a single symbolic expression. Just as one might dream about an animal that has human traits, myths contain strange combinations of creatures, such as the Sirens, often depicted as women with the bodies of birds. In myths as well as dreams, a symbolic element can be substituted for a different object or abstraction. A golden fleece means kingship, or an apple signifies immortality. Finally, feelings can be transmuted into visual images. The winged horse, Pegasus, seems to embody the ambition and exultation of his rider, Bellerophon, much as dreams of flying express the feelings of discovery and joy. Psychoanalytic criticism has been best in interpreting the ugly and bizarre elements in such stories as the birth and succession of the gods, which feature chaos, castration, and swallowing of children.

C. G. Jung, the second major figure whose theories touch on myth, was a Swiss psychologist, and friend and collaborator with Freud from 1907 until 1913, when their differences over the role of sexuality in neurosis drove them apart. After the break, Jung developed the influential notions of "archetypes" and the "collective unconscious." The "archetypes" for Jung represented an archaic level of human consciousness that gave rise to specific, regularly recurring types of motifs and images in both myths and dreams. Whereas Freud had seen in dream imagery an unsystematic, uniquely personal expression of one person's psyche, Jung saw signs of a shared, "collective" psychic structure. Some of the many instinctual "archetypal" images Jung identified include those of the mother and father, the trickster, the wise old man, the hero, and the *animus* or *anima*. This last pair is a unique contribution by Jung, referring to the unconscious images that women form of men (*animus*) and men of women (*anima*). In another formulation, Jung describes the *anima* as the "feminine side" of a man, and even attributed problems of violence and war to the underdevelopment of this facet in the modern world.

Whether or not Jungian theory explains the *origin* of any given myth does not alter the success that his theories had in psychotherapy. Patients can be taught to handle relationships through recognizing how their unconscious reliance on or resistance to archetypes blocks psychological wholeness. Jung's influence was overwhelming in the work of a recent American popularizer, Joseph Campbell (1904–87). In *The Hero with a Thousand Faces* (1949) and many subsequent books, Campbell rummaged through worldwide mythology to construct a "monomyth" of the hero, knowledge of which, he claimed, can help each person discover his or her individuality. A spate of Campbell-inspired self-help books and workshops has now turned the individual's quest for "inner" heroes and heroines into a profitable segment of popular psychology. To some, this is simply an updated form of the ancient method of turning myths into coded narratives, stories that systematically conceal their "real" meanings under the guise of heroic or supernatural events.

## SOCIOLOGICAL APPROACHES

The most recent mode of interpreting myths relates them to society. This work is an outgrowth of two traditions. One in France dates its modern beginnings from Émile Durkheim (1858–1917) and his collaborators on the journal *Année sociologique*. The other is a "functionalist" position most famously developed by Bronislaw Malinowski

(1884–1942), the Polish anthropologist who influenced a generation of scholars through his renowned seminars at the London School of Economics. Durkheim's central ideas—that religion is a symbolic expression, or "collective representation," of underlying social structures, and that all the cultural expressions of primitive societies are tightly knit together—had a great influence on several generations of French classical scholars. Malinowski, a social anthropologist who felt the powerful influence of J. G. Frazer when young, did intensive fieldwork in the Trobriand Islands of Melanesian New Guinea during the later years of World War I. This experience led to his formulation of a distinctive approach to the role of myth within culture. For him, myth codified the beliefs and morals of a given culture, and was an active force in holding together the social fabric. Myth, wrote Malinowski, was a "charter" for social beliefs.

In the study of actual myths, ancient or modern, the notion of "charter" opens up new perspectives. In the cosmogonic stories of Hesiod's *Theogony,* we can now see that the tales do nothing less than authorize a society's gender roles, agricultural practices, family structures, economic exchanges, and legal procedures. What the functional approach does *not* do is explain the variety and change within myth systems. Why should there be multiple versions of a story within one society if in fact the myths continually prop up social roles that all people acknowledge? Here, more attention has to be paid to the innovations made by a person telling the myth aloud. Because stories work with a limited number of symbols and narrative paths, not unlike a language with its finite resources of grammar, any "speaker" can become adept enough to manipulate the system. By making a story the tribe controls itself, true enough; but a subgroup, or even an individual within the society, can gain power in the same way, through myth. Herodotus reports that Peisistratus took charge as a tyrant in sixth-century B.C. Athens by claiming that Athena (as she did in myths) was accompanying his heroic return, riding in a chariot before him. Because of his propaganda parade, the Athenians welcomed the tyrant, a fact that dismayed Herodotus. The rationalistic critics in the fifth century were already having trouble understanding the way myth worked in their own culture just a century before.

## COMPARATIVE MYTHOLOGY

Another method differs from the broader use of comparisons made by anthropologists and sociologists studying major institutions—sacrifice, taboo, matrilinear descent, and so forth—in various cultures. The idea of "comparative mythology" is a descendant of the modern discovery that languages, like flora and fauna, occur in historically related families descended from common "parent" languages. This idea gave birth in the early nineteenth century to comparative historical linguistics. As did anthropology and sociology, comparative linguistics grew in connection with European colonial expansion. A British judge in Calcutta, Sir William Jones (1746–94), is credited with first bringing to the world's attention the resemblances among Sanskrit, Greek, and Latin. The insight that these languages "have sprung from some common source, which, perhaps, no longer exists," heralded a century of intensive work by linguists. It is now known that the Balto-Slavic, Celtic, Germanic, Indo-Iranian, and Anatolian language families, along with Greek and Latin, are descended from a single parent language, probably spoken in the area of southern Russia around 3000 B.C. Just as we would have to assume, on the basis of similarities among French, Italian, Spanish, and Portuguese, that something like Latin once existed, even if no texts of that language survived, so we presume the existence of an "Indo-European" language. No texts survive from the language, and we can only guess what concepts it expressed from an analysis of shared vocabulary in the daughter tongues.

Early comparatists often cast wide nets with their reconstructions. Max Müller (1823–1900), a German Sanskritist who spent most of his scholarly life at Oxford, was the first scholar to extend systematically this sort of linguistic detective work into the realms of comparative mythology and religion. Nowadays, he is remembered chiefly for the idea that mythical gods were originally natural phenomena—the sun, moon, dawn, rivers, and so forth—which had been described by primitive "Aryans" in metaphorical terms that later were misinterpreted and taken to refer to persons. (The linguistic misreading thus implied led Müller to call myth "a disease of language.") Müller gives the example of the story of Daphne, a nymph changed into the laurel tree in order to escape Apollo, who once pursued her. Her name, he claims, originally signified "shining." Apollo, he says, was worshiped as a sun god; thus Apollo's pursuit originally signified the driving away of dawn by the sun. In case after case of this type, Müller's use of the philological method not only knit together the myths of Vedic India, Greece, Rome, and other cultures, but neatly overcame the apparent scandals in many ancient stories. Through this reading, Apollo changes from a lecherous nymph chaser into a more properly Victorian meteorological explanation.

In this century, the French scholar Georges Dumézil (1898–1986) almost single-handedly revived the study of comparative mythology. He conducted numerous studies of older literature in Indo-European languages, as well as work on myths from the Caucasus region. Dumézil was a student of Marcel Mauss and Marcel Granet, two associates of Émile Durkheim. He thus brought to the study of myths a much more sophisticated theoretical outlook than had been available to Müller. Dumézil's "new comparative mythology" makes brilliant and detailed equations among mythic motifs in Irish, Greek, Roman, Indic, Iranian, and Norse traditions. The parallels that he draws between the Greek hero Herakles, for example, and the Scandinavian warrior Starkadr—both of whom are known for violating the rules of their respective cultures—place these figures in an entirely new light, as characters that define the structure of society. Dumézil's abiding concern has been to show how these Indo-European myths embody a specific *social ideology*. For Dumézil, as for Malinowski and the followers of Durkheim, myth represents one strand in a tightly knit web of social institutions. Unlike his predecessors, however, Dumézil dealt with cultures that an anthropologist could no longer observe, and ultimately with a "culture"—Indo-European—without an identified physical location or artifacts, one deduced solely from the reconstruction of linguistic forms.

## CONTEMPORARY ISSUES IN GREEK MYTH

The study of ancient stories is often a barometer of modern concerns. Thus it happens that two politically charged and controversial approaches to the origin of Greek culture and its myths have recently gained attention. Both approaches have drawn support from broader research on groups that had been widely neglected in academic circles until the mid-twentieth century: women and African Americans.

Feminist criticism, which has changed the face of Classical studies, especially in the areas of Greek and Roman social history, gives prominence to the experiences of actual ancient women, their roles, contributions, and creative expressions. In the analysis of myth, the impact of feminist scholarship can be seen in the many innovative studies produced in the last quarter century on certain collective categories (goddesses, heroines, nymphs) and on such individual figures as Helen, Medea, Penelope, Circe, and Calypso. While most of this research has found ready acceptance, one question remains fiercely debated—whether Greek myths as we know them show traces of a suppressed, pre-Greek "matriarchal" culture in which women were dominant.

The late Marija Gimbutas of UCLA, an archaeologist of prehistoric Europe, attempted to prove that successive waves of invasions across Europe in the period from 4000 to 2000 B.C., by speakers of "Indo-European" (the parent language of Greek, Latin, Germanic, Slavic, Celtic and other dialect groups), led to a clash of ideologies and mythologies. In such studies as *The Language of the Goddess* (1989) and *The Civilization of the Goddess* (1991), she claimed that the original inhabitants, with a sexually egalitarian society and worshiping one primary goddess associated with earth, were eventually subjected to a male-dominated hierarchical social structure devoted to a masculine sky god. The goddess in her various forms was absorbed into the invading religion; her powers were split and reconfigured under the names of different wives, daughters, or consorts of the new male pantheon. Traces of an Old European goddess cult survive in folklore and customs, especially in the Baltic region, according to Gimbutas.

It is not difficult to see how this vision, which has roots in the mid-nineteenth-century writings of Bachofen and other scholars, might be fitted to progressive social views in the present: women's equality would count as a return to a forgotten golden age. Archaeologists, however, have given the work of Gimbutas a skeptical reception. The major objection is that such work is speculative, claiming to reconstruct a world of thought from the mute remains of carved symbols and figurines. To deduce that Old Europeans strongly believed in regeneration, from the evidence of some graves that she interprets as "egg-shaped" or "uterus-shaped," or that are decorated with concentric circles, begs a number of questions. In the absence of documents, such equations can remain only a vague possibility. Even the alleged worship of Mother Earth in prehistoric Europe is moot.

Another controversial figure whose work touches on the study of Greek myth is Martin Bernal, professor of Chinese studies and of government at Cornell. *Black Athena: The Afroasiatic Roots of Classical Civilization* (1987), the first book of a multivolume study, gained attention far beyond the field of Greek studies with its claims that deep-seated racism and anti-Semitism among Classical scholars had for more than a century suppressed the truth about the origins of Hellenic civilization. According to Bernal, those origins were to be sought in the older civilizations of Egypt and Phoenicia. He has made many claims based on supposed linguistic borrowings from Egyptian and Semitic languages into Greek—by his estimate, more than a third of the vocabulary of Greek would stem from such sources. Myth, as well, is called on to support his arguments. For instance, the stories that Kadmos from Phoenicia colonized Thebes in Greece, or that Danaos came to Argos from Egypt, are seen by Bernal to contain a core of fact. Decrying what he calls the European or "Aryan" model, according to which non-Hellenic sources played no role in the birth of Greek culture, Bernal advocates a return to an "ancient" model of Greek cultural development. Bernal notes in defense of this model that prominent Greek thinkers themselves, especially Herodotus and Plato, credited Egyptian culture with many of the distinctive traits of their own civilization.

In 1996 a group of twenty experts sought to rebut Bernal's theses in a collective volume, *Black Athena Revisited* (edited by Mary Lefkowitz and Guy Rogers). Among their many counterarguments were demonstrations that Bernal's linguistic equations lacked plausibility or precision, and that ancient art and artifacts did not bear out his claims. At the same time, no one now denies that some central myths of early Greece—such as the Kingship of Heaven cycle in Hesiod—owe much to earlier stories from civilizations of Asia Minor, especially that of the Hittites (on which see Martin West, *The East Face of Helicon,* 1997). But the idea of massive influence of Phoenicia or Egypt cannot be sustained.

Bernal has recently defended his ideas anew in *Black Athena Writes Back* (2001). Meanwhile, his views have been welcomed by Afrocentrist scholars, who make even wider claims that Greeks stole nearly all their major cultural institutions—democracy and philosophy included—from Egyptians (claimed to be black Africans, as were, they assert, Socrates and Cleopatra). Despite overwhelming scholarly evidence against these ideas (marshaled in the 1996 volume by the Wellesley classicist Mary Lefkowitz, *Not Out of Africa: How Afrocentrism Became an Excuse to Teach Myth as History*), the issue still sparks heated debate. At any event, discussions like these remind us that one of the abiding gifts of Greek culture has been the tools with which we can sift through the residue of *muthos,* or "traditional utterance," by means of *historia,* or "research." The Greeks themselves were the first to appreciate the essential differences between these two ways of looking at the world.

## INNOVATING, ENTERTAINING, AND THIS RETELLING

As we have said, myths are stories. Put simply, they tell the enthralling narratives that people in any culture want. For the nineteenth century, the closest art form to myth was the novel. Readers modeled themselves on fictional characters, and the society depicted in stories became an ideal (or distorted but alluring) reflection of life. People could communicate with one another through reference to "Werther" or "Heathcliff." For the past few generations, movies have taken on a similar role in shaping society's imagination. But in the days before either of these forms of mass entertainment, storytelling sessions and public performances about supernatural beings and great men and women of the past were an important part of community life, as they still are in many parts of the world. Myth familiarized the world, but also made it strange, unpredictable, and exciting.

Where myths come from, precisely how they work, and why they use such fantastic and oddly compelling images and narratives will never be completely explained, even though scholars and artists have thought and written about these powerful stories for two thousand years. On one point we can be certain, however. The teller of a myth is always both a reteller and an innovator. Paradoxically, the more closely involved in the remote past and its stories the teller becomes, the more liberated he or she is to tell them afresh. The story material is there; the rest is up to the narrator. Even the earliest authors known to us from Greece—Homer and Hesiod—are clearly taking advantage of their authorial freedom, as we can tell from the cases in which multiple versions survive for a given story. In their cases, the resources of a richly developed, age-old Greek poetic language (one that can be traced in part back to the third millennium B.C.) gave performers a vast choice of phrases and motifs whereby they could elaborate their mythic performances.

Retelling through innovation marks the treatment of Greek myths throughout antiquity. A later Greek poet, Callimachus, said of his mythological poems, "I sing nothing unattested." At home in the extensive royal Library and Museum ("shrine of the Muses") at the great cosmopolitan city of Alexandria in Egypt, he had hundreds of papyrus scrolls preserving previous writings to consult when he retold the mythic stories from his Hellenic heritage. Most likely, he could draw as well on a strong, living oral tradition. These stories would have been still circulating in the Greek communities of North Africa, or were being brought to the new metropolis by traders and visiting scholars, soldiers, and slaves. Given this material, Callimachus clearly felt free to embellish.

My own retelling, though nowhere near as elegant, is equally hybrid. On the one hand, I do not invent versions. Each tale in this book is attested, and my narrative follows the leads given by one or several ancient sources. Most often, the source is from the archaic or Classical period of Greece (800–300 B.C.), although I sometimes include later ancient variations that appeal to me. In every case, I have gone back and reread the evidence we have in Greek or Latin. I have cited my main authorities in the headnotes. Those who wish to find more detailed accounts of the available mythic versions can consult one of the handbooks listed in the bibliography.

On the other hand, I have felt free to invent dialogue and novelistic touches where I thought this helped the telling. When the narration turns into a straightforward translation from the ancient sources, it never occupies more than a paragraph or two. Usually, my retelling is a combination of summarizing and more cinematic reimagining. Those familiar with the original texts will notice that I splice together various sections of such standard narratives as the *Theogony* and Apollodorus with more dramatic renditions from Homer, Pindar, the lyric poets, and Athenian tragedy. I have added transitions and, most important, an overall framework for all the stories, in the hope of lending some clarity and consistency to the material without distorting the shapes of the individual tales. At times I choose a specific chronology, although it is clear that ancient sources often wavered on the issue. Thus, for instance (with hints from Ovid), I associate the Silver Age with the coming of the Flood (Apollodorus reports that it destroyed the Bronze Age). The various births of the gods and stories of their encounters with mortals are arranged thematically. The heroic sagas—Herakles, Theseus, Jason, and the rest—are arranged by generation, with cross-references where possible. An alert reader may still notice a few anachronisms that have been left unaltered (for instance, in the career of Medea). Ancient tellers of myths were generally cavalier about strict accuracy in such matters, and so on occasion I am, too. My goal has been to allow readers, as far as possible, to grasp and retain the stories as parts of a whole, a world of mutually supporting and illuminating narratives that can, in turn, illuminate and support our own lives.

I leave to them judgments about my narrative voice. I strove to keep in English something both "traditional"—the occasional poetic inversions, lyric passages, and older diction—but also readable or, rather, hearable. My ideal was the speaking voice of a storyteller—admittedly a quirky teller who has all sorts of odd bits of lore in his or her head and sometimes stark opinions, and one who is situated somewhere in Greek lands in later antiquity (and thus is both closer to the material than us, but has enough distance to be occasionally ironic). The voice is as much a creation of this enduring body of stories as it is a shaper of the tales it tells.

# BOOK ONE

## THE BEGINNINGS

WE STILL MAKE STORIES ABOUT the way the world came to exist. The tales we tell nowadays have to do with mysterious creatures— black holes and big bangs, ever-expanding cosmic bodies, "quarks" and "superstrings." Before the science of physics, the stories were different.

In mythologies around the world, there are two central types of creation stories: automatic, in which the elements arise by themselves, and architectural, in which a supernatural being or trickster figure creates and shapes the universe. Greek myths are of the first type. Out of Chaos—the essence of nothingness—come two divinities, a place (Earth) and a force of attraction (Eros). In the physics of myth, these are enough to generate the rest of creation, including the divisions of day and night, the features of sky and landscape, and even such social forces as memory (Mnemosyne) and divine order (Themis). There is no principle of evil—unlike other ancient mythic systems—but Greek tales acknowledge that there are all sorts of bad influences and misfortunes in the world, including the shortness of human life. In the manner of genealogical expression that is characteristic of early Greek myth, such evils come from Night, who is daughter of Chaos, the original emptiness. Here, as in general, Greek myth does not attempt to explain the existence of pain and suffering. They are simply a given.

Evolution marks the origin story told by Hesiod's *Theogony*. Three generations of passionate conflict and violence are required before Zeus finally takes power and establishes his eternal order among the gods of Olympus. Before his triumph, Zeus' grandfather (Ouranos) and father (Kronos) attempt in vain to prevent change by refusing to let the next generation mature. The various repressions by these primitive gods backfire, and they end up dismembered or dismissed. There is both psychological and political wisdom embedded in this family saga. It turns out that Zeus' abilities to foresee trouble, to take advice, to be cautious, and to make alliances are what gain him victory. It helps, of course, that he also controls the weaponry of the sky, with his lightning and thunderbolts. These save the day against the final dark threat of Typhoeus. His superior physical position explains as well why Zeus wields sovereignty over his brothers, Hades and Poseidon, although they have theoretically equal thirds of the universe (the underworld and the sea).

Until the early twentieth century, it was thought that Hesiod's story of the struggle for divine kingship was uniquely Greek. But the discovery and decipherment of clay tablets containing much older Near Eastern myths, from the second millennium B.C., now suggest that many details of the Greek myth complex are either borrowings or at least shared beliefs. For example, the Babylonian poem *Enuma Elish* ("when on high"—its opening words) tells the story of the creation of gods from the mingling of two divine beings, male (*Apsu*) and female (*Tiamat*) waters. One of their descendants, Ea, god of wisdom, learns of Apsu's plan to obliterate the newer generation, and so kills him. His own son, Marduk, goes on to destroy the monstrously inflated Tiamat and become king and shaper of the universe. Even closer parallels to the Greek succession myth occur in the tales of the Hittites and Hurrians, early inhabitants of what is now Turkey. The god Kumarbi castrates his father, Anush (as Kronos did Ouranos), and produces a son (Teshub, like Zeus, a storm god), who then overcomes a dragonlike, mountain-high monster (Ullikummi) threatening his realm—compare Zeus' struggle with Typhoeus. The full implications of such close analogies between Greek and Near Eastern mythologies have yet to be worked out. In any event, it is worth remembering that the Greeks were never out of contact with the older cultures to their south and east, from Egypt to the Tigris and Euphrates rivers. Narratives might easily have passed back and forth.

Conspicuously absent in Greek myths of origins is any story of how humans came to exist. The Babylonian stories feature a craftsman god who forms people out of clay (albeit to be slaves of the divinities). In Greek myth, Prometheus comes closest to this role, although the idea that he, too, fashioned humans from clay occurs relatively late. Possibly, this was a well-known tale that simply does not survive in our patchy early sources. The evidence from religious cults tells us that potters at Athens worshiped Prometheus. More prominent is the complicated story of his duel of wits with his cousin Zeus. As this brings about the establishment of three key Greek institutions—meat sacrifice, agriculture, and marriage—it can be said that Prometheus creates the human condition, regardless of how people actually came to be.

Yet another myth with regional parallels is the story of the Flood. Unlike the biblical Noah, Deukalion and Pyrrha are saved merely because they are given advance information, not on the basis of righteous behavior. On the other hand, the motif of the watery destruction of humanity for offenses against the chief god unites the Greek with the Hebrew narrative. The tale of Lykaon (told here following Ovid's version) clearly taps into an additional source, the age-old belief in werewolves.

## 1. THE WORLD BEGINS

How did this world of gods and mortals come to be? Here is what the Muses tell:

In the beginning was an emptiness called Chaos—the yawning gap. Then Earth—or Gaia—sprang, without parents, into being. Her broad bosom provided a sturdy seat for the gods to come. And suddenly there appeared Eros, the fairest of immortals. At his touch bodies melt; he destroys will and reason, not only for humans but even for gods. In the beginning, then, were these all-powerful three.

What came next? From Chaos arose Erebos (the Darkness) and inky Night. By joining in love with Darkness, Night gave birth to Aither—the shining of the sky—and Day.

Earth brought forth Ouranos, the Sky, to be her cover and protector and a place for the blessed gods. He was filled with stars.

She bore, by herself, tall Mountains, where gods and nymphs delight in their dwellings, and then Pontus, the tireless, rushing, swelling sea. She went to bed with Ouranos and made Ocean, with its deep currents. From their further matings eleven more children were born from Earth; we call them Titans. These were Koios, Krios, Hyperion who goes on high, Iapetos, Theia the shining, and Rheia. With them were Themis—high law—and Mnemosyne, or memory, Phoibe with her gold chaplet, lovely Tethys, and finally her cleverest son—cunning Kronos.

Earth and Sky also produced six uglier, yet mighty, offspring. Three were the arrogant Cyclopes—Thunder, Lightning, and Flash—like gods, except that each had just a single eye in the middle of his forehead. Also were born three Hundred-Handers—Kottos, Briareos, Gyes—each of whom boasted fifty heads.

Now Ouranos, the Sky, seeing these children of his, was anxious that they would one day overthrow him. As soon as one would come to be born, he used to hide it away from the light of day by placing it deep in a hollow of its mother, Earth. He took pleasure from these evil deeds. But the Earth, vast as she was, was soon packed full. She groaned continually, to no avail. She had to come up with a way to stop him.

One day Earth crafted a great harvest sickle out of the hardest stone. Showing it to her children, she called on them to be brave: "If you want, we can get back at your father. We can end this outrage of his." All the children were struck with fear. No one spoke. Finally, Kronos, with his crafty wits, answered her challenge. "My mother, I promise to carry out the task. I don't care a thing about our cursed father. After all, he was the one who started this awful practice."

Overjoyed, Earth hid Kronos in a place where he could wait in ambush, and armed him with the great jagged-tooth sickle. Immense Ouranos arrived, bringing on the night. He desired Earth, and clasping her, he began to stretch himself out. All at once his son grabbed him with his left hand, holding the sickle in his right. In one stroke he sheared off the member of his own father and threw it behind him into the sea.

Earth took into herself the bloody drops that rained down. Within a year she gave birth to the powerful Erinyes, the Furies. The Giants, too, with their bronze armor and long spears, sprang from that shower, as did the ash-tree nymphs. From the immortal flesh that fell into the surging sea there arose in time a white froth, or *aphros*. Inside the foam was nurtured a lovely girl. First she floated toward holy Kythera, and then to Cyprus pounded by the sea. Out she stepped from the waves, a queenly beautiful goddess, and around her slender feet fresh grass sprouted. They call her Aphrodite, from the foam in which she was born, and also Kythereia, since she had drawn near to that place, and Kyprogeneia, since she was born on wave-washed Cyprus. Eros and handsome Desire accompanied her as she entered into the gods' company. From that time she has had control over maiden talk and love smiles, cheating, sweet pleasure, delightful loving.

## 2.   NIGHT AND SEA

Loving and Deception, which Aphrodite knows so well, had their own parentage. Night, the daughter of Chaos, was their mother, and they have brothers and sisters aplenty: Doom and Death itself, Sleep, and the tribe of Dreams. Night the dusky goddess slept with no one and yet produced more offspring: Blame and Grief with all its pains; the bane of Nemesis; Old Age, that destroyer; and Strife with its harsh heart. It was Night who gave birth to the Fates—Klotho the spinner, Lachesis the lot-giver, and Atropos, whose name means "no turning back." When a human being is born, these sisters decide how much good and evil each will have in life. Afterward, if a mortal—or even a god—goes astray, the Fates follow, ever angry, until the wrongdoer is given his comeuppance. The Hesperidae, creatures of evening, who live beyond Ocean tending the Golden Apples and the fruit trees of the far west—these too are daughters of Night.

Out of this dreadful brood, Strife presented her mother with the most grandchildren: Labor, Forgetting, Famine, piercing Pains, Clashes, Battles, Murders and Manslaughters, Quarrels, Lies, Arguments and Wrangles, Bad Government, Disaster (these are related evils), and finally Oath. He afflicts humans most of all: look what happens whenever somebody willfully swears an oath, then breaks the promise.

But trustworthy speech also found its place in that early world. Pontus, the Sea, had an eldest child, Nereus, who never lied. This master of truth is known as the Old Man of the Sea, since he is just and mild, never does wrong, and remembers the right ways of acting, like an elder. Nereus married a daughter of Ocean, the world-encircling river, and they had fifty daughters, who had traits of both parents, and whom all men desired for wives:

*Firstborn, Well-ordered, Saver, Amphitritê,*
*Goodgift, Thetis, Calm, and Gray,*
*Waverush, Cave, Swift, and lovely Salty,*
*Allgoddess, Pleasant, Goodwin with rosy arms,*
*Graceful Honey, Goodharbor, Glory, Giver,*
*Floater and Bearer and Power and Cliffie,*
*Islander, First-in-charge, fair Galatea,*
*Bestower, Allvoice, Steedswift the beautiful,*
*pink-armed Maremind,*
*Wave-taker, who calms the surge on the misty deep*
*and soothes the blasts of wind, with her sister Wave-end,*
*Wave and Shore and fair-crowned Sea-knower,*
*Gray-ways, Mainford (all smiles), Smooth-sailing,*
*Good-talking, People-ruling, Much-minded, Self-willed,*
*Slip-queen, Goodprow (the beautiful and blameless),*
*Sandy (charming form), divine Horse-stayer,*
*Islet, Bon Voyage, Tradition, Prudence.*

And then there is Unerring (she makes fifty-one) who has her death-less father's mind. Such were the daughters of Nereus, and they all knew excellent crafts.

## 3.   THE COMING OF ZEUS

The sea had taken form. The beings of the sky and air were in place as well, because Shining Brightness (Theia) had borne the great Sun, brilliant Moon, and their sister, Dawn. This lovely daughter, in her turn, married the Starry One (Astraios) and gave birth to the stout-hearted winds: Zephyr (the Western), Boreas (the Northerly), and Notos (the Southerly), as well as the Dawn Star, who announces his mother's arrival each morn, and all the other lights of the heavens. Still, the world was not the way we know it.

Sky and Earth, as you recall, had brought into the world the first gen-eration of divinities, the Titans. Kronos, the cleverest of these, had put an end to his father's evil oppression. When he grew up, Kronos became powerful in his own right. With Rheia (a Titan herself), he had glorious children: Hestia, the hearth goddess; Demeter, goddess of grains; Hera; Hades the pitiless; Earth-shaker Poseidon; and—last but not least—Zeus, the cunning god, whose thunder and lightning batter the wide world.

In Kronos was a broad streak of his father's violence. His own mother, Gaia, had foretold that one of his sons or daughters might usurp his royal power. So when each of his own offspring was born, Kronos swallowed the child whole.

Rheia was consumed with a mother's grief. What could she do? She was pregnant again, and the baby was due. She begged her aging parents, Ouranos and Gaia, to come up with a way that she could give birth without her husband seeing the child. The old couple knew what was to come, and they told her how her brave son could survive and eventually overthrow Kronos. Late one dark night they bundled her off to the high mountains of fertile Crete. There, deep within a cave on a lofty peak (some say Mt. Ida, others Mt. Dicte), she gave birth. But instead of presenting the child to its father, Rheia tightly wrapped a large rock in swaddling clothes and handed that to her lord and husband Kronos. He took it in his hands—and shoved it down his throat.

It took a year or so before Kronos, whose devious mind had been so deceived, threw up. Out came the stone first of all and then his children, one by one. Zeus, who meanwhile had grown up miraculously fast, safe in Crete, strong of limb and crafty, took the rock and set it in the ground at Delphi, where you can see it even now, a marvel and sign of his power. Then Zeus freed his Cyclops uncles: Thunder, Lightning, and Flash. For a long time they had lain in chains, since being bound by their father, Ouranos, in the gloomy depths of Tartarus. In gratitude, they gave Zeus what were to become his trusty weapons (named after them). Armed with these, he began the final struggle.

## 4. BATTLES OF THE GODS

The older generation of gods did not give up their power easily. The Titans rallied around their king, Kronos, atop Mt. Othrys, while Zeus and the younger gods made their base on snow-crested Olympus. Ten years they battled one another, equally matched, the war drawn taut as a tug rope and with no end in sight. Once more it was the ancient, wise Earth goddess Gaia who suggested a way out. In his early days, her husband, Ouranos, had imprisoned not only the weapon-forging Cyclopes; he had also put under the earth in unbreakable bonds the huge Hundred-Handers. "Remember them," whispered Gaia to her grandson Zeus. "With their help, glory and victory are yours."

Now, Zeus was a clever schemer as much as a warrior. He found a means of secretly releasing the Hundred-Handers and of sharing with them the food and drink that the gods of Olympus enjoyed—ambrosia and nectar. Each day their strength and will to fight grew greater. Then Zeus made his plea. "You fine sons of Earth and Sky, listen to what I have in mind. For a long time the Titans and children of Kronos have been warring to win control. The time has come for you to remember how it was *our* plotting that brought you up to light from the murk. Show the Titans that invincible strength of yours in deadly combat."

Kottos answered for the three brothers. "You are right. It was you who freed us from our unrelenting chains. And we know, too, that you have the wit, the brains; you were born to be the gods' defender. We will fight the Titans in terrible battle, fight with our minds intent and our will unfailing, and claim power—for you." All the Olympians heard this and cheered. Gods and goddesses, all set about to further stoke the fires of war.

Their allies were terrible to behold, each with one hundred arms growing from his shoulders, and on each of their necks fifty heads. They seized great boulders and held them aloft. The Titans waited, strengthening their fighting lines. Then the boundless sea screeched, the earth resounded, the wide-open sky let out a groan and shook. Tall Olympus itself was quivering from the ground up under the onrush of immortals. The quake struck deep, all the way down to Tartarus, and you could hear the powerful weapons hum and thud and clash. Voices from both sides reached the starry heaven as they came together with great war cries.

Zeus held nothing back. His power blazed forth. He leapt from Olympus, blasting away with thunderbolts, the flames shooting thick and fast from his mighty hand. Below, the earth caught on fire, all the forests crackling. The ground sizzled, and the Ocean stream around the edge of earth. The Titans were surrounded by suffocating smoke. Licks of unquenchable fire reached the bright upper air. The flash of white-hot lightning blinded them, strong though they were. Indescribable waves of heat overwhelmed Chaos itself. It looked and sounded as if Sky had crashed down on Earth.

The battle turned. The Hundred-Handers had been fighting in the ranks, but now they advanced to lead the assault, Kottos and Briareos and Gyes, insatiably hungry for war. They hurled three hundred boulders at a time, wave upon wave, until they completely overshadowed the Titans and drove them off to Tartarus. There, as far beneath the earth as sky is above it, the Hundred-Handers tied them up in chains the Titans could not break, for all their might. If you threw an anvil out of heaven, it would take nine days to reach earth, and another nine to drop down to where they ended up.

## 5.  THE FINAL STRUGGLES OF ZEUS

Rewards were in order. First, the Olympians cast lots for supreme rule. To Zeus went lordship over the sky. Poseidon got control of the sea, and Hades won the regions beneath the earth as his domain. Styx, the daughter of the great cosmic river Ocean, who was the first to volunteer her help in the recent battle, was granted the honor of being the oath by which both gods and mortals make their solemn agreements. She lives now deep under the earth near Hades in a stone house with tall silver columns. Whenever one of the gods makes a promise, Iris, the rainbow, is sent from Zeus to fetch up water from Styx in a golden pitcher. If a god pours that water while swearing the oath and later breaks his word, terrible things happen. He can't breathe, he lies speechless in bed, he can't take nectar and ambrosia, and an evil sort of coma overcomes him. And when he recovers from that, more punishment awaits. For nine years he is deprived of the company of the other Olympians, can't go to their council or their fine feasts. Only in the tenth year may he or she return. That is how powerful Styx and her waters can be.

Until now Gaia the Earth had been a kind protector. Without her advice, Zeus would never have survived beyond birth or defeated the Titans. Perhaps she still felt something for those Titan children whom she had conceived with Sky. Or maybe she was pained from the injuries she received in the great battle between divine generations, when the blazing bolts of Zeus ranging over the plain of Thessaly had scorched her body. Whatever the reason, Gaia showed another side. She became the enemy and began to send hostile offspring against her royal grandson.

First came the Giants, who had sprung from her when she was splattered with the blood drops from Ouranos. They were terrible in appearance, with long hair and beards drooping down, armed with long spears and shining body armor. Their tall legs ended in snaking dragon tails. As if to taunt Zeus, they threw huge rocks and burning oak trees at the sky. Porphyrion was one of the chief Giants and the other was Alkyoneus, who could never be killed as long as he stayed in the territory where he had been born. Each time he was knocked to the ground there, Earth herself revived him.

Gaia, as usual, knew about the future. She had learned—as had the gods—that the Giants would not be defeated unless a mortal joined with the gods to help. To protect her huge sons, even from such a puny being, she began to search for a magic drug, something from her own store of herbs. But Zeus beat her to it. He told Dawn and Sun and Moon to hide their light while he himself found and cut the herb that would have made the Giants invincible.

They clashed, the Giants and the gods, with Zeus at their head. Porphyrion lunged to assault the goddess Hera, but Zeus struck him with a thunderbolt and he fell. The other divine ones used their chosen weapons: Apollo the archer knocked out the eye of the Giant Ephialtes with a bowshot. Dionysus used his long stalk, the sacred *thyrsus*, to kill Eurytos; Hecate singed Klytios the Giant with her torches, while Hephaestus the smith god slung pieces of hot metal at Mimas, killing him.

Noticing one Giant as he tried to escape, Athena picked up the island of Sicily and threw it on top of him, pinning him beneath. Yet another, named Pallas, she captured and flayed, taking his skin off to become her own protective covering (for which she is sometimes called "Pallas Athena").

Hermes, Artemis, Poseidon, and the Fates joined in the slaughter, until the earth was rid of Giants, except for their chief, Alkyoneus. How did he die? Some say Herakles was already born by then, and that it was he, the greatest hero among humans, who overcame Alkyoneus—that, without Herakles, the gods could not have succeeded. The Giant was hurling boulders, demolishing every chariot that rode against him, when Herakles tackled him. He dragged him away from the plain of Pallene, where the Giant had first seen the light of day and the battle was raging. Once Herakles had severed his precious bond with Earth, he aimed his arrow and shot him dead.

However the final Giant's death came about, there is no doubt that Zeus' troubles were not yet over. The Giants were defeated, but Gaia had one more monstrous threat in store. By the power of Aphrodite she lay with Tartarus, deep under the earth, and brought forth Typhoeus. He had one hundred horrible snake heads growing out of his neck, each one flicking forth a black serpent tongue. Fire glowed from all his glaring eyes. His voices, one from each head, were unspeakably awful. At times the gods could actually understand words coming from him, but more often his heads made a bull-bellowing, lion-roaring, snake-hissing cacophony, which the tall mountains would echo back.

Typhoeus might have toppled the new reign had not Zeus the Father acted at once. He thundered loud and hard. The earth and the sky and the Ocean, even the deep roots of earth, reverberated. Olympus shook beneath his mighty strides. Withering heat engulfed the purple sea as Zeus brandished his lightning and Typhoeus emitted his jets of flame. Ground and sky and sea boiled furiously; high waves crested over the headlands. Even Hades in his underground house and the Titans imprisoned deep in Tartarus trembled with fear at the unquenchable din.

In his armor Zeus leapt down upon the monster and incinerated every head. Then he whipped him, and the mutilated beast fled, smoking still from Zeus' lightning strikes, so that the forests caught fire and earth began to burn. You've seen tin melting, when the bellows blow on it in a crucible, or iron, the hardest metal, when Hephaestus the smith heats it in a mountain forge. That is how earth started to melt under the rays of fire from Typhoeus' body. Zeus in his disgust seized the monster and hurled him to Tartarus. From his rotting body arose the wet winds that beat down on the misty sea all of a sudden, scattering ships and killing sailors and battering down the lovely crops on earth: *typhoons*.

## 6. THE MARRIAGES OF ZEUS

After that, Gaia gave up. "Make him king," she told the Olympians. At last secure in his power, Zeus, son of Kronos, son of Ouranos, ruled unchallenged. He remembered, however, what had led to the downfall of his father and grandfather—cruelty and violence, yes, but also stupidity. Each had tried to suppress the next generation, and each had made a fatal miscalculation. No child of Zeus would overthrow *him*. This is how he made sure.

Ocean and his wife, Tethys of the golden crown, had fifty daughters and numerous sons. They were mainly streams, springs, and rivers. The Nile was one and Scamander near Troy another. The oldest was Styx, the stream of the underworld, who had aided Zeus in his struggles. In the new ordering of the world, the children of Styx—Contention and fair-ankled Victory, Force and Strength—lived with Zeus, never leaving the vicinity of Olympus.

One of the fifty girls was a beautiful young goddess called Mêtis. She represented a different kind of power. In some ways she resembled her cousin Nereus, the wise son of Sea. She knew more than any other god or human, and for this she was well named "Cunning Ability"—for that is what Mêtis means. Any mortal who drives a war chariot, steers a ship, or makes an intricate piece of craftsmanship does so through her sort of practical wisdom: knowing what step to carry out and when to do it.

Zeus learned from Gaia one final secret. To prevent being overthrown, whether by a son or any other god, he must master Mêtis. Any offspring of hers, it was said, would be outstanding for cunning. So he married her, his first bride of many to come. But that was not enough. When Mêtis was about to give birth, Zeus, again with his grandmother's advice, coaxed her with wheedling words—and then swallowed her whole (. . . like father, like son, you might say). Yet this did not prevent the child from coming into the world. With Mêtis in his belly, Zeus began to feel swollen. The pain was not in his stomach; it was his head that hurt. Hephaestus, his son, was summoned, and as Zeus sat still on his throne, Hephaestus split his head open a bit with an axe. Out jumped a daughter—Athena, goddess of craft and wisdom, already fully armed (thanks to Mêtis, who provided all from within). War, after all, is also an occupation for the cunning, and Athena is as good at casting spears as she is at weaving. Her mother remains within Zeus still, a source of good advice.

Zeus took as his next wife the sleek and lovely Themis. She bore him the Seasons, who are named Orderliness, Justice, and Peace. Some say it was by Themis, not Night, that the Fates came into being as well, which would make them daughters of Zeus rather than ancestral powers. Another daughter of Ocean named Eurynome presented Zeus with the three lovely-cheeked Graces—Aglaia (Delight), Euphrosynè (Cheer), and the desirable Thalia (Bloom). Demeter bore him Persephone. Hephaestus had become his son, yet his latest wife, Hera, had produced him without the help of Zeus, one time when she was enraged (as she often was) with her lusty husband. Hera and Zeus together had Ares, the war god, Hebe (eternal youth), and the midwife goddess Eileithuia.

## 7. THE BIRTH OF APOLLO AND ARTEMIS

Eileithuia was old enough to be a helpmate at the birth of her half brother and sister, Apollo and Artemis, which took place on the tiny, rock-strewn island of Delos. Their mother was the mild and beautiful Lêto. Made pregnant by Zeus, with her pains coming on, she wandered over the world looking for a place that would welcome and care for her. From Crete to Athens, the peaks of Mt. Pelion to misty Lemnos in the northeast corner of the sea, down the coast past Khios, Samos, Karpathos, she went, circling the entire Aegean (as it would be named later). No land would have her, no matter how rich. They all trembled in humility and fear at the thought of seeing mighty Apollo born on their soil. At last she came to Delos. Lêto, exhausted, set foot on her and begged: "Delos, if you would only be my son's refuge, the site of his rich temple, no one else will ever take you over. Apollo won't forget you, either. It doesn't look to me as if you can raise cows here—or sheep, or vines, or anything else, for that matter. Ah, but if you have Apollo's temple, people will be bringing hundred-cow sacrifices, feasting and holding fairs, and the smell of meat will spread all over. You'll feed off the fat of the land—and I must say you are pretty skinny yourself."

After she made her plea, Delos beamed with delight and said: "Lêto, you who are so glorious, the daughter of great Koios . . . I'd be overjoyed to receive your son. It's true. I'm unattractive otherwise, and this way I'd be brimming with honors. But there's one thing I am afraid of, Lêto—I won't hide it. They say Apollo is going to be overwhelming in power, that he'll be the one who gives order to gods on high and mortals on the wheat-covered earth. So I'm terribly frightened that when he sees the light of day, he'll spurn me (I *am* just a little rock cliff) and he'll give me a kick, tip me over, and shove me under the sea. Then a big wave will always be washing over my head, while he goes off to some other land that he likes more and builds his temple there and all his shady sacred groves. And me—I'll be home for octopuses and black seals.

"Here's what I want. Swear by Styx that he'll build his first beautiful temple *here* . . . before he goes anywhere else, as I know he will." And Lêto did. "I swear by great Styx—so help me, Earth and Sky— Apollo's fragrant altar, his sacred enclosure, will be here, and he will honor you, Delos, above all others."

When this contract was completed, Delos was happy. Lêto, however, felt her pains come on sharper than ever. For nine days and nine nights she was pierced by labor pangs. All her goddess relations came to her: Dionê, Rheia, Ikhnaie, Themis, Amphitritê who lives in the groaning deep, and all the others—except Hera, who knew the birth was the result of her husband's affair. Worse, she knew that young Lêto, with her lovely curls, would have a towering, famous son.

Hera was jealous, and she made up an excuse to keep Eileithuia busy on Olympus, up in the golden clouds. Back on Delos, the other goddesses became desperate. They sent Iris the rainbow to fetch the midwife, promising her a lavish gold and amber necklace, and they told Iris, "Don't let Hera find out." So Iris shot off up to the sky, reached the high plateau of the gods, and stood at the doorway of their golden house. "Eileithuia," she whispered, trying not to be noticed. The young goddess excused herself and hurried out. Iris explained the situation, with such urgency that Eileithuia was swayed, though she was taking a risk. Like a pair of white doves the two descended to Delos. At the very moment Eileithuia stepped onto the rocky shore, Lêto felt the birth begin. She knew this was the time. She threw her arms around a slender palm tree growing all alone by the side of the gentle slope of Kynthos. She pressed her knees into a spot of soft meadow grass. Beneath her, Earth smiled. Out the baby leapt toward the bright light. The goddesses all together let out a high-pitched shriek of joy. *"Ololololê!"* They bathed baby Apollo in pure waters, wrapped him in white linen, fine-spun and shining, and put a thin gold band all around it. Lêto did not suckle him; Themis instead fed him nectar and ambrosia. His mother gazed at her infant and was happy and proud because she had produced a strong boy, a real bowman. His twin, Artemis, who also favored archery, was born the same day, but with less fanfare.

## 8.   PROMETHEUS AND THE HUMAN WORLD

Like Zeus himself, Lêto was a child of Titans. Zeus got along quite well with the women of that clan, but the men kept giving him trouble, even after his victory in the great battle. He had an uncle, Iapetos, brother of Kronos, who had four sons, Zeus' cousins. Two were known for strength (good and bad) and two for their wits (that is, for having them and lacking them). Atlas was the son with the most useful physique, and Zeus, sometime after the Titan war, set him at the far

edge of the world, where the clear-voiced Hesperides live, to stand there forever and on his muscular shoulders bear up the wide sky. With his strong legs rooted beneath the depths of the sea, Atlas, big as a mountain, keeps the heavens from crashing onto the world below. Menoitios, his brother, had been a boaster and a brawler, and nobody missed him when Zeus hurled him down to the netherworld with a thunderbolt in battle. Of the other pair, Prometheus was the intelligent one—too clever, some would say—while his brother, Epimetheus, was all too dumb.

Some say that Prometheus, the Fore-thinker, first created human beings, while he was experimenting one day with clay and water. Like a potter, he kneaded the earth and built up his creation. He fired these clay models with life and let the newly made men and women go forth on their own. But he was always looking after them, even though the Olympian gods could not be bothered much about humans.

Wherever people first came from (and there are many stories about that), in the beginning human beings and gods lived in harmony. In a way, after all, both sides were descended from the same mother, Earth. Gods would fall in love with mortal women from time to time and produce half-divine sons and daughters. In those early times, all enjoyed coming together and feasting. One day their gathering place was set at Mêkonê, not far from where Corinth is now. Prometheus was to make the meal. Now, this cousin of Zeus was an excellent butcher, but an inveterate trickster. He always did things differently. On that day he brought a big ox to cook. Happily, he set out preparing. When he had killed it, roasted part, and grilled some other pieces, he slyly divided the food into two portions. For Zeus, and the other gods, he bundled up the ox flesh and the meaty parts in the animal's paunch, to make it look unattractive. For the humans, he laid out the white bones, but nicely dressed them up in sleek, shining fat.

Zeus took one look and said, with an edge to his voice: "It looks to me like an uneven split, my dear son of Iapetos." So Prometheus, in his twisty-minded way, smiled and said, "Zeus, almighty, glorious, ever-living god, pick the portion you want." Zeus had caught on already, but he played along, because he had plans of his own. He reached out both hands and took the glistening fat package, found it was only bones covered up, and exploded with anger. He had to live with his choice. (That is why nowadays humans still burn on the fragrant sacrificial altars the white bones for the gods—and eat the tasty meat themselves.)

"Never without your tricks, Prometheus," said Zeus—that was all. But Zeus got his revenge. He refused to give humans the fire they needed (for things like cooking or pot making). When people tried to produce sparks by rubbing together sticks from ash trees (which fire inhabited—so they thought), nothing happened. It was as if all the power of Zeus' lightning had gone out.

Prometheus, seeing how his poor mortal friends suffered, devised a plan. There is a plant that grows in marshy places, called *narthêx*, or fennel, tall like bamboo, but with a whitish pith inside it, all the way down. Breaking off one of these stalks, Prometheus secretly made his way to Olympus, stole back fire from where Zeus had hidden it, and returned to the humans, with the flame safely smoldering inside the fennel stalk.

When Zeus saw, at a distance, the unmistakable brightness of fire burning on humans' hearths, he was angrier than ever. He went off to design something really evil to pay them back. He had Hephaestus make out of clay a figure that looked like a bashful human maiden, with a human voice and looks that would rival those of a goddess. Athena dressed her in a silvery gown, adorned her with jewelry, and on her head placed an intricately worked veil, topped with a crown of lovely blossoms. She also taught her to weave at the loom, as women should. Then Zeus had Aphrodite give the maiden grace and charm, the kind that leads to melting desire and wrenching heartache. The Graces and Seasons and Persuasion joined in. And Hermes he ordered to make her thieving and shameless. Hermes named her as well: Pandora, "All gifts," because all the gods and goddesses had presented her with something.

Pandora was made to bring men pain. Some say she was the first woman, and that from her came the race of women (to some men, the gender does appear to be a separate race). It seems she was the first bride, at any rate, and with her began the custom of marriage.

When the immortals had finished adorning her, Zeus sent Hermes to bring this lovely "present" to Epimetheus (the less bright brother, aptly named After-thinker). Epimetheus had been specifically warned by Prometheus: "Don't accept any gifts from Zeus. Send them back, or something awful will happen." But when he saw lovely Pandora on his doorstep, he forgot all that and took her in. Only when the harm was eventually done did he remember.

All during the time when gods and men dwelled in harmony and enjoyed shared feasts, humans lived on the earth without experience of labor, or any evil, or killing disease. But then Pandora came, and with her she brought a big jar, like the kind women use in the storeroom to keep grain or oil. Whether or not she knew what was in this jar (it could be that Zeus told her not to look but had also made her curious), Pandora one day, living in Epimetheus' house, lifted the lid. Out flew disaster, voiceless sicknesses that haunt the night, and ten thousand other ills. The sky and sea became filled with them. Pandora tried to reseal the jar again, but not until everything had escaped. All, that is, except for Hope, which, being small, could not manage to get past the lip of the container. So, in one way, Hope is safe. In another, we don't have much hope out in the hard world. And, come to think of it, since it was stored up in that jar of evils by the gods, perhaps Hope is less beneficial than one supposes.

## 9. PROMETHEUS PUNISHED

No one tricks Zeus and gets away with it. Sooner or later the father of gods catches up. Before long the burly henchmen of Zeus, Force and Strength, the sons of Styx, paid Prometheus a visit. Together with

Hephaestus, who makes chains, they dragged Prometheus off to the far northeast, to a mountain named Caucasus, and there meted out punishment. They bound him hand and foot with unbreakable bonds to a rocky outcrop. Hephaestus was hesitant. "I can't bear to look at a fellow god being tied up like this." But the two brutal brothers did their job, warning Hephaestus, "Do not pity Zeus' enemies overmuch, or you may be the next one to be pitied." And they mocked Prometheus as they tied him all the tighter: "Now you won't be so arrogant, stealing the gods' rightful honors and sharing them with those creatures of a day. Now see how your philanthropy has been repaid." Then they went away and left him.

Alone, Prometheus called out:

> *"Shining bright sky, breezes swift as birds,*
> *River sources, laughing waves of the sea,*
> *All-mothering Earth, Sun observing all:*
> *Look at me, see how gods force a god to suffer."*

As he moaned over his condition, he caught a scent as of perfume and an echo of voices. "Here I am chained, a sight for my enemies to mock," he thought. "What god or mortal is coming to have a look now?"

Up came a group of young girls, of the age when they are just learning to do their choral dances all together. They had heard the blows of hammer on metal and, being curious, had persuaded their father to let them track down the sound. As they gazed at this stranger and heard his story—how he had helped mortals, even stopped Zeus from wiping out the human race, and been punished—their eyes filled with tears. Yet their innocent minds could not fathom the matter. "Well, you did something wrong; now you just have to think of a way out," said one. Prometheus was gentle but bitter, and said: "What wrong I did, I did willingly. All my discoveries have brought me pain! I wanted to be a protector of my people. Never did I think I would find myself pinned to a cliff with no humans in sight."

Just then the girls' father arrived on the scene. It was Ocean—a kinsman of Prometheus—and these were some of his many daughters. He sympathized, he advised, he philosophized, but he could do nothing to help. Besides, Prometheus did not encourage him: "Think of what happened to Typhon when he rose against the new order, hissing terribly, glaring, determined to overthrow Zeus. One thunderbolt and he was ash, his body buried under the mountain of Sicily, still sending up puffs of smoke and streams of fire throughout the island. Don't take such a risk."

Only with difficulty could Prometheus make them understand the extent of his good deeds, all the inventions he'd made for man: metal-working, star tracking, counting, letters, ox yokes, chariots, boats with sails, how to interpret dreams, to find useful herbs and remedies, to listen to sounds, watch birds in flight, or read the livers of sacrificial beasts to tell the future. "Any craft they have, they have from me," he sighed. But his listeners, never having worked or suffered, did not see the point of the god's lament.

Eventually, they drifted off. Prometheus on his crag thought deeply. He nearly became one with the rock. Humans, far away as they were, gradually forgot him. It is not clear what was the worse punishment, the torment of mind or body, their forgetting him, or the last cruel touch that Zeus added. Every day he sent his favorite bird, the eagle, to seek out Prometheus where he stood chained, pierce him with its beak, and peck at the lobes of his liver. Every night his liver grew back and every day the eagle came. It went on for nearly forever, until one day a mortal hero set him free. But that is another story.

## 10.   THE GREAT FLOOD

In the days when Prometheus was still cheerfully inventing crafts and devices for his beloved humans, he had a wife (either Asia or Hêsionê was her name), and the couple had a son, Deukalion. He was an ordinary boy, not a trickster like his father, and no one expected that he would grow up to be famous. But then again, no one thought humanity, except for Deukalion and his bride, would be washed from the face of the earth. It happened this way.

When human beings were first created, they lived in perfect peace, like gods. It was before the coming of Zeus, when Kronos was still ruling over all. Old age, hard work, and sadness were unknown. They died, in good time, after some hundreds of years, as gently as falling asleep. They had all they could ever want to eat and drink, and the earth brought forth good food without plowing, sowing, or harvesting. It was a Golden Age, now that we look back. When people of that age went to their rest beneath the earth, their spirits continued to go about the world, clad in mist and invisible. Even now they are keep-

ing an eye on us, whoever does right or wrong, dispensing justice—
that is their special role.

Another generation succeeded them, as different as silver is from
gold, and like silver of less value. They took a hundred years to grow
up. All that time they stuck by their mothers like witless infants. Nor
were they any smarter full grown. These Silver People kept on doing
one another harm, and worse, they insulted the gods. After the incident at Mêkonê, toward the end of the Golden Age, gods and mortals
no longer shared meals as equals. The humans were supposed to cook
meat and offer part to the gods, and they in turn (since they did not
eat anything but nectar and ambrosia) took delight in the smell of siz-
zling meat. But this newer generation failed to sacrifice, or did it pro-
fanely.

Zeus came down from Olympus one day to see for himself the evils
of the age. As the evening shadows were falling, he crossed Mt. Kyllene and arrived in wild Arcadia, the land of a certain king named
Lykaon. Though the god was in disguise, all the villagers he met
treated him with reverence—except Lykaon. The king thought to test
the divinity of Zeus, in the lowest sort of way. He cut the throat of a
prisoner and at the mealtime he presented cooked human flesh to
almighty Zeus as if it were a delicacy. Of course Zeus knew, and as
soon as the dish was served, he demolished the king's house, brought
it down right on top of the banqueters. Lykaon escaped, panting as he
ran into the woods. But he was punished all the same. In the dim forest light he saw his arms and legs begin to bristle with thick gray hair.
When he tried to speak, he could only let out a howl. His eyes
gleamed and he felt a craving for the raw flesh of sheep flocks. He had
become a wolf.

As Zeus later told the story, it was then he decided that the age
that had produced a Lykaon must perish. Using fire was too dangerous. He remembered the end of Typhon, when the universe had nearly
gone up in flames. So water seemed best.

Prometheus heard of the decision in time to warn his only child:
"Build a stout wooden chest, like a coffin," he told Deukalion, "and
when it starts to rain, stock her with supplies and board her." As the
sky got blacker, Deukalion worked harder, until the makeshift craft
was ready and he clambered into it with Pyrrha, his wife (the daughter of Epimetheus and Pandora). The heavens opened up, and rain
pelted down, whipped sideways by competing winds. Greece was soon
covered with raging flood waters. Cattle and houses, horses and peo-

ple, were torn from the land and swirled about in the muddy waves. The daughters of Nereus, swimming atop the flood, gazed down on what had once been towns and woods. Dolphins dove among the tops of oaks, seals changed places with grazing goats, the wolf paddled along amid the sheep. And still it rained.

After a time, all was submerged. Only the twin peaks of Parnassus stuck out above the plain of water. On one of these peaks, Deukalion's wooden box came to rest, and he and Pyrrha disembarked. Before anything else, they paid homage to the local nymphs, and to Themis, whose oracular shrine stood in that isolated mountain spot. Zeus was happy seeing this; the clouds began to scatter with the cold North Wind, and the waters to subside. Gradually the couple realized that they were the only ones left alive. It was up to them to remake the race. But they were stunned, without direction. "If only I had my father's skill at shaping people out of the earth," said Deukalion in despair. Frustrated, the couple could only sit and weep. Finally, they decided to seek guidance from Themis and went to consult the Titan. The oracular reply was shocking: "Leave this temple and throw over your shoulders the bones of your great parent." For a long time the pair pondered this dark saying—what could it mean? At last the son of Prometheus came to a conclusion: "The oracle could not have commanded something so impious. Unless I am mistaken, by 'parent' it means Earth; by 'bones,' the rocks."

Pyrrha was persuaded. Together, they gathered as many rocks as they could. Then, standing close, they threw the stones one by one over their shoulders, without looking back. If they had, they would have seen the stones hit the ground and immediately lose, in part, their hardness—that became flesh—and in part, retain it—that turned into bone. The rocks thrown by Deukalion changed into men, and Pyrrha's into women. Which is why we humans are a flinty lot.

# BOOK TWO

## SINGERS,
## PLAYERS, AND RIVALS

"MUSIC" COMES TO US FROM Greek *mousikê*, the "art of the Muses." The important status of these goddesses of song, dance, poetry, and verbal skill is clear from their genealogy. As daughters of Zeus, they have the special task of always praising his regime and encouraging harmony through their performances. A Greek audience would see in them the divine mirroring of a common civic institution, a chorus of well-born marriageable young women who were trained to perform the songs, dances, and myths of their city-state. That the Muses' mother was Memory itself (Mnemosyne) reminds us how late, in terms of cultural development, was the use of writing. In the period when Greek myth developed and flourished, poets and speakers composed as they performed, relying on a knowledge of traditional phrases, motifs, and plots to make new stories. This sort of "oral" culture, dependent on memory rather than recorded words, can be paralleled in a number of small-scale societies today, particularly in Asia and Africa.

Since myths were composed and transmitted primarily within performances, it is important to try to understand how Greeks thought about the origins of song and music. After all, what we might recognize as poetry (language with rhythm) was almost always sung or accompanied by instruments in ancient times. The notion of bare narrative notation, or texts to read in private, would have been foreign to the composers of myths. In this context, the elements of competition and cooperation in performance appear particularly significant. Musicians and singers vie with one another (Apollo and Marsyas, Thamyris and the Muses), something we know occurred in actual Greek social life. At stake in such stories is a relative ranking of the genres, contents, and types of performances represented. Thus, the tale of how Apollo defeated the Phrygian reed player encapsulates deeply held attitudes among the Greek aristocracy concerning the appropriate kinds of musical modes. We know that Plato and Aristotle disapproved of *aulos*-playing (the art of Marsyas) because it excited emotions too easily and led to passionate excesses. The lyre was the favored symbol of harmony and calm, and thus became associated with Apollo, whose job it was to organize and manage the world according to his father's will. The story that Hermes, a trickster and thief, invented the lyre may be a propaganda counterthrust on the part of a less exalted social group to claim a role in supporting Apollo's art. At the same time, this tale, wonderfully narrated in the *Hymn to Hermes,* seems to acknowledge the elements of improvisation and craft (as well as craftiness) in musical and poetic art.

If Hermes, the brother of Apollo, embodies a genial joking spirit, one that employs music to create familial peace, Pan, the goat-god son of Hermes, represents the wild, asocial, and irrational aspects of the art. His instrument, the *syrinx* or "Pan pipes," belongs specifically outside the boundaries of the city-state's civic space, having power over the wild hills that the goat-god haunts. He himself is half animal, of course. And his music shades into something noncrafted and noncultural—pure sound itself—as the story of Echo seems to say. Perhaps it is not accidental that his myths are linked with the story of Narcissus, who has given us a word for self-absorbed behavior. For both Pan and the handsome youth fail, at key moments, to interact with society, tending instead to extremes of terror or love.

The figure of another outdoor performer, Orpheus, has long been powerful and evocative. Stories of this mythical singer, whose command of song charmed all nature, most likely circulated through the songs of bards who claimed some link with his enchanting art. Because he was said to have gone down to Hades to retrieve his wife, Eurydice, Orpheus became associated with beliefs about the afterlife. Small groups of Greeks in many city-states, from the sixth century B.C. well into the Christian period, appear to have followed rituals and practices, such as abstaining from meat, which they claimed came from Orpheus, in order to ensure happiness after death. Some texts buried with devotees—like the fourth-century B.C. papyrus found in a northern Greek tomb in 1962—refer to an elaborate and exclusively "Orphic" tale of the origin of gods (in this retelling, placed in the mouth of the singer). In this noncanonical version, Eros hatches from an egg laid by Night and helps produce the world. After a succession of gods, Dionysus, son of Zeus, is killed, cooked, and devoured by the Titans, who in turn are incinerated by the divine father's thunderbolt. Human beings come from the ashes.

## II.    THE MUSES AND THEIR OFFSPRING

Now let us celebrate the Muses and all other famous singers, the players of lyres and flutes, dancers and pipers—for without them, no banquet or wedding feast, sacrifice or grand funeral, is complete. Nor would any stories of the gods and heroes ever reach us. The Muses were there, they saw all, they remember. Fame is passed down only through song. Bronze Age followed Silver, and the heroes of legend came, for a few glorious generations, warring at Thebes and Troy, before our present age—the gritty, lawless Iron Age—began. Through all of those times, through their chosen poets, the Muses have sung.

To the north of Mt. Olympus lies Pieria—"Fat Land," they called it. There a sister of Kronos, Mnemosyne, or Memory, gave birth. Nine nights Zeus had left the company of the other gods and visited her bed, resulting in nine daughters, the Muses, who make one forget all ills and put an end to cares. They create delight by singing and dancing, playing music, and praising their father's world, as their very names say: Clio "makes famous," Melpomene "sung about," Euterpe and Terpsikhore "delight" and "dance-delighting," Erato "lovely," Calliope "fair-voiced," Thalia "blooming," Polymnia "of many hymns," and Ourania "of the sky" (these last two names describing their father's royal position). The sisters have their dancing places and fine home near the peak of Olympus, not far from the houses of the Graces and Desire. At all the gods' feasts they lead the songs and perform, celebrating their immortal kin just as poets celebrate the gods.

Sometimes they make joyful processions in the hills, binding peak to peak with their trail of sacred songs about their father, recalling how once he overcame Kronos, how he rewarded the gods and assigned their roles. Sometimes they dance on their soft white feet around the dark springs in the mountains or circle, dancing, around the altars of Zeus. Then you can see them descending like mist from the hilltops. Once they met Hesiod the shepherd as he pastured sheep on Helikon in Boeotia—and they were not so gentle. "You shepherds, you are always sleeping out in barnyards. You are an utter disgrace, nothing but scrounging bellies. *We're* the ones who can tell lies that sound like truth. And we know how to sing the truth as well—when we want to." They chose him, breathed into him and taught him song, and as a sign of his new powers they gave him a staff cut from blossoming daphne. They told him to sing about the gods and always to put the Muses first. And so poets still do.

The most influential of these daughters of Zeus is Calliope. Her gifts are prized not just by singers, but also by kings, for being a good speaker, with a clear, loud voice, is what is needed to persuade and control the people. In general, the person on whom the Muses look kindly at birth will grow up to be a poet or a ruler—two jobs not at all unrelated, requiring skill to please and hold crowds, and wizardry at language. Then again, poets are like doctors. If anyone is sick with grief, his or her heart quite parched, the poet will sing of the immortals or the great heroes, and right away the patient loses memory of the painful experience. Such is the therapy of the Muses.

Like many an immortal woman, Calliope was married to a mortal man, a combination that never seemed to end up well. She and her husband, Oeagrus of Thrace, had two sons. Not surprisingly, since their mother was a Muse, they were both excellent musicians. So good was Linus, the first son, at singing that he was killed by the god Apollo, who could tolerate no rival to his own art. Because the young man's singing had been widely beloved, mourning for him spread all the way to Egypt, and the "Linus song" of lament was passed down for centuries. (Others say that this Linus was Apollo's own son, and that he was slain not by his father but by the young Herakles, when Linus was too strict as a music teacher to him.)

The second son, Orpheus, was even more renowned for his music. When he played on the strings of his *kithara*, the beasts of the field and the wild, predator and prey, gathered to listen, transfixed by his song. Trees and even the stones themselves moved at the music of his lyre; birds in the air and fish in the sea leapt and soared to the rhythms played. He was a sage as well, versed in the ways of the gods. Charms and purifications, cures and means to avert divine wrath, were invented by him. The mysteries of Dionysus, some say, were brought to Greece by the poet Orpheus. Like Dionysus himself, who brought his mother, Semelê, back from the dead, Orpheus once made the journey to Hades. But it did not end happily.

Orpheus was married to the beautiful Thracian nymph Eurydice. Not long after their wedding, as she was running happily one day through a low-lying meadow, she stepped by accident on a water snake, was bitten, and died. Overcome with grief, Orpheus traveled to the land of the shades. He entreated Hades and Persephone, the rulers of that realm, to give his wife back. As he spoke, in tears, his voice changed from pleading to lamenting, and his fingers ran softly, by instinct, over the lyre strings. All the famous dead, even those like Sisyphus, engaged on eternally fruitless tasks, paused to listen. The dreaded Furies themselves began to weep.

This was too much. Hades, lord of the dead, relented—but on one condition. Orpheus could not look behind him once as he led Eurydice forth to the light of life. The journey was long, the pathway steep. Orpheus was tense with delight, and the desire grew to gaze once more on his beloved wife who followed behind. After they had gone on for what seemed like hours and hours, he became apprehensive—was Eurydice really there? Or was this a trick of the gods, who could be so cruel to humankind? He could not restrain himself. Looking over his shoulder, Orpheus caught a glimpse of his love—only to see her face fill with sudden sadness. Her back was turned to him as she was forced to retreat forever to the world below. Reaching out wildly to grasp Eurydice, he touched only the empty air.

## 12.   THE SONG OF ORPHEUS

This man who had moved the very rocks with his playing now found the gods of the underworld unyielding. For seven days he sat on the banks of the Styx, unfed and unkempt, begging and pleading to be allowed back over. Charon, the wiry old ferryman of the dead, each day collected his souls to transport across the wide stream, but when Orpheus tried to clamber aboard, he would swing his oar at the singer's head and with a curse drive him away. Hungry and exhausted, half-dead himself, Orpheus at last trudged back up to the portal (it was within a cave at Taenaron, at the tip of the southern Peloponnese, where he had first descended) and from there made his way north, home to his native Thrace.

He could not be consoled. For years he shunned human company. The world the way it was became intolerable, and so he changed it all utterly with his tortoiseshell lyre. A broad field full of harsh sunlight Orpheus transformed into a grove. A few melodies from his lyre strings, and soon, where nothing but scrub had ever grown, there flourished ilex and oak, beech, laurel, ash, birch, plane, hazel, myrtle, ivy, arbutus, maple—endless profusion of woods. That is how he repaid the world for its harshness.

All this time he held in his head a long song, on which he worked day by day like a crafted piece of wood, a house within his mind into which he built rooms and labyrinthine passages. It faintly resembled other songs, but as a distant echo, faded and disturbed. It went like this:

*What was there in the beginning? Mud.*
*Mud and water made earth, earth and water*
*Time, a bull lion, son of slime,*
*Snake with a face like a god.*

*Time with Chaos made pure Aither,*
*Time made an egg in her, silver, round.*
*The egg split open, out came Phanes,*
*Shining One, First Born, maker of all.*

*Phanes the brilliant, gold were his wings,*
*Bull-headed, marvelous, female, male—*
*All was within him, all in her,*
*Every name was right for this pair.*

*Cities, mountains, mansions, men,*
*Homes for gods did Phanes fashion,*
*Night was his daughter, Night his wife,*
*Night took his mind and scepter.*

*Night had Heaven, Night had Sky,*
*Heaven and Sky made Titans.*
*Zeus came along in the usual way,*
*Zeus ate Phanes and grew stronger.*

*All in his belly roiled and grew,*
*Ocean, underworld,* aither, *sky,*
*Zeus the Maker made all new,*
*Zeus the Start and Finish.*

*Korê he wanted, Korê took;*
*made a son Dionysus.*
*Him the Titans hated and killed,*
*Lured him to death with playthings.*

*Each Titan smeared his face with clay,*
*White-masked, they found the toddler.*
*"Have a mirror; here's a nice ball."*
*He took the toys and they slew him.*

*Zeus made Apollo piece back the body;*
*The heart, saved by Athena,*
*Zeus put again in Dionysus,*
*Dionysus, reborn at Delphi.*

*Titans had tasted his tender flesh, though,*
*Grilled it and boiled the tidbits.*
*Furious Zeus flashed forth his lightning,*
*Burning the Titans to ashes.*

*What was there in the end? Ashes; men:*
*Mortals rose from those ashes.*
*Mostly Titans, but part a small god,*
*Mortals must hail Dionysus.*

That was the strange song that came from within Orpheus, the
burden of his grief emerging in the weird music that went with it.
Some say he killed himself soon after losing his wife to death the second time, but that was not so. This instead was his strange death:

Shrouded in his grief, Orpheus appeared to be neglecting Dionysus, odd as that might seem, since all his singing used to conclude
with the name of the god of intoxication. To tell the truth, it was the
female worshipers of the god whom he spurned, for he had no interest in women. Despite this—perhaps because of this—they loved
him, some passionately. But he was immovable as stone. Scorned, the

Thracian women began to spread evil tales. They blamed Orpheus with leading astray husbands, who followed him the way nature itself had trailed him once, for his music and his mysterious learning, his stories of the underworld. Whether moved by neglect of their homes, their rituals, or themselves, the women of Thrace had their revenge.

One day, spying him from a height amid the trees and beasts who listened intently to his ethereal music, the women, already frenzied from their Dionysus rites, attacked. One, clad in a leopard skin, threw her long, sharp-pointed ritual stick, the *thyrsos*, just grazing Orpheus' face. Another picked up a huge rock and aimed it at him, but before the rock could hit, his song paralyzed it in midair (for Orpheus could stop stones as well as move them). The assault grew fiercer. In a mad lust to kill, the women took clods of earth, tree branches, hoes, and clod hammers. They swarmed around him like hunting hounds cornering prey. Overwhelmed, he was shoved to the ground, but still held out his small lyre to shelter his head from their blows. Like the Titans of his own creation song, they tore Orpheus limb from limb.

But that was not the end of his singing. He had a sort of resurrection. Done with their bloody deed, the women tossed his head and lyre into the Hebrus, which flowed with the fragments of the singer down to the sea and entrusted them to the waves. In a few days the gray, lapping waters brought what was left of Orpheus to the shores of Lesbos, at Methymnê, where some fishermen found the head and lyre and buried them in a tomb. From the grave, people say, kept on coming beautiful music and singing to the lyre, so that the island would sometimes be filled with sound and a strange voice. That is why it is to this day the most musical of places, the home of Sappho and Terpander and Alcaeus—all the finest singers and instrumentalists.

Orpheus' spirit descended to the underworld it had once seen and, united with Eurydice, roamed happily in the Elysian Fields— at least some say this. The Thracian women, meanwhile, were punished by their menfolk. Grief-stricken and angry, they decided to tattoo all the females, so that they would bear on their bodies purplish signs like the bruises they had inflicted on the gentle singer. And the custom persists.

## 13.   THE MUSES VICTORIOUS

Orpheus never meant to offend. His art came from the Muses, and he never boasted of his powers as if they were anything other than a divine gift. That was not always the case with other singers, and at times the Muses had to remind mortals of the real sources of song.

There was a handsome man named Thamyris, whose parents were Philammon and the nymph Argiope. Himself the son of Apollo, Philammon was a superb lyre player, and his son, too, became skilled in the arts of music. So accomplished was he that some later said his real mother was a Muse, Erato (nor did Thamyris discourage the rumor). In fact, the Muses turned out to be his antagonists.

Like many a poet and singer, Thamyris traveled far and wide, spreading the latest events through his verses, and celebrating great heroes. Kings and warriors were sometimes willing to maintain a full-

time bard, as long as they were praised. There were plenty of patrons in those days for good performers, and many a contest at fair days to see who was the best.

Once, Thamyris was on his way back from visiting a relation of his, Eurytos, who was also a grandson of Apollo and lived in Oikhalia, to the north of Mt. Parnassus. Eurytos was skilled in archery—another of his grandfather's special gifts—and his confidence with the bow would eventually bring him to a bad end. Thamyris was already nearing Dorion, in the western Peloponnese, when he came across nine beautiful young women in the hills: the Muses.

He recognized them at once and decided—fool that he was—to have some fun. "Let's see who is the best at singing to the *kithara*. Here is my challenge," he announced. "If I win, then I have my way with you—each and every one. If you win, take from me whatever you will." He began, almost violently, to pluck the strings and sing a long heroic tale. It is not known who could have judged them in that wild and lonely spot. The Muses had their turn and, of course, handily won at the singing; they were, after all, daughters of Memory and endlessly inventive. The prize they chose was the mortal's eyes. These eyes were not just beautiful, but highly unusual as well, for one was black and the other white. They put an end to his singing also (for blindness, they knew, sometimes made bards even better). They took away his gift of song and made him forget even how to play his instrument. Thamyris was ruined.

Nor were the Muses any kinder when women were their rivals. Another time they were challenged by nine stupid sisters, the daughters of Pieros from Macedonia, who traveled as a sort of choral group through Thessaly and Achaea, entertaining and impressing all by the sublimity of their blended voices. They found the Muses on one of their favorite mountains, Helikon in Boeotia, and began to mock the goddesses, saying, "It is easy enough to gull the country bumpkins hereabouts. Let's see who are the real singers. We'll have a song duel. Let the nymphs judge. And the losers have to take to the road and leave their homes behind forever."

Each side chose soloists, for whom the rest then sang along as a choir. The Pierides began with a dreadful parody, a *Battle of Gods and Giants* in which the Giants won, and the Olympian divinities slunk off to Egypt, of all places, where they became various birds and beasts of the type one sees there in pictures. When the last note echoed, the Muses took their turn—a long and intricate song, telling of the sorrow of Demeter, enough to make any audience weep, except their rivals. The nymphs had no doubt of the winner, but the Pierides kept on with their mocking, poor losers that they were. "Your challenge was bad enough. Now you go too far," hissed the goddesses. In the midst of their complaining, their cackling and rude laughter, the mortal sisters began to sprout wings and feathers all over. The Muses made them magpies.

## 14.  APOLLO'S RIVAL

Not only the Muses disliked mortal rivals in music. Apollo, the lyre player, who often struck up tunes to lead the Muses in circling dances on their mountain home, detested overweening performers.

His own musical sons were not a threat, for these young men (called the Corybantes) played a different instrument, the broad, shield-size skin drum named *tympanum*, hardly a match for the lyre in anyone's estimation. Thalia the Muse was their mother, some said. Others claimed that the Corybantes came from the Great Mother, Cybele, and that was why they were larer worshiped at her lofty shrine on the misty northern island Samothrace. Only those initiated into the Mother's mysteries there could learn their real father's name. In any case, these boys bore an uncanny resemblance to Apollo. The Corybantes even had powers to drive one mad, or to heal illness, and it is well known that Apollo is a healer, too. They spent most of their time over in Asia, in Phrygia, to be precise.

From this same place came Apollo's challenger. His name was Marsyas, and most people think he was a satyr, having pointed ears and the tail of a horse (while the rest of him looked mostly human). His instrument was the *auloi,* the double pipes with a thin reed mouthpiece. Unlike the Corybantes, who made the first drums, however, he was not clever enough to have invented the *auloi*. Athena had recently made the first ones, and Marsyas merely picked them up when she discarded them.

What happened was this: the hero Perseus (about whom more later) had Athena's divine aid in slaying the Gorgon named Medusa. Athena heard the way in which Medusa's sisters wailed in mourning, their snake-entwined heads emitting eerie sounds that seemed to come from the many reptilian tongues themselves, although they were actually Gorgon voices. Proud of her young hero, and of herself,

Athena decided to imitate the voices of this monstrous lament. What was a funeral song for Medusa would become a victory song for her.

Always the clever craftswoman, she drilled holes in lengths of box-wood, fitted the pipes with reeds, and produced a convincing imitation, "the many-headed tune," as she called it, weaving in and out of it the varied wails of snaky voices. Yet as Athena played, her cheeks all puffed up to make the high, screaming notes, she happened to glance into a nearby stream and saw her reflection as in a mirror. "What an ugly, shapeless face!" she gasped, and threw down the pipes in disgust, never to play them again. Marsyas later came sauntering along, picked up the instrument from the turf by the riverbank, fiddled with it, found he could make different notes by covering the holes with his fingers, and (since he had nothing else to do) became a fine musician.

So good was Marsyas at the *auloi* that he made the mistake of challenging Apollo to a music contest. They played for the usual terms—winner does what he will with the loser. They matched each other tune for tune. Note for note, Apollo was shadowed by Marsyas, who had a natural gift for imitation, and could even make his pipes mimic the lightly plucked strings. It was a duel of instruments, really—which was better, soothing lyre or wild *auloi*? Then Apollo had an inspiration. Flipping his lyre upside down so that the tortoiseshell was up near his chin and the string-board pointing down, he started strumming a dance tune and shouted out, "Imitate this!" Now, no one, no matter how good an aulete, can play the pipes turned upside down. Marsyas was beaten. Apollo, the winner, hung him on a nearby pine tree and stripped the skin off his body, which is why pine trees still bear a reddish bark.

## 15.  HERMES TRICKS APOLLO

It may seem like a low-down trick, not worthy of Apollo, this reverse playing by which he defeated the satyr. Yet it shows that the god had learned a few things from his younger brother. Apollo had not always claimed the lyre as his own. Here is how he came to have it:

Zeus once loved a nymph, a daughter of Atlas, named Maia, who lived in a cozy, shadowy cave in Arcadia. She gave birth to a lying, cheating, dream-inducing, night-strolling, little baby, Hermes. In many ways he resembled his mother's uncle, Prometheus. He was a trickster, from the moment he first opened his eyes.

The day he was born, Hermes managed to climb out of his cra-

dle and toddle toward the opening of the cave, where he met a tortoise, which was munching some tender grass at the entrance. The baby chuckled and said, "How lucky I am today! You beautiful thing, lovely lady who goes to dances, how nice that you've come! Where did you ever get that nice shiny shell you wear, and why are you hiding it away up here in the mountains! Come in  You can really help me out." To himself he added: "When you're dead, that is—then you'll make some fine music." With both his baby hands he lifted up the tortoise, carried this new toy inside, and in a flash had scooped it right out of the shell. He cut some reeds, made a frame, stretched a cowhide over the shell, added a yoke for the two upright pieces, and finished by stringing it with seven twisted cords of sheep gut.

Then Hermes tried out his new invention, plucking it with a pick and singing a little improvised song:

*"Zeus and Maia made me;*
*Once in love they fell.*
*Nice cave! Nice slaves!*
*Nice tripods here as well!"*

It was not a very good song, but he was just a baby and had to versify whatever was in his surroundings. His mind was already racing toward other topics. Meat, for instance.

Hermes tucked his lyre into the cradle and, like a burglar in the night, made off for Pieria, the homeland of the Muses, where Apollo kept his cattle. When he arrived, he cut fifty cows out of the herd. Instead of driving them off, though, he made sure to confuse their owner by walking them backward so the footprints would point the other way. Meanwhile, he disguised his own trail by tying little bundles of leaves and branches to his feet.

Over mountain and hollow and plain he drove them, until Night was giving way to Dawn, who calls people to their labors. By that time Hermes had reached the river Alpheus, in the western Peloponnese. And he got to work as well. Herding the rest of the cattle into pens, and giving them dewy grass to eat, he settled down to build a fire. He took fire sticks (he was the first to make them), rubbed them, started a flame, and then fed it with tinder and kindling, piling on logs when it was burning nicely. Then he took two of the cows, gently mooing, and with one great swoop flipped them onto their backs. He butchered them, spitted the meat, collected the innards and blood, and stretched the hides over a nearby rock (where they can still be seen, petrified).

Now it was time to eat. The baby cut up twelve portions and laid them out, as for a feast of the Olympians. But savory as the smoke was, and hungry as he had become, Hermes did not eat. After all, he was a god, not a mortal craving food. He left some of the cooked meat as a mark of his successful theft, quenched the coals, and went home. He slipped into the cave like a mist and wrapped himself up in the cradle blanket, holding the lyre. But Maia was not fooled. "Where have you been in the middle of the night, you shameless little one? You're such a worry. I'm afraid Apollo's going to come and tie you up and bundle you out of here." To which Hermes replied, "Why are you treating me like an infant? I'm about to launch a career that will raise both of us. Why should we two be stuck in this hole, without sacrifices and suppliants coming to us? Why not live a rich, full life, mingling with the other immortals? Besides, I'm going to get a great honor from Apollo. Either my father will get it for me or I'll drill a hole into his temple at Delphi and steal gold, and iron, and clothes and tripods. Just you wait and see."

While they were conversing, Apollo was already on Hermes' trail. He made some inquiries, consulted some bird signs, and found out that the newborn child of Zeus and Maia was the culprit. As he came closer, Apollo noticed hoof marks—but they were heading the other way. The traces in the dust next to them looked like no human's he had encountered. At last he reached the Arcadian cave of Maia. Sensing her divine fragrance all around him, he stepped over the threshold into the coolness.

As soon as Hermes saw him, he burrowed deeper into the blankets, like a coal in the ashes, and tucked his lyre closer to his body. But Apollo was not deceived. He started checking, but found nothing in the cedar chests but nectar, ambrosia, gold, silver, lots of clothes—what a god's house usually contains. Then he turned to Hermes. "You in the cradle—show me the cows, right now. Because if you don't, I swear I'll hurl you to Tartarus, deep and dark, and your parents won't be able to bring you back. You can play the smart one down there—big boss of all the little boys."

Hermes had a clever answer ready. "Son of Lêto, why are you looking for cattle here? I didn't see any, hear of any, witness any theft—nor, frankly, do I resemble a thief. I have only soft blankets, warm baths, and mother's milk on my mind. Imagine what the other gods will say when they find out you go around threatening babies. I was born yesterday. My feet are tender and the ground is rough. Do you want me to swear an oath? I myself never stole or saw anyone else steal your cows—whatever 'cows' really are. I've only heard the word."

Apollo was having no more of this. He reached down and grabbed the baby. Hermes, thinking fast, let out, in quick succession, a fart and a sneeze—and Apollo dropped him. Back and forth they argued, and Apollo countered every dodge Hermes could make. Finally, the baby took off for Olympus and their father's house, while Apollo followed behind.

When they reached the fragrant halls, with the immortals gathered around and the scales of justice set up before them, Zeus asked, "Phoebos, where did you find this excellent prize, a young boy with the looks of a herald? This is a serious matter, no doubt, you bring before the divine assembly."

Apollo proceeded to tell all about the tiring trip he had made to Arcadia, the confusing tracks, the clues, the baby's denial. Hermes spoke in turn, swearing an oath that he never left his mother's cave, never stole the cattle, concluding: "Believe me. You are my father, so you say. Aid the weaker side." Zeus looked at Hermes, who had been holding his baby blanket up to his cheek all this time and peering around, and he laughed at the little liar. "You two, go together and look for the cows. Hermes, you lead. Show him the place you penned them. And no tricks." And so they did. When Apollo found out that Hermes had not only taken the cattle but butchered a pair of them, he was angry and tried to tie up the thief. But Hermes caused the willow-branch cords to fall off his body, and they took root and grew magically all around the cattle. Apollo was dumbstruck.

Before the older god could react, Hermes slyly pulled out his lyre, struck up a tune, and sang in a lovely voice a praise song about how all the gods came to have their honors. First (like a good bard) he named Mnemosyne, mother of the Muses, and then all the others, in proper order, with all the right details. By this time Apollo was overcome with longing. "You cow murderer, this thing you've devised is worth fifty head of cattle. Who taught you this art? It's joy, it's passion, it's repose. I know the Muses and lead them in dance; but the dancing, the piping, the songs at feasts—they are nothing compared to this!" And he kept praising Hermes' performance, promising to make him respected and famous.

They concluded the business like this: Apollo could take the lyre for his constant companion, since he was so eager to play and sing and carry it to dances and banquets—"but be gentle with her," said Hermes. He also took an oath, at Apollo's insistence, that he would not steal the instrument back again. In exchange, Apollo gave Hermes a beautiful staff, the right to herd cattle and flocks, and full control over the Bee Women of Apollo's mountain Parnassus, who make prophetic utterances once they have eaten wild honey (and, unfed, tell lies).

## 16. PAN THE GOAT-GOD

When Hermes was grown up, he preferred the outdoors amid the rough mountains of Arcadia, especially Kyllene, to the homes of the gods on Olympus. The country was full of rivulets and watercourses and, therefore, full of nymphs as well, who always dwell near them. One nymph, the daughter of Dryops, Hermes found particularly attractive. So great a melting passion for her overtook him that he, though a god, consented to work as a shepherd for her father just to be near the girl. In time the two married, and the nymph (whose name may have been Dryopê) gave birth. The baby was even more of a surprise to its mother than Hermes had been to his. Seeing it for the first time, the nymph screamed in terror and ran out of the house. The nursemaid did the same. Then Hermes bent over the cradle and peered in. What appeared to his eyes had a baby face—with a beard and a leering smile. He had two budding horns coming out of the forehead, little hooves where feet should have been, and a short tail.

Hermes was mightily pleased. He tenderly lifted the goat-child and wrapped it in the softest hides of a mountain hare. Holding the baby to his chest, he set out for Olympus, to introduce his new son to the other gods. All of them were absolutely delighted, especially Dionysus (whose companions already included a number of half-goat and horsey figures). Since *all* were made happy by the infant, that is what they called him: "All"—or, in Greek, *Pan.*

The boy Pan proved to be a happy, lusty, randy, roving creature—like a goat. He would climb the steepest hills where only goats could clamber up the rocks. For hours he would look out from the heights over the valleys, sniffing the air, his beard lifted by the breeze. He was a great one for dancing with the nymphs, able to cavort for hours on his tough legs, hooves stomping out the rhythm. He liked to sing and to hunt. On occasion he would let out a *whoop* that could be heard all over the mountain, echoing from glen to glen. Any human being unlucky enough to be alone in those wild places might shrink in fear hearing this powerful uncanny sound, an uncomfortable feeling that people began to call "panic," after the goat-god who caused it.

Pan also was a musician and invented the shepherd's reed pipes—the Pan pipes—after a lost love. Once on his way home from Mt. Lycaeus, where the dancing had gone on that day, Pan thought he saw the goddess Artemis. He was not afraid of having fun with divine beings. Once he had even turned himself into a lamb with a beautiful fleece and managed to draw the moon, Selene, from her proper place in the sky, down into the deep Arcadian woods, at least for a night. So Pan started his usual sweet-talking. This was no goddess, though, but a shy nymph. Soon Pan was no longer jesting. As his passion began to grow, the nymph grew more afraid. She ran down through the trees toward the plain, Pan in full pursuit, his hooves clattering, the pine-branch crown he was still wearing from the dance slipping down over his sweaty forehead. She reached the river Ladon near collapse from exhaustion, but still hearing Pan's approach, and terrified of the violent goat-man. "Sisters! Help!" she screamed to the river nymphs. Instantly she vanished into the reeds growing on the marshy bank. Pan reached the very spot but could not see her. Instead, he heard only a low reedy sound, as the wind blew over the stream and swirled along the riverside. Pan clutched at the reeds to catch her, but came up with only woody stalks. "At least I can have your voice," he thought, and he cut the stalks, trimmed them to different lengths, bound them with wax, and breathed into them, reproducing the melodious sound, if nothing more, of his love, Syrinx—whose name he bestowed on the instrument. Now he plays every day on the pipe, and the goats, at least, are happier.

There is a third tale about Pan and mysterious voices, also the story of a nymph. Her name was Echo. When Pan chased her, she gradually disappeared, rather than vanishing into thin air, until only her resonating voice remained—or was it just Pan's own? He had taught himself to imitate Syrinx; untutored, Echo now perfectly mimicked him. A more unlikely version holds that Pan was so angry at being rejected by the nymph that he let out his terrifying holler and drove the mountain men into a panic, so the shepherds and goatherds, acting like wild dogs, tore Echo to pieces. Her scattered remains kept putting forth her voice, which haunts the mountains still.

Perhaps we should believe the further variant, that Echo, having escaped Pan's attentions, used to play with the other nymphs, and when Zeus was interested in spending time with one of her friends, she used to distract his wife Hera by chatting with her for as long as was needed. Hera realized what was going on and punished the girl appropriately, making her unable to speak unless she repeated the last words she had heard. Then it was Echo's turn to suffer passion, the story goes. She desired with all her heart Narcissus—sixteen, blond, and handsome, but utterly uninterested in love. Echo lingered unseen in the woods where Narcissus liked to hunt with his companions. Noticing something moving in the brush, he called to his friends, but it was not they who answered:

"Will you come over here?"

"Over here."

"What, can't you find me?"

"Find me."

"Look, I can't stay all day."

"Stay all day."

Now Narcissus knew his friends had their weapons poised to spear their prey, and he didn't fancy getting mistaken for a boar or deer.

"This game is getting risky. I don't want to run into your arms."

"Run into your arms!" came the delighted reply, and with that Echo, who had been waiting for this invitation, rushed from her shady hiding place and embraced her love.

Narcissus was horrified. Perhaps he had heard of men carried off at noon by nymphs, as often happened. "Let go. Get away from me. There's no way that I'll do your will."

Heartbroken, Echo fell away, saying softly, "I'll do your will." She spent the rest of her days up in the hills, mourning for that lost chance, and withered away until only her voice was left.

Narcissus came to pay for his aloofness. One day, tired and hot from the hunt, he paused to drink from a secluded pool. As he bent down to touch the glassy surface, he found himself facing a handsome youth, with curling hair like Apollo's, a fine ivory neck, shining eyes, and the hint of a blush. Transfixed, he stared for hours. Whenever he tried to touch that perfect face, it fled beneath the waters. He pined, he ached with fever, his strength dwindled, and like wax in the sun, his heart melted with love—of his reflected self. Even when he finally died on the spot, his spirit, in the underworld, spent all his time gazing into the waters of Styx. When his sisters, the nymphs of the area, went looking for Narcissus, they found, instead of his young body on the grass, a beautiful white and gold flower—now named for him.

# BOOK THREE

## LOVERS MORTAL
## AND DIVINE

GREEK GODS AND GODDESSES seem particularly susceptible to love affairs—a fact that did not escape the ancient Greeks themselves. By the sixth century B.C., Xenophanes, a poet and philosopher from Ionia, was already complaining that the myths about gods depicted them as immoral, as thieves, deceivers, and adulterers. How is this divine behavior explained?

The allegorical method (see the Introduction) tried, in various ways, to rehabilitate the gods' reputation. If "Zeus" was really an animated way of talking about the weather, then his frequent encounters with nymphs or women on earth could be read as explanations for fertility and irrigation. More probable is a sociological interpretation that would view the many tales of Zeus' amorous errands as political assertions by powerful clans claiming that their heroic ancestors were the sons or daughters of the chief god. Certainly, a number of aristocratic families in the archaic period traced their descent from Herakles, son of Zeus. Aeneas, said to be a son of Aphrodite, was revered as the founder of the Roman people. The myth continued to prove useful for propaganda as late as the first century B.C., when Julius Caesar and Augustus claimed the Trojan hero as their ancestor.

Besides the obvious political advantages to such love stories, there was, doubtless, high entertainment value, playing on the fascination ordinary folk have often had with those who are fantastically power-ful, unreachable, and good-looking—an Adonis, Aphrodite, or Ares. Seeing them subject to the same passions as mortals may have been particularly satisfying to Greek audiences. On another level, there seems to have been a theoretical, even philosophical, urge behind such tales as the loves of Apollo and Zeus that produced Asklepios and Dionysus. How else could such beneficial phenomena as healing and wine enter into the world of humans if not through divine interven-tion? Apollo especially is often depicted as bringing order or shape to the world through his passions. Embodied in such myths is deep reli-gious feeling, a recognition that good things come from the gods— but also that encountering gods can be dangerous.

History and ritual also must be taken into account when we try to interpret such myths as Demeter's search for Persephone, or the death of Pentheus. The former story is linked with a key religious institu-tion, the festival of the Mysteries at Eleusis, twelve miles west of Athens. Each autumn, for nearly a millennium, thousands of people flocked to this site to become initiated in rites that, to this day, remain secret. The tale of Demeter's grief over Persephone's abduction, told in the *Hymn to Demeter*, is clearly connected to the agricultural cycle, to the growth of crops over which the goddess presided. It could orig-inally have explained why the seasons occur. Fertility rituals through-out Greek lands were tied to the myth, just as they were connected with the stories of Adonis, another dying youth. The Mysteries at Eleusis may have elaborated this basic story and ritual complex into an allegory about human death and rebirth, promising initiates a happy afterlife.

As for the death of Pentheus, at the hands of women driven wild by Dionysus, another religious phenomenon intersects with the myth. Seasonal festivals throughout Greece commemorated the god of wine, intoxication, and ecstasy. At Athens, one such festival was the main occasion for performances of comedy and tragedy, which originated in informal processions and skits honoring Dionysus. Apart from such civic celebrations, there were also private rites, usually observed by women, who went to the wild uplands to perform ecstatic dances. These women were called "Bacchants" (after Bacchus—another name for the god) or Maenads ("the maddened ones"). As crystallized in Eu-ripides' tragedy *The Bacchae*, the mythic version depicts such women as dangerously violent, able to tear apart large animals, and eager to eat raw flesh. Mythically, Bacchants play a role not unlike that of the male-threatening Amazons, the women warriors from the east. In the actual rites, it appears that small pieces of raw meat were offered to the god, but there is no evidence for anything wilder. If anything, maenadic associations in the historical period resemble social clubs.

The mystery and sacredness of mountain land, glimpsed in the Pentheus story, are best represented in Greek myth by Mt. Olympus, where the gods and goddesses were thought to dwell. Here they lived in a divine version of the palaces inhabited by early Greek kings and their courts. Even the location—atop a towering peak—seems to be a fantasy based on the fact that human kings, in the Bronze Age, often had their houses on the high point of a territory, the local acropolis. On Olympus, each divinity had quarters, beautiful rooms made of bronze and gold by the smith Hephaestus. A wall surrounded the entire complex, containing a great gate, wide enough for divine chariots to pass through when gods wanted to drive out and intervene in earthly matters. From the cloud-wreathed peak, Zeus and his family kept an eye on human affairs, and the chief god's lightning bolts flashed forth to punish transgressors.

In early sources, Olympus is in fact not easily distinguished from the upper sky, and seems to be a clear, lucid space, far above rain, snow, or wind. Only occasionally do we hear that it is a mountain rooted in the earth. Several mountains in Greece, Asia Minor, and Cyprus were named Olympus, but the gods' home seems to have been located by most Greeks on a snow-covered peak not far from the present-day city of Thessaloniki. This Olympus is actually a series of peaks, the tallest of which towers nearly 9,500 feet. Archaeologists have discovered several religious shrines on the mountain range, but no single complex that would give any historical grounding to the myth that this was home to the gods. There is little doubt that Greeks in antiquity could and did ascend the mountain—the climb, popular among modern hikers, can be made in a day. Did they question belief in their gods when failing to see golden palaces at the climax of their ascent? Or did they imagine they could discern the very dwellings of the gods shining forth in the cold mountain air? No ancient Greek who made the climb left behind anything to enlighten us.

## 17.   THE LOVES OF APOLLO

It is hard to love a god. It is easy for them, on the other hand, to fall in love with mortals, usually with fatal results. All the same, this is the way—through the passions of the Olympians and lesser divinities—that the world has been shaped and settled and named.

When the hillsides are all ablaze with color in the spring, every tree and bush and flower brings to mind a story. You may find Narcissus is there or Cyparissus—the cypress (once another handsome boy). And then there is the hyacinth.

Hyacinthus was a fine young man who lived in Amyklai, not far from Sparta. He loved hunting and music and sports. In these last two, at least, he was like Apollo, the divine lyre player at whose sacred shrine in Delphi famous athletes came from all over Greece to compete. His music making must have been impressive, since people came to say the Muse Clio was his mother, though everybody knew he was the son of local gentry. Perhaps it was this skill that first attracted Thamyris, the unfortunate bard, who doted on him once. Later, Apollo made Hyacinthus his favored companion. Neglecting his shrine and oracle, he would spend entire days roaming the woods with the young man, learning about traps, setting nets, or keeping the hounds leashed until the hue and cry went up.

One day, tired of the hunt, the pair turned to other amusements. Oiling their bodies, they strode out to a sandy stretch of ground to hurl the discus. Effortlessly the god hefted the heavy circle, curled about, coiling his strength, and then lofted it high into the air. Hyacinthus nearly lost sight of the discus as he followed its path toward the sun. He spotted it descending, and he ran to see the length of the god's magnificent cast and mark the spot. The discus touched ground but skidded, hopped and rebounded, headed upward again, and struck him hard in the head.

Hyacinthus lay crumpled on the grass. All of Apollo's doctoring—herbs and compresses—was in vain. Blood continued to trickle from the wound. But where it fell, instead of stains, grew a beautiful flower, like a lily but purple. As his young companion's spirit ebbed, Apollo determined to make his lament eternal. The sharp sigh "Ai Ai" that rose from his chest would not die, for he inscribed it on the petals of the flower that bloomed before him. And so it stays.

Apollo also figured in the tale of Daphne. He had not planned on falling in love with the girl. Years before, he had set out from his island birthplace Delos, through Euboia and Boeotia and up through rough country to Krisa and Parnassus. He had settled on a spot there for his oracle, where he was to share with mortals the mysterious divine will of Zeus. But the place—near a gorge and spring, with a splendid eagle's eye view of the gulf—was already occupied. A huge snaky creature, age-old and ugly, lay guarding the waters. It was the Python, to whom long ago Gaia had entrusted the young monster Typhoeus in her last attempt to ruin Zeus.

Apollo moved forward cautiously. He had never yet used his shining golden bow. This was his first time. The dragon slumbered, occasionally an eyelid lazily opening and a snaky tongue lashing out, from habit more than anticipation. When he was just within range, the young god bent his bow, notched the arrow, aimed at the beast's head, and let fly. The Python screamed, an unholy cry that would have terrified any mortals within hearing. Her snaky length coiled and uncoiled in pain. She grew weaker and weaker and closed her eyes and died. "Rot here!" shouted Apollo, with a savage pun on the snake's name (for "Python" means "Rotter"). Slowly the dragon dissolved in the heat of the noonday sun.

From that day Apollo was called "Pythian," after his first kill, and his priestess and mouthpiece, the woman who speaks his oracles when in a trance, bears a similar name: the Pythia. The shrine he established needed priests to supervise the endless sacrificers who were to visit Apollo's temple, so he looked all around, from his lofty position, to find some. Catching sight far off of a ship full of men, on their way from Knossos in Crete to Pylos, Apollo dove into the sea and took the form of a dolphin. He swam right up to the ship and leapt aboard, flopping around wildly until the timbers shook. The crew was dumbfounded. As they sat there, a strong wind filled the sails and drove the ship at top speed straight around the Peloponnese to Krisa, where the wind dropped and the vessel put in to land, all on its own, the helmsman helpless to guide it. Apollo shot from the ship like a burning comet. He landed high up the mountain in his own temple, casting light all around, then blazed back to the harbor and took the form of a beautiful youth, revealing himself to the anxious sailors as the god he really was. Amazed and persuaded, they followed his lead uphill, high-stepping and singing Cretan songs, no longer scraping by at sea, but guardians of a holy site.

All this had happened some years ago, but Apollo was still proud of his shooting. Therefore, when he happened to see the boy Eros one day at play with bow and arrow, the older god could not resist some barbed words. "Leave that to me, son. I killed the Python, after all. What do you know about archery? Taking aim at lovers?" Eros said, "You'll see." Winging his way to Apollo's own mountain, he aimed two very different arrows at two targets and shot: Apollo he hit with the gold-tipped (causing love) and Daphne, daughter of the river Peneios, with the lead-headed (expelling love).

Apollo burned, like chaff that has ignited, with passion for Daphne, who fled from his advances. She was not impressed by his status and prestige—son of Zeus, god of Delphi, healer, lyre player, prophet, all of which he cited for her. Yet as she ran away, hair and dress blown by the wind, blood rushing to her cheeks, she grew even more desirable. Apollo kept up his pursuit. Soon he was nearly touching, his breath at her neck. He would have won her, but they had reached the river (her father) and she prayed, "Help me, ruin my beauty." He did: before Apollo's eyes, she was transformed into the trunk and branches, roots and crown, of a bay laurel tree. Still the god thought her lovely, for he loved her, and took her leaves to wreathe his lyre, his hair, his arrow case.

## 18.   FIERY BIRTHS: ASKLEPIOS AND DIONYSUS

Phlegyas lived and raised horses on the broad plains of Thessaly. He had a daughter, Koronis, the most beautiful girl in the territory. The brilliant Apollo, so often unlucky in his loves, also chose her, but he was no more successful.

A mortal man, Iskhys son of Elatos, lived near the horse farm. He was newly arrived from Arcadia, getting to know the flatlands, and he came to visit more and more often as he saw the fine young woman in Phlegyas' house. Koronis, meanwhile, had not been seeing her divine admirer very often because the god always had other pressing concerns. And what role, anyway, could she ever play among the Olympians, she a girl from Thessaly, they living up on the mountain in golden houses? Why not at least be kindly to a handsome neighbor? One thing led to another, and soon the two young people became more than friends.

Now, Apollo may have been absent, but the pair was not unobserved. In the vicinity was a raven—at that time, a beautiful, glossy white bird (officious and chattersome as now, however). The spying raven caught sight of Koronis in the arms of Iskhys, and it hurried off to tell the master of all bird signs at his shrine in Delphi, "She is unfaithful!" Deep in his heart, Apollo had already begun to realize this. After all, he cannot be deceived. Yet this harsh news from the raven was the final blow. In a jealous rage Apollo picked up his bow, found Koronis, and shot her in the chest. As her breath grew shorter and her body turned cold, the girl gasped: "Our child." But it was too late to save her. Apollo was torn with grief and guilt—how could he have acted so rashly, egged on by gossip from a bird?

The villagers were already piling oak logs for her pyre and the flames were leaping up the sides of the girl's last wooden bed when Apollo stepped forward. The fires parted, opening the way for the god. Reaching out, he snatched his baby boy from its mother's womb. He brought the child to Cheiron, who lived on Mt. Pelion, not far away, so that the wise Centaur could raise the boy and teach him cures for every painful human disease. Asklepios was the name he gave his son. As for the raven, Apollo turned him black.

Dionysus, like Asklepios, is a great help to humans, as his gift of wine heals body and mind. Oddly enough, he had the same sort of birth. Zeus was his father; his mother, Semelê, was a mortal woman, one of the daughters of Kadmos, the founder of Thebes. All might have gone as with the birth of Hermes and the Muses—nighttime wandering of Zeus followed some months later by discreet childbearing, somewhere in a distant spot. But Hera found out that Semelê was pregnant, and determined to make her pay.

On Olympus, she entered a golden cloud that soon touched down near Thebes. Then Hera disguised herself as an old woman, the nursemaid who had tended Semelê for years, and went to see the girl. They chatted about this and that until the name of Zeus came up in the conversation. "He is the one who comes to visit," said the girl to her trusted friend, with a blush. "Are you sure?" said the false nurse. "Why not find out—there are so many impostors—by asking him to come to you in the form he takes when loving Hera?" The next time the lovers met, Semelê did just that, after first making Zeus promise he would grant her whatever she wished.

Zeus was seized with despair. He knew what the end would be. Nevertheless, even the king of gods is bound by the oath of the Styx. So the next night Zeus came to Semelê's bedroom, mounted on his chariot, thunder clashing and bolts blazing fire. The poor girl died of fright and the house was incinerated. Such was his promise of love.

Before his beloved's corpse could disintegrate in the room that had become its pyre, Zeus took his premature son from her body, slashed
himself open, and placed the baby in his own thigh—thus the new
god's name, "Zeus-thigh," in Greek: *Dio-nysos*.

In four more months the child was ready to be born. But Zeus
lived in fear of Hera's revenge. What if she found the baby? It was a
nightmare his own mother must have had fleeing to Crete to avoid the
ravenous, crazed Kronos. Secretly, Zeus unknit the stitches in his
thigh and drew forth the baby. He delivered the child to its aunt, Ino,
and her husband Athamas. "Don't even let him dress as a boy," Zeus
warned them. That was not enough, for Hera learned the truth. The
enraged goddess induced such madness in Ino and her husband that
Athamas, thinking his older son had become a deer, hunted him
down, while Ino took the younger son, Melicertes, and threw him into
a basin of boiling water. Whether she ever realized what she had done
and regretted her act of madness is unknown. Perhaps she did, and for
that reason, cradling the boy's body, she leapt into the sea. Mother and
son live there still, as immortals now. The sailors, whom they help
weather the storms, call Ino "White Goddess" (Leukothea) and her
child "Wrestler" (Palaimon).


## 19.   THE GOD OF ECSTASY

Eventually all who encountered Dionysus felt something akin to madness. Those who resisted the power of his gifts were driven out of their
wits more often than not. Those who welcomed and worshiped him
experienced joy and excitement such as they had never known. Even
those who merely watched the rites of the god were strangely moved.

While Hera was causing havoc with the guardians of the young
Dionysus, driving them to murder and suicide, Zeus managed to
hurry the child out of her sight by turning him temporarily into a
goat kid. In that unexpected form he brought him to the nymphs of
Mt. Nysa in the east, and they took him in, gave him milk, and raised
him. In the meantime, back in his birthplace of Thebes, a rumor circulated. Semelê had really slept with a stranger, a man not a god, and
covered her shame by blaming Zeus. That's why the great god of the
sky struck her down with his bolt, because she had defamed him.
There was no child, it was claimed, and even if one had survived, he
was not divine.

Dionysus was very much alive, however, and wandering the distant regions of Asia in the company of his former nursemaids, now his followers. He visited Persia, Phrygia, Bactria, the Black Sea, Arabia, Syria, Egypt, places that for most Greeks were just hazy images and names. (Some say that Hera had found him and driven him in a maddened state throughout the world, but it was actually his choice to wander.) Everywhere he went spread the cultivation of his discovery: the grapevine.

Now a young man in his full strength, with blue-black hair and beard, Dionysus made his way west toward his mother's royal house. Thrace was the first place he arrived within Greek lands, but there he was not welcomed. Lykourgos, king of the Edonians, who lived beside the river Strymon, spurned his gifts, insulted him, and finally attacked the young god and his nymph companions with an ox goad. The young women dropped their ritual sticks in terror and fled, while Dionysus dove headlong into the sea and swam down to the underwater home of Thetis, daughter of Nereus, who gave him refuge.

Doomed Lykourgos had not long to live, for Dionysus, though distant, drove him insane. Imagining that his son Dryas was a sprawling grapevine, the king pruned his arms and legs with an axe. Then the land withered, as if it, too, had been assaulted and killed. In desperation, the people of the kingdom went to seek an oracle. "The king must die," was the response. So, by the will of Dionysus, the Edonians led Lykourgos up the mountain and, having tied him between two horses, tore him apart.

After this misadventure Dionysus was more cautious. If mortals did not want the intoxicating joy, the release from ordinary life, the merging with wild nature that he brought—then it was not he who would suffer. He disguised himself when he came to Thebes. There he noticed, first, the flame that still burned at the site of his mother's ruined house. Her father, Kadmos, had kept this alive as a memorial to Semelê, turning the land around it into a sacred enclosure. Kadmos had stepped down from the kingship, letting his nephew Pentheus rule instead. The stiff-necked, priggish, younger man was proud of the law and order he enforced throughout Thebes. No eastern cult, with its newfangled music and ecstatic rites, was about to disrupt his city—so he thought.

But just about the time of the stranger's arrival, odd goings-on began to occur. The women of Thebes, starting with the daughters of Kadmos, even Pentheus' own mother, Agavê, seemed to have gone mad. (It was noted, by the way, that the first victims were precisely those who had mocked poor Semelê and her story about being loved by Zeus.) As if driven by gadflies, they rushed up into the woods of Mt. Kithairon, clad only in fawn-skin coverings and crowns of ivy, with *tympana* and long sticks topped with pinecones, just as if they were imitating the "maddened ones" (as people called them), those dangerous followers of Dionysus. For days they did not come back to town. They danced in the hills all day and at night fell down exhausted and slept under the stars, like animals. Even more mysterious tales circulated: that these crazy women of Thebes were suckling the young of wild animals, deer and wolf cubs; that they struck the earth and made fountains of milk or wine or water flow; that their long sticks dripped with honey, a sign of sweet fertility.

Worse, a royal messenger confirmed the rumors: "But it's not what you thought, Pentheus—no hidden love affairs, no carousing with wine up in the hills. If you could see these miracles, you'd fall on your knees before this god you're so set against. But when my boys and I thought we'd have some fun and chase them—maybe even do you a favor by catching your mother—it was chaos. She started calling her friends 'racing hounds,' shouted that they were trapped. Then all these women rushed at us and we fled. But they didn't stop. They got hold of a heifer and—I don't know how—ripped it apart with their bare hands. Whole cows, even bulls they tore into—hooves and ribs were hanging from the pines, with blood all over. Then they swarmed around like birds and took off for the local villages up there—Hysiai, Erythrai—and broke into all the houses, plundered them. Carried off babies, pots, iron goods. Put live coals on their heads and didn't get burned. The village people were enraged. They got their spears and started hurling them, but these women were unstoppable. No spear cast drew blood, but those sticks of theirs, they wounded many a man—I still can't believe it—men were beaten by women! Pentheus, whatever god they're worshiping you'd better welcome him."

The messenger left. The king was instantly ready to lead his troops against this female threat. "Wait!" said the newcomer, the long-haired stranger whom Pentheus had been regarding with suspicion. "Don't fight them with force—you'll never win against the god." Although Pentheus had been bent on violence, the stranger—for it was the god in disguise—gradually, fatally, turned his mind. "Don't you want to see their revels? Dress yourself up as a woman and spy on them first. I'll bring you there." So Pentheus donned a linen shift, a hairpiece, a snood, and other feminine attire. Dionysus approved (he was, after all, to become the god of theater). Pentheus was already strangely exultant. He claimed that the stranger now looked to him like a horned bull, and said he felt that he himself could lift up the whole of Mt. Kithairon with his hands. With the god's madness slowly working on his brain, Pentheus obediently followed the stranger into the hills.

Soon they caught sight of the "maddened ones" peacefully making crowns of flowers in a glen. Pentheus wanted to see more clearly. "Here, climb on," said Dionysus as he bent to the ground the trunk of a tall pine. Pentheus rode the top of the springing tree as it straightened out, high into the sky, and became visible to the women. At that moment the god's voice boomed out, "I have brought your man, the one who mocked us. Punish him!" The women, in god-induced fury, swarmed up the hillside to the spot where Pentheus had perched. Yet they failed to bring him down with stones and branches. "He must not escape and spread our mysteries," shouted Agavê, and she led them all in surrounding the trunk and clawing it up, whole, from the earth. Her son plummeted like a falling star. The fall did not kill him; instead, his mother, out of her mind with Dionysus, planted her foot on his chest and ripped off his arm. Her sister, Autonoe, worked on his other side. Like wild dogs at a kill, they tore and shredded the Theban king. They brandished pieces of his corpse like prizes. And his mother proudly brought Pentheus back to town as the stranger had promised that she would. He had not said how: with Pentheus' head (she insisted it was a mountain lion's) stuck atop her *thyrsus*. Thus Dionysus had his revenge.

## 20.   DEMETER AND PERSEPHONE

Dionysus had many other encounters with mortals as he spread his gift of wine through the world. In a place called Ikaria, not far from Marathon in the territory of the Athenians, he met up with Ikarios, who was a likable, clever farmer who soon learned how to care for the vine shoots that the god gave him. When he had harvested the grapes and pressed them and fermented the juice—all according to Dionysus' instructions—Ikarios was overjoyed with the results. It was truly a divine drink, and he wanted to share it. Nearby were some shepherds with their flocks, and Ikarios, when the sun set, went to visit them. They tasted the wine and asked for more, and then more, pouring it down their throats without bothering to water it down, the way civilized people do, so pleasing was this new concoction. Their bodies soon felt different—light, dizzy, uncontrollable—and they were struck with fear. "He put a spell on us!" one shouted, and the rest, believing it, attacked poor Ikarios and killed him.

The next morning, the shepherds woke up to find their friend's body, and slowly, painfully began to remember the night before. Filled with shame and guilt, they hurriedly buried Ikarios in a wooded spot and moved on. He would have lain forgotten, but his daughter Erigonê refused to believe that her father would just walk off and disappear. When he was working in the vineyards, Ikarios used to tend the rows with his old dog Maira, his inseparable companion. The day after her father had failed to come home, Erigonê heard Maira, far off, howling. She followed the sound and discovered the old dog pawing the loose dirt of a makeshift grave. Now she knew. Erigonê could not bear to live without Ikarios and, numb with grief, hanged herself on the spot.

Before long a mysterious disease began to spread throughout the villages in Attica. In distress, the people asked the oracle of Apollo at Delphi what they should do. They were told "worship Dionysus and those who died for him." And so they do still. Every year at the time the new wine is opened, they put up masks and figurines that sway in the breeze, and also suspend from the branches swings for young girls to ride, attempting to turn away the sorrow of that earlier hanging.

In this same period, when Pandion was king in Athens, another great gift from the gods came to mortals: the growing of grain. This gift, too, was intertwined with grief for a lost loved one, but this time it was a goddess who mourned for her only daughter.

Demeter's girl was called Persephone. Her father was Zeus, and it was his overbearing will that started the chain of events. For Zeus shared power, you recall, with his brother Hades, who had been given control over the dark regions beneath the earth. Hades, seeing his brothers comfortably settled, decided the time had come for him, too, to take a wife, and so he went to Zeus. The king of gods and men was happy to do a favor. Perhaps he thought as well that a bond of marriage would give him an advantage in future dealings with the lord of the dead. In any event, Zeus promised to give his brother Persephone as a wife. This was done without Zeus bothering to consult the girl's mother.

One day Persephone was gathering flowers with her companions, the young daughters of Okeanos. Violets, roses, crocuses, hyacinths—all grew abundantly in the meadow. Suddenly they noticed a new, marvelous plant, shining with many petals in the sun and perfuming the air all around with the sweetest scent—a narcissus, which Gaia had caused to grow here to help Zeus and Hades with their plan. When Persephone reached out for the beautiful flower, the earth gaped open. Up flew dark Hades in his chariot with black horses from the depths below, seized the girl, and dragged her, screaming, underground. She called pitifully to her father, never knowing he had approved all this. But there was no one nearby to answer her cry.

Yet her plight was not unnoticed. There is a strange and revered goddess, Hecate, whose powers go back to a time before Zeus became king. She was honored even by the Titans, and Zeus allowed her to retain her role as the helper of mortals. Warriors and kings, athletes, herders, fishermen, the young—to all who pray humbly to her she gives success. She frequents the crossroads, those special places where anything can happen and decisions must be made. Some say she can even summon ghosts and perform black magic, but people who maintain that are probably jealous of the luck she has brought to others. In the cave that is her home, Hecate lifted her sheer veil a moment and then heard, more clearly, Persephone's scream. And Helios, the sun above, saw Hades' deed.

Demeter herself caught an echo of her daughter's cry, and it seized her heart. She flew like a bird over land and sea. Nine days she roamed the earth, searching with blazing torches in her hands, but no human, bird, or beast could tell her what had happened to Persephone. Unfed, unwashed, grief-stricken, and exhausted, she finally met Hecate, who said, "Someone has taken her. Who it is, I don't know. I heard the cry, but did not see." Together, both with torches, they went to Helios and stood before the chariot in which each day he rides the sky. Demeter begged him to tell her who had taken her sweet girl. "None other than the brother of Zeus," replied the sun god. "But don't be sad. After all, think what a glorious and powerful son-in-law you now have." Whipping forward his horses, he flew off.

Now the ache in her soul grew even keener. She avoided the company of the Olympians altogether, and traveled instead among the cities of men, in appearance like an old woman, one who has endured many sorrows, who has reached the time when she is through with love and children. Her lush, thick hair was thin and gray, her face wrinkled, her arms and legs like bones. In this state she entered the territory of Keleos, at Eleusis, not far from Athens, and sat down to rest in the shade near the Maiden Well, where the women of the neighborhood came daily to draw water. Four beautiful young women, like goddesses in their tender flowering, arrived with bronze jugs. Of course, they did not recognize Demeter. "Who are you? Why aren't you inside at home instead of wandering far out here?" they asked. And Demeter replied, "Children, whoever you are: listen to my tale. I came from Crete—but against my will. Pirates stole me away, looking to sell me as a slave somewhere. But when they put in at Thorikos and started making supper, I secretly escaped—I won't be sold! What country is this, anyway? Who lives here? Well, my dears, I hope you all get handsome young husbands and have children to make a parent proud. . . . By the way, you wouldn't know if someone needs a housemaid and a nurse for babies? I can still do both—look after the rooms, spin, comfort a child in my arms."

Kallidikê, one of the girls, thought a moment, looking at this sad and confused old woman. "I sense something about you, I don't know what—something highborn. Not one of the people in the big houses hereabouts would turn you away. In fact, wait here and we'll go ask our own mother. Metaneira is her name. She just had a baby boy, at long last, what she had prayed for. You might help to raise him." So the girls filled their bronze pots with the water, picked up their skirt hems, and ran off up the rutted wagon path, skittish as fawns or calves, to tell their mother. Demeter walked more slowly behind, veiling her head and face, the edge of her dark blue gown trailing over the ground.

The mother sat next to a column inside the dark hall of the house, holding her dear son. As Demeter stepped quietly over the threshold, suddenly the doorway filled with light. For a second she looked no longer like a wizened old woman, but tall and fair. The mother turned pale, overcome with awe and fear. She offered this strange woman a chair, but Demeter refused, preferring to stand silently, her eyes downcast. At last she did sit down on a small stool that one of the servants brought, but she would not talk or eat, filled with remembering and longing for her own fair daughter. Finally, the servant Iambê, who was full of jokes and mimicry and stunts, managed to get the goddess to smile a little and almost laugh. When Metaneira tried to get her to drink wine, however, she raised her chin—"No"—and asked instead for some water with mint, which they brought her.

Metaneira had been looking at her the entire time. "I see from your

eyes that you have a certain gracefulness and know how to respect people and thank them. Stay and help with this baby that the immortals
have finally given us." Demeter said, "Thank you, madam. May the
gods give you all good things. I'll see he never gets the worm or the
toothache. I know very well how to ward these off. I have excellent
remedies." Still talking she took to her bosom the young child, baby
Demophon, son of the king.

Day by day he grew bigger and stronger, remarkably fast. He soon
looked like a young Apollo. Stranger still, he never seemed to eat anything. Demeter was forever rubbing him with ambrosial oils. At
night, when no one could see what she did, Demeter held him hidden
like a coal in the warm ashes of the fire. That is why he grew so godlike. She would have made him ageless and immortal in this way had
not Metaneira one night awoken and discovered the nurse stretching
the baby out over the hearth. "She's burning you!" cried the mother,
slapping her thighs in grief. At this, Demeter, becoming angry, threw
the child to the floor, away from the fire, shouting, "Stupid, witless
humans! You don't even know what's good for you! Now he will have
to die, like all other mortals. Yet deathless fame and honor will be his,
since he has been privileged to rest in my arms. Know this. I am
Demeter, mankind's greatest joy and aid." As she spoke, the goddess
changed appearance, until she looked her divine self, taller and more
fair, her golden hair flowing over her shoulders. A sweet fragrance
wafted from her clothing and a gentle glow pulsed from her skin, filling the whole house with light. With a last command—that the people of Eleusis should build a great temple on the hill to seek her
favor—Demeter left the hall.

Metaneira was too shocked even to pick up her precious baby,
whose cries eventually brought his older sisters running. They cud-
dled him, washed him, tried to soothe him, but nothing these girls
did would ever match the loving care of his former nurse. All night
long the villagers, shaking with fear, prayed to Demeter to be forgiv-
ing. The next morning, Keleos ordered that the great shrine be constructed.

In its innermost room, fragrant with cedar and boxwood, Demeter
stayed for an entire year, apart from the immortals, mourning her lost
daughter. On earth, it was the worst year ever. The land would not
produce a single plant because Demeter kept hidden the seed beneath
the ground. The people grew thinner and more haggard, and all humanity would have perished, as in the Flood, if Zeus had not observed

what was happening. He sent Iris, the rainbow messenger, to summon
the grieving goddess. She would not budge. Then Zeus sent all the
gods, one after the other, to persuade her to relent, without success.
Until she could see her daughter face-to-face, Demeter would neither
approach Olympus nor let crops grow.

When he had heard her ultimatum, Zeus decided to send Hermes
to persuade Hades to allow his bride to return from her misty, dank
new home. Hermes found the couple sitting unhappily together, the
girl upset and missing her mother terribly. With a glance at her, he
addressed the king of the underworld: "Lord of the dead, Zeus com-
mands you to send Persephone back. Demeter plans destruction for all
of us. Never mind the strengthless races of humankind—if the crops
do not grow, there will be no sacrifices for immortals!"

Hades lifted his brows and smiled ever so slightly. "Go on, Persephone, go back to your mother. I don't want you to be down-
hearted. But you should realize what you are losing. I would not be

a bad husband at all. I'm the brother of your father Zeus. Stay here, and you'll rule with me all that lives and breathes. You'll have power, too. People will offer sacrifices to you, and if they don't, you can take your revenge."

While he was speaking, Persephone had jumped up with joy, eager to go back with Hermes to her mother and the world above. "Just a moment, dear. Take something for the journey," said Hades, and he offered her a ripe pomegranate, which she took, and would have saved, but Hades insisted, "Eat a bit now."

The trip did not last long. With Hermes guiding the horses, they fairly flew until they reached Demeter's new temple. Seeing her daughter, the goddess rushed out to meet her like a "maddened one" of Dionysus, and Persephone, catching sight of her mother's beautiful eyes, leapt down before the chariot had stopped and ran to throw her arms about Demeter's neck. It was too good to be true.

Of course it was too good. Demeter, still trembling, when she had found the courage, asked what she did not want to learn. "My child, you didn't eat anything below, did you? Because if you did not, you'll stay with me and Zeus forever. But if you did . . ." She could tell by the look on her daughter's face what the answer was. "A pomegranate, Mother, that's all. I'm sorry. It was so cool and sweet." On she rushed with her story, naming all the daughters of Ocean with whom she had been playing, picking flowers in a meadow; the narcissus; the dark man in his golden chariot; her cries that no one heard. The women, mother and child, warmed each other with talk, and Hecate even joined them. Then Rheia, the girl's grandmother, came from Zeus to tell her, gently, what Demeter had already hinted. "Because you have eaten, you must return. A third part of the year you must spend with Hades. The two other portions you will be with the gods above, with your mother. In spring, when flowers break forth, you will rise. And now, Demeter, do not be angry—you have seen her. Make the crops grow."

Demeter could no longer disobey. All over, the broad land began to blossom. To ensure that the crops would never fail again, the goddess revealed to the king and the men of his family—Keleos, Triptolemos, Diokles, Eumolpos—the secret rites, her Mysteries, which only the few may know. Happy is the one who becomes initiated, and so becomes blessed after death.

## 21.   DANGEROUS HUNTRESS

One odd thing Persephone told her mother was that Athena and Artemis were present when the rape (or "marriage," if one takes Hades' view) took place. It is not strange that these two, sworn to be virgins forever, loved spending their time with dance groups of young women (and all young Greek women learn chorus dancing as part of growing up). What seems peculiar is that they failed to use their divine power to fight against the lord of the dead and keep Persephone from his grasp. But then no one, immortal or not, can change Zeus' will.

Artemis was known to be a fierce guardian of her own virginity and that of the nymphs who attended her. She was as expert with a bow as her twin brother Apollo, hunting often in the wilds of the mountains, and yet, like him, she also could lead the dance of the Muses and the Graces, adorned with delicate golden jewelry. When women die, either in childbirth or when older, people say it is the arrows of Artemis that kill them—a way of acknowledging that she cares greatly for women but can also be swift, deadly, unexpected.

Once, when caught defenseless, she took a brutal revenge. Agavê of Thebes, whose son Pentheus was to suffer so, had a sister, Autonoê, who also had a son. His name was Aktaion, and Cheiron the Centaur, the great old half-horse sage, taught him to hunt. One day Aktaion and his companions, other young men of Thebes, were out with their dogs on the mountainside. The day was growing hot; they had been up since early morning and already had snared many hares and even a small boar in their bloodied nets. "Let's rest for today," said Aktaion, and began to lead the way home, but along a new path he had long wanted to explore.

Artemis had been hunting that day as well. In a cool, shady spot, beneath the pines deep in the woods, was a spring and pool of crystal-clear water, where she and her nymphs went to bathe after their morning's labors. One bound up the long, honey-colored hair of her mistress, who had already let slip from her white shoulders the short hunting dress she wore. Others, standing on a rocky ledge, began pouring cool water from stone jars over Artemis' head and neck. Suddenly they heard the sound of twigs breaking in the nearby woods, and into the clearing Aktaion emerged. It was difficult to say who was more surprised. The nymphs shrieked and ran to cover their lady's nakedness, while Aktaion stared, transfixed, at the perfect body of the goddess.

Blushing and angry, Artemis wished she had her bow at hand to teach this intruder a lesson. But she had only the water in her cupped hands. "Lucky hunter! You've stumbled on big game," she cried, and threw the water at Aktaion. He was instantly transformed. Antlers sprouted from his forehead; his hands grew hooves. When he tried to jump away, he found he had leapt six feet. He knew he was a stag, but his mind was still that of the young Theban prince. And so he felt even more the terror when his own hounds, well trained to sniff out and bring down deer, caught his scent. They were good dogs, Spartan and Cretan bred, and did not tire from their chase. They knew the woods as well as Aktaion. Blackfoot and Tracker led the pack. Killer and Sable took a shortcut over the hill. Chomper, Swifty, and Sharpy were first to launch themselves full force at the stag and pin him down, while the rest—Spot, Whitey, Barkley, Flash; he knew them all, he tried to call to them—ripped open his haunch, his flank, his neck. By now the other young men had run up. "Hey, Aktaion, come on, you should see this! Where's Aktaion?" they yelled. But the excellent stag—their friend—had breathed his last, before their eyes. "That one will never tell he saw me nude," thought Artemis as she listened to the howling and then stalked off.

She was cruel, too, though perhaps more justly so, when two huge hulking men sought to win her and Hera. Otos and Ephialtes were sons of Poseidon, handsome boys, and troublesome from the start. By the age of nine, they were nine feet wide and nine fathoms tall. They thought they could gain a place on Olympus by climbing up to it on a sort of mountain ladder. First, they made sure to get Ares, the war god, out of the way, so they ambushed him and put him in a big bronze jar (where he was stuck for thirteen months until Hermes managed to steal the jar and break the seal on it). Meanwhile, they piled leafy Mt. Pelion on top of Mt. Ossa, and would have made it into the sky had not Apollo threatened to kill them. Some think the son of Lêto did in fact take his bow and shoot them down, so young, before they had even grown beards. But seeing him armed, they gave up the attempt, and that's when they started dreaming up another way of joining divine society: namely, marrying goddesses.

Their courtship was intolerably bothersome. For one, they were even bigger and more loutish by the time they reached the age for wooing. Also, Hera was already the wife of Zeus, and Artemis, his daughter, had made a pledge long ago, sitting on his lap, to remain always unwed. There was no way for the young giants to enter Olympus this way, either. Yet they persisted, until Artemis had the clever idea to lure them to the island of Naxos. Knowing their weakness for hunting, she changed herself into a golden hind and dashed right between the two bullies. When they tried to bring down the game, Otos and Ephialtes speared one another.

After these brothers, the next most handsome son of a god (though not as tall) was Orion. He, too, was Poseidon's, by Euryalê, a daughter of Minos from Crete. His father gave him a marvelous gift: the ability to walk on waves as if on land. Eager to try this out, Orion made his way overseas to Chios—and his feet never sank beneath the surface. But there he was brought low by another sort of gift, the wine of Dionysus. The intoxicating god's own son, Oinopion—"Wine Drinker"—lived on the great island with his daughter, Merope. Wild animals were creating havoc in the vineyards. Orion was hired to clear them from the land and he did a fine job. In the evenings, he ate in the house and stayed with the family. But Orion, a child of water, could not hold his wine. One night he became horribly drunk and assaulted Merope. When her father found out, he summoned the satyrs of Dionysus. With their help he tied up the handsome visitor, blinded him, and cast him out.

Orion had to swallow his pride and do what many sightless ones do: he took up begging, and so made his way to Lemnos, the volcanic island where Hephaestus has his forge. As in most towns, the smithy is where travelers, poets, and beggars (sometimes all the same person) end up. They can keep warm there and pass the time in talk. Hephaestus, hearing Orion's story, took pity on him, and told him of a cure, from his blacksmith's hoard of secret knowledge. "Take my helper, Kedalion, on your shoulders, and keep walking in the direction he tells you." They traveled east all that day and night. At dawn the sun came dashing up the sky over Asia, striking Orion full in the face with his rays—and with that, he regained his sight.

"Now for my revenge," said Orion to himself. He rushed back to Chios. Try as he might, though, he could not locate Oinopion (for his fellow Chiots had hidden him underground). Orion gave up the search, went back to Crete, and took up hunting. This is where Artemis comes in. She and her mother, Lêto, were pleased to have the glorious son of Poseidon back on his home island, and they even helped him hunt, yet for whatever reason—maybe because of his half brothers' boastfulness, inherited from their bluff father, the Earth-Shaker—Orion was not content merely to accompany the goddesses through the woods. He bragged to them and all who would listen, "I am going to slay every wild beast the Earth produces." But Gaia, the old Earth, happened to hear this. Furious, she sent a scorpion, large and swift, to sting Orion dead.

Artemis mourned, either from love for him, or because she liked all bold hunters. So she persuaded Zeus to place brave Orion in the stars. There the great hunter forever can chase the Pleiades (the seven girls of Atlas he tried to win on earth, and whom Zeus rescued and turned into stars). Zeus put the scorpion up there as well, forever chasing Orion—just to remind mortals, I suppose, that there are limits to their killing.

That, at least, is the kinder version. Some insist that Orion, overstepping mortal bounds, tried to take Artemis herself, and it was she who sent the scorpion, or pierced him with an arrow. Or else, Dawn wanted Orion for her own, he was not unwilling, and Artemis, being jealous, shot him, whether by accident or by design. Indeed, any one of these stories would suit her character. Even more likely (given her protective nature) is the tale about Opis, one of the young girls who adored the goddess of the wild. When Orion tried to take Opis against her will, they say, Artemis felled him with a single fatal bowshot. But maybe this is a story told to young men, to scare them from making free with young dancing girls and make them mind their manners while courting.

As for the girls, here is a tale for them to ponder as well. Once Zeus, visiting Arcadia, was overcome with passion for a maiden he saw there, one of Artemis' devoted followers named Kallisto. He caught sight of her when she was resting alone in a glade, and he approached the girl, disguised as Artemis herself (when Zeus is infatuated, nothing is beneath his dignity). Thinking it was her beloved lady, Kallisto hugged and was hugged; kissed affectionately, like a sister, and was kissed in return, but much differently. Now she knew something was wrong, that this was a trick, but Zeus was too powerful. He took her and left her filled with shame and hurt. She tried to hide her condition from the others in the hunting band of Artemis, but as time went on, this became harder. When nine months had passed, and the nymphs were bathing with their goddess, Kallisto's body gave her away. Artemis firmly told the girl she must leave the group forever. But she did not kill Kallisto, as some would have you believe. It was Hera who nearly did that.

Observing Kallisto without her usual fond companions, she avenged herself for the insult of being upstaged by this country girl, and turned her into a bear. Kallisto, though transformed, still brought the child to term: Arkas was his name. Hermes, acting on Zeus' orders, gave the boy to his mother, Maia, to bring up, and he was raised, like any other Arcadian, to be a mountain man and hunter. His fifteen years' maturing were, for his mother, fifteen years wandering in deep forests. Kallisto's father, Lykaon, had meanwhile found out who had ruined his daughter, though he never found her. That's why, when he got the chance, he served the culprit, Zeus, such an unspeakable meal. Some even say it was his own grandson, Arkas, who served as the victim for that horrible sacrifice, but that is not so. Arkas survived and one day came face-to-face with a bear whose gentle eyes stared at him in a weirdly human way. He was shaken by the encounter. As the bear tried to approach him, he became afraid and picked up his hunting spear, but was stopped. Zeus saw all, and rather than watch a son kill his mother, the father of gods swept them both into the sky to become the two prominent Bears, Great and Little. Hera, it turned out, had one small piece of revenge left. Through her persuasion, the Ocean stream never lets these enemies of Hera touch its cool water. They never set, wheeling constantly in mid-heaven.

## 22.   HEPHAESTUS THE SMITH

How Hephaestus came to be is somewhat of a mystery, as obscure as the trade secrets of the master craftsman himself. One tale holds that when Zeus gave birth to Athena through his own head, Hera decided that she, too, would produce offspring outside the normal way, and went off and bore Hephaestus, without ever coming near Zeus or any other god. Yet it is well known that when Zeus swelled up with his child-to-be, the only solution was to have Hephaestus split his head with an axe—so Hephaestus must have been born already. Maybe there is more truth to the nastier rumor that Hera gave birth to him before ever marrying Zeus (who was the father) and tried to conceal her shame by claiming she had produced him all by herself.

Hera was the one who shaped her son's career, at any rate. When her labor was over and the result was revealed to her, she drew back in horror, saying, "He's all twisted in the feet!" Before anyone could stop her, she picked up her son and hurled him off Olympus, straight into the sea. Hera was a proud goddess and could not stand to have any child of hers be less than perfect.

That would have been the end of the story had not the sea nymph Thetis, the daughter of Nereus, been sunning herself that morning. She caught sight of a very small object approaching, like a falling star, from the northwest sky and watched it plummet in a flash into the water a few yards off. Diving under, she was able to reach the little bundle before it hit the bottom. While she swam back to the surface, Thetis felt wriggling and kicking from the soggy lump of swaddling clothes. She brought it to one of her favorite smooth sea caves and opened it, uncovering a tiny god. So was Hephaestus saved and tended, with Thetis and her friend Eurynome, daughter of Ocean, taking turns at his care. The child grew quickly, as gods do, and showed his talents early. By his ninth year, Hephaestus was crafting elaborate necklaces, tiaras, bracelets, and earrings, all of which delighted his foster mother and the nymphs.

Hera never knew her lame son's fate—she never gave him a second thought. But Hephaestus knew about her. Thetis had passed along to him stories she picked up in her travels, bits of information gleaned from her father, the wise old sage of the sea. These made Hephaestus eager to meet his birth mother, though mainly to take revenge. Thetis noticed that the boy (now nearly like a man) spent more and more time in his cave workshop, nights and days, emerging only now and then for some nectar and ambrosia. At last, one day he came to her with his crooked smile and said, "I've made a present for my mother. Can you deliver it?" Proudly he brought her to see his masterpiece: a gleaming black throne, with gold inlay on the back and arms, tiny delicate scenes depicting all the stories of the gods, their victories and loves.

Thetis went off with this marvelous piece of furniture to Olympus, where she found Hera. The throne was placed before the wife of the supreme god, somewhat near the edge of a ridge, so she could have a view. Pleased with this anonymous gift, Hera took her seat and stayed for a long time, entranced by the meticulous workmanship of the miniature stories that decorated it. Finally, she went to get up—and found she couldn't move. Invisible ties held her down. Worse, the throne began to rise on its own, as if lifted by some gust of air that was becoming stronger every moment. As the chair floated out over the cliff edge, Hera abandoned all attempts at regal repose. "Release me," she screamed, and tore frantically at her clothes, trying to find the hidden bonds that gripped her tight. Somehow, the other gods (they had all come running by now) lassoed the throne and tethered it, but failed to pry Hera off it. Then the truth began to dawn on them—this was no ordinary piece of work. Only a god could have devised it, but who?

Thetis came forward to explain—she had no idea, she thought it was just a fond son's gift. Yes, Hera's son—now she should know—a smith and the finest jeweler ever. The gods debated how to bring this unheard-of god, Hephaestus, to release his mother. For a long while no one spoke. Then Ares, the god who loves fights, offered, "I'll get him!" Off he went to the cave where the smith god worked. But Hephaestus drove him off with flaming fire brands, saying, "Let Hera rot." Meanwhile, Hera was in a terrible state, trembling in fear that she would spend eternity tied down. (Nor did it help that she recalled the fate of Prometheus.) When Ares came back shamefaced, Dionysus then volunteered. The god took plenty of intoxicating supplies with him, found Hephaestus, and without mentioning his mission, began to ply him with strong wine. It did not take long before Hephaestus was ready for anything, although he was too drunk to walk. Dionysus summoned his satyr friends, obtained a donkey, and with flutes play-

ing and cymbals crashing, the whole parade marched back to Olympus. "Hera goes free only if Hephaestus can stay—that's the bargain," announced Dionysus, on behalf of his incoherent new acquaintance. All agreed (it was not the first time a new young god had blackmailed them, mumbled Apollo). So the cunning smith fiddled with the throne a minute and sprang the locks.

Hera's ordeal was over. She owed Dionysus for this release, and she knew what he would probably ask for in return. His own wanderings, since the unfortunate incidents at Thebes, had taken him far and wide on earth and under it. He had accomplished what Orpheus could not. He brought back to life a beloved one from Hades—namely, his mother, Semelê, whom he renamed Thyone. He himself had been captured and bound once when pirates kidnapped him on his way to Naxos, thinking him a fine king's son who would fetch a good ransom. But their chains had magically fallen off the young god as he lay in their empty ship. His dark eyes glistened, and the ship suddenly filled with flowing, fragrant wine. The mast turned into a sprouting grapevine, heavy with fruit, while the dark ivy of Dionysus curled its tendrils all about the halyards. Then the crew, already frightened, got the scare of their lives. They thought they saw a lion in the prow and a hairy bear amidships. Rushing to the helm for safety, they heard the beasts (or thought they did) pursuing them. To a man, they leapt overboard and were transformed into dolphins.

The helmsman, who had begged the others to let the young captive free, remained at his post. To him Dionysus made his epiphany, promising him a blessed, happy life. To many other mortals as well Dionysus had been mild and kind. But the wine god was still not yet accepted on Olympus, precisely because Hera knew about his origins. At last, after this victory, she was forced to accept him as a member of the divine company, one of the great twelve gods dwelling forever on their snowcapped mountain.

## 23. APHRODITE'S LOVES

Life might have stayed serene and undisturbed among the gods—not to mention mortals—if not for Aphrodite. Pain and desire had led to her watery birth, and were left in her wake, it seemed, wherever she went. That was the price of such unearthly beauty.

Each time she entered the gatherings of gods and goddesses was like the first time, her stunning arrival from Cyprus. The Seasons, with their golden tiaras, dressed her in perfumed, sheer, and shimmering sea-blue garments. She wore a gold crown and elaborate, cunningly worked earrings made of precious gold and orichalch. Delicate golden necklaces lay on her soft neck and fragrant, shining breasts. As she stepped lightly among them, every god secretly prayed to have her as his own.

Ares had been promised her, and Ares she eventually went with. But the unexpected appearance of this young lame blacksmith with his threatening powers complicated matters. For it turned out that acceptance on Olympus was not the only reward Hephaestus desired after freeing Hera. He wanted Aphrodite as well, and Ares could not stop him. Hephaestus, of course, provided wonderful bride gifts—all sorts of jewelry, golden tripods, silver bowls, lifelike statues, even a new house. So Aphrodite was given to him as wife by the cautious Olympians, albeit reluctantly.

Whether it was unrequited love or the indignity of being bested that drove him, before long the war god started secretly to court the new bride. He gave many gifts and soon was disgracing the bed of his rival Hephaestus. Helios, from his high vantage point, saw the goings-on and told the smith. As soon as he heard the depressing news, Hephaestus took himself off to his forge, mulling over thoughts of betrayal and revenge. Furiously, he pounded out on the anvil lengths of chain—air-thin, unbreakable, impossible to loosen. Full of anger against Ares, he snuck back to the bedchamber. From the high ceiling he strung the gossamer chains, making a circle, lightly suspended, right above the bed.

"I'm off to Lemnos to see how some work of mine is going," he casually announced next morning to the other gods. Ares smiled to himself and kept watching until the coast was clear. Then he went to Aphrodite's room and motioned to her. Without a word she followed him to the bed, where they began to take their pleasure. Neither heard the soft sound, like a breeze, of the falling net, and only when they began to get up did Ares and his lover find themselves trapped. "What have we here?" came the voice of Hephaestus from the doorway. He had never had any intention of leaving and had stayed nearby, waiting for this moment of satisfaction. "Zeus, come here and see how your Aphrodite disgraces me, cripple that I am. She fancies Ares, so fine and light on his feet. Take a look at these two wrapped up in my sheets. I don't think they'll be doing much sleeping after this. In fact, they're going to stay put until Zeus pays me back every bride gift I ever gave him for this shameless bitch of a woman."

Ares was blustering so much that the other gods began to gather and (while the goddesses, imagining something shameful, modestly stayed home) had great fun mocking the stuck couple: "Hey, Slow-poke wins the race." "Ares pays the penalty." Apollo elbowed Hermes, saying, "Wouldn't you like to get squeezed in chains going to bed with that golden Aphrodite?" To which his brother responded, "Would I ever! Give me three times as many chains, with all you gods looking on into the bargain—just so I'd have her!" And they all roared with laughter— all except Poseidon, who kept begging Hephaestus to let them up. "I myself will pay whatever is needed. I promise," said the sea god. But Hephaestus replied, "What if Ares reneges on his bond? How am I ever supposed to tie *you* down?" He had a point, since the god of waters was notoriously slippery. At last, however, he took Poseidon's word and un- chained the guilty couple. Ares left immediately for Thrace, while Aphrodite hurried away to her temple at Paphos, in Cyprus, where the Graces soothed her with a long bath and olive-oil massage.

Aphrodite's connection with Paphos had a long history. The city had been founded by Kinyras, who claimed as an ancestor, five gener- ations back, Eôs, the goddess of dawn. Kinyras married Metharme, the daughter of the king of Cyprus, whose name was Pygmalion, and his story was also bound up with that of the love goddess. A sculptor, he shunned the women of the island, preferring the ideal female that he could shape from ivory with his own hands. So beautiful was the smooth white body he crafted, with its delicate features and tender limbs, the very image of Aphrodite herself, that Pygmalion fell in love with it, treating his creation as real, bringing gifts of colored stones and flowers, amber and little birds, and even clothing the statue in fine robes and jewels. One morning, on the greatest feast day of Aphrodite, Pygmalion prayed at the altar of the goddess, "May my wife be this girl of ivory . . . a woman like her, that is." The goddess knew that he desired none other than the likeness itself, and granted his unspoken wish. When Pygmalion returned home and began, as he often did, to caress the ivory woman, warm flesh met his touch. He could feel blood rush in the veins he had so realistically sculpted. The lips of ivory responded to his kiss. The statue moved and breathed— and Pygmalion had his bride.

In an odd and awful coincidence, Kinyras, too, was joined to his own creation—his daughter, Smyrna. The girl failed to honor Aphrodite properly and therefore suffered the wrath of the goddess. Because she refused to let herself fall in love with any of the frequent suitors who begged for her hand, Smyrna was afflicted with an uncontrollable passion for her own father. She tried to conquer it, but all her efforts to deny the feeling failed. On the point of attempting to hang herself, she was discovered by her old nurse, who probed her to find the cause of Smyrna's despair. When it became clear at last, the old woman could not conceal her horror. Yet she was a devoted servant. She devised a plot to get for her beloved girl what she wanted.

The yearly rites of Demeter demanded that the wife of Kinyras, and all women who worshiped the mourning mother, abstain from lovemaking for nine nights. This was the time the nurse chose to arrange for poor Smyrna to mate with her father. The old woman told him the conditions—a certain girl (she made up a name) would visit him for love, but she was bashful. All lights would have to be extinguished, and he could never look upon her face. And so the defilement took place, not once, but night after night, the king often half-drunk, and assuming his companion was a local courtesan. Finally, his curiosity led him to wish to find out more. He lit a lamp one night as his bedmate slept. When he saw who lay there, he froze with fear, anger, and disgust. He drew his sword to kill her, but Smyrna awoke and fled. After wandering for nine months, she reached Arabia, not caring whether she lived or died. The gods took pity on her, transforming her into a tree with fragrant sap, the myrrh. The child growing within her still lived, however. In a short time the trunk of the myrrh tree burst open. The baby, Adonis, emerged into the light.

This boy, born as a result of Aphrodite's anger, lived to bring her both joy and grief. When he was still an infant, she realized that he was to be more beautiful than any mortal. She chose to hide him in a painted wooden chest, out of the sight of the other gods, knowing how jealous divinities can be. Or perhaps she did not want the sordid story of Smyrna's incest to reach Olympus. At any rate, Aphrodite entrusted the chest to Persephone. The queen of the underworld took one look at the boy in the box and decided to keep the handsome child for herself (as she and Hades never had any children). Aphrodite, however, did not give up her claim. Taking the matter to Zeus, she asked for his judgment. "There are three concerned here, and so I decree three divisions of the year," the father of gods announced. "During one third Adonis stays with Persephone; another third with Aphrodite;

and he has the last third by himself, wherever he wishes." Adonis, however, gave his own share of time to Aphrodite, so that he was with her eight months out of twelve.

For the gods, time means nothing, but for mortals, everything. The extravagance of Adonis in giving his time to the goddess of love was rewarded by her constant attention to him, though his own time was to be short. Her thoughts were always with him, and she feared for him even as she faithfully accompanied Adonis in all his hunting and roaming the woods. Her last words to him before she mounted her swan-drawn chariot to visit Olympus one day were, "Be not too bold—beware of lions and all the other savage beasts. No love or beauty can charm them." But he was young. No sooner had she left than Adonis with his hounds roused a wild boar in the undergrowth. Rather than running from it, he tried to bring it down. His javelin pierced the huge beast, but not deeply enough. The charging boar gored Adonis with its deadly tusk. Aphrodite, in midair, heard his cries and turned back, only to find him dying on the ground. Where his blood dripped, she sprinkled nectar, and from the spot grew flowers red as blood and, like Adonis, quick to sprout and lose their blossoms to the wind: anemones. As she promised him then, Aphrodite made sure that every year women in all the towns would reenact the lament for her beloved, weeping and filling the air with cries of "O my Adonis!"

## 24.  COSMIC COUPLES

For Aphrodite, the brief time spent with Adonis was an ending, the final result of her own wrath against a girl who had hesitated to enter her realm, that of love and marriage. It produced nothing except sad memory and regret. On the other hand, the second mortal love for which she was known brought forth, in the course of time, an empire spreading thousands of miles and lasting millennia.

Zeus could not often resist the appeal of fine-looking mortal women, try as he might to honor Hera, his lawful wife and a beauty herself. But it was not all his own doing, so he felt. All that Aphrodite represented—soft garments, clouds of scent, glancing eyes, melting looks, seductions—worked easily on his body and mind. (Of all the divinities, only Athena, Artemis, and Hestia, the hearth goddess, had failed to fall under her spell.) Yet in turn Aphrodite laughed at them and boasted of how she had driven gods to mate with women, but never herself had wanted a mortal's bed. Zeus decided he'd change that.

He filled Aphrodite with sweet longing for Anchises, who lived in the rugged uplands of Mt. Ida near Troy. He was a handsome young man with a common trade: herding cattle. One day she was sitting on Olympus, assured of her powers, smugly looking over the world, when she noticed him. That was all it took. Aphrodite instantly began to feel the pangs of desire for this unsuspecting youth. She hurried to Paphos and her temple there, filled with the scent of cypress. She gently closed the shining doors of the inner chamber and undressed, bathed luxuriantly, then clothed herself (with the help of the Graces) in a gown permeated with the most alluring perfumes. Then she rushed north toward Troy, striding high above the clouds, until she set herself down on Mt. Ida. The place was well known as "mother of beasts," and as soon as she set foot there, they came out to greet her. Gray wolves that fawned at her feet, lions with glaring eyes, bears, leopards. Aphrodite was delighted seeing them, and by her very presence she infused them with the joyous urge to love. Two by two the animals went to lie and mate in the shadowy woods.

Meanwhile, she made straight for the summer huts of the men who worked the mountains. The rest were out putting the cattle to graze in the fields, and Aphrodite found Anchises alone, casually plucking a lyre and singing with a clear, strong voice, the way mountain people do.

She came before him. To all appearances, she was a young, innocent girl at the point of marriage (a disguise, for she did not want to scare him). Anchises took a long look and was filled with growing wonder. Sheer shining gown that blazed like a flame. Beautiful silver earrings and finely wrought bracelets. And on the neck—it looked so soft to the touch—gold necklaces studded with jewels. Was this some country girl he had overlooked? Not likely—she was more like the sun or moon. He spoke first, a bit rapidly, out of nervousness.

"My lady—whichever of the goddesses you might be—Artemis, Lêto, Aphrodite, Themis, Athena. Or one of the Graces. Perhaps a nymph? One of the ones who live here around the springs and river sources? Whichever you are, I promise I will find a grove and build you an altar and sacrifice at every season—not just summers. Please be kind to me. Make me a noble man, prestigious in Troy, with a flourishing bloodline, and let me live long and happy among my people." (Such was the routine to follow on meeting a goddess.)

Aphrodite replied, "Dear Anchises, you most glorious of men on earth. I'm no goddess at all—why compare me to them? I'm just a mortal. I have a mother, like everyone else. Otreus is my father. He is pretty well known, too—have you heard of him? He is in charge of all of Phrygia. Oh, I see, you're wondering why I know Trojan, then? Well, I know both languages, you see. I had a Trojan woman . . . as nursemaid?" (She had a pretty, rising inflection to her voice.) "Yes, she took care of me when I was little—and that's how I know Trojan and Phrygian, both."

"Interesting," thought Anchises. It got more and more intriguing. "Just now," the goddess in disguise continued, "Hermes the Argus-Slayer, with his golden wand, came and snatched me out of the dance group of Artemis (who has a golden bow) right at the time when we girls were performing and there was a crowd of people watching! He took me over fields and no-man's-land, and I could see wild, hungry animals going through the shadowy woods. And I didn't even seem to touch the ground with my toes." She gave him a wide-eyed look, as if to say, "Do you believe it?" and went on. "Hermes kept telling me I was going to become the bride of Anchises and give him beautiful babies. He pointed me toward you, then he went back to Olympus. And here I am. But please, I'm begging you, by Zeus and your parents, show me to your mother and father and your brothers. They'll see, I won't make a bad daughter-in-law at all. Also, could you send a messenger down to Phrygia and let my parents know I'm all right? They'll send shipments of gold and woven cloth. You'll be wonderfully rewarded. After that, we'll prepare the marriage feast, precisely what gods and humans consider proper."

This little speech aroused Anchises, as Aphrodite had wanted it to, and he answered, "If you are a mortal—with a real mother—and Otreus is your father, just as you say, and you arrived here because of Hermes, and you're going to be my wife for all the days to come—there's no one on earth, man or god, who could stop me from joining in love with you this very minute. Not even if Apollo were to take his silver bow and shoot me. I'd want it that way—to die and go to Hades, as long as I got to climb into bed with a woman like a goddess!" So saying, he grasped her by the wrist. Aphrodite bashfully looked down at the ground and turned her head to the side—but followed. Anchises had a high-built, soft bed inside the hut, with bear skins and lion skins strewn on it, from beasts he had killed himself. Slowly, she took off her earrings, then her necklaces and bracelets, revealing more of her glowing skin. He untied her silken waistband and her shimmering clothes fell down (so beautiful were they that he took time to place them on a chair nearby). Then, because the gods wanted it this way, a mortal lay with a goddess, little though he knew it.

All afternoon he slept, until the rays of the sun going down the sky filtered in through the chinks in the hut's wall. Aphrodite had dressed herself in all her fine clothes and stood, tall and stately as a goddess, her head nearly touching the roof-beam, immortal beauty radiating from her face. She woke Anchises, saying, "Now have a look and tell me. Do I seem the same as when you first laid eyes on me?"

Anchises let his gaze follow her words, and saw, astonished, her lovely neck and fine, bright eyes, and the divine glow only a goddess possesses. Quickly, he hid his own face in the bedcovers. "I knew! As soon as I saw you, I knew you were immortal, but you did not tell the truth! Now I beg you, by Zeus, do not leave me unmanned, strengthless among humankind. Pity me. I know that mortal men who sleep with goddesses lose the warmth of life."

"Anchises," she answered gently, "take heart. Don't be afraid. The gods are on your side. You'll have a son who will rule among the Trojans, and the children of his children, and their descendants will extend far into the future. His name will be Aeneas, because an ache so terrible (*ainon*) came over me, having fallen for a mortal." Then she reminded him that the race of Trojans had been always dear to the gods, recalling how Ganymede was snatched up by Zeus himself—he was so handsome, he had to be among the immortals—and he now has the role of steward for the Olympians, pouring out their red nectar from a golden mixing vase. And when Tros, his father, was frantic with worrying where the sudden squall had carried off his boy, Zeus had taken pity and given Tros, as compensation, horses that carried the gods themselves. Another handsome Trojan—Aphrodite continued—was Tithonos, whom Dawn of the Golden Throne took to be her own. She had sought from Zeus that the young man be deathless all his days, and Zeus agreed to this wish—foolish though it was! Dawn had not thought to ask for eternal youth for him. As a result, the pair were delighted in their love, with Tithonos living at the edge of the world, near Ocean, where Dawn would arise each morning from their common bed. But then his hair began to go gray, and his beard lost its black sheen. As he aged, Dawn stayed away more and more, though she still took care of him, feeding him nectar and ambrosia, seeing to it that he was clothed like a god. He continued to decline

until he was really old. He could not move his arms or legs or even
stand up. So Dawn put him in a bedroom and shut the door. He shriveled, more and more, down to the size of a cicada, and like the insect,
now he merely makes a shrill, strengthless whirring.

"I wouldn't want that to happen to you," said the goddess, reaching out to touch him tenderly on the arm. "If you could remain just
as you are—strong and healthy and young and beautiful—I'd want
you to be my husband, and for all to know it. But eventually old age
will shadow you, too, pitilessly. That is what happens to you humans—wasting, painful old age that we gods despise." She sighed.
"As it is, I'm going to have to endure jokes and insults on Olympus
because of my weakness for you. All those gods that I tricked into loving mortals! I won't ever be able to mention your name there, let alone
say I conceived a child by a man. In fact, when this boy is born, I'll
have the mountain nymphs care for him and raise him. They live a
long, long time, being in between goddesses and mortals. They take
part in the dances with the gods, and Hermes and the satyrs make love
to them in mossy caves." (Anchises had heard these stories from the
older shepherds, so he nodded in agreement, though he wasn't sure
where this was all leading.)

"At the birth of nymphs, the gods plant trees—pines, oaks with
high crowns—and no one may cut these sacred groves. When the time
comes for a nymph to die, the tree connected with her life loses its
bark and branches, bit by bit, and her soul leaves the sunlight." These
creatures, so close to divinity but knowing death, would guard his
son, said Aphrodite. "When he is growing out of boyhood, they will
bring him here and show him to you. You'll be pleased when you see
his godlike bloom of youth. That's when you should take him down
to Troy. But if anyone should ask, 'Who is this boy's mother?'—say
what I tell you: 'I'm told he belongs to a nymph of the holy mountain.' Because if you should ever be so mindless as to boast you slept
with Aphrodite, Zeus will strike you down with lightning."

That was the last conversation they ever had. She took one last
look at him, and left him staring with joy and dismay.

# BOOK FOUR

## THE TALES
## OF ATHENS

ONLY IN THE EARLY NINE-
teenth century, after the War
of Independence against the Turks, did
Athens become the official capital of Greece.
From the fifth century B.C. on, however, this
city, out of the many Greek-speaking regions,
most often had the distinction of being the cultural
and intellectual center of the Hellenic world. Part of the
reason for its success lay in the Athenians' capacity for making up compelling stories about themselves. And of course, it
helped that the invention of drama as we know it came about in
this ancient city-state in the sixth century B.C. As a consequence, a
high proportion of the myths that reach us either have to do with
Athens and its kings, or were filtered through an Athenian consciousness, as mythic material was crafted into plays.

The one motif most conspicuous in Athenian myths is "autochthony"—that is, the belief that one's race was born from the very
earth on which it lives. This must have been a convenient notion to
have when competing claims were being made for territory, as often
happened in early Greek history. Among Native American peoples,
the Pueblo, Navaho, and Apache tell a similar story of emergence
from the soil of the Southwest. Instead of featuring the appearance of
full-grown humans out of the ground, however, the Athenian stories
speak of a king or kings (Erechtheus and/or Erichthonius, often con-

fused in the sources) who came from the earth as a baby. Snakes, sacred in Greek religion, were associated with the earth, and so autochthonous beings are characterized as partly serpentine; lameness is another marker of the earth-born. So important to the Athenians was this ideology that, we are told, aristocratic men of the older generation used to wear in their hair golden pins shaped like cicadas—the insects most well known for emerging from the ground.

Not only origins, but features of the contemporary city, too, are given mythical foundations through the stories told of Athens. The "charter" function of myths, first studied by the anthropologist Malinowski (see the Introduction), appears on the surface here. The tale of a contest between Athena and Poseidon not only explains why the olive is cultivated in the region, but gives authority to the predominance of the goddess and her cults on the Acropolis. The story of what happened after the original inhabitants chose the patronage of Athena supports such social practices as the exclusion of women from citizen life and the naming of children after the male line. And the myth of Ares' trial for homicide confirms a divine origin for the chief Athenian law court in the archaic period.

Alongside such politically charged stories are the tales of passion and women's misfortune represented in the myths of Prokne, Prokris, Kreusa, and other Athenian ladies. We owe to Ovid the fullest and most pathos-soaked versions of these, although probably, in more cases than we can now prove, he followed the lead of once extant Athenian dramas. One play that still survives, Euripides' *Ion,* tells the story of Kreusa and her son by Apollo. The depiction is finely attuned to Kreusa's viewpoint, at the same time as it explains a genealogical problem—how it is that the Ionian Greeks are closest to Athenians in language and culture. What unites these myths is a concern with the proper treatment and place of women, whether in the extended family or the city-state. As we can see from other sources, whether historians (Herodotus), philosophers (Plato and Aristotle), or dramatists (the tragedians as well as Aristophanes, the comic playwright), the role and status of women was one of the leading issues of the fifth century in Athens. These myths, seeming as they do to make room for the expression of the inner states of the "other" gender, complicated and enriched the social debates.

## 25. ATHENS ARISES

Aeneas was born and raised exactly as Aphrodite promised Anchises. His family was connected with Troy, though not with the ruling house, that of Priam—and so it was only natural that he would end up fighting for the defense of the great citadel when, in later years, the Greeks of the mainland arrived with their ships and battled the Trojans over the strange stolen woman, Helen. Troy would fall and Hector die, but Aeneas would survive to lead a remnant of his people from the burning city, carrying the aged Anchises on his back, and after many adventures land safe in Italy. There his own descendants, some three centuries later, founded a settlement on seven hills, named Rome. The rest is history, or, if you prefer, history wedded to myth. But all of that was still to come, the great western empire sprung from the goddess of love.

Athens was another small town that would become a great city in times to come, and would have its own brief, glorious empire. Like all the Greeks, Athenians had stories concerning their origins. Unlike most others, they claimed to come from the very earth beneath their feet.

The first king of Athens was an *autokhthôn*—that is, born of the soil. His name was Cecrops and his closeness to his native ground was visible in his very body, which was, from the waist down, that of a snake. During his reign Athens got its name, from the goddess Athena. The gods had decided to choose for themselves what cities they wanted to offer them worship. "There's a likely spot," thought Poseidon of Cecrops' town, and he proceeded to place his mark on its acropolis by striking the great rock with his trident. (You can still see the imprint.) Where he struck, a water source bubbled up, leaving a deep well that had the scent of the sea—a miracle, since the rock is miles from the shoreline. "Now, that proves this place is mine," Poseidon said.

"Not so fast," said his brother's child, Athena, who had also come along and chosen this place. "Watch this," said the goddess to Cecrops, and she immediately caused a beautiful olive tree to shoot up from the rocky soil, its silvery slender leaves glinting in the strong sun. The two gods began to argue over their respective rights, who was stronger, what was more useful (olives seeming to have the edge over seawater), and so on until Zeus intervened. He summoned the rest of the twelve chief gods as a divine jury. Cecrops gave witness that he favored Athena's gift—the very first olive tree—to his new town. And so Athena gave the place her name, and the inhabitants enjoyed the fruit of her tree forever after. Poseidon, meanwhile, took the loss poorly. "Don't want water, eh? Then take this!" The plains all around Athens were flooded, making the craggy Acropolis look like an island. But gradually the water subsided, and Poseidon stalked off in defeat.

There is another story (as usual) that made the god's loss even more upsetting, since the decision was even closer. Instead of the gods, the judges of the contest for patron of Athens were none other than the inhabitants themselves, so the tale goes. They held an assembly to decide whether Athena or Poseidon should be honored. In those days women could vote, and they did, every one of them in favor of Athena. The men cast their votes for Poseidon. As it happened, the number of women was just one greater than that of men: therefore the victory went to Athena. At this point an angry Poseidon unleashed his powers, punishing the territory with a tide like a great tsunami. The waters did not go away on their own. Instead, the Athenians determined that the only way to make Poseidon relent was to take away two privileges that women, up to that time, had: the right to vote and the right to have their children bear their mothers' names. Pleased with these new restrictions on his rival's city, Poseidon withdrew. And Athena's society remained the domain of men.

Cecrops, the snake-tailed king, had three daughters, who disobeyed and got into trouble. They were called Herse, Pandrosos, and Aglauros (names that signified three different forms of dew), and their downfall had to do with moistening of earth. Although Athena had vowed to have no contact with males, human or divine, her lame and lusty half brother Hephaestus paid no heed to that. One day, finding her alone in the vicinity of her new city, he tried to force himself on her. The goddess held him off and his seed fell on the ground. Among the divine, no energy is wasted. Just as long before Aphrodite arose from the fertilized sea, so now Earth produced from the smith's sowing a son: Erichthonius (whose name means, appropriately, "Earthy"). Some called him, for short, Erechtheus. Athena received the child at its birth, but could not be a mother to the infant. So she put him in a wicker box, making sure he could breathe even when it was sealed up, and set beside him two guardian serpents. She gave the box to the daughters of Cecrops with a stern-eyed warning not to open it.

As anyone who knew these young headstrong girls would have realized, Athena might as well have said, "Open this box as soon as my

back is turned." Because that is what they did. Prying open the lid, the sisters peered inside and glimpsed the writhing watch-snakes (they were fairly large, with yellow eyes) and what looked like a third snake, only with a baby's head. They screamed in utter terror. Driven out of their minds by fear—or, as some say, by Athena, who wished to punish them—they dropped the box, and all three girls leapt to their death from the height of the Acropolis onto the Long Rocks below.

Perhaps the girls were not so young when this happened, since there are stories about them having children by gods, although who knows whether they are true. The Kerykes ("Heralds"), who are an important clan responsible for carrying out Demeter's Mysteries at Eleusis, claim as their founder the hero Keryx, whom they say was the son of Hermes and the sister Pandrosos. Some say that Hermes also loved a second sister, Herse, and that she bore a son, Kephalos, who was carried off by Dawn and established the royal line that ended with the unfortunate Adonis. And the third sister, Aglauros, is said to have been the mother of Alkippe, by the god Ares. This Alkippe was stunning, an object of desire for gods and men alike. Once, a son of Poseidon went beyond admiration, attempting to take her by force, and for his crime was struck down by the war god Ares. That presented the dwellers on Olympus with a dilemma. "He can't get away with this!" Poseidon insisted. "I'm indicting Ares for the murder of my Halirhothius." The other gods decided to put the question to a jury, composed of themselves. The murder trial was held where the crime occurred, in Athens, on a craggy outcropping just down from the Acropolis. Ares was acquitted, and from then on, the hill and its Athenian court that met there were named Areopagus ("Ares' hill").

## 26. CRIMES IN REGAL BLOOD

Eventually, Cecrops, the old king of Athens, passed on, returning to the soil from which he had come. As often happens, there was fierce contention for the throne. First Cranaus (another *autokhthôn*) succeeded, only to be driven out by Amphictyon, who in turn lost the kingship to earth-born Erichthonius, the one whom Athena had put into the wicker box when he was an infant. He had been raised (after the unfortunate incident with Cecrops' daughters) in the goddess' own precinct on the Acropolis, the place now called the Erechtheum, home also to her sacred snakes. Erichthonius grew up to be a brilliant leader. Immediately on taking the kingship, he established such festivals as the Panathenaia, the great holiday dedicated to Athena that the townspeople celebrated forever after. He introduced chariot racing, a favorite event at the games. He crafted the olive-wood image of the goddess to adorn her shrine. He married a nymph named Praxithea, and the couple had a son, Pandion. After a long reign, he died in peace and was buried within the sanctuary of the goddess he so revered, Athena.

Pandion came to the throne next. About him not much can be said, other than that he, too, lived to see his daughters suffer a sad fate. Their names were Prokne and Philomela, beauties both, regal and tall.

Pandion's people, like those in most Greek states, were regularly involved in border skirmishes with neighboring cities. The latest threat was from Thebes and its king, Labdacus (whose story we will reach further on). Pandion realized that he needed an ally, and so called upon Tereus, a prince from the wild lands of Thrace and—most helpful—a son of the war god Ares himself. Of course, with this help Athens won, and Tereus was rewarded in the usual way, with a daughter of the man he had come to aid. He was given Prokne.

When a girl marries, the wedding feast often has the overtones of a funeral. Gone from her parents' house for good, carried far off to a place they may never visit, be it her husband's village or his palace, the bride is escorted partway down the road from home by friends and relations with a mixture of joy and sorrow. So it was with Prokne. She was happy and proud, a queen now in her own right, in the far northern region where her husband came to reign, with their young son, Itys. But she missed her home. "If only they could come here or I go there!" she thought to herself more and more. Finally she mustered the courage to beg her husband. "I am lonely. I miss my people. Please, let me return to Athens, just for a while. Or, if not, would you go and fetch my sister? Tell my father not to worry, she'll come back soon." And so Tereus set out southward by ship, in a few days came to the harbor of Piraeus, and headed inland several hours to the king's house, where he was royally welcomed.

Prokne was a rare beauty, but until then Tereus had never seen her younger sister. One sight of her in Pandion's gleaming marble palace, and he fell violently in love with her—or his lust convinced him it was love. On their way back to Thrace, Philomela was so absorbed in the prospect of seeing her sister once more that she did not notice at first that Tereus had taken a turn and was driving the chariot full speed up a small byroad. Instead of questioning her brother-in-law, she merely sat gazing as fields and olive trees, goats, sheep, and rough stone walls flashed by. As they got deeper and deeper into the country, and the road became more rutted and overgrown, it became obvious this was not the way to any palace.

At last they halted before a low stone house with whitewashed walls and a few hens straying in the yard. Philomela waited for Tereus to help her down from the high seat, but after the king had jumped off, he disappeared around the back of the house. He returned, talking intently to a worried-looking peasant, who then hurried down the hill to the west, where the sun was about to set.

She was thinking, yes, she could use a rest and a cool drink, but she felt somehow that this was not the place for either when she saw Tereus approach. His expression was changed. His blazing eyes were fixed on her, but he looked through her, as if blinded by some fire in the mind. Philomela shuddered. She was drawing her lavender shawl tighter around her body when Tereus bounded forward to attack. The look he had, one she had never seen before, was of lust and violence, arrogance and greed, all intermixed. This stop at a forlorn house—she now realized—was for Tereus to satisfy himself with her.

Painful as it is to relate how Tereus shamed and hurt Philomela, it is harder still to mention what came next, how the monster concealed the rape by cutting out the tongue of his victim, so she could never tell. Tereus made up a story for his wife, Prokne, when he returned home without her sister. The details were variously elaborated, but the gist was she had wandered off at their last stopping place, only twenty miles from the palace. Every day the lying king pretended to go out looking for the "lost" girl. Each time he would visit the hovel where he kept her under guard. Each night he would return exhausted, as if he had spent himself hunting in earnest, but found no trace of her. Gradually, his excursions grew less frequent. Prokne lost hope. And Philomela was put to other uses. Now that he had lost interest in her, Tereus let her occupy her time with weaving and embroidery.

All would have been forgotten had not a woodsman arrived one day at the halls of Tereus when the king was out on business, and handed Prokne a neatly wrapped package. He had been given it by a peasant, the man said, over the mountain. Inside, the queen found a long white cloth, like her mother's wall hangings, cunningly decorated with exquisite detail, depicting what, at first sight, looked like a tale of love. As Prokne peered more closely at the fine needlework, she froze. The figures had above each of them neatly stitched names, and the story told was not at all about love. Here was her sister; unmistakably there was Tereus; in ordered procession a chariot, a house, a bed, a knife. And a final phrase, floating above a weeping maiden, in red thread: *Sôson me* ("save me").

It was not difficult to leave the palace, even though Tereus returned that evening. "We celebrate Dionysus tonight, dear. The girls and I will dance," she said, and slipped off in her fawnskin outfit, carrying her tambourine. She had arranged for horses, and in less than two hours she was sobbing uncontrollably in her sister's arms. But pity and heartbreak only last so long. Now that she had rescued Philomela, Prokne was overcome by her bloodred rage. The women returned late at night to the palace and entered by the back rooms. On the ride home through the hills Prokne had made up her mind and devised her entire plan. All was done in a few minutes—finding in the dark her little son Itys, Tereus' pride, his small bed, the long knife. In his sacrifice was the best revenge.

She and her sister took the boy's limp body to the kitchen and worked through the next few hours until dawn, then slept. Tereus stirred only once in his heavy sleep, when he thought he heard a scream in the night. "Foolish Bacchants," he muttered to himself. "Who knows what those whorish friends of hers are up to in their so-called rites?" He woke up after noon and called for his main meal, which arrived quite quickly. As he hungrily tore into the meat, feeling invigorated, he asked Prokne (who was not touching her food), "Where's that lad of mine?" She looked without wavering into his dark eyes. "Closer to you right now than he'll ever be again." And at that moment the king saw Philomela emerge from behind the door.

Tereus made a sound like a wounded animal, like a bull being slaughtered. He leapt up and grabbed down his war axe from the wall, taking aim at his wife. But she and Philomela were already running. Some say they ran as far as Daulis in Phokis (a place destined to be linked with murder later on). Tired from the chase, on the verge of being caught, the sisters prayed to the gods, who changed them instantly into birds. Philomela is the swallow, who swoops in the evenings soundlessly. Prokne is the nightingale, who trills in mourning constantly "i-toos i-toos"—her son's name. And Tereus, although he had not asked for escape, became the hoopoe, who chases the other birds, angrily asking for his boy "pou"—which is the Greek for "Where?"

## 27. TALES FROM THE VIRGIN'S CITY

Perhaps because it was the city of Athena Parthenos—ever a virgin—Athens witnessed many a catastrophe or near disaster among those of its royal house who became married. Take, for instance, three grand-daughters of Pandion, through his son Erechtheus II.

Prokris, the first girl, married Kephalos, but two months after they were wed, Eôs, the Dawn goddess, saw him one morning as she was peering over Mt. Hymettos, fell in love, and whisked him off to her own lands in the east. Their union led to a dynasty in Syria, as you have already heard. But soon Eôs tired of her new lover's continual pining for his wife. The goddess told him, "If she's so wonderful, go back! But don't be surprised if you regret it." So Kephalos made his way home to Athens, ready to take up again with Prokris. But he was haunted by the suspicion, planted in him by Eôs, that she had not been faithful while he was away. (Kephalos' own affair did not count, he figured. After all, how could he resist a goddess?) He remembered an idea Dawn had once told him, how to test his wife, and he decided, before making his homecoming public, to disguise himself and try to seduce her.

Every day when Prokris went out (never alone), she saw a handsome, well-dressed stranger near the square. Eventually, he sent word, through her maid, that he might know something about her missing husband and could he visit her? Prokris took the bait. Their meetings became more frequent, especially as she realized that this traveler did know details, sometimes startlingly accurate, about the lost Kephalos. When the stranger began to press her for affection in return for his news, however, Prokris resisted staunchly. "I belong to another still, my only love." So it went for weeks on end. At last, the pretend seducer was about to give up. Making as if to leave Athens, he met Prokris once more and set down before her a bag the size of his traveler's hat, brimming with gold, and said, "This is for you, not that you owe me anything in return." As he turned to leave, he caught a tenderness in her eye, a moment's lingering hesitation in her farewell. That was all the proof he needed.

"So, perhaps I should stay?" Kephalos began in a quiet voice. Then louder: "Or, maybe you should know that I belong here, you faithless slut!" and he tore off his disguise. "You were ready to fall for a rich man, eh? That was what you were waiting for. How many more have there been?" Around the room he raged, as if expecting to find imaginary lovers in the corners. Meanwhile, Prokris had melted in tears. Dodging the grasp of her jealous spouse, she fled from the house and straight into the woods. There, they say, she became one of the brave girls who accompany the Huntress, Artemis, and shun all contact with men. Eventually, after a contrite Kephalos had begged forgiveness, she came back to him and the pair lived happily for a time.

In all fairness, you should know that there is another version of the story, namely that while Kephalos was away in the east, Prokris was courted relentlessly by one Pteleon, took his offering of a golden crown, and slept with him. When found out by her husband on his return, she took flight for Crete. Minos, the king at Knossos, was delighted at this turn of events, for he was a notorious womanizer. So mad for women was he that his wife, Pasiphae, found it necessary to put a spell on him, to ensure that his attempts at lovemaking would scare off any casual companions. (His body released scorpions and millipedes instead of seed.) Prokris overcame the problem through drugs she had somehow got from Circe and enjoyed the favors of Minos, until the king's fierce wife made her anxious, whereupon she decided to return to Kephalos. This version sounds like an excuse, though, a rumor started by the friends of Kephalos.

At any rate, Prokris returned—either from Artemis or Minos—with two gifts: a beautiful, sleek dog, a hunting hound that could outrun any beast; and a gold-tipped javelin made of a marvelous, smooth wood, a hunter's weapon that never missed its mark. Kephalos, always fond of hunting, now spent all his time in the hills above Athens, delighting in these new companions. He rose at sunrise and returned at nightfall. But he rested each afternoon in a cool spot near some wild cherry trees. Sweaty and exhausted, at these times he would urge the breeze to come fan him: "Let me feel your breath on my face, you who love the deep woods." One day he was overheard talking this way, and Prokris soon heard gossip that her husband talked sweetly every day with a wood nymph named Aura (which is the word for "breeze").

After all they had been through, Prokris was not about to trust mere rumors. Yet she was as worried as her husband had once been. Sneaking to the woods, she lay down behind some bushes one afternoon, bordering the spot she had been told was the trysting place. Sure enough, Kephalos came to rest, and she could hear his voice, whispering urgently, "Aura, come!" At the name Prokris automatically gave a start. At the same time, her husband, hearing a rustling like an animal astir in the dead leaves, aimed his javelin and let it fly. Unerringly, the sharp point found its victim—his fond wife. Kephalos reached her as she was struggling to wrench free the shaft of the weapon, her gift to him, but it was too late. Such are the snares of love.

Prokris had a sister, Oreithuia ("Rushing on the mountain"), who became another abductee. This time it was the burly North Wind, Boreas, who spied her one summer day as he was beating down lustily over Attica and the islands. She was playing by the grassy banks of the Ilissos, not far from the Acropolis. At this time of year the river was barely a trickle. The girl was happily skipping over the stream and back, practicing delicate steps for the day she would dance in the chorus of Artemis, like her older sister. Boreas played about, rustling her linen skirt, teasing her hair. Then he puffed harder and harder, until she began to rise into the sky, just as you feel yourself flying in a dream. He took her to his northern home and made her the mother of four children: the girls Kleopatra and Khionê ("Snowy" her name means), the boys Zetes and Kalais, handsome fellows with sky-blue hair and tawny golden wings jutting from the shoulders, so tender to the touch. When they grew up they sailed with Jason after the Golden Fleece—but we'll get to that later.

The third sister, Kreusa, also bore a famous child, although she did not know for years that he had survived beyond a few days after birth. Like her siblings, she also had a close relation with the divine. Apollo, the golden god, the perfect youth, lay with her in a cave on the steep slope of Athena's sacred hill. Nine months later, she returned to the spot and tearfully abandoned the love child she had borne. How could she know that Hermes, hours later, would snatch it up and bring the boy to be his father's temple servant at Delphi?

Years went by. Kreusa's own father, Erechtheus, became embroiled in a war with the people of Eleusis. To reward his ally, a warrior named Xuthus, he gave the hand of his daughter in marriage. It was a good match, thought the king. After all, Xuthus had a superb ancestry, since his father was Hellen, son of Deukalion and Pyrrha, the only survivors of the great Flood. All the Greeks to this day bear the name of "Hellenes" after the father of Xuthus. Of course, there was pressure to see that such a lofty bloodline continued, but Kreusa and Xuthus failed to produce a child.

On the verge of despair, the couple did what any Greek in their position would, even the humblest peasant: go to Delphi to ask the god what should be done. They made the trip overland to the mountain peaks of Parnassus. Xuthus posed the question, and Apollo, through his oracle at the high shrine, replied, in his usual ambiguous mode: "Going out immediately will appear the person that is your son."

You can imagine the joy of Xuthus on meeting, as he exited the shadowy temple, at the golden portico, a handsome teenage boy. Nor is it hard to imagine the confusion felt by this temple servant, suddenly accosted and told he was a high king's son. When asked what his name was, he said "Ion," which means "Going-out."

Kreusa was more doubtful. "This is some bastard of Xuthus, no doubt, gotten on a local girl when he was up here years ago sowing wild oats." Nor did she have much use for Apollo's oracle—wasn't he the god who seduced her? And now this nonsense about "the first one you will meet is your son." She would not be dishonored, not a royal princess whose very name meant "Ruling." So she plotted to "welcome" this Ion into the family with a feast, in which the drink was to be special—a poison potion just for him. All would have gone as planned had not a bird—one of the swallows that always dip and soar around the peaks—swooped down to the banquet table and sipped from the chosen cup. The bird dropped like a stone, in full view of everyone. Kreusa was caught in the act, and her son—for Ion was, of course, the boy she had once abandoned—was saved.

The gods put all right. Xuthus and Kreusa returned to Athens with their new heir. Ion in time became the father of four sons, and these produced the tribes of the Ionians who brought the culture and dialect of the Athenian Greeks to the coastlands at the eastern edge of the Aegean Sea.

# BOOK FIVE

## THESEUS, LORD
## OF ATHENS

WHEN ATHENS ADOPTED A democratic regime in 510 B.C., the founder of the new government, an aristocrat named Cleisthenes, mounted a propaganda campaign. As had his predecessor, the tyrant Peisistratus, he chose myth to convey his political message. To express the ideals of the new system, Cleisthenes championed the young hero Theseus instead of Herakles, the burly fighter favored by other Greek city-states. Suddenly Theseus appeared everywhere, his exploits illustrated on painted pots, on the new Athenian treasury at Delphi (where Cleisthenes had connections), and in frescoes around the Athenian business center, the agora. The boldest art schemes put Theseus right in the picture with the older hero Herakles, or juxtaposed the two to generate an unmistakable message: the Athenian king was every bit as valiant as the bluff Dorian, and more civil to boot.

Recent developments in Athenian life—the use of coins, elaborate festivals such as the yearly Panathenaia, the uniting of scattered communities around one civic center—were said to be, in fact, institutions that Theseus had first started. The authority of "tradition" was granted even the newest schemes. Perhaps it is not an accident that Theseus, the great civilizer and "culture hero," bore a name meaning "the one who arranges."

The replacement in popular imagination of Herakles by Theseus could seem natural because the two men were, after all, cousins. Aithra, mother of Theseus, was the daughter of Pittheus; this wise king's sister, Lysidike, was mother of Alkmene, the woman whom Zeus cunningly deceived one night—visiting her bedroom in the guise of her husband—to beget Herakles.

On his mother's side, Theseus could claim direct ancestry from Pelops, the famous charioteer and favorite of Poseidon. His father's heritage was somewhat more complex: Aegeus, king of Athens, could trace his lineage back to Erechtheus, the king who had been born from that city's very soil (thus making his clan "autochthonous"—born from earth itself—as Athenians never tired of telling people).

Only in the twentieth century did the most famous exploit of Theseus begin to seem more like history than myth. In 1900 the great British archaeologist Arthur Evans uncovered at Knossos in Crete the remains of a vast palace complex, dating to before 1700 B.C. Here were twisting corridors and hundreds of apartments, storage rooms, and porches clustered around a central court. What is more, the sign of the ceremonial double-axe—the *"labrys"*—was common throughout this newly found pre-Greek site. Most intriguing of all, frescoes, figurines, and gems were soon found that depicted bull sports—daring acrobatic jumps over the animal's head—being performed by graceful young men and women. The "Minoan" culture (so Evans called it, after King Minos) had declined following a tremendous volcanic explosion on the island of Santorini, north of Crete, around 1480 B.C. But the memory of this vanished civilization must have survived among the Greeks who came after it, in their stories about a powerful sea king, his maze-like "labyrinth," and a monstrous bull.

## 28.   THE SWORD UNDER THE STONE

History repeats itself, especially in Athens. Royal names were passed down over generations. There was even a repetition of the near poisoning of a royal son, but the young man—Theseus—was to escape death and become his country's greatest hero.

Erechtheus II, father of such interesting daughters, had also three sons, the eldest of which, named Cecrops (after the early king of Athens), lived a less eventful life, assumed his father's kingship in time, and in turn fathered a royal heir, Pandion II. The son was less lucky. Ousted by his cousins, he fled west—not too far off—to the dusty old town of Megara, and ingratiated himself with the local ruling family, eventually marrying into the clan, amid another round of slaughter and sedition.

In exile, Pandion II fathered four sons. After his death the sons— Pallas, Aegeus, Lykos, and Nisos—conquered "Attica," their ancestral land, and divided it among them, with Aegeus winning the territory around Athens itself. Pallas was jealous, and dangerous as well, since he had no fewer than fifty sons to help him do battle, should it come to that. Aegeus, on the other hand, was childless, a problem that he attempted to solve by consulting the oracle of Apollo at Delphi. He journeyed over the mountains to the northwestern town, and arriving at the shrine, he asked the Pythia—Apollo's mysterious spokeswoman—for advice. As usual, she replied in obscurely significant verse:

> *"Greatest leader, do not loose*
> *the wineskin's jutting foot*
> *until you come to Athens once again."*

Puzzled by this answer, Aegeus sought an interpretation from clever Pittheus, who ruled Troizen in the Peloponnese. "He does not understand the metaphor in these verses," thought Pittheus when he heard the conundrum, so he proceeded to arrange for Aegeus to "loose the skin's foot" immediately by getting the Athenian to sleep with his daughter—a dynastic decision. Aithra, the girl, became pregnant. Aegeus instructed her that if she bore a son who could, on reaching his teenage years, lift a certain heavy rock, the boy should be sent to Athens to take up his rightful royal crown. He would be recognized, Aegeus said, through the tokens he had hidden in a hollow in the rock: a pair of sandals and an ivory-hilted sword. And so the baby who soon arrived was called Theseus ("Arranger") because Aegeus had ordered things this way.

Like his cousin Herakles, Theseus' paternity carried an air of ambiguity. Someone—Pittheus, or Aithra herself, perhaps—put out the story that the god Poseidon, not Aegeus, had fathered this handsome child. Some even claimed that Aithra, after lying with Aegeus, waded to an offshore island and that same night made love to the sea god. Aegeus, as it turned out, was by a sad mishap to give his name to the Aegean Sea. Was there in his younger days already something fishy about the king, something godlike and marine? At any rate, the boy Theseus became a great swimmer, yet at a crucial moment in his youth scorned the sea.

As did many a young hero with an absent father, he dreamed of the day that he could show everyone how important, how loving was the missing man in his life. As soon as soft down began to darken his chin, Theseus put his shoulder to the great stone and shifted it, took the tokens Aegeus had deposited, and headed off to claim his throne at Athens. But he did not go by sea. That would have been too easy, since Athens was a short sail across the gulf from home. Instead, he chose the circuitous mainland route along the seacoast and across the Isthmus, precisely because it was so perilous, filled with fearful creatures and villains his cousin had failed to remove. At the time, Herakles was in Lydia, doing shameful slave labor for the exotic queen Omphalê. It was the moment for Theseus to win his own fame.

Not far from Troizen is Epidauros, a place that would become prosperous and famous for its great hospital at the healing shrine of the hero Asklepios. In Theseus' day, however, Epidauros was a backwoods spot. Here he met his first opponent, "Club-Man" Periphetes. A son of the crafts god, Hephaestus, he robbed travelers by threatening them with his heavy wooden weapon. Theseus overcame him with his bare hands. He took the ruffian's club—so he, too, had a weapon like Herakles'—and moved on.

Next he met Sinis "Pine Bender," a son of Poseidon (a half brother?), who would rip apart the unwary traveler by tying him between two flexible, bent trees which he then let go. Theseus treated him to a taste of his own treatment. The third obstacle he overcame was inhuman in another way: the man-killing sow Phaia, which terrorized the township of Krommyon, west of Megara. (Some declared later that this was not a sow, in fact, but a female robber so nicknamed on account of her piggish lifestyle.) Then there was Skiron, at Megara. He seated himself athwart a narrow pass and demanded of those on the road, "Wash my feet!" and when they bent to do so, he booted them off a cliff into the Saronic Gulf, where a giant turtle ate them up. Thanks to Theseus, this menace gave the sea beast its last big meal.

Twelve miles from Athens is the holy place Eleusis, where Demeter once sat in mourning for her daughter. At this spot the young hero defeated Kerkyon in the wrestling match all travelers had to face from him. Finally, he encountered the most dangerous man of all. "Hammer," "Cutter," "Pain's Son," "Beater"—Procrustes had many names, but his behavior remained always the same and it horrified the hospitable Greeks. Offering "guests" a place on which to sleep, this inconsiderate host used to pound out their legs to lengthen them or chop them short to fit the bed. To Procrustes, Theseus repaid the favor *before* settling down for the night.

Having in this way done others a great service by making travel safer, Theseus reached his father's city, confident of an illustrious career. What he did not know was that Aegeus was now living with a foreign wife, a powerful woman whom he had first met at Corinth the very year of Theseus' birth. Her name was Medea. There is much to tell, in its place, about her own story.

Aegeus had no idea who this handsome stranger was, nor did Theseus, a cautious young warrior, rush to reveal himself. Medea, on the contrary, needed only one look to discern the truth: this was the son who would one day rule Athens, displacing her and shattering her dynastic hopes for her own offspring. Luckily, when she had left her home on the far side of the Black Sea some years back, Medea had brought with her a supply of aconite.

Once, when Herakles dragged the hellhound Kerberos up from Hades, the horrifying dog shook its multiple jaws near a place in Scythia, scattering rabid canine saliva over a wide area. Where the flecks of spittle fell, there grew noxious plants—right out of the bare earth—and from these "dustless" (*akonitos*) shoots, the locals discovered, a useful poison could be made.

Medea convinced Aegeus that this newcomer was a danger to the realm, a plotter and a rabblerouser. Then she let her husband try his own method of elimination first: the test of the Bull of Marathon. That wild animal, roaming at will, had already slain some strong young men. But of course, Theseus killed the beast, won the thanks of the community, and strolled back the twenty-six miles to town. That is when Medea chose to use her own means.

The fatal cup was prepared. Medea kept it hidden, to be sure no stray animals would take a sip and give away the result. To make the ruse more convincing, she handed the cup to Aegeus so that he would be the one who offered the drink to Theseus at the evening's feast. "We have heard of your bravery, boy, even before this wonderful bull-slaying feat. Now may this be the shining moment," said Aegeus, "for which you will be remembered hereafter." Theseus took the cup, holding it high so that the gold reflected the torchlight. "And I have a gift for you," he said. He reached for the sword he wore, to present it at last to this unknown man they had told him so much about. "First, a toast," said Theseus, and put the cup to his lips.

But Aegeus in that moment caught a glimpse of the weapon the younger man had started to unsheathe, an ivory hilt with unmistakable characters inscribed thereon—his personal sign. With a crash he leapt across the table and knocked the great cup from the hands of Theseus, sending it clattering across the floor. "Sorceress!" he screamed, whirling around, for he guessed the whole story. Medea, however, was already gone, snatched by a whirlwind she had whipped up with a spell. She transported herself back east, not to her birthplace but farther south. There her last child, Medus, became ancestor of a race that centuries later tried to destroy the Athenians. But the Medes—as the Persians were called—failed as miserably as Medea. Later heroes who came, like Theseus, to Marathon took the credit for their defeat. The victorious warriors of Athens sent word by swift runner from the plain near the sea back to the town. And they told later of a vision in the midst of battle: Theseus, gigantic in form, rising out of the earth to urge them onward.

## 29.    THE CRETAN ADVENTURE

Athens was filled with the sounds of flute and lyre, of the smells of incense and sacrificial meat. All rejoiced that the king's son was at last among them. But beyond this scene of joy lay a darker horizon. The people of Athens were suffering under an even greater burden, a problem that had begun back in the time that Aegeus himself first came to power.

The "All Athens," or Panathenaic, festival was the greatest sporting event in those parts. It vied with the renowned games of Zeus at Olympia and of Apollo's shrine at Delphi. Athletes from all over the Greek world competed, not for material reward (though they did win an amphora of Athena's olive oil), but for the fame, the glory that came with victory there. When Aegeus conducted these celebrated games for the first time, a powerful young man named Androgeos turned up, and he defeated his opponents in every single contest, from wrestling to broad jumping, the footrace to the javelin toss. Then, as now, glory induced jealousy. The grumbling started immediately. "Unfair!" said one. "Fixed!" said another. "Who is this stranger coming in here and winning all the prizes?" Dark mutterings led to threats and threats to a shameful ambush. For, it is said, a gang of the losers waylaid Androgeos as he started out for the next festival, the Laius games at Thebes. (These contests were held to honor the king who had recently been struck down by a young man who would not give way for the royal chariot—but that story can wait.) Other rumors said that Aegeus himself, probably chagrined that Athenians had not won anything, dispatched the winning athlete to go fight the Marathon Bull, which meant sure death. Whoever did the murder, Athens was blamed, since it stemmed from the festival there.

Androgeos' father was the owner of the most powerful fleet in the world: the king of Crete, Minos. The sea was in Minos' blood, you could say—at least, his personal history had much to do with the water. His mother was Europa, a granddaughter of Poseidon. As a girl of fourteen, living in the land of the Phoenicians, she went one day with friends to the seashore, where they caught sight of a beautiful white bull. The animal was playful; one girl draped its shining horns with a flower garland, while another patted its glossy shanks. They fed it sweet grass. The bull lowered its neck, just like the beasts she had seen her father sacrifice to the god, and Europa, braver than her playmates, climbed onto its back.

Now the splendid leader of the herd began to shamble off. It was great fun—until he turned in the direction of the sea and kept going. Soon waves lapped at his flanks. Deeper and deeper he went. The girls' expressions of delight turned to surprise and then alarm. They rushed to the sea, but only went in the water up to their ankles, and called to the bull to come back. What more could they do? Europa, meanwhile, proudly riding the white beast, one hand on its right horn, as if to steer, the other holding aloft the end of her long veil, which bellied out like a spinnaker, regally steamed off toward the horizon.

The bull was Zeus—in another of his love disguises—and he took Europa over the sea to faraway Crete, the large mountain-filled island where he himself had spent his childhood days. The girl would have a continent named after her, but Crete is really just the edge of that region, being nearly equal in distance from Africa, Europe, and Asia Minor. Here Zeus embraced her, in his normal form, and left her the mother of twins—Minos and Rhadamanthys.

Both boys grew up to have a legal turn of mind, which could also stem from their ancestry, since, as the old folks say, "The sea is the most just." Until he emigrated to Boeotia, Rhadamanthys formulated laws for the Cretans. Even when he died he continued this career, as judge and ruler in Elysium, the fair land of the afterlife. Minos, the brother who stayed in Crete, took over the lawmaking. Some said he would consult personally about legal matters with his father Zeus every nine years, and for that reason the Cretan system in time to come became a model for other legislators.

Minos' personal life was rather less orderly. His penchant for beautiful women has already been mentioned. He populated the island by means of various nymphs, even chasing the favorite of Artemis, named Britomartis, until she jumped off a cliff into the sea, where fishermen caught her up in their nets (so she was addressed as "Diktynna" or "Netty"—as was Artemis herself sometimes). His official wife was a daughter of the Sun, named Pasiphae ("All-shining"), and it was by her that Minos had Androgeos, the ill-fated athlete.

The king went to visit Paros, one of his many subject island-states in the Cyclades, north of Crete. He was in the middle of a sacrifice to the Graces when news came that Androgeos had been murdered. After the messenger had spoken, Minos, with a deep groan, ripped the ritual garland from his head and ordered the flute player to stop (which is why in Paros now they sacrifice with neither music nor headgear). "This is war!" he declared, and immediately laid plans to punish Athens, and Megara as well (since the cities had close ties).

The latter was easily taken. Minos used his charm on the daughter of the Megarian king, Nisos, a young woman called Skylla. On Nisos' head there grew, amid the black curls, a single lock of purple hair. An oracle had foretold that if Nisos lost this lock, he would lose his life. At Minos' request, Skylla snipped the hair, risking all for her love of the Cretan king. In return, she got nothing but his revulsion and scorn. "Imagine, killing your own father—treacherous woman!" was all he had to say. He proceeded to keelhaul the girl, hanging her off his ship's stern until she drowned.

Athens required a drawn-out siege. No matter how many ships and men Minos brought, the clever Athenians found ways to keep supplied. In disgust, he finally prayed to Zeus: "It is not right for a father to go unavenged. Help me to get my due!" The prayer worked. Soon, Athens was overwhelmed by a plague. Hundreds died, so quickly that the living could barely keep up with the burials. The water was polluted, a cruel irony since that was all that the victims craved. Corpses and dead animals choked the streets and even tainted the sacred places of the gods. At the end of their wits, the Athenians even resorted to sacrificing virgins, as they had once before in the time of Erechtheus. But that, too, failed. At last they asked Apollo's oracle what they might do, and were told, "Do whatever Minos wants."

Minos, as it happened, wanted a revenge that would never end. Every year the cream of Athenian youth, seven picked young men and seven young women, had to accompany him to Crete, to be fed to his dreaded Minotaur. They could fight the beast in its labyrinth if they chose—provided they brought no weapons. The Minotaur—or "Minos bull"—was the monstrous result of an earlier time when Minos had his prayers answered. Back in the days when he was claiming the kingship of Crete, his stepfather having died childless, and with many rivals for the throne, Minos alleged that the gods themselves had granted him, and only him, the island. "Watch," he told his skeptical competitors. "Whatever I want, I get," and praying to Poseidon, he asked for a bull from the sea. Sure enough, a beautiful animal appeared and trotted out of the waves onto the beach. But Minos, instead of sacrificing this bull, as he had promised, kept the divine animal, and substituted an inferior specimen from his herds. Poseidon, angered by this trickery, made the bull wild and impossible to control. To top it off, he made Pasiphae, the wife of Minos, fall in love with the bull so madly that she yearned to mate with it.

A harmless fantasy, perhaps—maybe it did not help that she had heard so many stories about Zeus and Minos' mother. But, unfortunately, the means to fulfill her wish were soon at hand. The architect Daedalus, an exiled resident of Athens, and distant relation of Theseus, crafted an extremely lifelike hollow cow, out of wood and skin with wheels beneath it, put Pasiphae in it, and obligingly trundled the contraption to the roving bull's favorite meadow. The offspring of the ensuing union was a ravenous, ugly creature: it looked like a man but had a bull's beastly face.

The next puzzle, how to keep the damnable creature from roaming the island, was also neatly solved by Daedalus. He was good at such challenges, and immensely proud of his talents. His exile from Athens had come about because a young apprentice, his nephew Talos, had appeared to be more talented than himself, and he did not like that. Once, Daedalus discovered that the boy had invented a fine-tooth saw, using a snake's jawbone, and could do fancy scrollwork on a stick of wood. Jealous, he threw Talos off the Acropolis. (He landed near Dionysus' theater, where the Athenians can show you his grave.) The Areopagus court convicted the architect of murder, and he fled to Minos' land. The solution for imprisoning the bull-man was something Daedalus called "the labyrinth"—a devious, sprawling building, with a central room, the rest entirely made of intersecting, winding, branching, crisscrossing corridors, designed to make any exit impossible. They put the Minotaur in first, and built outward and outward until he was trapped.

Now this was to be the death chamber for the young of Athens. After his humiliation of the city, Minos came the next year for his first sacrificial boatload, and the next year for the second. The third year was the one in which Theseus came to Athens. Hearing about the tribute to the cruel king, he volunteered to go as one of the seven young men, against the wishes of his newfound father. This time the Athenians sent their own ship, carrying a black sail, a sign of sorrow for the doomed youths. "If you somehow survive," said Aegeus, "you must let me know as quickly as you can. As soon as you come within sight of the Acropolis, on your return, run up this white sail, and I'll see it and rejoice." So Theseus agreed, and the ship set out for Crete.

On arriving, they met Minos. "Lovely maidens this year!" was the first thing he said, in his coarse way. "You'll make a fine meal for the bull-man," and he started to handle one of the maidens, Periboia. Theseus told him to back off, but Minos leered more: "Oh, are you her boyfriend?" and kept on with his harassment. "I'm the son of Zeus. I can do whatever I want, and Zeus will back me up," he said to Theseus. "Zeus," he roared out to the sky, "cast down your bolt!" A white lightning shaft shot down from the blue sky, and Minos, smiling, turned to Theseus. "See?"

"So I have heard," said the young man, "but perhaps you don't know that my own father is Poseidon, who lay with my mother Aithra. She still has the gold veil the Nereids gave her in remembrance."

"Oh, really? Then why don't you dive down to your father's house for this?" snarled Minos, and threw into the choppy sea his gold ring. "Then we'll see if he helps his sons."

Without a further word, Theseus leapt from the stern of the Athenian boat, plunging down like a shearwater until he disappeared. He was under so long that the other young men and women thought he was surely dead. But dolphins bore him to the bottom and brought him to the god's deep-sea home. He saw the daughters of Nereus dancing, their legs and arms streaming phosphorescent flashes like fire. On her throne was Amphitritê, Poseidon's wife. She smiled kindly, inviting him, as if to stay forever. She presented Theseus with a cloak dyed purple, like the sea itself, and tenderly placed a gold crown on his curly hair. And of course, he retrieved Minos' ring. Then Theseus shot back to the surface—that alone would have killed any other diver—and emerged resplendent with clothes and jewels from the gods. All his companions, huddled on deck, gasped and then broke out in song, a *paian* of thanksgiving to the gods. "Try not to lose this again," said Theseus, and tossed the hammered gold ring at the Cretan king's feet.

Minos turned on his heel, in silent disgust, and stalked off with a sidelong growl to his bodyguard: "Take them to the labyrinth."

Theseus knew what their two choices were: slow death if they entered as a group and then scattered. They would all wander endlessly in the nightmarish building until the Minotaur sniffed each out and ate them. Or one at a time. The third possibility—to kill the Minotaur and escape—was equally hopeless, for without a diagram—and there was none, since the plan existed only in the head of Daedalus—no one could leave the labyrinth.

The night before the ordeal, an answer arrived. Theseus and his companions had been left free to roam one wing of the palace. There were no weapons available, and no one could escape. All access was barred. Yet the daughter of Minos, the slender Ariadne, slipped into the Athenian quarters, found Theseus, and presented him with an offer. "From the moment I saw you break the waves, when you came out of the sea, all shining and smiling, I think I fell in love with you. I will show you how to escape tomorrow if you promise to take me away from here and make me your wife." For a long time Theseus could not speak, only stare at this tender, lovely girl. Love did survive even in such places, and a kind of justice, too. Minos had led another woman once to betray her father, and now he was being paid back in kind.

He accepted the offer. Later that same night, Ariadne returned with the secret. Daedalus had told her that Theseus should take with him a ball of linen thread, tie one end to the front doorway of the labyrinth, and unwind the skein as he went in. When he had accomplished his task, the thread would lead him out.

That is exactly what he did. The next day, as his companions watched, Theseus entered the maze. Even they did not see that he had hidden the thread, or noticed that he tied a knot while pretending to bend and lace his sandal. He worked his way inward, almost by instinct, to the final room, where the bull-man was sleeping. Before the

Minotaur could stir, Theseus battered him senseless with his bare fists. He knocked him hard once more against the floor, and made his way out by the guide thread.

Ariadne and Theseus' companions were waiting by the door. The guards had already gone off to rest, expecting never to see that particular Athenian again. By the time night fell, the group had sailed, making the harbor at Naxos. Theseus led his band of companions in a dance of joyous celebration, using steps that he had dreamed up while he worked his way into the labyrinth—left, left, right, over and over in a mazelike, shifting mode. Now the accounts get most confused. Either Ariadne was killed by Artemis, at the urging of Dionysus—but no one can explain why he would want her dead. Or else Dionysus, while the dance went on, stole Ariadne, took her to Lemnos, and lay with her: local clans on that island swear their ancestors resulted from the event. Or else, Theseus and his crew woke up the next day and sailed off to Athens without a second thought of

Ariadne—either they abandoned her because she had served her purpose, or they just forgot—and Dionysus found her later, consoled her,
and made her his wife.

When Theseus approached his home, after sailing another night,
and headed up to the harbor, he forgot something else: the white sail
his father had given him, the signal of victory. Some say he was too
sunk in grief at losing Ariadne to think of his promise. The old king,
his father, had risen early that morning, as on every morning since the
youths departed, to seat himself on the western tip of the Acropolis,
gazing out at the sea, miles off. Today he spotted a sail—and though
far away, the color was visible: black as the night that had just passed.
His last hope gone, Aegeus threw himself off the city's high rock,
plunging to his death. There are those, too, who say he waited closer
to the sea, and that his dive to death gave the sea its name: Aegean.

## 30. LIFE AFTER THE LABYRINTH

It was with a mixture, therefore, of exultation and grief that the Athenians came to meet Theseus and the miraculously returned youths as
they disembarked. For the young leader, the blow was severe. He had
hardly known the man who had been responsible for his birth. Was
that boast to Minos about his having a divine father somehow a cause?
Or was it a part of his psychology? Had he really wanted then to deny
the influence of any man that would have tied him down to the earth?

As if to avoid questioning himself, Theseus plunged into activity.
First he faced an all-out war with the fifty sons of Pallas, who saw an
opportunity to overthrow the man they had always called "the outsider." Theseus killed them all. Then he had the task of organizing
Athens. To strengthen the city, he incorporated all the outlying villages he could, making up stories when he had to, in order to explain
to all these people that they were meant to be one community. Finally,
he allowed himself some heroic adventures. He joined forces with his
cousin and boyhood idol, Herakles, to launch a raid on the mysterious
eastern race of women called Amazons.

No one knows where these expert warrior women came from.
Scythia, Thrace, Asia Minor—all had seen their incursions, and tombs
of their great queens marked even wild landscapes. It was not true
that they hated men—they simply had little need for them, and lived
in all-female encampments. Nor did they mutilate themselves in

order to throw the javelin better; that was merely someone's guess at explaining their name, which to a Greek sounds like "one-without-a-breast" (*a-maz-on*).

Herakles got from them the object he had come for, the heavy, jewel-encrusted belt of Hippolyte, the Amazon queen. If this conquest of his was largely symbolic, the victory of Theseus had more real consequence. The Athenian hero carried off, as a prize of war, Antiope, an important Amazon fighter, slinging her over his shoulder as lightly as a shepherd hoists a lamb. She went with him to Athens, and they had a child, Hippolytos. All went well for a few years. Then word came that the Amazons had regained their strength and were on the warpath. A few months later the rumors proved true. One summer day an Athenian scout reported to the king that a fierce band of women warriors were at the borders of Attica. Immediately, the fighting men of the newly united city fortified the Acropolis. When the Amazons arrived, thousands of women strong, they encamped beneath the rock, all around the Areopagus. Never before had such an invasion force threatened the city. It was all the more ironic that these worshipers of another virgin goddess, of Artemis, should undertake the attack on Athena's city. They had come to avenge the abduction of Antiope.

A terrible battle erupted. Neither side could maneuver their horses well in the rocky, steep places where they had chosen to make a stand. Hand-to-hand fighting was the rule, and men shuddered to see their companions cut down, all the more because they died, shamefully, at women's hands. But these were more like superwomen, or some unknown hybrid breed. They had to be respected and feared. With increasing desperation, and prayers to the gods, the men of Athens, led by Theseus, finally routed the Amazons. But it had been a close call.

Some think that Antiope died in this battle, at the hands of Theseus. Either she had joined her former sisters-in-arms, or in the rout and confusion he struck out at her by mistake. But another version, perhaps more believable, places her death somewhat later. It seems Minos had now left Crete in the charge of his son, who wanted to patch up relations with Athens, and learning of the loss of Ariadne, he promised a sister in marriage to Theseus. The match was made, and Phaidra, the brilliant woman (as her name means), arrived by boat in Athens soon after for the wedding rites. The tables were set, the lyre players were tuning up for the dancing, and the wine pourers hurrying about, when an uninvited guest appeared at the door: Antiope.

Theseus had neglected to inform her of his impending new marriage, and she was understandably upset. The servants said she had been heard threatening murder. Greek men did not respect "barbarian" women (and all who did not speak Greek well were called "barbarian" because their words, to the cultivated Hellenic ear, all came out "bar-bar-bar"). Jason had already paid for just such a misstep, and the lesson was not lost on Theseus. So Antiope was quietly invited into a private room, forced to leave her Amazon companions outside with their weapons, given a meal, then put to death.

Phaidra and Theseus began their life together. In a few years they had two sons. Meanwhile, the boy born from Antiope was reaching manhood. Theseus was traveling more often, adventuring with various hero friends. Hippolytos, the young man, had always lived in the palace, and Phaidra could not help but notice how strong and handsome he had grown. Later on, after the disaster, older folks blamed her family background. "What do you expect? Look at her mother and that bull." Others made similar remarks about the habits of "Cretan women." Later tales say that she tried to force herself on him, and when rejected, she tore her dress ragged, broke her door down, and told all it was a rape. In actuality, Phaidra appears to have done all she could to resist her growing passion for her stepson. When word leaked out (through a stupid old nurse) that she loved Hippolytos, the young man was furious. He was unusual, for Greek men: devoted not to Aphrodite, but (like his mother's clan) to Artemis. Shunning women in general, he was always talking about "purity," channeling his energy into the hunt. He righteously scorned Phaidra, called her all sorts of names. And she, in shame, hanged herself, but not before taking a step in revenge. On a wax letter tablet, she wrote the whole tale. Only she gave her version: that Hippolytos had wanted her, but she would have nothing of it. When they found the body, this tablet was dangling from an arm. Theseus, arriving back at exactly this time, read the story it contained, and exploded in rage and disbelief. "My own son gained my marriage bed by force!" Despite the young man's protests that he had never been with any woman, Theseus exiled him, calling down destruction on his head—one of three powerful curses that Poseidon once entrusted to him. Before the day was out, Hippolytos was targeted. As he drove his chariot away from home, the sea, on his right hand, roared and a gigantic wave, a hundred feet high, rose up and towered over him. A huge bull rushed out of the wave, straight at the chariot. Hippolytos wheeled this way and that, but the bull managed to stay along-

side his vehicle, no matter how fast he drove. Finally, at a sharp turning, Hippolytos was forced off the road. The chariot turned onto its
side, still dragged at top speed by the terrified horses. Hippolytos, entangled in the reins, was smashed against the roadside rocks. Too late,
Theseus realized his mistake. Artemis assured him that his son had
been innocent. His body was brought back to town for burial. To this
day, the young women of Troizen (where it all took place) sacrifice
locks of hair to chaste Hippolytos the night before they wed.

The second episode for which Theseus is remembered from his
later career also involved improper love and weddings gone wrong.
Ixion, a man of Thessaly, once offered a magnificent bride price for
Dia, a beautiful young woman of the region near Larissa. Her father
was delighted, so much that he agreed to come and fetch the rich
goods in person. Knowing the route he would take, Ixion constructed
a pit and filled it with hot coals so that his would-be in-law perished
horribly. He himself fled to Zeus—no one else would purify him of
this awful crime—but even on Olympus, Ixion did not conduct himself any better. Having forfeited a human wife, he now tried to take
the goddess Hera, the wife of his host. She told her shocked husband,
who contrived to catch Ixion in the act. Zeus made a beautiful repro-
duction of his spouse, constructed entirely from fluffy clouds. Em-
bracing this fake Hera, Ixion thought he had achieved perfect
happiness. Instead, when Zeus saw the proof of the mortal's arrogance
and ingratitude, he lashed Ixion to a wheel that turns round constantly in the heavens, flashing fire as it rotates.

Energy is never lost among the gods, however. The cloud Hera,
even though a decoy, brought forth children who reflected their
mixed-up heritage. From the front they looked like human men, until
one noticed that their backsides stuck out five feet and resembled
horses. The manly torsos, with hairy flanks and horsey legs and tail,
looked comical or, perhaps, were a lesson—that a man's ambition of
marrying a goddess was, like these Centaurs (so they were called), un-
natural and absurd.

Some time before his crimes, Ixion had fathered a wholly human
son, Peirithoos. This young man had heard about Theseus and ad-
mired the Athenian immensely. As a way of getting an introduction,
he stole some cattle, from Marathon, to see how Theseus would react.
When the king chased after him and tracked him down, Peirithoos
surrendered, and the two became close friends. Peirithoos invited
Theseus to his wedding with Deidameia. Out of courtesy (for he was

the opposite of his father, Ixion), the young Thessalian sent word to his half brothers that they, too, should come. That was a grave mistake. Centaurs are fine when allowed to live peacefully on Mt. Pelion (their preferred range), racing and hunting. But certain aspects of civilized life are beyond them. An example is wine, which marks every Greek feast, especially weddings. The Centaurs became drunk after the first few sips that Peirithoos gave them. In no time, their animal nature got the better of them, and they started pawing all the women present, including the bride. The Lapith men (the clan of Peirithoos) could not stand by idly. A ruckus ensued, one of the most famous battles of its kind, and many Centaurs died.

Among the Lapiths there were fewer fatalities, but one in particular deserves mention. Kaineus, a brave fighter, had once been a woman. The story goes that in his teenage years Kainis (her former name) had been astoundingly beautiful. As usual, gods noticed her as much as men did. Before she came to marry, as she walked one evening on the beach, Poseidon assaulted her. "Now, my love, what would you like? I will give you anything at all," the god promised after their encounter. And Kainis replied, shivering, "That this never happen again. Make me a man so that it won't. Make it impossible to hurt me." Poseidon fulfilled her wish, and Kainis became Kaineus.

In the battle with the Centaurs, one beast recalled the story and taunted the Lapith fighter with it. Kaineus slew him on the spot. The other Centaurs slashed at him with javelins and swords (weapons they had picked up and were not quite used to). Nothing hurt Kaineus: swords shattered, spears bounced off. "Bury him!" screamed Monykhos, another Centaur. And the beast-men obeyed. They ripped fir trees right out of the ground and tore off whole cliff sides for pounding rocks. Even when they had battered him halfway into the earth, Kaineus survived, driving the Centaurs even wilder. Finally, they heaped so much wood and rubble on his head that he could no longer breathe and gave up the ghost.

Theseus distinguished himself in the Battle of Lapiths and Centaurs. With a wine vat he smashed the skull of Eurytos, the Centaur who had started it all by trying to steal the bride. Peirithoos should have been grateful to have his new wife back, and content with his new friend. But the two men, as often happens to heroes, did not take well to simple contentment. One began to grow restless, then the other. One night, over lots of wine, they hatched a plan for the best

adventure yet—or so they thought—little suspecting, or caring, that it would put an end to all their roving.

"My father," began Peirithoos, "was not all that wrong, you know. Women—the ones we court, and we fight for, and work for—get old quickly. A woman's season is brief, like a flower's. That's why Ixion did what he did, I'm sure of it, now that I've seen more of the world. And even if he did not get an immortal goddess as wife, still, he's got a kind of fame. All the world knows about my father." Theseus was getting uneasy, but could not hide his interest, as his friend went eagerly on: "Here's what I say: we did all right getting fine mortal wives. Let's try the next step. And let's not anger Zeus by trying to court his own wife. Instead, I want to make a pact: by this time next year, we'll each have taken for ourselves a daughter of Zeus—something no human man has yet accomplished." The older hero's mind blazed up at the prospect: "Son-in-law of Zeus! Imagine, if old Minos could hear that!" They swiftly swore an oath to choose the right women and carry out their plan.

By this time Theseus was fifty years old, but rather than instilling caution, his increasing age seemed to make him more reckless. He knew already the girl he wanted, for he had heard of her amazing beauty and birth. Her father, Tyndareos, lived in Sparta, although he had acquired his wife, Leda, while in exile. The couple had been blessed with two daughters, Timandra and Phylonoe. One day Leda was resting by the banks of the Eurotas when she caught sight of a perfect white swan, which came right up to her—but gently, unlike most swans, which are, as you know, aggressive birds. The swan allowed itself to be stroked and nestled up to Leda, stroking her neck in turn with its own. This game went on for a while, pleasantly enough. When Leda tried to leave, however, she found herself pinioned by the bird's powerful wings. Soon she was overpowered, unable to fight back. For the swan was the lover of mortal beauties, Zeus.

Some say that Leda caught on a bit earlier, and when she fled Zeus' advances, she was transformed into a goose, which he then caught up with. That would explain more easily how Leda came to lay an egg. Whatever the facts are, the egg, which an embarrassed Leda left in the marshland, was discovered by a shepherd following a stray lamb, was taken to the palace, placed in a special box (since it was so impressive in size), and in due time hatched. Out came a baby girl—Helen (whose name is tied to rushes and willows). Because Leda had three other children at the same time, there are various accounts as to the number of eggs and what they contained. Her sister Klytaimnestra was said to have broken out of a second egg, and along with each girl, a boy emerged. The boys were called Kastor and Polydeukes, but since they were always together, they usually went by the name "Dioskouroi," "Zeus' sons." Because Leda had been loved by the father of gods (as also by her own husband the same night), half the offspring were immortal: of the boys, Polydeukes, and of the girls, Helen.

This was the remarkable girl that Theseus chose. The drawback was that she was at the time only twelve years old. But the graying Athenian king wanted to steal her now, while his strength held out, then wait a few years to have the proper wedding. With Peirithoos, he swooped down on Sparta and carried off the fair young blond girl as she was dancing in the chorus of Artemis Orthia. He hid her in Aphidnai, leaving her, untouched by any man, in the care of his old mother, Aithra.

After the successful raid, now it was Theseus' turn to help his friend. Theseus had thought his own choice ambitious—a young virgin, surrounded by kin, in a remote mountain stronghold with few ways out. The challenge that Peirithoos came up with was ten times harder—foolhardy, if the truth be told—but that made the challenge more appealing. "I want Persephone," he said. "You are a true son of Ixion," commented Theseus. "Still, a promise is a promise." So the two set out for the underworld and the bride of Hades.

They found the way down easily enough and managed to slip past Kerberos, the hellhound. On some pretext they made their way into the presence of the royal couple, the king and queen of the dead. "No questions! Food first, and drink," said Hades. "Then we'll see what brings you boys here." The heroes politely declined food (having heard, no doubt, what had happened to Persephone when she accepted long ago). Drink they did take—the dead are always thirsty, it seems, and the drink was plentiful. But before they could relate the elaborate lie that Peirithoos had dreamed up, the two friends noticed that their seats were becoming less comfortable. Trying to shift position, they found with horror that the rocky thrones on which Hades had seated them held them tight. The living stone, like a stalagmite, had fused itself with flesh. "I thought we wouldn't bother chasing after you swine later, but get right to the punishment," said Hades coolly. "You see, I knew what you had in mind."

That was the end of the Lapith hero Peirithoos, bound for eternity, like his father, because he overstepped what is human. Theseus, too, would have stayed rooted forever, if not for his former idol, Herakles, whose own journey to the underworld neatly coincided with this misadventure. Herakles intended to rescue both. After he wrenched Theseus free, he went to pry loose his friend, but at that moment the earth quaked, as if the wreck of the second stone chair would cause all Hades' realm to cave in, so he gave up, taking only Theseus back to the light. As it was, Theseus left behind part of himself on that hellish throne, which explains why, even today, Athenians have such slender buttocks.

## 31.  FINAL FALLS

You cannot leave a kingdom behind and expect to find it months later safe and sound. Especially, if like Theseus, just before going you provoked an international incident. The brothers of Helen, the Dioskouroi, wasted no time in taking advantage of the king's absence from Athens. They invaded along with experienced warriors from Arcadia and Sparta, chased out the two young sons of Theseus, who had been left in charge, rescued their lovely sister Helen, kidnapped Aithra, her guardian, and restored to the throne Menestheus, an aristocrat who had been waiting in the wings ever since Theseus returned from Crete. Theseus tried to set things right when he came back from Hades, but finding the people had already turned against him, he gave up and took himself into exile on the island Scyros. He thought he had a friend in the king of the place, Lycomedes. However, true to his name ("Wolf-planner"), his host, in showing him the local views, suddenly seized Theseus and threw him down into a gorge, where he perished instantly.

Ironically, the old enemy of Theseus met his death through a false host, too. The very day that the Athenian youths had fled the labyrinth, with Theseus and Ariadne in the lead, Minos had started investigating, and he soon decided that Daedalus had been the culprit. Only he, after all, knew the secrets of the maze. Now he would get to learn the labyrinth from the inside—with no thread to help him out. Minos shut up the cunning architect inside the hopelessly complicated building, along with his teenage son, Icarus. He provided a little food, and even candles.

Daedalus, always ingenious, set to work on his escape. Even if he could have found an exit, the entire building was now surrounded. His only choice was by air. Each night before extinguishing their candles, father and son carefully gathered up the soft wax. Every day they spent their time wandering the maze, which was open to the air, and they picked up feathers shed by passing birds. Minos knew from his guards about this activity, but assumed Daedalus was simply going crazy, in a harmless way. Then one day father and son vanished.

Daedalus had made wings for their escape, patiently gluing with wax the hundreds of feathers they had found. "Follow me," he told Icarus just before their flight, "but take the middle course. If you fly too high, the sun will melt the waxen bonds. If you fly too low, the sea's moisture will weigh the feathers down." And he took off, executing a few preliminary climbs and dives to show Icarus how it should be done.

Soon a fisherman on the Cretan Sea was gazing up at two tiny winged figures as they made their way across the sky. "Gods, on some errand," he thought, and made a silent prayer. Icarus did indeed feel like a god. Soaring and gliding, circling his father and veering off on the updrafts, he felt as though he would never want to touch earth again. How high could people fly with these? He was not *really* that high now, and he started to ascend.

What Daedalus noticed first was the silence. Up to now there had been the swish and flap of artificial wings, his own steadily beating, his son's erratically but sure. Now all he heard was a distant cry like a gull's. Not wanting to look up, he nevertheless forced himself, and saw what looked like a little flame, a small white star, falling and flapping its naked arms. Icarus had gone too far and could not be helped. His father watched as he plummeted and sank beneath the waves of the sea (after that, called Icarian).

His spirit crushed, Daedalus still pressed on, coming to Sicily, to a place called Camicus, and its king, Kokalos. There, he found shelter in obscurity, inventing various useful, humble items. Meanwhile, Minos was determined to track him down, wherever he was. He suspected that Daedalus would flee to Athens, his birthplace, but knew the cunning architect would never go directly there, so the Cretan warlord traveled to all the countries bordering the sea. He brought along an enticing trap. At every place he came to, Minos would show a polished, whorled seashell, the kind that has one flared opening and a spiraling inner chamber that winds around and ends at a narrow tip. "To the first person who can thread this shell and pass the thread right through, I'll give his weight in gold!" declared the king. No one could, and few even tried, until Minos came to Kokalos. "That looks easy enough. Wait a moment, please," he was told. Within an hour, Kokalos was back with a perfectly threaded shell. "It just required an ant," he said, and showed how a hole had been bored at the tip, and a piece of thread had been stuck to the insect, which then marched dutifully through the corridors of the shell. "May I now have that gold?"

But Minos detected the hand of his former engineer at work behind the scenes. "Forget about the gold. I know who you're hiding. Why don't you hand him over, before I declare war?" Kokalos had to surrender Daedalus. Yet the rites of hospitality could not be ignored. "Tomorrow, he'll be safely aboard your craft. He can't escape. So, my king, relax. We shall feast, and while things are cooking, my daughters will prepare your bath." Maybe it was his slight emphasis on "cooking" that gave the girls the hint. Perhaps, as some say, Daedalus secretly made the suggestion. As it happened, when Minos was happily stretching in the bath, the efficient daughters of the king, pretending to rinse him off, poured over his head boiling hot water (some say, hot pitch), and that was the end of the dreaded son of Zeus.

# BOOK SIX

## HERAKLES, GREATEST OF HEROES

"BY HERAKLES!" YOU MIGHT hear an ancient Greek say when anything amazing or disturbing happened. How did this man's name come to be used like a divine oath? Was he himself a god become man? Or did it work the other way around? Why was someone called "Glory of Hera" so relentlessly harassed by the goddess herself? And did his final apotheosis ("making divine") provide the model that other heroes expected to follow? These are just a few of the many puzzles surrounding the original superhero, the man whom Greeks knew as bigger, stronger, and more dangerous than any other legendary warrior.

His "labors" emphasize several characteristics of Herakles' distinctive identity. First, there is his uncommon involvement with the natural world. He encounters lions and wild boars, birds, snakes, and a divine deer, among other creatures. The lion skin that comes to be his symbol of prowess sometimes makes Herakles appear to be half beast himself. On a number of occasions he does battle with Centaurs, as if drawn to these other half-human forms by a similar nature. Second, there is his link with the otherworld. In his travels to the ends of the earth to find the Golden Apples of the Hesperides or the cattle of Geryon, we can see Herakles winning the essence of immortality and depriving Death itself of its possessions. The story of his stealing of the hellhound Kerberos gives a more obvious example of the same theme, as does the tale that Herakles brought back the brave Alkestis from her tomb. Walter Burkert, a Swiss scholar of ancient religion, has suggested that Herakles' dual connections with animals and the otherworld link the hero with age-old traditions of shamanism that may once have been practiced in Greece. Shamans are ritual experts in archaic hunting societies (as are still found in Central Asia). To ensure that their tribe has enough game for food, they enter into trancelike states in which their spirit travels to the realm of the gods to seek animals. If Herakles continues the figure, if not the function, of a shaman, this may explain another peculiarity of the hero: his occasional murderous fits. His music teacher, his first family, and Iphitos are victims of a sudden rage, one that the myths attribute to Hera's bad influence. Perhaps this motif stems from a misunderstanding, on the part of storytellers living centuries later, of an original hunter-shaman's trance states.

Alongside the stories of a hero who roams the boundaries of nature and death are the practices that place Herakles at the center of the city-state. He was the patron hero for young men reaching maturity, the hero most associated with the gymnasium, with training the body for powerful feats. One tradition claimed that Herakles himself founded the Olympic games. Hero shrines of Herakles often featured full-scale dining facilities, for men's eating clubs, it appears. This corresponds with the image, frequent in myth and drama, of Herakles as a glutton. Since the strongest hero made a good protector, communities and individuals often prayed to him for help. As a heroic model, his image was everywhere. At the centrally important religious site of Delphi one could see depictions of him on the Siphnian Treasury (530–525 B.C.) and the Treasury of the Athenians (500–490 B.C.). In Athens you could glance up from your business in the agora to see his image on the temple of Hephaestus at the edge of the market. If you traveled to Olympia for the great athletic games held once every four years, the entire story could be read off from the scenes sculpted around the top of the imposing temple of Zeus, his father.

The story of Herakles' hard service on behalf of his cousin Eurystheus, and his immortalization, was eventually given a moralizing message by Greek philosophers, who presented it as a tale of suffering that leads to final reward. Cynics, Epicureans, and Stoics adopted Herakles as an emblem of virtue, a man who made the choice of a difficult, devoted life instead of one of idle luxury. Most important, even for later Christian allegories about Herakles, was his fiery death followed by reception into the company of the gods. His death on Mt. Oeta, commemorated by a peak sanctuary to him there, was unique in myths about heroes. Yet it expresses a fundamental religious belief that underlies the concept of heroism in ancient Greece: namely, that such figures achieved immortality through the local community's memory and continuing esteem for them. Heroes and heroines were worshiped as a category of supernatural being, through rituals at what were believed to be their tombs, in hundreds of spots throughout Greek lands. Modern archaeology has shown that a number of such sites where worship began in the ninth or eighth centuries B.C. centered on actual burials dating from four or five centuries earlier. Hero cults might have begun as a kind of ancestor worship by communities that once traced their descent from great local warrior figures. It has been suggested that the noun "hero" (*hêrôs*) comes from a word root related to English "year," and so reflects the seasonal nature of the dead hero's worship. If the divine name Hera also stems from this source, Herakles, the most conspicuous of the category, and his divine nemesis might be even more closely linked with each other. In any event, without Hera's constant antagonism, the hero would never have been driven to do the deeds he did, and the goddess' power would not have been so obvious to the world. For both reasons he embodies the "glory of Hera."

## 32. THE GLORY OF HERA

The man whom Theseus idolized and imitated, who rescued him from Hades (as he had others), was the greatest hero of the Greeks, Herakles. So numerous are his feats, so far-flung his destinations and descendants, it would take a year to relate them, and there would still be more to tell. But a simple urge unites these, the Labors, the Deeds, and the Incidents: to survive gloriously, even though a goddess was dead set against him.

Once there were four brothers, sons of Perseus and Andromeda. Mestor had a daughter, Hippothoe; Electryon had a daughter, Alkmene; the third brother, Alkaios, had a son, Amphitryon, and the fourth, Sthenelos, had a son, later in life, named Eurystheus. All their fates would intertwine.

Hippothoe, as often happened to beautiful girls living near water, attracted the attention of Poseidon, who carried her away. He fathered a son with her, called Taphios, who became king of the Teleboans, and in turn had a son, Pterelaos. Poseidon made this grandson immortal by planting in his scalp a golden hair.

The boys of Pterelaos were less gifted. With no promise of eternal life, they wanted land. So they traveled back to the kingdom of Electryon, centered on the great citadel of Mycenae, and there they demanded their old ancestral grounds. Electryon, now well along in years, ignored them—why should he owe a niece's great-grandsons a thing? To make their presence more felt, the Teleboan lads stole all the Mycenaean cattle, and when Electryon's sons tried to stop the raid, a battle broke out. All but one of the lead warriors on each side was killed. The remaining Teleboans hustled the cows aboard ship and sailed off to the western side of the Peloponnese.

Those cows would prove to be the death of Electryon. He wanted them back, and he wanted to punish the killers of his sons. Since his only remaining boy was too young, he engaged his nephew Amphitryon to track the cattle to where the Teleboans hid them, and lead them home. At the same time, he readied himself for war. To Amphitryon he promised as wife his own daughter, Alkmene, and entrusted the kingdom to him until his return. But he died before he could begin the campaign, in the following odd way. Amphitryon managed to retrieve the cows. When he was driving them to the yard, however, one broke from the herd. The animal came directly for him. Amphitryon hurled at it what lay close at hand—his club—but the weapon glanced off the beast's horn and struck Electryon, who was watching the cattle drive, hard on the head.

"That was no accident," said Sthenelos when he heard about his brother's death. "I know you aimed that club, thinking you'd get his kingdom once and for all. But that won't happen." He exiled Amphitryon, seizing the opportunity to grab Mycenae and its sister city Tiryns for himself. Alkmene knew her fiancé was innocent, and with her father dead, she inherited the vendetta. Uppermost in her mind was one object—to avenge her slaughtered brothers. She accompanied the man she loved into exile northward, and at Thebes their marriage was celebrated but not consummated. "Not until you crush the Teleboans," Alkmene solemnly announced.

It so happened that Thebes and the area all around was being troubled at that time by a fierce marauding fox. This was no ordinary vixen, for it could not be caught, by some reason known only to the gods. Though Amphitryon tried, even he, with his tracking skills, failed. The fox stole not only farm animals but even children, and the desperate Thebans had taken to sacrificing one child a month as a designated victim for the terrible fox, thinking she might thereby be satisfied and spare others.

"If I end this bane, will you give me an army to fight the Teleboans?" Amphitryon asked Kreon, who was then ruling Thebes. Winning his consent, the exiled hero sent word to Athens, to Kephalos, whose wife had given him the famous dog. He promised a large share of the booty that would be won (so he was sure) from defeating the killers of Electryon's sons, and Kephalos came. Amphitryon had engineered a metaphysical conundrum. When an uncatchable fox is chased by a hound that cannot fail to get his prey, who wins? Not even Zeus, husband of Mêtis, intelligence itself, could solve that puzzler. So Zeus made the whole matter moot—or at least delayed answering the problem—by turning both vixen and dog to stone.

You might say, then, that Minos had a hand in producing Herakles, because the dog—some said—had been his present to Kephalos' wife. More strangely, an act of Minos was repeated in the war that now began—or was it Minos who copied Amphitryon?

The Teleboans were still ruled by Pterelaos, and there were many of them, though only one of his own sons survived. He had a daughter, Komaitho, who proved to be his undoing. When the battle surged back and forth for days, with the Theban force weakening each day, while the native Teleboans stoutly battled on, Amphitryon, who had come to learn that he had an admirer among the enemy, asked her— the girl Komaitho, who burned with love for him—to perform the unthinkable and cut her father's golden hair. She must not have known of the fate of Skylla, whom Minos once asked to do the same dark deed. And Amphitryon was no less cruel in this case than the Cretan. Once she had ended her father's life, and lost her people the war, Komaitho was quickly slain by the victors.

In triumph Amphitryon marched back to Thebes, arriving late. That particular night was three times as long as usual for the time of year, and for good reason. Zeus made it so, in order to prolong his affair with Alkmene. The king of gods had fallen hard for the young wife of Amphitryon and, in the husband's absence, had changed his own appearance to look exactly like him—not difficult for a god who can transform himself into swans and bulls when he desires something.

"My darling, you're back! You've won!" Alkmene exclaimed on seeing the false husband at her door. "Now at last we can complete our marriage." That was exactly what Zeus wanted to hear. Thirty hours later—it was still night—Alkmene was confused when the real Amphitryon knocked at the door. "My darling, I'm back! I've won! Now at last we can complete our marriage," he called out, but he noticed Alkmene was less than enthusiastic. Few things are more disorienting than to learn that one has already been where one hasn't. And so, when Alkmene kept insisting that her husband had in fact already slept with her, had told her already all about the victory over the Teleboans, and so forth, he took action. Going to the seer Teiresias, he inquired about this strange apparition of himself, and was told about Zeus' divine deception.

As happens in such cases, the woman bore twins. One was the son of his father, the other son of Zeus. But which was which? Amphitryon yearned to find out, even though he knew he might be disappointed. When the twins were eight months old and starting to sleep through the night, to their parents' relief, the king tried an experiment. He crept to the nursery door and shook out of a wicker box two hefty snakes. The serpents slid inquisitively toward the infants, up the crib side, and onto the tiny bodies, slowly curling themselves around the babies' limbs. Just then Iphikles woke up with a start and wailed. That woke his baby brother Herakles, who opened his eyes wide but uttered not a sound. Instead, he grabbed both snakes just below the head and strangled the life out of them. "Well, *that* one's not my boy," Amphitryon sighed.

There is another version of what happened that night, according to which it was Hera who slipped the snakes into the room, because she wanted to destroy her husband's latest offspring. That seems more believable. It fits with another fact, one which was to have the greatest significance for the hero's life. On the day that Herakles was to be born, Zeus looked out from Mt. Olympus and beamed proudly. "The son of my bloodline through Perseus who comes to light this morn will rule over golden Mycenae and all its realm." Hera heard him and asked, "Do you swear an oath to that, dear?" "Indeed, I do," was Zeus' reply. That was all she needed. Hera sent for the goddess of childbirth. "Eileithuia, go to the house of Sthenelos. His wife, Menippe, has a seven-month child in the womb. Begin the delivery, and when the pains have started, go to Thebes, to slow Alkmene's birthing. You know how." Eileithuia did as she was ordered. After inducing labor in

the one, she halted the process in the other woman, by taking the "binding" pose outside Alkmene's house. Sitting in the courtyard, at the house altar, with her legs crossed, she interlocked her fingers and chanted over and over a secret spell.

For seven days Alkmene strove to give birth, but was held in check. How long this might have lasted is anybody's guess. A serving girl, little, efficient red-haired Galanthis, happened to be working around the house. As she hurried back and forth, she noticed the strange woman and knew this was no ordinary suppliant. Suspecting that Hera had a hand in all of this, Galanthis approached and slyly spoke: "Didn't you hear? The mistress has had twins just now. It's time to go wish her well!" Eileithuia jumped up. "No! How could that be?" Too late, she realized she had been duped into relaxing her spell. At that same moment she heard the cries of newborns in the house. "You little busybody. Now you can dart around people's houses forever," she hissed at Galanthis, and at a touch transformed the girl, still laughing, into a small, rust-colored lizard.

Due to Hera's meddling, the child born on the day Zeus swore his oath was Eurystheus, the son of Sthenelos, and not the boy whom Zeus had fathered. Technically, the oath was correct, since both children were ultimately descendants of Perseus. But forever after Herakles would be subject to the wishes of his cousin, once removed. It seemed, therefore, a cruel joke, an added insult, that the name he was destined to bear meant "the glory of Hera."

## 33.   THE HERO GROWS UP

Apollo's priestess and prophetess at Delphi, the Pythia, was the first to confer the name on him, when he was in his early twenties. Up to that time Herakles had been called Alkeides, "descendant of Alkaios," his father's father. He had led—by heroic standards—a fairly ordinary Theban life. His human father provided nothing but the best in the way of education. Archery was taught by Eurytos, a grandson of Apollo, the archer god himself. Autolykos ("Real Wolf") instructed him in wrestling, a cunning sport with all its tricks and holds. His father, Amphitryon, taught Herakles how to drive the chariot, and Linos, a brother of the singer Orpheus, was in charge of lyre practice.

Herakles had many talents, excelling in every kind of physical feat and sport, but he was not especially musical. In fact, he could not hold a tune and, with his powerful hands, was clumsy with the *plêktron* when he tried to pluck the lyre. "Phrygian mode! Phrygian! How many times do I have to say it?" Linos shouted one day as his slow pupil struggled to produce the right note. In exasperation, Linos, a master of the old school, gave Herakles a hard slap on the side of his head. It was shame and embarrassment more than the hurt that caused Herakles to react. As would happen many times, he flared up with passion first, and thought, if at all, only considerably later. He lifted his polished lyre, and with one swift blow to the forehead, he knocked his music teacher dead on the spot.

Outraged, the kin of Linos had the boy tried for murder, but Herakles got off, citing before the court a law of Rhadamanthys, which said that killing one who started an unjust fight was justified. Still, his parents thought it best that he be sent away. They could see he was hot-tempered and feared lest a similar incident occur. So Herakles was sent to Amphitryon's cattle ranch and grew up there, fiercely strong, powerfully built, and loving action.

When he had just turned eighteen, Thebes and another town in the region, Thespiai, were faced with one of the worst threats cattle ranchers could have—lion attacks. Night after night, a big animal that had its lair on Mt. Kithairon descended to the plains and killed cows. Even kings could not afford such a loss of stock. Herakles volunteered to eliminate the lion. He set up base at the house of Thespius, king of the other town. Every day Herakles went out to the hunt, and each night when he returned, Thespius treated him to a bath and banquet, followed by drinks. He also made sure that the young man did not sleep alone. With his breeder's instinct, he put to bed, for fifty nights, a different one of his fifty daughters with the hero, to get offspring from him.

At last Herakles cornered the lion on Kithairon, overpowered it, and skinned it on the spot. The pelt and head, with its gaping mouth, he took for his own use, wearing them like a one-piece cloak and helmet. When seen from a distance, he looked like a cross between man and beast—appropriately enough, since he had the keen senses and strength of a powerful animal.

It was cattle, again, that involved him in his next adventure. Sometime back, a king of the Minyans, a local clan, had been struck and killed by a stone that a Theban charioteer slung at him. Erginos, the king's son, started a war over the death, concluding it only when a treaty had been reached under the terms of which, for twenty years, Thebes should send him a hundred cows. Herakles was on his way back from his first glorious kill when he encountered two heralds of this man Erginos. Seeing them, he was engulfed with anger. "So, you have come for the tribute again, have you? Go back to your master and say here's this year's bounty," he shouted. With that he sliced off each man's nose and ears, hung these around their necks, trussed up the pair with ropes, and sent them packing. Of course, such an outrage immediately led to war—perhaps what Herakles wanted after all. In the battle that followed, his father, Amphitryon, was slain. Yet Herakles fought valiantly, routing the Minyans and forcing them to pay back the tribute at double the amount. For his services to Thebes, Kreon gave Herakles his eldest daughter, Megara, who was to bear him three children.

Now came the happiest and saddest phases of his life. The young married couple lived well for some years at Thebes, with their sons, Therimachus, Kreontiades, and Deikoon. His twin brother, Iphikles, lived very close by, with his own older son, Iolaos, and two little children by a second marriage. You will not have heard of any of the young ones, because they never reached maturity. Herakles burned them all in a roaring fire during a manic fit produced by his enemy Hera. Temporary insanity, it could be said. Though he could not recall what happened, he could not excuse himself, either, for this horror. He decided to go into voluntary exile. This is how he came to Delphi, to be led by the oracle's command, wherever the god might wish.

"Glory of Hera," he heard himself pronounced. "You are to be immortal at the end of a series of labors. A dozen years you must serve first, subject to Eurystheus, and live at high-walled Tiryns."

## 34. THE LABORS OF HERAKLES

Herakles had instincts like an animal, with a special affinity for the wild. Eurystheus, by contrast, was a man of the city, living behind the solid battlements of Mycenae and sending orders to his cousin in nearby Tiryns by way of Kopreus, his personal herald. Some say that once Herakles began to have success at the various kills and captures arranged for his ordeal, Eurystheus would not allow him into the city, but made him hang up the carcasses or pen his prey outside the gates. He is even said to have constructed an underground shelter, like a huge bronze pot, to hide himself from whatever beast Herakles brought back. This was the type of man the hero worked for.

The first task was another lion. Hera had stirred up a dangerous one, at Nemea in the northern Peloponnese. Typhon or Ekhidna was said to be its parent, and Eurystheus wanted the skin from this animal. Herakles set out with confidence. "Give me thirty days," he told a workman whom he met at Kleonai along the way. "If I come back, we'll sacrifice to Zeus. If I don't, make the offerings to me, a black sheep by night, as to a dead hero." His first attempts at reconnaissance showed that the lion in question had an impenetrable hide. Arrows bounced off it. A sword would be of no use. So Herakles cut himself a stout piece of wood from an old tree near Nemea and shaped it into a heavy club. He also discovered in canvassing the neighborhood a cave with two entrances. After he walled up one, he began the chase in earnest. The Nemean lion took refuge in the cave, just as Herakles had planned. He went around to the other entrance. Cornering the lion, he started pummeling it with his club. The blows dazed the large beast long enough for him to circle its neck with his arm and choke it to death. Then, using the lion's own claws to skin it (no human knife would work), he hoisted the bulky hide on his shoulders and headed for Mycenae. At Kleonai, he found Molorkhos, the poor workman. He was about to sacrifice a sheep over a pit—the way we make offerings to the special dead—but Herakles stopped him. Together they slew a white sheep in honor of Savior Zeus, and sat down to a joyous meal.

Eurystheus had not wanted his cousin dead, although Hera may not have minded. He was so useful for making the world safe. The second labor, for example, was to reclaim a swamp that had been taken over by the Hydra. No one knew where this creature had come from, or even exactly what it was. They called it "water snake." It used to venture from its lagoon, mauling cattle and crushing crops. No one could stop it, as it had eight heads, mounted on a massive, scaly body, and a ninth head, set in the middle of the others, which was immortal.

When Herakles sighted the Hydra at Lerna, it backed into a cave. This time, though, he preferred to fight in the open. He smoked it out with flaming arrows, then started clobbering the heads. All the while, a giant crab (sent by Hera) kept nipping at Herakles' foot. He swatted it with his club, crushing the shell. (Hera later rewarded it by making the crab a constellation—Karkinos, or as the Romans call it, "Cancer.")

Meanwhile, for each head Herakles smashed, two others sprang up to take its place. Fortunately, he was not alone. His nephew, Iolaos, son of Iphikles, had acted as charioteer on the journey. "Burn the woods! We'll cauterize this fiendish thing!" Herakles yelled to the youngster, and Iolaos obeyed. Now each time Herakles destroyed a Hydra head, Iolaos instantly scorched the stump with a burning torch. Herakles lopped off the last one, the immortal head, with a sword, then buried the ugly, slimy piece under a heavy rock. Before they left, Herakles had one last idea. Slicing open the Hydra's body, he dipped his arrows in its poisonous black blood. "It may be useful later on," he told his nephew.

Next he captured two live animals, at Eurystheus' command. The first, the hind of Keryneia, had golden horns, and had been dedicated to Artemis by a mountain nymph from Sparta named Taygete. Artemis used four such hinds to draw her chariot. This one escaped (or Hera made it run away). Since this unusual specimen belonged to the goddess, Herakles could not even try to wound it. So he pursued the hind until it grew weary, though this took an entire year. He finally caught it resting at the river Ladon. He was carrying it back to Mycenae when the goddess and her brother Apollo met him, as they were out hunting. "You arrogant human, trying to kill my sacred animal! Give that back!" said Artemis, tugging at the hind and slapping its captor. But Herakles explained he was just doing what he had been asked, and the divine children of Lêto at last relented. In return, once he had displayed the hind to his cousin, Herakles let it go free.

The other animal was an enormous boar. This was no contest— Herakles simply drove it high up Mt. Erymanthos, where it was living, slowed it down in some deep snow, and when it was tired, he threw a net over the creature. Eurystheus, when he saw it coming, started flailing his arms wildly and dove headlong into his bronze pot for safety.

The fifth labor was less enjoyable. "Go to Augeas of Elis," Kopreus told the hero one morning at home in Tiryns. "His cow barn needs cleaning." Augeas, son of the Sun, had a thousand cattle, and never once had he cleaned their stables. Herakles was told to do it—within one day. The hero set out for Elis, in the west of the Peloponnese, where the deed was to be accomplished. His solution was simple—no dung heaving needed to be done. Instead, he used a pickaxe to break the wall of the yard at either end, then went off to reroute two rivers. He managed to divert the Alpheios and the Peneiös, and as it was that time of year when both were in flood, the gushing streams soon carried off the mounds of filth.

The sixth task, the midpoint of the ordeal, was even simpler. At the lake of Stymphalia, hundreds and hundreds of birds had gathered. People said they were trying to avoid capture by wolves. That seemed unlikely, since the birds—according to some—had the ability to shoot their feathers out like arrows. Perhaps neither detail was correct.

No one really knew why they had roosted, just that they were a nuisance. Herakles realized his club wouldn't help. He could shake the trees, but that would probably be fruitless as well. Casting about for ideas, he recalled for some reason his cousin ridiculously cowering in his metal container. If this citified type trusted bronze so much, maybe nature would be repelled by it. He obtained from Athena bronze castanets (which she got from Hephaestus), and by clashing these together, he scared the birds off the trees long enough to shoot them down.

After that Herakles was sent farther afield. The Peloponnese was running out of dangers. He began to beat the bounds of the known world. First, he went to Crete to capture a bull, the very one that Minos had once preserved when he substituted for it an inferior sacrifice. Herakles caught it, brought it to a nervous Eurystheus, and let it go. It ended up in Marathon, where Theseus later killed it. The eighth labor was the mares of Diomedes. This Thracian king was a son of Ares, and his horses had the habit of eating men alive. Herakles, some say with assistance, carried out the roundup. Or else he did it alone, feeding the mares their master, whose flesh made them quite tame. At any rate, he managed to bring them dutifully to Mycenae, where Eurystheus released them. They moved into the foothills and were killed off by predators.

For the ninth labor, Herakles was sent to Hippolyte, queen of the Amazons, with instructions to steal the royal belt. The tribe of warrior women lived in the northeast, having little contact with the rest of the Greek world. Nevertheless, they worshiped Artemis, and Hippolyte's wide war belt was a gift from Ares. Eurystheus actually had no interest in this object, preferring to tame the natural world. His daughter, Admete, had heard of the treasure, and she persuaded him to have it fetched. This was the only mission Herakles undertook with Theseus, though aid was not at first needed, for the queen gladly promised them the belt. Then confusion set in. Hera started a rumor that the men had really come to abduct the queen. That led to an all-out battle, and Hippolyte was slain. Herakles stripped off her armor and took what he had come for.

His journeys and missions became stranger after this, as if, on the way to immortality, he had to learn its secrets. The quest for the cattle of Geryon took Herakles to the edge of the known, to Erytheia, an island in the world-encircling river Ocean. On the long trek westward, the Sun beat down on the hero mercilessly. Burning and parched, Herakles raised his bow and threatened to kill Helios. "Such manliness is impressive," thought the Sun. Instead of snuffing out the cocky human, he presented Herakles with a golden goblet. In this boat-sized cup (which the Sun himself would use to float back east each evening after setting) Herakles crossed the waters to his destination.

Geryon had three bodies, united at the waist. His dog, Orthos, had two heads. His herdsman, Eurytion, looked fairly normal. The cattle themselves were a deep shade of red. Herakles killed the dog, guardian, and master, drove the cows into the goblet, and sailed it back to the mainland, making sure he returned it so the Sun could rise. It was on this journey that Herakles set up his famous Pillars, one in Europe, the other in Africa, to commemorate the farthest outward trip taken by a mortal. He made his way home on the European side of the sea, which accounts for several features of the landscape. Why are there so many boulders on the coastal plain? Because when the natives tried to steal the cows from Herakles, he prayed to Zeus, and his father rained down stones. Why is Italy called what it is? Because on his cattle drive a bull broke away at the region where the Tyrrhenians lived, and their word for "bull" is *italos.* Why is the river Strymon hard to navigate? Because, when Hera drove the cows astray near Thrace, Herakles blamed the river and filled it with rocks. Why are there wild cattle in Thrace? Because Herakles never found all the cows he lost.

At last, Herakles made it back from this, his longest quest thus far. Eurystheus received the cattle and sacrificed them to Hera.

Eight years had passed since Herakles had begun his labors. Weary as he was, he wanted to complete his service. And he was curious too to see what further obstacles Hera could throw in his way. The eleventh labor was connected with the goddess, since the Golden Apples of the Hesperides were originally a wedding gift from Earth to Hera. She grew seedlings from these and had them transplanted to the gods' garden, which lay near the spot where Atlas forever was holding up the sky. Opinions varied as to the exact location. Herakles had to wrestle Nereus, the Old Man of the Sea, to get him to reveal the secret spot. He caught Nereus napping and held tight as the wiry ancient prophet turned himself into various slippery shapes—water, fire, ferocious beasts. When he finally regained human form, Nereus blurted out the route: "Go to Libya, Egypt, Rhodes, Arabia. Thence to the Caucasus and the far Hyperboreans."

That was another edge of the world, for the Hyperboreans, as their name shows, lived "beyond the North Wind." Herakles readied himself for the journey, thanked the local nymphs, daughters of Themis, who had pointed out where Nereus liked to sleep, and started for the northern shore of Africa. At that time the country called Libya was ruled by a paranoid tyrant, Antaeus. He considered any stranger a threat. He could not afford to let his people know that other ways of living, other kings, existed apart from his own parched realm. To keep the land "pure" he would find and kill any travelers. But to make it all look fair and square, he used to challenge these passing foreigners to a wrestling match. Antaeus would inevitably win, and the losers lost their lives. Their skulls went to decorate the roof of the temple Antaeus maintained in honor of his father, the sea god Poseidon.

From a distance Herakles caught sight of the gleaming white bone roof, shining in the desert sun. He wiped his brow, trying not to think of what his own head would look like, mounted like a bleached cow's skull atop the ornamented building. In his mind he rehearsed wrestling Antaeus. He remembered what his old teacher Autolykos had said: "Use not brawn, but brains, boy—keep your head." The advice took on new significance in the contest he was about to enter. Antaeus knew that he was entering the territory. Ill-concealed spies had been following him ever since he landed on the coast. Again, he tried to concentrate, to think what Real Wolf would do in this situation.

"So, the great Herakles, your fame precedes you." Antaeus, when he finally met him, was surprisingly smooth. "I am sorry I missed you last time you crossed through Libya, but then again, I'm sure you had much to do." His attitude was too self-assured. Nor was his build at all a wrestler's—in fact, he was scrawny, observed Herakles. There must be a secret. He began to suspect that Antaeus had some hidden help. But by the next morning, when the match began, Herakles had not yet discovered what the secret was. The two men eyed one another. Herakles was the first to make his move. Using a weight-shifting trick he learned from Autolykos, he quickly threw Antaeus and pinned him. "This is going to be easy, after all," he thought. But as he held his opponent to the ground, he began to feel something like a minor earthquake. It was Antaeus himself, quivering, his muscles straining and hardening with newfound strength. Before Herakles could change his position, Antaeus erupted, tossing off the hero as though he were an insect atop a volcano.

Over and over, Herakles went on the attack, twisting, pinning, slamming his rival down and clamping his own bulk down on him. And each time, like a lid on a boiling cauldron, the seething energy beneath forced him to fly off. Perhaps the rumor about being "a son of Poseidon" was a trick; it was Earth, obviously, that gave Antaeus strength. Once Herakles thought this through logically, the solution began to come to him. The opposite of wrestling was what was needed. At the next clench, instead of doing what the first rule called for—pinning and keeping your opponent down—Herakles lifted Antaeus off the ground, hefting him on high like a sack of barley. He could feel the power draining from the tyrant's limbs. The longer he held him, the lighter and weaker he seemed, until, with a final toss, Herakles could hurl him like a shot put. Antaeus hit a nearby hillock and cracked in two.

With one danger put to rest, he passed directly to another. In Egypt, yet another xenophobic king insisted on getting rid of each newcomer. Busiris was the king's name. He, too, was said to be Poseidon's son. His habit of killing strangers as if they were cattle had itself a foreign origin, as it turns out. Once, when Egypt was barren for nine years, and no crops grew throughout the land, a seer arriving from Cyprus had an answer. This wise man, Phrasios "the Thinker," declared that every year the Egyptians should seize a stranger and sacrifice the victim, with full rites, to Zeus. Busiris immediately decided that Phrasios would be first and had him slaughtered. The sacrifice worked, just as the deceased had said it would. So every year thereafter, anyone who landed on Egypt's shore might be sent to the altar and the sacrificial blade.

Herakles was duly arrested, for being Greek. Stout hemp ropes were twisted around his hands and feet. A team of lackeys dragged him to the altar—of Zeus, the hero noted grimly—his father, his protector. All the official arrangements were in place—a crown for the hair, a flute player to drown out inauspicious screams, lustral water, a bowl for the blood. Never before had Herakles felt so cowlike, despite the lion skin still worn on his back.

They had left him his second skin! It was going to save his own skin this time. Herakles could see that one of the lion's feet, although fastened down tight, was close enough to the bonds around his upper arm that enough straining and wriggling, done inconspicuously, might bring the razor-sharp claw into contact with the restraining rope. Pretending to be quaking with fear as he sat propped up near the place of sacrifice, he contracted and expanded his muscles, working

the hemp closer to the cutting edge. At last, thanks to the inter-
minable prayers of the Egyptian priest, Herakles had worn down and
burst the rope. He waited until Busiris drew near, then reached out
and strangled him. In the fray that followed, he slew the king's son,
his herald, and all the attendants. For now, Egypt would be safe to
visit. For good measure, some say, he sailed down the Nile and killed
the king there, too—Emathion, son of Tithonos.

There were also lighter moments on this journey east. As he had
been instructed, Herakles crossed over to Rhodes, and stopped awhile
at the seaside city of Lindos. He was hungry from all his travels. Seeing an ox cart, he untied the yoke, helped himself to a bullock, sacrificed and ate it. "What do you think you're doing?" yelled the cart
owner when he saw what was going on. Unable to stop the burly hero,
he climbed up the cliff near Athena's temple and cursed Herakles
until his voice gave out. To this day, whenever the Lindians make offerings to Herakles, they accompany the ritual with loud, angry
curses.

Another time—most believe it happened near Ephesus, which would
have been on Herakles' route—his hairy backside caused amusement.
There were monkeylike boys living nearby, troublesome to all. Their
mother warned them: "Someday Black Rump is going to get you!" But
the monkey boys laughed it off, and kept on with their thieving and
general hooliganism. Herakles was resting one day when they were on
the prowl. They thought it would be a great idea to steal his club and
sword. But they accidentally woke up the hero, who seized each boy
by the foot and tied both malefactors upside down to either end of a
pole, like the ones used to carry water buckets. Then he walked
around, dangling the Kerkopes (for that was their name) behind his
brawny back. Their mother had been right: they got a good view of
Herakles' rump then. But the boys nonchalantly started making jokes
about his posterior. It wasn't their wit so much as their pluck that
started Herakles laughing himself at the pair of them. They lightened
his mind so much that he relented and set them free, and they scur-
ried off to their next act of delinquency.

Now, all the time that generations had been living and dying in
Greece, ever since Zeus first took up his reign and mortals stopped
dining with the gods, Prometheus, the proud Titan child, whose love
of humans led to grief, had remained strapped to the mountain called
Caucasus, in the far northeast. That is where Herakles found him, and
saw the eagle that gnawed his liver day by day. He stood awhile in

awe. He had come so far that he was back at the very origin of things, gazing on the earliest of events, as if space and time had spread out from a center, and at the edges one could see what had been. Yet he could change events, if not reverse time. And so he did. Herakles lifted his great curved bow, and with a prayer to archer Apollo, he shot the eagle. The arrow sheared through its body and it dropped. He had not given thought to what might happen to him for destroying the bird of Zeus. But Zeus was his father, and he was related to Prometheus, too. He would face whatever came to him.

As it turned out, the consequences were largely symbolic. First, Prometheus himself, now released, was required to wear a finger ring, crafted from the iron fetters and holding a chip of the rock that once held him, so that one might say he was never completely free. And people on earth wear rings today because of this, to recall Prometheus, their greatest benefactor. Next, Herakles, too, had to wear a token fetter. He chose a crown of olive leaves, his favorite tree. Finally, because Prometheus was supposed to have stayed fixed to his desolate rock until he died—even if it took thirty thousand years—Herakles was made to find a substitute victim, someone to serve in the trickster's stead. He did that, quite unexpectedly, as we shall eventually see.

When he had come back into time, his gaze adjusted to seeing on a human scale, his voice again audible, Prometheus gave advice to Herakles. "Don't risk the final step. The Hesperides are only girls. So they pose no threat. But the tree on which the Golden Apples grow is guarded by a scaly creature, a dragon-snake with unblinking eyes in all one hundred of its heads, and voices pouring from each throat. It's much worse than the Hydra." (Herakles had been telling him of his previous adventures.) "Listen to me. Instead of going yourself to the land of the Hesperides, ask my brother. Atlas will be happy to get away. We both know what it's like to be forever in one place." Herakles agreed.

Herakles came to the country called Hyperborean. Atlas was delighted by the request. There was only one problem—who would support the sky? "I'll do it, of course—it's the least I can do," said Herakles. He carefully took the burden from Atlas' back and shoulders. Trembling and groaning like a champion weightlifter, he held up the heavens. Atlas was not gone long. The Hesperides—Aigle, Arethusa, Hesperia, and Erythia—were very generous, or simply naive. No one had ever asked them for the apples before. Before much time had passed, Atlas was back. "Look, let me take these myself. I've never seen Mycenae—or anyplace else, for that matter," he begged Herakles. But the hero was wary. Unlike Atlas, he knew there was a lot to do in the world. What if this hulking son of Iapetos never came back? On the other hand, he *had* been unusually helpful. He had to think fast. "Just a moment—you can go, but let me put a pillow on my shoulder here. I don't think I can do without one." Atlas graciously put the apples on the ground and stepped back into his old stance—just for an instant, as he thought. But no sooner had he hoisted up the sky than Herakles snapped up the golden fruit and hurried off. "I'm sorry," Atlas heard from a distance.

It could be that final trick, in this version of the story, or the well-known fact that Eurystheus and Herakles had already quarreled about the method of calculating labors—the former ruling out Augean stables and the Hydra killing because, as he alleged, "You had help." Whatever the reason, some claim that Herakles bypassed Atlas altogether, fought the dragon, and got the apples on his own, without assistance. That would make a simpler story, but maybe one not quite as good. One fact all agree on: the apples were returned. After Eurystheus approved the deed, Athena carefully carried the perfect fruit back to its guardian maidens at the world's wild edge. The apples

might bring immortality—who knows?—and humans were not going to be getting any of that.

Finally, the twelfth labor. Eurystheus had pondered a long time to come up with the idea. This time Herakles would go not just to the ends of the earth, but under it. He would bring back the fiercest animal yet. So it was that the weary hero was sent off to fetch Kerberos, the hound from hell.

Some claimed that the dog had fifty heads, but that is an exaggeration. He had only three that properly could be called heads. Confusion arose because, in addition, his back was covered with the writhing, hissing heads of various snakes. Instead of a dog tail, he sported a serpent as well. Chain in hand, lion skin on his broad back, Herakles started off for the entrance to the underworld, at Taenarum, the very tip of Lakonia. It was late one evening when he reached the cave that led to the portal of the realm of shades. As the gloom deepened, Herakles descended. The way down was steep and gravelly, like a gorge in the mountains, and the walls dripped constantly with bitter-smelling water. Finally, when his torch was almost extinguished, Herakles reached bottom. He gazed around in wonder.

Here was the bleak home of all who had ever lived. A river—the Styx—flowed near his feet, and in the distance, on the other shore, he could see the ferryman, Charon, approaching in his skiff, ready to carry over the latest of the dead. Herakles shivered. "He's coming for me." But his thought was interrupted by a more terrifying vision. The head of a woman, her mouth open in a fierce scream, her hair a mass of swarming snakes, rushed before his face. As it circled and made another pass, even closer, he lunged with his sword, only to see the blade slice through the disembodied head like smoke. It was a phantom Gorgon, a mere imitation of the monster that his ancestor Perseus had long ago slain. A real animal, no matter how fierce, he thought, would be preferable to such ghostly apparitions.

Charon was surprised to find a living, breathing man at his landing instead of the pale shade he expected. "Well, get in," he grumbled. Then his face brightened. "Since you're so healthy, how about taking a turn at the oar?" For the first time in eons, Charon didn't have to work. Herakles guided the boat to the farther bank.

Now the full panorama of Hades' kingdom opened before him. From a slight rise, Herakles could see within the walls, and he caught sight of a man struggling to push a boulder up a hill. As Herakles looked on, the figure strained and leaned with all his weight, until he at last stood, shoulders sagging, at the crest. But the huge rock that he had managed to move there teetered on the narrow peak. Suddenly it began to roll back the way it had come, the man leaping out of its path just in time to turn and see it crash to the bottom of the hill. Slowly the distant human figure trudged down. Herakles knew exactly what came next. The same uphill agony, the same downhill roll, endlessly repeated. For this was Sisyphus, the clever Sisyphus, king of Corinth, about whom he had heard even as a boy, and this was his punishment for having twice cheated Death.

The first time, Sisyphus made the mistake of informing on Zeus, who had taken it into his head to carry off Aigina, a river's daughter. When the distraught father, Asopus, came looking for his lost child, Sisyphus told him what had happened. Zeus got angry and sent Death to his door. But the Corinthian king hoodwinked Death, bound and gagged him. For a time, nobody could die. Then Ares was sent to rescue Death. Now Sisyphus was sure to pay—or so all thought.

Before Death called the second time, Sisyphus whispered to his wife, Merope, "When I'm gone, just cast the body out. Don't perform any funeral rites—although you can lament if you want." Without asking why, she did what she was told. Meanwhile, Sisyphus went off to Hades. "My lord of the dead," he exclaimed on seeing the master of the realm. "I know that this is where I belong, and that your rule is just and eternal. Because you recognize all that is right, however, I must beg you to correct an earthly injustice. Look how my cursed wife has treated me! Without funeral torches or offerings of oil, grain, and honey, I was cast out, like a leper—I, the king of Corinth. It is only proper that I go back to haunt her, to reproach her for being the worst wife in the world." Hades, always one for propriety, agreed. So Sisyphus made his triumphant return to the light of life—and of course stayed, living out his years in Corinth until he died naturally of old age. The task that Herakles saw him engaged in was Hades' way of making sure the trickster would never escape him again.

Farther off, Herakles spied a gigantic form stretched upon the ground, his arms and legs pinned to the earth with fetters. This was Tityus, whose offense was that he tried to take Lêto by force. Being shot by the twin offspring of the goddess would have been too kind. Instead, Artemis and Apollo saw to it that Tityus was forever tormented by twin vultures, who nibbled at his liver, one on each side.

Beyond this instructive sight, Herakles could make out another figure, alternately stretching his arms and ducking his head. As he looked more closely, he saw the reason for these movements. A tree with luscious-looking fruit spread above the man, who obviously hungered to get at its branches. But every time he reached, the fruit moved, as if swayed by a breeze, just out of his reach. When the branch rose, so did the water at the man's feet, all the way to his chin, at which point he eagerly bent to sip—he was clearly parched with thirst as well. The water sank at the moment he would touch it, and of course, just then the bough above bent down. Tantalos—for this was his name—was thus eternally "tantalized." Herakles had heard various explanations for this punishment. Most believable was that the gods had once shared nectar and ambrosia with this one mortal, but he repaid their generosity by stealing the divine food and sharing it with his cronies. (A darker story said he even tried to turn the gods into cannibals, as we will hear in time.)

Fascinated by this theater of the great sinners, Herakles nearly forgot why he had come. A horrific barking and growling brought him to his senses. Some unlucky soul was trying to exit the realm of Hades, and Kerberos, so docile when shades entered, was making sure no one could leave. Herakles could see, as he rounded a corner of the great wall, the three furious dog heads yapping, snarling, lunging, in sequence, as a terrified shade flitted back with a batlike squeak, resigned to hell forever. Slowly, the hero crept nearer. In one hand he held a stout chain he had brought to be the leash for this hound. The other he held out, as if to pat the creature on the head. Kerberos sensed him immediately and started sniffing the ground with one head, while the others gazed intently in opposite directions. But Herakles was not scared. Although he was almost within the dog's range, and Kerberos was furiously leaping at the end of his tether, howling in triple voice, Herakles confidently held out his hand. A remarkable change came over the guard dog. He began licking eagerly, one tongue after another, and Herakles had no problem slipping the leash onto his neck. He had tricked the dog by taking the precaution of rubbing raw beef all over his palms.

Hades and his bride, Persephone, were not upset that Herakles wished to borrow their hound. He promised to bring Kerberos back. They were more concerned that he succeeded in tearing loose Theseus, whom they had wanted to punish for his abduction plan. At least Peirithoos was left behind, and since there would never be another Herakles, no more humans would be carrying out rescues of the dead.

Orpheus had failed. And Herakles, though he could not know, would himself soon enough perish.

## 35. THE LAST YEARS OF HERAKLES

When Herakles returned to Mycenae with the hound of Hades, Eurystheus dove for the shelter of his great bronze pot. His quavering voice resounded from inside: "Magnificent, cousin! Well done—now please return the beast." The time of purification for Herakles' homicide had ended. On his way back to the underworld, Herakles realized he no longer knew what to do with his life. There had always been another labor. Now that he was free, the loss of his family began to sink in. He could not go back to his wife, Megara, but he wanted to see her taken care of. Returning to Thebes, where he had once been so happy, he handed her over to his faithful nephew, Iolaos. Then he set out to begin a new life.

There was news that his old archery teacher, Eurytos, had challenged all comers to a bride contest. Whoever could defeat him and his sons with the bow would be given the privilege of marrying the beautiful Iole, daughter of the king. Herakles remembered her as a sweet, small child. He traveled to Oikhalia as much from curiosity about how she had grown as from any desire to engage in this new contest. But when he saw her at a welcoming banquet—an exquisite young woman, still shy but with passionate, wild eyes—he wanted nothing else than to defeat all other suitors and take her as his own.

When the day came for the contest, man after man stepped to the mark, aimed, and let fly their swift arrows. Those who managed to outdo the sons of Eurytos in shooting at a target then faced the king himself, and invariably lost. Herakles took his turn. He easily beat the sons, even at the most difficult events, like winging a dove tethered to the top of a tall pole. Then he met his former master. The test was to shoot cleanly through a narrow alley of close-set, upright javelins. Herakles went first. Gripping his massive bow just as he had been taught years ago by the man who was now his opponent, he bent it into an arc and launched his arrow straight and sure down the passage. Not a javelin swayed. Eurytos had the last shot. Whether it was his hand that trembled, or his eyesight that faltered, his arrow winged its way two-thirds down the row, grazed a javelin stock and flew out of the course. He had lost the contest—but gained a new son-in-law.

Or so Herakles thought as he saw his teacher fail. Iphitos, the eldest son of Eurytos, enthusiastically greeted Herakles as a brother. But the other men of the family, including the king himself, stood their ground, staring coldly at the hero from Thebes. One spoke for all. "If Iole goes to him and bears him children, their blood will be on our hands. Never will we let her marry this child killer."

Herakles backed away and once more took to the road. It was during this time, some say, that he came to Pherai and, cheated out of the new wife he deserved, helped Admetos recover a wife that man seemed unworthy of. The story had begun a little more than a year before, and was connected with Herakles' old friend, Theseus. As you remember, the son of Theseus, Hippolytos, was unjustly accused, dying horribly because of his father's curse. Artemis, whom Hippolytos had worshiped to excess, was grief-stricken and appalled at the disaster (for which jealous Aphrodite was ultimately responsible). She sought out the best physician in all Greece, the son of Apollo, Asklepios. As a young man, he had studied under Cheiron, the wise Centaur, learning the secrets of healing herbs, some so powerful they were said to revive the dead. Now he was in his prime, the father of a glorious clan, with two warrior sons, Makhaon and Podaleirios, and three rosy-cheeked daughters, Health (*Hygieia*), Healing (*Iaso*), and All-Cure (*Panakeia*). Artemis appealed to a father's heart—what would he have done if one of his own was afflicted? How could he stand by and let this happen? Asklepios was nervous, for he knew the iron law that governed mortals. And hadn't his own mother died a fiery death at a god's hands? But the insistence of the Huntress won him over. He went with her, opened the tomb, and brought her favorite back to life. Artemis whisked him away to Italy, to her shrine; the local people never knew Hippolytos lived again. But Zeus knew. "How dare any mortal breach the wall between life and death, the only barrier that separates humans from gods?" he fulminated, and with one resounding thunderbolt he blasted Asklepios straight to Hades. "No man can live twice."

Apollo, out of his mind with grief, raged, "I'll kill him! I don't care if he is my father, king of gods. He murdered my son!" He rushed toward Olympus with his bow. It took all the gods to restrain him. Zeus was safe—of course, he could never die, but a clash with Apollo might throw the cosmos into chaos. His anger diverted, Apollo took it out on another target, the old companions and weapon makers for Zeus, his political allies when young, the Cyclopes. After all, they had manufactured the bolt that killed his son. He hunted down the brawny gang of craftsmen, singled out three, and killed them.

As with mortals, so with the god. Murder of a family member requires purification (for the Cyclopes were distant divine relatives). Just as Herakles had to endure slaving for his cousin, so the god Apollo went into servitude, a year's hard labor, incognito, on a mortal's farm. The man he went to, Admetos, found his new servant to be extremely clever, hardworking, a good musician, besides, after their evening meals, and even better, a good-luck charm. The cattle multiplied three-fold; the crops grew twice as high that year. Admetos treated the disguised Apollo as well as his own son, and Apollo in turn was thankful for his master's kindness. "What lies in store for my friend?" he asked one day of the Moirai, who know the fates of all human beings. "Nothing but good, prosperity, fame, I hope?" "Nothing at all, in a short while," was the answer from the primeval women, daughters of Night. "Your mortal's thread of life will soon run out. We cut it short the day he was born." This time Apollo knew better than to fly into a rage. There was another way around the old crones. "That's unfortunate," he said, acting unconcerned. "Perhaps we can share a drink? No use crying over humans." He poured out for them some unmixed Cretan wine. After a few more rounds, the Fates were getting tipsy. Klotho decided to make a deal. "Your man gets to live—just let him find a replacement."

Apollo brought the news back to the farm. Admetos immediately set out to find his substitute. He begged his mother, but she refused. His father, Pheres, only replied, "There's no law that says fathers have to die for their sons. I love the light of day as much as you." No kin would make the sacrifice. It was his wife, Alkestis, who lovingly volunteered. And though he sighed and wept and clung to her at the last, Admetos let her die for him.

The very day Alkestis was carried out for burial was the day Herakles happened by the palace in Pherai. He had no idea what had happened. He saw servants and townspeople in black, heads shaved, no sound of a lyre or flute. Obviously a death had occurred somewhere. Yet Admetos welcomed the hero, clapped him on the back, led him into the great hall, and ordered great helpings of food and drink. After a good many cups, Herakles began asking the servants, who seemed on the verge of tears. "Cheer up—it can't be that bad. Who died, anyway?" Then the truth came out—actually, Herakles had to nearly strangle it out of the cupbearer, who was under orders not to tell. "It's the master's . . . wife."

Astonished, Herakles pulled on his lion skin as he strode toward the door. It was not yet completely dark, and he could still find the way to the tomb. He hoisted his club and strode off in the twilight. A few hours later, he was back at Admetos' door. "I want you to take this girl," he told his host, indicating the figure of a veiled woman some steps behind him. "There was a contest. Quite a struggle. Everybody else got horses, tripods, cattle. I won this—take her, I'm told you need a new wife." Admetos was horrified. He had promised never to remarry. And even if he had not, this was grotesque—to wed again the day a first wife went to Hades? But Herakles said, "I insist—as a guest," and Admetos, as the host, reluctantly accepted. "*You* take her hand," directed Herakles, "and don't give her to some servant. You might as well look at her," he said as he lifted the veil. Admetos stared into the face of his bride, his first love, Alkestis, for whom Herakles had just wrestled with Death himself, and won.

On his way back from Pherai, Herakles met up with Iphitos. Some time had passed since this young man, alone, had stood up for Herakles' right to wed his sister Iole. "Now my father wrongs you again," he explained as the two walked along. "His cattle were stolen and he says he knows you did it." Herakles thought about that. "Maybe I should have, but it wasn't me. From what you say, it sounds like the Wolf." (His intuition was faultless—Autolykos was in fact behind the raid.) "I told him it wasn't you, but when he kept insisting, I left to find you on my own. Together we'll recover them, right? I'll clear your name." Iphitos glanced at him with the expression Herakles had come to recognize in so many aspiring heroes, young men who yearned for adventure, a companion, the wild.

"Certainly," was his simple reply. "First, let's go home," and he led the way back to Tiryns. They didn't talk much. The closer they came to the city, with its towering, thick walls (the ones men say the Cyclopes made long ago), the darker it seemed Herakles' mood became. What happened next is unclear. Later, people tried to pin the blame on Herakles, saying it was revenge, implying he was as shifty and ruthless as Real Wolf himself. They claimed he lured that poor young man up to the highest point of the massive, brooding walls, as if to offer him the best view of the plain—then threw him off. Or that Iphitos was after horses, twelve mares stolen from his father, and Herakles murdered him so he could keep them for himself. Some even say Herakles himself stole the cattle, or the mares, or got them secretly from Autolykos, who had done the deed. But the truth, as usual, is more likely to be the least well understood. The hero, as once before, was driven berserk, from the madness tainting his blood.

Herakles could not escape punishment. The family wanted his head, and no doubt a vendetta was in the offing. But worse, he had violated the law of Zeus, who defends guests and strangers. The blood of his visitor, Iphitos, would cry out to the sky. Already, the aging hero could feel his body change, his skin redden, blisters, boils, and sores erupt. It was as if his flesh, and not the dead man's, was meant to putrefy. Only a god or a man with the god's touch can purify, and only one from another clan. So Herakles, in desperation, traveled to Pylos, "the gate" (some said, gate of Hades), where Neleus reigned. From his shadowy palace on a hill, in the far southwest, this king could gaze on his father's realm, the sea—for Poseidon had begotten him and his twin brother, Pelias. He was a remarkable man. They said his mother, Tyro, had abandoned the boys, from fear, and that Neleus was nursed by a dog, Pelias by a horse. Animals figured prominently in their later lives. When Pelias was a grown man, with a daughter of his own— the very Alkestis, of whom you have heard—he forced her suitors to undergo a bride test, yoking to a chariot a lion and a boar. Neleus, meanwhile, had a son Periklymenos, to whom Poseidon gave an unusual ability—he could change himself into an ant, a bee, a snake, or an eagle.

But Neleus, when Herakles arrived, was adamant. Hurt your enemies and help your friends—that was ever the Greek custom, and he stood by it. Herakles was the enemy of Neleus' friend—the king of Oikhalia, whose son had been murdered. There was going to be no *katharsis* here. Herakles, unpurified, hurried off. He was fuming, outraged—but vengeance would come later. He made his way north again, across the gulf to Delphi. There, he begged the holy priestess of Apollo to tell him how to cure his dreadful disease, the homicide's curse that was eating his flesh. The Pythia kept her silence. Herakles felt control slipping away. His life was completing a circle. Here he was back at the start, face-to-face with the woman who had first announced his mocking name: "glory of Hera"—the goddess who had lashed him constantly during his life. He felt the room sway. He had come to the center of the known world, the spot marked by the glistening navel-stone. And there was only silence. Then he broke.

"Oracle, I've suffered enough to make my own predictions! I know the world, the whole breadth of it. What does Apollo know of suffering, or you, ugly heartless crone? Sniffing your vapors, pretending the god is within. The god is here!" he shouted, and he snatched up the sacred tripod, the seat of oracular power, from beside the hearth. Who knows what might have happened had Herakles escaped the temple that afternoon. He turned to rush away, but caught sight of Apollo. The founder god moved menacingly, his bow glinting in the half-light that filtered through the door into the darkened inner sanctum. "I'll take that, Alkeides," he said quietly, advancing toward the polished brazen tripod. But Herakles gripped it tighter; Apollo, knowing better than to kill a son of Zeus, joined in a tug-of-war. Although a god, with divine reserves of strength, he found it difficult to overcome the burly hero. If not for a lightning bolt from Zeus, crashing between them and filling the temple with sulphurous smoke, Herakles might have put an end to the prophecies forever.

At the god's bidding, the Pythia answered at last. "Do as my lord did. Become a slave to redeem your life, for three years. And this time your master shall be a woman." So it was that Herakles was sold to Omphalê, queen of Lydia, his disease ended, and he endured the humiliation of being a household servant, carding wool and spinning. Some would have you believe he even dressed in ladies' clothing, and was regularly beaten by the queen with a sandal, but those were just his enemies' malicious lies.

After his servitude, Herakles was hungry for combat. An attack on Troy was followed by an attack on Augeas, the cattleman (who, said Herakles, still owed him payment—part of a complicated bargain). The brother of Augeas, a warrior named Aktor, brought forth his Siamese-twin warrior sons. Herakles retreated, but when the time was right, he ambushed them at a sacrifice, and finished his mission by destroying their uncle's city. Then it was time to return to Pylos.

His future battles became all the more surreal. At the gate, Herakles fought with Hades himself and wounded him—or did he just imagine that? Periklymenos defended his father's land, mutating from insect to reptile to bird, and killing Herakles' allies on all flanks. During an eerie lull in the fighting, Herakles noticed a small black fly rubbing its forelegs atop the very tip of his own war-chariot beam. With a prayer to Athena, he lifted his bow and shot, slicing through the pesky shape-shifter just as he was about to strike again. After that, it was as if a spell had been broken. The hero ranged across the battlefield and slew men by the dozens. Among them were Neleus and all his other sons, all except the youngest, Nestor, away from home among some kinfolk. Nestor would live to see Troy fall, but the war that most haunted him was this one he never had a chance to fight.

## 36. A WEDDING AND A FUNERAL

The campaigns of Herakles spanned the years that turned out to be his last on earth. It was as if he needed constant action. He had ended his labors, but where was the final glory, the immortality he had been promised? He had managed to stay alive despite Hera's best efforts. But he felt compelled to seek death, over and over, as if testing the limits of his existence. Perhaps he already had been given eternal life and didn't know it.

Soon after losing the chance to wed Iole, when her father reneged on his promise, Herakles found himself another marriage partner. On his trip to the kingdom of Hades, Herakles had encountered by the banks of the underworld river Kokytos the shades of many heroic dead. They whirled about, weightless, like the leaves on Mt. Ida when the autumn winds blow over Crete. Chief among them was the warrior Meleager, who came to rest near Herakles and related his whole sad story:

"Son of Zeus, men on earth can never turn aside your great father's intentions. And his daughter, Artemis of the white shoulders, is just as inflexible. My father, Oineus, once forgot to sacrifice to the goddess goats and ruddy cattle, and in Artemis was born a deathless grudge. She went and roused up a wild boar—a huge one, strong and savage—against our town, Kalydon. The beast ripped into our best steers and, when anyone tried to corner it, gored the man to pieces. We called for a hunt. Soon all the best of the Greeks arrived, and we set out. Six days we were tracking that horrible creature. We never got close enough for a shot. But then it would rush out, completely without warning, and take down whoever happened to be trailing. I lost my younger brothers, Ankaios and Agelaos. And Artemis never let up.

"At last we managed to corner the giant boar between a thicket and a rocky outcrop. All of us closed in and speared it at once, crazy for first blood, lunging and screaming. We hated that animal. But when we had skinned it, the trouble really started. Everybody wanted the tawny hide. It was Artemis who stirred the squabble into a war. Thestios was there with his boys, the Kouretes, from Pleuron—they are my mother's brothers. We fought them furiously. You know the chaos on a battlefield—everybody's confused, fighting blind, whatever god is looking on makes your javelin swerve. I swear I didn't want to, but I hit my uncles."

Here Herakles fought back the urge to ask a question. He had heard about the well-known fight, but he had been told another version, less to Meleager's credit, involving a love affair. The woman was Atalanta, a born huntress, not surprisingly, for her genealogy went like this: her father, Healer (Iasos), was son of Wolf-worker (Lykourgos), son of Sunny (Aleus), son of Generous (Apheidas), son of Arcas, the famous Bear, now a constellation, whose mother was the nymph of Artemis, Kallisto. You might say Atalanta was born to chase beasts. Word was that she herself, having been left in the wild to die because her father wanted only sons, was suckled by a she-bear and raised by woodsmen. Like Artemis, she spurned men (even to the point of shooting some would-be husbands) and loved the hunt. When she arrived with the best of the Greek men, Meleager fell for her, heart and soul. And when she wanted the thick hide of the Boar of Kalydon, Meleager got it for her—by slaying, on purpose, his own kin. So Herakles had heard from others. But he let the shade continue.

"The news spread fast, and my mother Althaia heard that her own son had killed her beloved brothers. She was as angry as any Fury that haunts a man who murders his own blood. She went to the fine chest that I had always seen in the house, and took out the charred log that was my life. The Moirai told her, the night I was born, that her son would live as long as that piece of wood was not consumed by fire. So she had snatched it from the flames that moment years back and kept the half-burned stump—and me—safe and sound. But in her rage she threw it onto the hearth blaze. The instant it happened, I felt my sweet life wither. I was stripping the armor from Klymenos when I felt myself weaken, and I knew my time had come, that these were my last few breaths."

People say that when Herakles heard this tragic tale, it was the only time he wept from sympathy with another. He answered Meleager, "The best thing for men is never to have been born and see the light of day. There is nothing we can ever do to change things. But tell me: is it possible you left at home a sister? If there's one who has even half your nobility, I would like to make her my wife." To which Meleager, in delight, replied, "There is. When I died, she was young still, with a beautiful long neck and fresh look, completely innocent of the charms of golden Aphrodite." And Herakles (more from pity than from love?) swore to wed the young woman as soon as he was able.

After his disappointment at Oikhalia, he went to Kalydon. What happened next was told later by Deianeira, the sister whom Meleager had so praised, in a lament she made.

> *I have a grievous and unlucky lot—*
> *A woman, if ever there was one of my country,*
> *who had the sickliest fear of marrying*
> *while I lived, still, within the house*
> *Of father, Oineus, in Aitolia.*
> *My suitor was a river; Achelôos, the god, I mean,*
> *Who begged me from my father in three forms:*
> *Coming as a bull as plain as day,*
> *Another time, a shimmering, coiled snake,*
> *Once more—a mannish torso—with an ox's front.*
> *From his thick beard a fountain's droplets rained.*
> *Awaiting such a wooer I would add on*
> *Prayer to prayer, forever, that I'd die—*
> *Wretch—before I'd reach this sleeping.*
> *In time—much later, though I was as glad—*
> *There came the famous son of Alkmene and Zeus.*
> *He falls straight to the contest-fight with him*
> *And sets me free. The style of their pains*
> *I could not tell, I don't know. One who sat*
> *Unflinching at the sight—that one might say.*
> *For I remained in fear, all paralyzed,*
> *Afraid my beauty would mean casualty.*
> *Finally, Zeus of the Contest put things well.*

Achelôos, this unmannered suitor, was in his bull phase when Herakles finally broke off one of his horns. The river god (for that was his ordinary mode) gave up, although he managed to retrieve his lost horn by offering in return the famous Horn of Amaltheia (Zeus' former nurse), a cornucopia that gave its owner all the food and drink he wanted. Herakles was interested only in the girl. She was more beautiful than Meleager had been able to convey. He felt his life begin to change for the better. For some time they stayed in the kingdom of her father Oineus, who, as his name implied (Wineman), toasted his new son-in-law with the finest vintages, the fruit of his grapes, night after night. One evening, however, as Herakles was sampling yet another variety, the serving boy came to pour water on the hero's hands, in preparation for the next course. Herakles never liked people to get too close, and the boy—his name was Eunomos—took him by surprise, moving in silently so as not to disturb his appreciation of the wine. Herakles reacted automatically, swinging out his powerful fist, bashing Eunomos with his bare knuckles. The servant fell down dead. Herakles, who never could control his own strength, once more had to pay for his powers. Since the boy was a relative of Oineus, and had been serving a few years in fosterage, as aristocrats do, Herakles felt especially guilty. Even though the father of Eunomos granted the hero pardon, Herakles nevertheless gathered up his belongings, and with his new wife he took himself into exile once again.

They headed toward Trakhis northeast of Delphi and a hard mountain trek from the bride's home in Aitolia. Herakles handled the chariot expertly, and Deianeira sat demurely on a box that contained all her finery. When they came to the river Euenos, they found it in flood. The autumn rains had made it impassable except by boat. Luckily, a ferryman emerged in the dusk. Or rather, a ferry Centaur, by the name of Nessos. "This boat you see"—he pointed proudly to the skiff—"was given me by the gods themselves, as a reward for my good behavior," he assured the couple. Herakles was suspicious, though. It was odd enough that a Centaur should be working the river, and even stranger that he had somehow won the gods' approval, since Centaurs were not generally known for their high morality, except for Cheiron, the teacher of heroes, who was called "most just" by all who had met him. Strangest of all was that a half-horse should be piloting a boat. His own past experience with the breed had also been unpleasant.

On at least two other occasions, he had run-ins with Centaurs. When he went after the Erymanthian boar, Pholos the Centaur, son of Silenos, had given him lodging one cold night, and even served roast meat (while the horse-man himself ripped into raw beef). When Herakles asked for wine, Pholos hesitated but gave in to his guest's entreaties. That's when the trouble started. The other Centaurs in the area sniffed the newly opened wine and gathered near the cave of Pholos, carrying their usual weapons (fir trees and boulders). Soon the temptation was too great for them, for Centaurs are mad for wine, but can't handle it at all. They pushed and shoved their way into the small cave, trying to get a drink. Herakles waved a torch to scare them off, but they got even wilder, prancing up and threatening him with their powerful hooves, and waving their thick tree trunks close to his head. He went on the offensive. Chasing them out of the cave with his bow drawn, he shot arrows at them as they ran off to Malea. The horse-men ran for their lives to Cheiron, who was a sort of chief and adviser to them. Herakles, in pursuit, thought he had a clear shot, finally, at Elatos, one of the more offensive of the herd. But Herakles watched in dismay as the arrow missed its target and instead pierced Cheiron— the one Centaur he would never want to harm.

Cheiron was badly wounded. Even the medicine that he gave Herakles to apply to the wound failed to help, and he felt more and more pain. But he could not die. His was an immortal bloodline, distinct from and higher than the rest of his companions', who traced their ancestry to Ixion and a cloud. So he stayed in his cave, immobilized and hurt, wishing only to be able to leave the earth. Herakles was the one who eventually made death possible. When Zeus demanded a substitute to die in the place of Prometheus, his former prisoner, Herakles, who had liberated the Titan child, suggested Cheiron. Prometheus gladly assumed the Centaur's immortality, and Cheiron, in turn, had his wish and perished.

Herakles recalled that Pholos had been so amazed at the power of arrows, an unknown weapon to his kind, that he plucked one from a fellow horse-man's corpse after that battle long ago, and dropped it on his own foot, foolishly pinning himself to the ground. What he did not recall, unfortunately, was the face of another beast who fled from the fight that evening. It was the face in the dusk before him now.

In spite of his worries and suspicions, the hero accepted the ferryman's offer. He made sure that he himself went first, taking the goods, just in case Nessos had a mind to run off with his possessions. Deianeira would follow. Herakles was thus on the far bank, waiting, peering across the darkened river through the mist, when he heard the plash of oars stop, and then a scream—his wife's. Nessos had not desired his belongings at all. The Centaur was trying to take his bride. Barely able to make out the shaggy horse form, Herakles nevertheless took a chance and let fly an arrow—one of the precious few he kept for desperate situations, an arrow tipped with the Hydra's own black blood. He pierced the heart of Nessos, ending the violent assault. Then he waded out toward the fast-moving current and grabbed Deianeira before the skiff was borne away. In the time it took him to reach his terrified wife, however, Nessos had managed

to whisper in her ear—and she, being young, believed in the truth of a dying Centaur's words. "Take my blood. It is a potion to win back love."

Deianeira was already learning what it was to be the companion of this obsessed, god-driven man. So she meekly consented when Herakles, now established in their new home, one day revealed that he was heading off again on the path of war. She never quite understood the details—something about a distant city whose king had once insulted Herakles, calling him all sorts of names and not even giving him some contest prize he really deserved—though Herakles had not said what the reward was supposed to have been. Frankly, Deianeira did not pay much heed. All the stories her husband used to tell her swirled together: talk of monsters and foemen, punishments and prizes. She sometimes wondered if he was altogether sane. She would nod, at those times, and smile and tend the children. And yet she loved him deeply, and when he was gone, pined for him.

This absence was a long one, more than a year. Then one day word came that Herakles was coming home. A few days later, Likhas, the loyal attendant of Herakles, arrived. His master was near, at Kê-naion, he said, preparing a magnificent sacrifice of thanks to his father Zeus at the god's great sanctuary in that place, at the northwest tip of Euboia. But who were these women that trailed behind Likhas, herded like slaves by an escort of soldiers? "The first fruits of Herakles' victory," he replied. "He fulfilled his vow. He crushed his old enemy Eurytos, the root of all his troubles, and he took the city Oikhalia. When he had burned it to the ground and killed the menfolk, these women remained—a sign of conquest. They're ours now, for fetching water and grinding grain." As he spoke, Deianeira's eye was caught by one young woman, taller than the rest, who had a regal look. "And this one? She's so different—who were her parents?" But Likhas said only that this girl was sad and shy, had never spoken the whole way back.

When Likhas had gone inside the palace, one of the soldiers approached Deianeira. "That one there, the girl you asked about? Either Likhas lied to you, or he lied before to the whole town, just this morning, passing through the marketplace. He was talking to a big crowd—I heard him—going on about his master's glory, and how Herakles had done in Eurytos. Killed him and wrecked his town, and all for Eros. I think it made Likhas happy that even a hero could be overcome. It wasn't Iphitos, he told them, that son who got killed, or Omphalê and the slavery Herakles had to go through for the crime, that drove your husband to it, but a passion for this girl. Her name is Iole—the dead king's daughter."

Her intuition had not betrayed her. Iole, poor girl. No wonder she was sad. Her beauty was her curse—her people slain, just because she was so fair! Deianeira felt more pity than anger. She knew that Herakles was a slave of passions, and here was this girl, so young and fresh, and she herself, weary with house tending and waiting, was drying up. Still, she would not have a rival in the house. She was the queen, mother of the hero's son, the rightful wife. Iole might stay, but Herakles would not love the girl—only Deianeira.

A brief while later, Likhas made ready to go back to Kênaion and assist his master in the victory sacrifice. "Before you take to the road," said Deianeira, "wait one minute. I have a present for my husband." She entered the shady palace and returned shortly with a metal box, tightly bound, the wax seal showing the mark of her signet ring. "A golden robe for my husband, from my own hand. Tell him that no one is to put it on except him. Do not let it see the light—and keep it from any flame—until Herakles dons it when he reaches up to heaven, at the moment of sacrifice. He deserves no less." Likhas, still trembling lest she should know his secret (not knowing that she already did), took the present and departed.

Herakles was pleased when Likhas handed him the box, but saddened at the same time. His dear Deianeira, always caring for him— how could he tell her? Like a coward, he had hidden the truth from her. Now Iole was in his house. He wanted both—wife and concubine. He was torn, the pain worse than any labor he had undergone. He could only pray that the sacrifice would cleanse him, and Zeus would somehow cure this wound, the wound that Herakles was even now inflicting on his house. All around him, ritual experts were preparing the bulls. Throats were slit, the blood flowing. The sweet meat smoke began to ascend to the sky. He opened the box.

The robe, heavy with golden thread, glinted in the rays of the blazing sun as his attendants helped Herakles put it on. The north wind was picking up, but the warmth from the garment protected him, reminding Herakles of the hearth and his home. As he stepped closer to the sacrificial fires, however, the son of Zeus began to sweat. He stretched his arms to let the robe slide off his shoulders, but it did not move. Instead, it clung tighter, winding itself around his upper body like a cobra. It began to burn his flesh, like acid. Herakles twisted right and left to escape its gnawing, but the robe only clung all the more. It was as if his skin had melted and his nerves were exposed to some poisonous liquid. Poison it was—for the blood of Nessos, which Deianeira had lovingly spread on this present, in her attempt to regain her husband, had been mixed with the Hydra's, by way of the hero's own killing arrow.

Even in the agony of being eaten alive, Herakles was still powerful. With a curse he seized Likhas by the leg and, whirling him around, tossed him off the cliff near which the altar stood. The attendant vanished into the white foam below, where the waves crashed against the sharp black rocks. Herakles looked around wildly to see who else was in on the assassination. "No!" shouted Hyllos, Herakles' eldest son. He had arrived from the palace with Likhas to meet his victorious father. "It wasn't a plot! My mother prepared this robe!" At this, Herakles groaned deeply. "Take me to Mt. Oeta and burn me on the pyre. But first let me see that Fury in my own house who murdered me." He was carried, raving with the pain, onto a small boat and brought to Trakhis, to curse his wife. But Deianeira, overcome with grief when word came back about her fatal gift of love, had already killed herself, stabbing deep with a sword. Herakles died never realizing her innocence.

The manner of his death was this. When they had reached the peak of Oeta, Herakles was barely able to breathe. With an effort he spoke to Hyllos, making the boy promise that he would wed Iole: "Let no other hero have her." At Herakles' insistence, they placed him on a makeshift pyre, hastily constructed from brushwood and leaves. But not a man among them had the will to kindle it. A passing shepherd, Poias, volunteered. Herakles, out of gratitude, ordered that his heavy bow be given to the man. Its polished wood gleamed in the flickering light as the shepherd gingerly lifted it. Thus, the weapon that would one day take Troy came to Philoctetes, the son of Poias.

Within a short time, very different stories spread about the final moments. Some say a thundercloud burst over the pyre just as the flames reached their fiercest heat, and that when the rain stopped and Herakles' men went to collect the hero's bones, nothing was left there. Others assert that they saw the cloud dip down, lift up Herakles, still alive, and then ascend to the heavens. Of course, some people claimed he was never cremated at all, that on the way to Oeta he threw himself into a stream to escape the awful burning of his flesh, and that the waters from that time on retained the terrific heat of his body, and gave their name to the locality, called Thermopylae ("Hot Gates"). Most of us like to think, however, that Herakles found the immortality he had been promised. He was taken up onto the heights of Olympus. There he met his divine father for the first time. Hera, his persecutor, also came to love him. He married exquisite Hêbê, goddess of eternal youth. And he feasts now continually among the gods.

# BOOK SEVEN

## ONCE AND
## FUTURE HEROES

U NLIKE THE MARTIAL AND tragic tales linked with Herakles, the stories of Jason and Perseus carry the aura of romance. Both are essentially about the early adventures, loves, and marriages of young heroes. We learn little if anything about the later life of either man. The focus is on growing up and undertaking great quests. Magic and monsters, supernatural powers and superhuman feats, abound.

The emphasis on youth in these myths may stem from an ancient connection between such stories and the social institution of male initiation. The details of initiation ceremonies vary from one culture to another, but anthropologists have detected a number of features that frequently occur in such rituals. The young man undergoes enforced separation from the community, often in groups with other youths. Ordeals, including physical challenges to endurance and the inflicting of pain or of symbolic wounds, are found. Also common are travel to the borders of territories; learning of secret lore, rites, music, or dances; decoration of the body; taboos on certain foods or behaviors, such as laughing; and pilgrimages to sacred places. In the Jason tale especially, we can see such characteristic motifs. The voyage of the ship *Argo* involves a test of young men journeying to a distant site to recover a sacred object under the guidance of older figures, one of whom (Orpheus) was thought to have access to secret wisdom.

In both the Perseus and Jason stories, the major hero is rewarded with a princess bride. Curiously, the young women in question (Medea and Andromeda) have names based on the same root, *med-*, meaning "to devise" or "to use powerful means." The name "Medusa" comes from the same source. This is not to say that the myths are simply allegories of a young man's coming of age and gaining power. Instead, myth ritual, psychological realities, and folktale narratives combine to create complex and enduring patterns. The "power" gained is both that of maturity and of kingship. The women represent biological but also social growth and command.

While the Argonaut story might yield to a ritual interpretation, psychoanalytic criticism has had more success with the explication of myths surrounding Perseus. The hero's boyhood as the sole child of a single mother, whose "husband" Zeus is not around, seems to condition his ambitious boasting. True to psychological type, he takes on the role of defender of the mother. Other males are seen by the youth as threats to the mother, whereas they are actually potential breakers of the maternal-child bond, and so dangerous in a different way to his own well-being. (The Telemakhos story in the *Odyssey* has hints of the same syndrome.) If we extend the method further, it is possible to read in the Gorgon Medusa a repressed version of a monstrous female embodying male anxieties concerning powerful women. Psychoanalytic critics have even viewed her gaping mouth and snaky hair as a hybrid of female and male bodily characteristics. Decapitation, in this complex, has been compared to castration.

On a different level, apparent in both myth cycles are numerous folktale motifs, including impregnation by magic means; magic objects (the invisibility cap, for instance, or Medea's herbs); the abandoned child; children raised by animals; and objects turned to stone with a single glance. Folklorists have found parallels for such plot devices in other stories told throughout the world. The standard references—*The Types of the Folktale* (1928) and *Motif-Index of Folk-Literature* (six vols., 1932–37), by Stith Thompson, a pioneering scholar in the field, indicate how widespread most of these elements are. Yet this does not detract from the distinctive Greek qualities of either myth. The role of the gods, the importance of cunning intelligence, and the localization in specific places of interest to Greeks in the archaic age, such as the newly colonized Black Sea area, turn the narratives into important culture-specific myths. Nor should we forget that both hero stories are interwoven into larger dynastic narratives about the kingdoms of Argos and of Iolkos. In other words, these are highly politicized "charter" tales as well as rich entertainments.

Depictions of the beheading of Medusa are among the earliest Greek vase paintings. The *Argonaut* myth as well is very old—the *Odyssey* alludes to it quite specifically—but the most complete and influential version, and the source used here, comes from later Greek literature, the third-century B.C. epic *Argonautica* by Apollonius of Rhodes (see the Introduction). Employing the resources of several centuries of Greek poetry, Apollonius paints detailed pictures of Medea's passionate love and Jason's shifting psychological states. Because he also knew well Euripides' *Medea* (431 B.C.), the poet can foreshadow in this tale about their first encounter the later tragedy that the pair undergoes. Even more than the story of the Argonauts, the commanding figure of one of its characters, Medea, came to fascinate later writers, artists, choreographers, and filmmakers, from Ovid in the first century A.D. to Martha Graham and Pier Paolo Pasolini in the twentieth. Ironically, the abandoned woman in the course of time comes back with a vengeance.

## 37. PERSEUS THE BOASTER

Herakles was the greatest hero the world had yet known. Ages to come would look back to the story of his life as a pattern to follow, an example of constant struggle and ultimate reward. What distinguished him from others, past and future, was not so much his adventures (remarkable as they were) as his lifelong striving, his refusal to quit. Others did wondrous deeds when young, then found themselves overcome by life's catastrophes or, like athletes past their prime, spent their remaining years in the diminishing glow of early victories and fame. Such was Perseus, the great-grandfather of Herakles (on both his mortal father's and his mother's side). Such, too, was Jason, his younger contemporary.

We must go far back to find the distant ancestor of "the Wrecker," Perseus. Inakhos, an ancient river, was the watery son of primeval powers, the cosmic stream Okeanos and his wife Tethys. He married a nymph named Ash Tree (Melia), and the couple had two sons, Phoroneus and Aigialeus. Upon the death of his brother, who left no offspring, Phoroneus inherited his father's land. You might say he was responsible for shaping the land itself. For the land around the great citadels of Argos, Mycenae, and Tiryns was always parched in later times—"thirsty," as the old folks said. That is because Phoroneus (who, the locals claim, was also the very first human being) once arbitrated a dispute between Hera and Poseidon over which divinity would be given pride of place in that country. Poseidon was always trying to flood new domains. He had lost Athens to Athena in just such a contest; now, in Argos, Hera was awarded worship. Poseidon consequently stalked off, disgusted, and caused the whole land to dry up, including the father of the king, the river Inakhos. Only in heavy winters does Inakhos fill with water.

Phoroneus married Teledike and had a son Apis and a daughter Niobe. She had the distinction of being the first mortal woman loved by Zeus (the first in a long line). Their offspring were Argos the First (who gave his name to the country) and Pelasgos. Argos married Evadne (another river's daughter) and she bore Ekbasos, who fathered Agenor, who in turn fathered Argos the Second—a monster. This junior Argos had eyes all over his body, a hundred moving, glancing eyeballs with as many blinking lids. "Panoptic Argos" they called him. He was not a bad sort. In fact, he proved to be quite useful at detecting murderers and cattle rustlers and thieves.

The streams of kinship start to converge here. Inakhos, an old river but still flowing, produced a daughter whose name was Io. She became the priestess of Hera. Since she was beautiful, with long wavy hair and alabaster skin, and Zeus had begun to seek out human women, it was not surprising that the chief god soon seduced his wife's quiet worshiper. He made love to her under a convenient cloud (which he himself caused to arise, since he is the cloud gatherer, Nephelêgeretês). That did not fool Hera. Looking down from Olympus, she spied the lonely wandering cloud. She leapt down, scattering the fluffy cover, and found—a cow. A heifer, to be exact. After enjoying their meeting Zeus had transformed his new lover just in time. Later, he figured, he would change her back.

"What a beautiful pure white animal! Never have I seen the like," declared Hera. "Where did it ever come from, Zeus?" "Oh, Earth just sent it up. Yes, an—autochthonous bovine," the father of gods spluttered. "Well, then, since it's a gift from our ancient ancestress, and since it seems to need attention (look how it's nuzzling your hand!)— I think I'd like to have it. Can I, my love? I'll take good care of it."

What could he do? To resist would invite suspicion. If it really was a cow, he could hardly refuse the gift. "Of course," Zeus cried magnanimously. "Where will you keep it, if I might ask? We don't have other cows at the moment on Mt. Olympus." "I'll find somewhere with nice grass," was his wife's reply. She never did reveal the location. For that, he had to employ his own sources of information. It turned out Hera had entrusted the heifer for protection to Argos, the all-seeing herdsman who lived, conveniently, in the immediate neighborhood. (Nor did Argos know it was his distant cousin that he was guarding.)

Zeus, seeing his lover tethered to an olive tree, pondered his problem. He sent for Hermes and told him to get rid of Io's guard. So the trickster put on his traveler's hat, stepped into his winged sandals, and picked up the rod with which he leads souls to Hades. He headed for the meadows near Mycenae, where Argos had taken Io to graze. In the form of a young goatherd he approached the all-seeing watchman. As he went, he played upon a set of reed pipes (the new invention of the goat-god Pan). Argos, being curious, as well as somewhat bored, made him sit next to him on the grass and entertain him with melodies—just as Hermes had planned. He played fast ditties; then slower ballads; then a few drowsier nocturnes; and then selected lullabies—until, eye after eye, Argos dropped off to sleep, his lid-covered limbs relaxed, and his head nodded heavily. When every pupil was safely shuttered, Hermes took Io from her halter. To make sure her former guardian would never wake up and miss her, he chopped off the freakish head of Argos, for which deed he became known as Argeiphontês ("slayer of Argos").

Now, Zeus would have had his way, but Hera, ever watchful, was no longer in doubt. This was no ordinary white heifer. Within hours, she partially avenged poor Argos by putting his eyes into the tail of her favorite bird, the peacock. And she caused Io to bolt from Hermes by sending a gadfly to sting her. Io, maddened by the persistent insect, ran aimlessly from one continent to another. She crossed a gulf (which thus became the "Io-nian"), then ran north to Thrace and east to the waters flowing from the Black Sea, crossing over into Asia (and thus giving this strait its name—Bos-poros, or "Cow-ford"). She wandered as far as the mountain in the Caucasus range where Prometheus was pinned, in those days before Herakles. There she paused to have a talk with the Titan child, who seemed like an amiable fellow. Then it was off to Scythia, Kimmeria, the Amazons, the Graiai, the Aithiopes, and at last Egypt. Zeus finally persuaded Hera that Io was no longer a threat to her position. She was changed back into a young woman just as before. She was pregnant with the child of Zeus, gave birth, and called the boy Epaphos ("Touch") because she had been touched by the divine power. The Egyptians learned to worship Io herself, under the name of Isis.

Epaphos grew up and married a daughter of the Nile (his mother, after all, had been a river's daughter). He named a city after her—Memphis. Their daughter was Libya—thus another place was named. She in turn lay with Poseidon and bore twin sons, Belos and Agenor. The latter (named after the father of Io's herdsman) moved east to Phoenicia, where he fathered Kadmos and Europa (the girl who rode a bull to Crete). The former stayed in Egypt, becoming the father (by another Nile daughter) of Aigyptos and Danaos. These twin boys always argued, even though they each inherited vast tracts of land and should have been busy enough, seeing as Danaos had fifty daughters and his brother had fifty sons. Nevertheless, faced with a small army of nephews and their difficult father, Danaos took the advice of Athena and struck out for another territory. He built a ship, embarked with all the girls, and sailed to thirsty Argos—his ancestral land.

On their arrival they searched desperately for water. They would have been doomed had Poseidon not taken a fancy to Amymonê, one of the young ladies, and showed her the secret springs at Lerna (later to become the haunt of the Hydra). With that problem solved, they soon faced another. The boys of Aigyptos had always imagined that their cousins would become their wives: the numbers, after all, were exactly right. At their father's urging, they, too, rigged up a ship and landed a few months later, eager to claim their brides. The daughters of Danaos, on the other hand, wanted nothing to do with their cousins. They fled for asylum to the local king, Pelasgos, in an hysterical state. "If you fail to take us in," they threatened, "we shall hang ourselves—right here," they proclaimed, pointing to his altars. "Anything is better than marrying those louts!" Pelasgos yielded. For a time he was able to protect the girls. But then, with war looming, he was forced to become harsher. If Danaos and his daughters wished to stay in their new home, he declared, they must submit to the sons of Aigyptos.

Danaos had to agree. Yet his heart was still with his daughters, adamant in their refusal to accept such a marriage arrangement. He went about the details of setting up a mass wedding. Daughters were systematically paired with their cousins, usually on the basis of their mother's race: for instance, seven sons of a Phoenician married seven daughters of an Ethiopian. Some matches were made by name—a Klitos got a Klite, Khrysippos got Khrysippê, and so on. Others were meant to bring together similar temperaments or skills. The eldest daughter of the exiled king was named Hypermêstra—"Surpassing Deviser"—and she wed Lynkeus. To all his girls Danaos gave a wedding present on the night of the great feast, a small gift, the same for each, and easily hidden: namely, a sharp Arabian dagger. Each daughter put her gift to use by stabbing her husband on their wedding night. Hypermêstra alone refused to kill her mate: he had been gentle, never trying to force himself on her, and she began to love him. For this weakness against his enemies Danaos punished her, confining her in the house. Meanwhile, the other, dutiful daughters buried their husbands' heads near the streams of Lerna. Zeus forgave and purified them, even though they had murdered guests, whose protection he was sworn to uphold. Then again, some claim the daughters paid for this violent rejection of being mastered by a man. In the underworld, it is said, the forty-nine Danaids are condemned to forever carry water from a spring—a task befitting serving women—in leaky jars.

They did consent to second marriages, arranged again by their father, this time with Argive youths. He sponsored a footrace: first prize was the daughter of the winner's choice, second the next, and so on down the line. Hypermêstra was allowed to stay with Lynkeus, who reigned over Argos after his father-in-law passed on. Their son, Abas, was in time the proud father of twins, Proitos and Akrisios. They were warriors—even in the womb of their mother they fought, and when they grew up, they battled fiercely for the kingship. (They were the ones who invented war shields.) Akrisios drove his brother out, at least temporarily. But Proitos, who took refuge overseas, returned with an army of Lycians, the subjects of his foreign wife's father. So the two came to an agreement. Proitos took Tiryns, the great citadel with its walls built by Cyclopes in ages past. Akrisios ruled over the city Argos.

In that hot, dusty town was his daughter, Danaê, born. Akrisios loved her, in his way. But all the time she was growing up, he kept wanting another child, a son to carry on his line. How could a race that traced its origin to Zeus be allowed to die out, to be swallowed up by another's lineage, nowhere near as glorious? He sought the oracle's advice. But the priestess at Delphi shocked him. "A son you will never have. A grandson, yes. Danaê, your daughter, will bear the one who will kill you." Akrisios could see only one solution. His daugh-

ter must never lie with a man. On his return to Argos he had an underground chamber constructed entirely of bronze, large and comfortable, but without an exit. There he put Danaê, who was not yet seventeen, and her aged nurse. Food and drink could be lowered through the roof, where there was a round opening, high up, for light and air. It rarely rained, so the hole was kept open.

Then, one day it did rain, but not in the usual way. A stream of gold, like a ray of sun but heavier, almost like a shimmering gold chain, poured through the opening, right into Danaê's lap, as the nurse looked on in amazement, her toothless mouth agape. Some cynics said later this "rain of gold" was a fabrication, a polite way of saying somebody bribed the nurse to be let in to see the girl. But no one could squeeze into that chamber, even if it were allowed. Only Zeus had found a way, coming to Danaê in this shower of gold.

The young woman's pregnancy was easy enough to hide. But once the baby was born, its cries could not be hushed. "Impossible!" swore Akrisios when he found the child. Danaê insisted that she had been loved by Zeus, but he treated the story with contempt and suspicion. He thought that Proitos was behind this. "At any rate, the child cannot stay," he concluded. "Perhaps it *is* the son of Zeus—so I will not kill it outright. It also needs a mother, so you will go with it, inside a wooden box, tossed onto the sea. The test by water will tell the truth of the matter. If the box stays afloat and you survive, maybe your story's true. But I for one am not convinced." Carpenters were called. They measured mother and son, cut air holes, even decorated the box, which resembled a wedding chest or a bulky coffin. And then, to protect his own life and power, Akrisios cast his daughter and baby grandson onto the waves.

Nighttime fell without a moon, and the sea was running high. Danaê was chilled with fear. But her infant, feeling its mother's warm body, was strangely, wonderfully, at peace. It was, for her, an illumination. She sang:

> *"Child, what trouble I've seen, what pain,*
> *And yet you sleep, my milk, my heart.*
> *The box is gloomy, with spikes of bronze,*
> *In the blue-black night, without a lamp,*
> *And yet you sleep.*
>
> *You do not fear the wave above,*
> *That sprinkles your tender head with salt,*
> *You do not fear the deep wind voice,*
> *Lovely face pressed to your blanket,*
> *Your little purple blanket.*
>
> *If ever you knew the trial we're in*
> *Your tiny ear would listen.*
> *But sleep, my child, sleep, you waves,*
> *Let my troubles go to sleep.*
> *Let Zeus reconsider."*

This last line she thought might be too bold, so she hurriedly added in her best ritual manner, "If that which I seek is neither justified nor appropriate, I humbly beg forgiveness." All through the night she sang her lullaby, while the wind and current carried the box to the southeast. Sometime the next day—she had begun to lose track of time—their craft came to land at the small island of Seriphos. A gang of fishermen, casting nets from the shore, hauled in the chest. When they discovered what it contained, they rushed to Diktys, whose house was on a nearby hill. He was the brother of the island's king, a sterner, older man named Polydektes. Kindhearted Diktys, seeing the infant and its teenage mother, took them in, for he had no family of his own. The girl and baby made his hearth less lonely.

Years passed, and Perseus grew to be a strong young man. No one knew who gave him the name "Wrecker"—for that is what Perseus means. It may have been a nickname invented by his playmates, who became used to the boy's bravado and his endless stories about his real father being Zeus. The boasts were his way of making up for his short-comings, or what he saw as shortcomings—the small house he lived in, the way his guardian had to grovel before Polydektes.

Diktys treated Danaê like a daughter. His brother the king, how-ever, saw her in a different light. He wanted to make her his wife, but Danaê—perhaps because she had heard of his cruelty—would not have him. And he could not abduct her. That wild son of hers, though just sixteen, was too dangerous. So he devised a ruse, letting the son's own boasts work against him.

"I intend to marry Hippodameia," the king declared one autumn day. "I am sure that her father Oinomaos will accept me—but I need bride wealth. I command every warrior on Seriphos to donate a horse. Those who do will be held in high regard." "A horse!" said Perseus when he heard this proclamation. "I'll do much better than that. I'll bring him the Gorgon's head itself." Of course, Polydektes soon heard this vaunting claim, and he told Perseus he would hold him to his word. Now the young man would have to make good on his offer. He had no idea where one could find the Gorgon, or what exactly it was, or if it even existed. He had heard the expression before—something like "milk from birds"—as a way of describing what could never be obtained. But now he would have to do so. Nor was it any longer just a matter of his reputation, since Polydektes had added, in his chal-lenge, "If you don't return with the head, I'll take your mother."

Perseus did not even have a boat, so unless the Gorgons lived on Seriphos, he was stuck. He walked all afternoon, until he found him-self at the western end of the island, the "uplands" as people called it, where he sank down on the beach in despair. Then, from a mist rising over the sea, he heard a voice and saw the figure of a man walking lightly over the water, a broad-brimmed *petasos* on his head and a golden wand in his right hand. "My brother," said Hermes, who had come to help. "Why are you so glum? Together we can accomplish all." The god led the way, stepping on wave crests, to the daughters of

Phorkos, three stooped and decrepit ladies named Enuô, Pephredô, and Deinô. This trio—called, collectively, the Graiai—had been old since the day they were born. So ancient were they now that only one aging eye remained among them, and only one tooth. They passed these around whenever they had to see or eat. There was not much to see where they lived, at the back of beyond, and they had outlived appetite, so their lack did not cause them any problem.

It did not take much ingenuity for Perseus (with advice from Hermes) to steal both tooth and eye—he just intercepted them as they were passing. "Give them back, give them back," the pitiful hags chanted in complaint. Perseus tried to calm them: "All right, I will—when you tell me where your sisters the Gorgons dwell, and the nymphs who can help me on my quest." They did, and he returned their precious parts.

At the next stop, the nymphs gladly provided him with all the magic gear he required: winged sandals (just like Hermes', only silver); a cap that made one invisible; and a sack for holding bulky objects, called a *kibisis*. From Hephaestus (via Hermes) he received a sharp adamantine sword, curved like a sickle. With these he flew to the edge of Okeanos, where the dreadful Gorgons lived. There were three of these as well, but only one was mortal—Medusa. The story went that she once had been a beautiful woman, with suitors from near and far begging for her hand. Her auburn hair was the feature of which she was proudest, combing it out and brushing it sleek and smooth for hours each day. Before any man could have her, however, Poseidon intervened. Their tryst he arranged to take place in Athena's temple, probably to insult that virgin goddess. When Athena found out, she transformed Medusa's fine hair into a nest of coiling, tangled snakes, and dispatched her to the edge of the world, where Sthenô and Euryalê—immortals with similar coiffures—already had their lair.

Perseus hovered over the spot, his sandal wings rapidly beating. The Gorgons were lying on a rocky ledge, deeply asleep. He was about to swoop down and kill the nearest of them when Athena stopped him. "You cannot even glance at their faces. One look from them, and you will turn to stone. Only Medusa—that one—can be slain. To do it, you will need this," she said, handing him a polished shield of bronze. Perseus savored the irony of using his grandfather's invention at a moment like this. He held the shield above his head, slightly to the left. The image of Medusa filled it, as in a mirror. With Athena's

help, he reached down, gazing at the shiny metal, and with one violent stroke chopped through the Gorgon's neck.

An unearthly howl arose, not from Medusa—who never felt a thing—but from her sisters, who caught Perseus' scent and began baying like hounds who have found their quarry. Their voices blended cries for vengeance with lament. (Athena later imitated this sound when she invented reed pipes.) Perseus snatched up the severed head with one hand, stowing it in his *kibisis* for safekeeping. With the other, he fastened on his cap of invisibility. Sthenô and Euryalê became frenzied, running all about. They rose from the ground—for they too had wings, large and golden, and big tusks and ugly, lolling tongues. All this Perseus saw in his war shield. He was already speeding back to the known world, while the surviving Gorgons tried in vain to catch sight of him. Meanwhile, a strange replacement appeared on the ledge he had left. From the decapitated trunk of Medusa two creatures emerged: a full-grown warrior with an odd, fixed smile; and a perfect horse, with elegant wings. These were both children of

Poseidon, by whom Medusa h'ad been pregnant when she died. The manlike figure was Gold Dirk (Khrysaor), who would eventually beget Geryon, herdsman of the west. The horse would later be tamed by another hero with the help of Athena. It was called Pegasus.

## 38. PERSEUS FINDS A WIFE

Like rivers, the careers of heroes wind and meander, looping back in unexpected ways. Belos, the ancestor of Perseus six generations back, had a brother Agenor, as you recall, who shook from his feet the dust of Egypt and headed east to the coastlands of Phoenicia. During the time the events were unfolding in Argos that led eventually to the brilliant conception of Perseus, generations of his kin in the east were being born and dying, as leaves flourish and fall. Of Europa, one of these relatives, you have already learned. Kadmos, her brother, we will hear of soon. Another relation of the line of Agenor was Kepheus, who married the beautiful Kassiepeia, and ruled the Ethiopians.

The queen was lovely and proud of it. Each day, when she went to the sea to wash (for in those early days, palaces were primitive, without running water), Kassiepeia would admire herself in a placid pool among the rocks. "Even the Nereids have not my hair, my cheekbones, my legs—I'm not sure they have legs at all!" she would muse. Since she was so near the sea when making these unwise comments, the Nereids overheard. Full of divine anger, they told their father, the Old Man of the Sea, who in turn reported to Poseidon the hubris of the Ethiopian queen. Poseidon promised to wreak revenge. First, he caused a giant wave to rush in from the sea and flood all the low-lying plains of the land of Kepheus. Then he found a suitable sea monster in the cold, murky depths and sent it to the coast to cause havoc. This *kêtos*—a cross between a shark and a whale—beached itself and started eating anyone in sight.

Kepheus was panic-stricken, as any loving king should be in such a fix. He dispatched a messenger to the oracular shrine of Ammon, in the desert (this was considerably closer than Delphi), and received the incredible reply that only one sacrifice would appease the monster: his own daughter Andromeda. "Kassiepeia may keep her beauty. But she must lose her child. Chain her to a rock in the sea, food for the *kêtos*. Then Ethiopia will be free." Kepheus refused to believe such a barbarous command, and would not do it. The Ethiopians, however, who were suffering more losses every day from the sea monster, demanded he make a choice. "It's her or you." So he agreed to expose his darling Andromeda.

It is curious how distant kin tend to share mistakes. An ill-timed boast and a king's fear had gotten Perseus into trouble, then made him a hero. The same combination was to lead to his marriage. He was flying home from his victory in the far east when, looking down from a great height, he saw a drama in miniature—what looked like a dragon plowing through the waves and, about a mile closer to shore, a tiny nude figure on a rock. Wanting a closer look, he descended until he could see that the figure was a young woman. She was the most stunning creature he had seen. He froze at her glance, which showed a mixture of despair and surprise. As though treading water, Perseus hovered in place, close enough to talk with Andromeda, and to learn her fate. Without a second thought, he called out to her parents, waiting in agony on the shore, "If I kill the monster, I must wed this woman." Of course, they consented.

By this point the *kêtos* was within a hundred yards, swimming toward the rock with its horrifying jaws wide open. Perseus, rather than using the Medusa head, chose to fight with his curved sword. He laid the precious Gorgon head on some tender seaweed at the water's edge, then flew up over the sea monster's bulky body. (Only later did he find the seaweed had turned to coral.) His shadow upon the waters confused the beast, which started thrashing, trying to maul the dark shape. Perseus edged toward the back of the monster, then dove, stabbed at the tail, then shot up. He dove again, jabbed the midriff, shot up again. The *kêtos* rolled over in a frenzy, trying to reach the gadfly tormenting it. At that moment Perseus dropped to the tender underbelly and hacked at it until dark purple blood spurted out and stained the sea for a mile around. Exhausted, he unshackled the girl, then slowly flew her to land, where the pair alighted. The corpse of the *kêtos* slipped without a trace beneath the waves.

The wedding of Perseus and Andromeda was magnificent—filled with processions and flutes and lyres, incense from the east, wagonloads of guests, and a banquet of heroic proportions. It came to an ugly end, however. Phineus, the king's brother, had been betrothed to Andromeda before the sea monster panic had set in. The bride's parents, naturally, had not taken into account this earlier claim in their desperation to have their daughter rescued. Nor, for that matter, had Phineus ever tried to stop the monster himself. At the time he was resigned to finding another wife. But now that this outsider with the winged ankles had saved the day, Phineus claimed his right. He gathered a gang of warriors and came to the feast hall ready for battle. His first javelin missed Perseus, hitting instead a loyal supporter of the king. Then all descended into chaos. Spears flew thick as hail, leaving men on either side wounded or dying. Perseus cracked skulls, broke jaws, and fought valiantly, but he began to lose ground. The wedding guests on his side had not come armed for a fight. Now their numbers were dwindling. It was time for his secret weapon. Reaching for his *kibisis*, while holding off two of Phineus' men with his sword, Perseus pulled out the snaky head and shouted, "Look!" Instantly, warriors were turned to stone, like so many marble statues in a sculptor's portico, posed in their lifelike positions forever. Phineus, who was cunning enough to suspect a trick, was discovered by Perseus in the silenced hall, cowering behind a purple-upholstered banquet couch. "Look!" the hero cried, jerking back his enemy's head by the hair. Then Phineus, too, turned to stone, a monument for later ages to recall the deeds of Perseus.

With Andromeda at his side, the young bridegroom returned victorious to Scriphos. He had not been gone long—only about two weeks—but he arrived just in time. Shortly after his departure, Perseus' mother Danaê and her guardian Diktys had been attacked by the arrogant Polydektes, and both had fled for safety to the altar of the gods. The tyrant still wanted to get his hands on Danaê, but it would be a terrible sin if he tore them from that sacred spot. Instead, he forbade anyone to give them food. Each day they grew weaker. None of the other islanders dared come to their rescue, since they were in terror of being caught.

Flying in from the east, Perseus gently touched down with his new bride in his arms, at the very spot he had first encountered Hermes. That seemed like ages ago. He did not go directly to the palace. In a few short weeks he had become cunning and cautious—the effect of Athena's guidance, no doubt. Only when he had ascertained that the roads were clear, and saw that it would be a moonless night, did he make his way inland. Andromeda came along; after her recent experience she could not bear to be left alone near the coastline. As they crept closer to the house of Polydektes, sounds of flute and lyres filtered toward them on the breeze. A feast was being held. Torches blazed in the hall. The king was in good spirits, eagerly anticipating his marriage to Danaê, as he imagined she could not hold out much longer. He and his friends were celebrating in advance. As casually as someone returning from a walk, Perseus entered the banquet room. It was as if all had turned to stone. He strolled to the couches at the back of the room, where Polydektes was reclining with his closest associates. Every eye followed him. No one was sure whether or not this was a ghost—how could the upstart have survived, if the Gorgons really existed?

Perseus paused in front of Polydektes, who had by now recovered a little of his color. "Back so soon, my boy? Your mother missed you so. I was just telling my friends how much she needs my consolation. Of course, she's mine now, according to our bargain. Or did you, by any chance, bring that head you were after?" With each sentence, his smile grew broader. "As a matter of fact, here it is," the hero coolly replied, yanking open his *kibisis* and holding up his prize, Medusa's frozen face. The smile never left Polydektes' lips. He was petrified, as were all the others who clambered forward to the king's aid.

His mission completed, Perseus returned the cap, *kibisis*, and sandals to Hermes, who gave them back in good order to the nymphs. The head he carefully handed over to Athena, who placed an image of it in the middle of her shield to terrify her enemies, while she buried the original in Athens beneath the marketplace. Then he appointed Diktys as the new king of Seriphos. Taking his mother and wife, he boarded a ship for Argos—no more flights through the air. But when they arrived, the townsfolk informed them that the old king, Akrisios, "the one who once had such a beautiful daughter, they say, and drowned her," had gone to Larissa. "He feared for his life," they explained. Perseus did not tell them that the woman beside him was that castaway girl, and that he himself was the cause for his grandfather's fear. It seemed the king had his own channels of information. For the townsfolk, on the other hand, Danaê had already passed into legend.

He set out immediately on his own to find Akrisios. Vengeance was not on his mind. Perhaps he was even eager to find the king. He had never known an earthly father. In fact, Zeus had been conspicuously absent in his life—unless it was the chief god who had sent his children Hermes and Athena to give him help. He was curious, more than anything, about his fabled grandfather. Would they recognize each other? Could they start all over?

When he came within a mile of Larissa, he saw crowds of people milling about in an open field. Rough wooden stands had been constructed. Mule wagons were trundling along toward the hubbub, packed with young men and women in their best-colored robes—saffron, sky-blue, crimson, white. From a group of men passing him on the road, Perseus heard that funeral games were being held today. The father of Teutamides, the local chieftain, had passed on. The games were for him, as if a dedication of strength and energy by young men could somehow keep vigorous the memory of the deceased. Perseus knew about the custom, but had never had a chance to compete. He did so now, putting himself forward for the discus throw.

When his turn came, he toed the line and bent down low to pick up the flat round stone. The crowd was excited, pressing in on the ropes to get a better look at this unknown athlete, who seemed to them like a god. He coiled himself for the toss, then with one smooth and powerful move, like a dancer, untwisted his body and flung the *diskos*. It flew toward the far end of the field. As Perseus watched, it skimmed through the air, along the ropes that marked the left-hand boundary of the course, sailing past the spectators at shoulder height. Then one man at the far end leaned—or was pushed—too far out. An old man, by the looks of it, with white hair and a blank expression. Perseus had only a glimpse of the head sticking over the ropes before the man was struck and knocked senseless by the speeding *diskos*. By the time Perseus registered what had happened and ran to the spot, the old man was dead. Somebody in the crowd knew his name—"He was a refugee. Akrisios." So Perseus saw his mother's father for the first and last time. The Pythia's warning had come true.

## 39. JASON AND THE VOYAGE EAST

Perseus did not have the heart to take over the kingdom left by the man he had accidentally killed. Instead of returning to Argos, he made an arrangement to trade realms with Megapenthes, the son of Proitos, who was by now ruling Tiryns. Andromeda bore him sons there: Alkaios, Sthenelos, and Electryon, from whose interlacing fates Herakles would one day be produced. He also fathered Perses, ancestor of the Persians, and ended his days, beloved but undistinguished, a former hero who once did something marvelous. If anyone knew how death finally took him, it was never recorded. It was too ordinary.

In the strange way that stories have, Perses, son of Perseus, would come to meet his own end because of the deeds of another hero who, like Perseus, reached his peak when young and died middle-aged, in a completely unheroic way. It is difficult to know exactly where to begin the story of this later adventurer, Jason. We could start way back, with Hellen, son of Deukalion and Pyrrha, the only survivors of the great Flood. From his fame all the Greeks, to this day, bear the name of "Hellenes." He had three well-known sons: Xuthus (the warrior who married into Athenian royalty); Doros, who gave his name to the Dorian tribe; and Aiolos, who was ancestor of another tribal division, the Aeolians, living in the rich horse-breeding plains of Thessaly. Aiolos had several interesting offspring—for example, Sisyphus, the rock roller of Hades, and Salmoneus, who mimicked Zeus. But the one who concerns us was called Athamas.

He was married three times. The first wife was Cloud (Nephelê), lighthearted and airy. With her he had two children, Hellê and Phrixos, before she disappeared one day. It turned out she was really a goddess. His next wife, Ino, was not a good stepmother. All her thoughts were for her own sons, Learkhos and Melikertes. So afraid was she that the older children would inherit the kingdom that she plotted to get rid of them, starting with Phrixos. She devised an elaborate plan. First, she persuaded all the women of the land secretly to parch the grain that was sown each year. When the time came for the crop to appear, nothing emerged from the ground, since scorched seed cannot grow. Like a good king, Athamas sent to Delphi to find a solution. Ino bribed the emissaries of the king to invent a horrifying reply: "Your eldest son must be sacrificed." The men of his country— who were ignorant of the parched-grain plot—forced Athamas to obey the command of the oracle, although he kept hesitating and delaying. Finally, his heart like a stone, the king called his son Phrixos. "Go to the royal flock," he instructed him, "and pick out the best sheep. Bring it here. We must make a special offering." The boy went off to the fields where they were grazing, unaware of his father's true intent.

It was not hard to find the most fitting animal. Amid the skittish, black-faced sheep, with their white woolly coats mud-caked from the fields, stood a ram, a head taller than the rest, with a coat that shimmered in the noon sun, all of gold. Nephelê had brought it there, having got it from Hermes. Though her son did not know its origin, he proudly led the ram back to town. When they were still some distance from the palace, and had stopped to rest in the shade of a low-branched olive tree, the beast lying in front of Phrixos with its front legs crossed beneath its shiny body, a strange thing happened. "Boy," the ram said. Phrixos paid no heed, thinking it was saying, "Baa." "Boy," came the sound again, more clearly this time, and he noticed that the golden animal was staring right at him. "Do you not know?" This time there was no doubt. The ram was addressing him. "I will not die today. It is you who are to be the sacrifice." Whatever marvel Phrixos felt at the sound of the talking sheep was replaced by fear, and he listened intently as the ram continued. "They will decorate my horns and sprinkle my head with the water and barley—the usual rites. But when you lead me to the altar, they will seize you. Take my horn then and leap on my back. Tell your sister also to come. And hang on." At that the ram fell silent, poked its fleece with its muzzle, and tasted some tender grass.

Everything went as the animal had said it would. His father led the procession to the altar, richly decorated with wool fillets. Hellê daintily carried the basket with the barley and sacrificial knife (which was always hidden, as if sheep might otherwise know their fate). At the moment when the ritual experts should have pulled the ram's head sharply backward and cut its throat, Phrixos saw their hands reach out instead for him. At once he jumped out of reach, onto the back of the ram, and helped Hellê onto the beast. Away it flew, soon becoming a golden speck in the sky to the dazed onlookers below.

Higher and higher the ram went, until it began to get very cold. They were heading due east and the sun was setting behind them. Phrixos was only half-afraid. But his sister was shivering both from fright and from the frosty altitude. Phrixos had all he could do to keep her firmly in place in front of him, trying meanwhile to keep his fingers locked in the curls of the ram's wool. They were passing over a body of water, the strait that runs between Europe and Asia, when Hellê suddenly lost her grip. In anguish her brother saw her drop down, down—a tiny white object splashing into the sea that forever after took her name: "Helles-pont."

The ram kept flying. His mission had been given him by Cloud herself, and he could not stop until it was fulfilled. As the sun rose again in front of them, animal and boy came to earth in Kolkhis. The king there was Aiêtês, son of the Sun. (His sister Pasiphae was wife of Minos, and another sister, Circe, lived on an island alone—some called her a witch.) At the ram's own insistence—he said this was the gods' will—Phrixos sadly slaughtered it. The Golden Fleece he gave to the king, who nailed it to an oak tree. The grove in which the Fleece shone belonged to Ares, and a huge serpent, bigger than a man, guarded this treasure day and night.

In time, Phrixos married a daughter of the king, Khalkiope, and lived happily with his wife and four children. Back in Greece, his own father had been less fortunate. After Hera punished Ino because the couple hid Dionysus, Athamas in a fit of madness shot his own son, and was banished from the land. He wandered for many months, until he found the spot that an oracle had foretold, "where the beasts of the wild treat you as guest." Coming upon some wolves that had torn a sheep into pieces, Athamas frightened them away. There was his meal, already divided into portions by these considerate animal hosts. In that place he founded a new territory and settled down, even marrying once more—this time uneventfully for all concerned.

So we could start Jason's story that way. Or we could go back to the time of Aiolos once more and take a different path. Another son of Aiolos was Kretheus, a mild-mannered prince. He married Tyro, his niece, and the couple had a son, Aison. Although her new husband did not know it, Tyro had also been an object of Poseidon's affection. Every day she used to go to the mouth of the river Enipeus to bathe. Her beauty was such that the sea god could not help but notice. One day he took the river's form and embraced Tyro, cresting in a fine light blue wave that covered the lovers until evening came. She became pregnant and gave birth to twin sons. She was young at the time and scared. She could not let her parents know—and, anyway, who would believe her story that a god had seduced her in a river's disguise? So the twins were set afloat on the river, their father's element, but unlike most children who are exposed they did not perish. Their little basket-boat came to rest on the banks where a horse meadow sloped down to the water. As they lay there, a mare trotted by, kicking over the basket and leaving a blue-black bruise on the face of one boy. The horse breeders in the field ran up and found the twins. The one with the mark on his face they named Pelias (from the word meaning "bruise"), and the other Neleus. They brought the pair home and raised them as their own sons.

When they were grown, the twins—both fine equestrians by now—drifted in different directions. Neleus headed for the far southwest, to Pylos, where he established a dynasty. Pelias went farther north to the fine natural harbor near the foothills of Mt. Pelion, where his mother's husband, Kretheus, had founded a seafaring city, Iolkos. He wanted to be recognized as the rightful heir, although Aison was officially next in line for the throne. No one could see why an un-known man with an ugly mark on his face should inherit the king-dom. When Kretheus died, a crisis erupted. Pelias drove out his half brother and took over.

Aison did not move far away. With his wife he went up to the wild hills above Iolkos. Although the woods were thick and hard to pene-trate, he took no risks. Pelias was a tyrant and would hunt down any-one he thought threatened his ill-gotten realm. Aison was powerless, no longer able to pose a challenge. But his newborn son gave him hope that the pain would be cured. In order to ensure that this boy, Jason, "the Healer," would survive, Aison brought him to the old man of the mountain, the ancient half-human Cheiron. Hidden deep in the forest, living in the Centaur's cave, Jason grew to manhood learning all the secret crafts and arts, hunting and music, medicine and the meanings of the stars, and of course horsemanship—and this last taught not by horse breeders (like his uncle's childhood guardians) but by a creature who was himself half-horse.

Pelias, meanwhile, wanted to have his own son, someone to whom he could hand on his city of Iolkos. As desperate people do, he sent to Delphi. He received no uncertain advice, but not about children. "One in the line of Aiolos, your own race, will slay you," the Pythia was reported to have declared. "Beware of the man who wears one san-dal." At first Pelias was merely confused. All his relatives had been ac-counted for; there were no disgruntled kin seeking revenge. Aison was childless, his spies had assured him. Where was the threat? Neverthe-less, with this prophecy weighing on his mind, Pelias began prepara-tions for a grand sacrifice to his father Poseidon. Perhaps through piety he could avoid his fate.

Up in the hills, Cheiron was finishing his education of the hero. "I have taught you all that I can. The time has come, lad, for the great-est test. You have always lived like us, a man in nature, part of the land. Now you must approach a city. The Earth-Shaker festival is coming round. Go to the flatlands where lies the kingdom—your fa-ther's by right—next to the sea. Bring to those people your wisdom from the mountain." Not without regret, Jason set off.

In order to get to the town, he had to cross the river Anauros. It was early spring, when the melting snows of the mountain feed the streams to overflowing. Even at a distance he could hear the rushing water as he made his way down from the heights of Pelion, and he could see the morning mist rising from the valley where the river ran out to the gulf. When Jason arrived at its bank, he found he was not alone. An old woman was waiting. Her black veil nearly covered her face, but Jason could see that she was silently crying. He asked what was her trouble and could he help. "My son," she said, "I came so far to see my sister over the mountain. And now I cannot cross this way at all. I have not the strength to go back and have no way around, nor anyone to take me in for the night." Her sobs broke out again—more like dry, wheezing gasps, as she could hardly draw the breath to really cry.

"Mother, take heart. Hold on," said Jason as he lifted her bodily— she could not have weighed more than a small goat—and carried her in his arms across the swirling waters. The stream was not deep, but the force of the current was enough to sweep a man off his feet, and Jason had to step carefully. They were just a few feet from the opposite bank when he slipped, caught himself in time, and managed to hold on to the ancient woman, who let out a sharp frightened sound, like a small dog. But they made it safely.

Once on land, Jason realized that the slip had cost him a sandal. He glanced back in time to see it being carried off downstream. Still, he was used to going barefoot. Some people even claimed that walking with just one foot shod was the best method for keeping a grip in mud, and he'd find plenty of that in the paths ahead. He turned from the river to check on the old woman, but she was gone. In her place stood a tall, elegant lady with the scent of jasmine, and a white veil that shone like a full moon. "Son of Aison, for your courtesy toward me, you had a small loss—but now a greater gain, the gratitude of a goddess, with which one never fails. Sovereignty is yours. Be brave. I am Hera." And with that, the figure vanished.

In this way did Jason come to Iolkos, bedraggled and wearing only a single sandal. It did not take Pelias long to notice him, even with the crowds and confusion of the festival. He stood out among the throng that milled around the altars, waiting for their portion of thigh or rib (for only at sacrifices did poor folk get the chance to eat beef). Now the account varies. Some say that they heard from others who were there that Pelias found out who Jason was, and that he had a rightful claim to the kingship of the land. Pelias, so these people assert, yielded his throne on the spot, but then called Jason aside and told him: "I am overjoyed that you have come to save the kingdom. I am old, too old to accomplish the feat that must be done. Every night now for six months I have been visited by the ghost of Phrixos in an awful dream. It comes to me and says, 'Take back the Golden Fleece,' and predicts disaster if I do not. You remember, he was the boy who rode a flying ram to Kolkhis. But I cannot undertake the journey to the east. Now you have become king: it is your duty to fulfill this task." In this clever way, of course, Pelias thought to dispose of his younger rival.

In the other story Jason resembles the hotheaded Perseus. Instead of devising the part about the dream, they say Pelias—who did not know Jason's identity, only that he was the foretold man with one sandal—asked his advice. "What would you do if you were king and someone had come to kill you?" Jason, not knowing he was cutting out the shape of his own future, answered: "Send him to get the Golden Fleece"—a mythical object, as far as he knew, but a trip sure to be packed with danger. Pelias replied, "The oracle never lies. It told me that man is you. Go get it or perish."

Whichever way it happened, Jason bravely undertook the quest. He sent for the finest shipbuilder, Argos son of Arêstôr. Work began at the docks north of town. Within a few weeks the *Argo* (named after its builder) was complete, the fastest ship ever propelled by fifty oars. In the prow of the vessel Athena had Argos carefully insert an oaken shaft taken from the sacred prophetic tree of Zeus in far Dodona, where the priests, who sleep on the ground, interpret the rustling of leaves and cooing of doves in the branches to tell mortals the will of the father of gods. This oaken beam itself had the power to speak.

Next came the "Argonauts"—sailors of the *Argo*—the bravest heroes of their time. First to arrive was Herakles, fresh from his latest labors. Kastor the horseman and Polydeukes the expert boxer, twin brothers of Helen, came together, as did Zetes and Kalais, the handsome winged sons of the North Wind, Boreas. Idas came forth with his brother Lynkeus, who had the power to see through any object, and could view even things buried underground. Idmon the seer, who told the future, joined the expedition, with Mopsos, another prophet. Ekhion and Eurytos, sons of Hermes, came. So did Periklymenos, the nephew of Pelias—a useful fellow, who could change his shape at will. From all over Greek lands, men flocked to Iolkos. Kaineus (once a woman); Laertes (who would later father Odysseus); Peleus (father-to-be of Achilles); Autolykos (Real Wolf), the crafty son of Hermes; Meleager, son of Oineus; Augeias, whose father was the Sun, along with many others. One woman joined them—the hardy Atalanta. For the helmsman, they chose Tiphys, son of Hagnias. And to set the rhythm for the rowers with his music, they called on Orpheus, the master of the lyre.

One day in early summer, the ship was finished. All the gear, food, and water were loaded. The crew marched through the streets of Iolkos on their way to the dock, wearing their bronze armor, which flashed in the sunlight. Crowds jammed the route. "How can Pelias send off the flower of our youth like this?" wondered some. Others prayed that Jason would return to avenge his father. A few thought, "It would have been better if Phrixos drowned along with his sister long ago. And the ram as well."

Jason looked like Apollo that day as he strode up the gangplank, his long hair streaming in the breeze off the water. The *Argo* swayed gently at the dock, like a living thing, a horse waiting to bolt from its stall. But first a captain had to be chosen. "Don't hold back—pick the best man," Jason urged the heroes. One and all, they looked to Herakles. He was the oldest and, as they all knew, the most experienced. But the veteran held up his right hand, saying, "I cannot take this honor. Let the man who gathered us together lead the expedition." So Jason was put in charge. If he minded being the second choice, he never showed it. He, too, realized that he was still young and untried.

They poured libations and offered prayers to Apollo, promising the god rich sacrifices of bulls, at all his major shrines, if they returned unharmed. Then Tiphys took his place at the helm, the heroes sat to their oars, and the sleek ship started off toward the rising sun. Soon they were skimming the dark blue waters of the Aegean. To pass the time, Orpheus began a song—his own "god-birthing" composition, as he called it.

"*Sky and Earth and salty Sea,*
*in the beginning, all were one.*
*Ill will split them, quarreling, anger.*
*Early on, they moved apart.*
*Sun, moon and stars, all took their places.*
*Mountains towered, rivers flowed.*
*Kronos and Rhea came to Olympus.*
*Daughter of Ocean with Snake Man*
*Yielded the kingship. They reigned among Titans.*
*Then came Zeus, an artless boy.*
*Yet the Earth-Born armed him with thunder,*
*the Kyklopes gave him glorious sway.*"

The music infused their bodies, strengthening them, helping them work. By this time they had rounded the ridge of Mt. Pelion. As they left the long promontory in their wake, nymphs from the mountain watched—they had never seen a ship. Cheiron stood, his right hand raised in farewell, the other arm tightly grasping a squirming toddler who had just been entrusted to his care—the son of an Argonaut, a blond boy named Achilles.

They rowed until afternoon, and as they left the shadow of the mountain, the wind began to pick up. They hoisted sail and sped toward their first landfall. Another two days of hard rowing and sailing brought them to Lemnos, the island of Hephaestus. The prospect did not look good as they approached. Bronze-clad warriors on the beach were brandishing swords and javelins. "Thracians," the crew whispered to each other. They had heard of these wild men from the north, a menace in the islands. But these were not men. When the *Argo* got closer, they saw that the figures were smaller and beardless. Even with their helmets on, they were clearly a troop of females. And not Amazons—of that, Herakles assured them.

Stranger still, the women warriors were cheering and smiling as the Argonauts beached their ship. They welcomed the crew and escorted them up to the palace, with Jason in the lead, swathed in a purple cloak with intricate mythic designs. He walked in splendor, like the evening star, that shines brightest in the heavens, the star that young women gaze at from their upper rooms as they dream of lovers to come. When they reached the royal enclosure, Jason expected to meet the king of the island. Instead, his daughter, Hypsipyle ("High-Gate"), emerged from her chamber surrounded by the scent of cedar.

"Do not be surprised, my guest-friend," she began. Jason noticed how young and vivacious the queen appeared. "You are the first men to set foot here for a long time." She went on to explain. When her father ruled, the men of Lemnos had gone on raiding expeditions against the Thracians, who lived on the coast of the mainland. They took not only cattle and grain but Thracian women to be their captives and concubines. Outraged, Aphrodite brought trouble down on them. Back on the island, the men neglected their own wives. They cherished the children of the foreign women more than their own lawful daughters and sons. For a while, the Lemnian women tolerated this. Maybe their menfolk would grow tired and change their minds. But the men persisted. The next time they were out on a raid, their wives on Lemnos locked them out of the city and, when they returned, told them to either come back to their homes or leave Lemnos once and for all. So the men left. "Now they are over in Thrace—and good riddance to them!" said Hypsipyle. "But you could stay with us if you like. It's a fine island—rich corn, plenty of fish and game." She was also thinking of what some older women had advised the other day in their assembly. Without a new generation of men, farmers and fighters, the island would be vulnerable to attack and the fields would lie fallow. It did not take much to persuade Jason and his vigorous crew. Soon, Argonauts and Lemnian women had all come to know one another. An entire year passed, marked by plenty of births.

None of the visitors knew that Hypsipyle's story was misleading. Nor did they seem to think it odd that there were no males around, not even little boys, on the island. Had they also gone on the raids? The truth was that Aphrodite had cursed the Lemnian women because they had neglected worshiping her. She made them smell, and the stink drove off their husbands, who soon found companions among the Thracians. Nor had they been locked out on their return. Instead, they were slaughtered by their wives, who then set about killing every last Lemnian boy so that no male would ever seek vengeance for the murders. Only one man—Thoas, the queen's father—survived. Hypsipyle herself smuggled him out of town, down to the beach, in the dark and packed him into a floating box; Dionysus—the old king's father—took care of him after that.

Happily ignorant of these events, the Argonauts kept putting off their departure. Herakles grew disgusted. "Have we lost our wits? We could have any wives we want—Greek girls, too, not these crafty foreigners. Is this why we sailed—to settle down like peasants, tilling Lemnos? Do you think the Golden Fleece is going to fly by itself over here to us if we wait long enough? Let's leave Jason in his comfortable bed. Let him populate this place on his own. See what glory that gets him." Not a man could deny the truth behind his words. Each lowered his eyes in shame. Jason, too, came to his senses. One morning the heroes said their farewells, and the *Argo* pulled away from the island forever.

They put in at the next island, Samothrace, at the urging of Orpheus. Sacred mysteries were celebrated up at a shrine hidden in the hills. Astounding displays were said to occur. One could, for example, see metal rings that clung to one another through some mystic power, forming long chains. Blazing lights could be seen, like the fire that runs up the forestays of a ship, the sign that, in our day, tells sailors the Dioskouroi are present. But those twins, Kastor and Polydeukes, were themselves crew members and witnesses back then, so the glowing light came from some other source. The Argonauts were purified, initiated into the secret rites of the island, and sent on their way with the blessings that protect sailors who worship the Great Gods of Samothrace.

Propelled by the winds from Thrace, they reached the Hellespont and passed up the narrow strait into the Propontis, the "fore-sea" that leads to the great expanse of waters to the east. Here further adventures awaited them. Kyzikos, king of the Doliones, a hospitable, god-fearing man, gave them a warm welcome on their arrival at his kingdom. The next day, they had a brief skirmish with some unruly earth-born giants, a remnant of the tribe that once fought the gods. With Herakles' help, they won easily. Another night passed, again with Kyzikos in his banquet hall, and the next morning they set out. But a storm came up, with rain pouring down so hard, the land was lost to view. The *Argo* was battered by the contending winds, blown every which way, until night fell, when the weather grew calm. Tiphys, at the helm, was unsure where to steer. A harbor at last appeared—as it turned out, the very place the Argonauts had left that morning. But this time their arrival was treated like an invasion. Kyzikos and his men, not realizing these were their new friends, swept down with a war cry on the landing party. A battle followed, in which the handsome young leader of the Doliones met his death at the hands of Jason—all of it a terrible mistake. The wife of Kyzikos hanged herself in grief. The Greek heroes lamented as much as did the natives. After that, head winds kept them in port, unable to put out to sea, for twelve straight days, as if the gods were angry. Mopsos, the seer, tried to determine the divine will. From a seabird, passing overhead, he heard a voice: "Worship the Mountain Mother." So he instructed Jason to take sacrificial animals to the hilltop of Dindymon and pray to Rhea (which is what Greeks called the local divinity). The rites were accomplished, the winds dropped to a steady breeze, and the Argonauts continued their voyage east.

They worked their way along the south coast until they reached Kios. Here they stopped, not from any interest in the land, but because Herakles had broken an oar in half as they were rowing hard in choppy water, trying to keep the ship off jagged rocks. While he went into the woods to select a suitable pine tree, one straight and slender, without too many branches, his young companion, Hylas, took the opportunity to find drinking water for the crew. Herakles located the tree he wanted, put down his bow, took off his lion skin, and leaned against the trunk with all his might. The pine tree snapped from the earth, roots and all, as easily as a mast topples when the north wind hits it with a sudden squall. Meanwhile, Hylas had wandered off with his bronze water bucket. He was the youngest Argonaut, a boy really, whom Herakles had taken under his wing after he wiped out the rest of his town and people, the Dryopians. There was a spring a mile or so inland. The nymphs of the woods and mountains went there frequently, when they were hot and tired after dancing with Artemis. One water nymph lived in the spring. She was just breaking the surface, to come out for the evening, when she saw Hylas by the light of the full moon, leaning down to fill his bucket. He was so sweet, a combination of man and child, that the nymph was filled with desire for him. She reached out gently to kiss his soft lips, and gently wrapped her white arm around his neck, pulling him closer, closer—until he fell headfirst into her watery home. Herakles was too far off to hear the splash or his friend's cry. Another sailor, Polyphemos son of Elatos, was closer. At the sound, he pulled his sword and rushed toward the spot. But there was no sign of danger, no wild beasts, no evidence that anyone had been in trouble. All the same, he was sure that had been the voice of Hylas. Polyphemos met Herakles on his return from the woods, the pine oar over his shoulder, and told him his suspicions. Someone had grabbed Hylas, bandits probably, maybe wolves. At the news Herakles threw down the oar and rushed off like a maddened bull, calling his beloved companion's name.

It was already getting near dawn when the crew back on the beach had stowed their fresh supplies and finished a meal. Tiphys checked the winds, then hurried the heroes on board. They took advantage of the rising breeze, raised the sail, and soon were well offshore. But when the sun rose and they sat down to the oars, they discovered that three spots at the rowing benches were empty. Herakles and the other two had been left behind. There was nearly mutiny. "You did it on purpose!" yelled Telamon at Jason. "You knew he would win glory and leave you in the dust. So this was your devious plan—abandon the best man!" He rushed at Tiphys to make him steer the *Argo* back to land. The sons of Boreas held him down, however (something for which Herakles would later punish them). In the middle of the confusion, a great wave smacked the side of the boat, and a booming voice startled everyone. "Men of the *Argo*!"—the rough voice came from the sea itself, where the huge head and torso of a bearded man had risen from the water. It was the prophet Glaukos, son of the Old Man of the Sea. "You must proceed. This was fated, the will of the gods. Herakles must return to Argos to endure his troubles. His destiny awaits. Polyphemos shall found a city in this place. Hylas—he whom the others sought—is now a nymph's husband." With that the sea god slid beneath the waves. A whirlpool of swirling white water marked the spot where he descended. So Telamon and Jason made their peace. The rowers set to work. All afternoon they sweated, until the night came and then they coasted under sail toward the next unknown landfall.

Without much further trouble—a boxing match with Amykos, a local ruffian (whom Polydeukes easily bested), and a skirmish with his friends—the Argonauts sailed through the Bosporos and into the vast Black Sea. They made a landing at Bithynia, where they encountered Phineus. He lived alone near a temple at the far edge of the town, an old blind man with a pathetic history. Once he had been a prophet; he had the gift from Apollo himself. But he told the future too well. He even revealed the sacred will of Zeus. So Zeus blinded him and made sure he had a long life, in which to endure his punishment. The king of gods and men allowed Phineus to receive, as before, splendid gifts of food, endless dishes, from his admirers, all those who still flocked to hear his predictions. But he balanced this blessing in a cruelly tantalizing way. Whenever the feast was laid out before him, and Phineus could have reached out for the most delicious foods, two screaming, ferociously ugly bird-women tore down from the clouds and carried off the offerings in their sharp claws and beaks. Harpies—"Snatchers"—they were called. They left some scraps, enough for the old prophet to live on. Yet even these bits of leftovers they polluted with a foul liquid. No one could approach, the smell was so bad, until the food was eaten or rotted away.

Phineus knew it was the Argonauts as soon as he heard the sounds of tramping feet and clanging armor. He hobbled out of his dingy hut, feeling his way along the path with a stick. "Best of the Hellenes," he called out to them. "You come on your journey at the king's cruel command to find the Fleece. In this I can help. But I beg you, by the gods, do not leave me here, helpless and unaided. Rescue me from my horrid fate." He went on to tell them of his woes. The two sons of the North Wind were especially touched. Phineus, it seemed, was a distant relative of theirs, from Thrace. "You are the most wretched man alive," said one of them, Zetes, "and we want to help. But the gods are jealous about their rights and powers. How can we know this will not bring their anger crashing down on us?" Phineus swore an oath and assured them that divine retribution was not in their future.

The Argonauts quickly prepared a meal, the last the Harpies would ever snatch. Phineus reached out his hand to pick up a bit of food. At that instant, like flashes of lightning, the hideous creatures descended and tore it from his grasp. But the crew shouted and clashed their spears on their shields. The Harpies fluttered around, screeching horribly, then took off toward the west. Immediately, the Boreads flew up to chase them. Zetes and Kalais winged their way over sea and mountains until they came to the Floating Islands, the ugly beast-women always just out of reach of their sword tips. Just as the brothers finally came within range, and were about to chop their monstrous wings, Iris, the rainbow goddess, messenger of Zeus, appeared. "It is not lawful to hunt the hounds of the father," she solemnly pronounced. "I will vouch that they will prey no more." She sealed her oath with a libation of water from the Styx, the underworld river even Olympians dread. She hurried back to Zeus, while the Harpies flew off and hid themselves in a remote Cretan cave.

While this pursuit was going on, Phineus was having his first dinner in years. As in a dream, he greedily ate and drank. When everyone was full, and still waiting for the Boreads, the aged prophet began to speak. "For you to learn everything is not allowed. Zeus does not let the entire truth be known. But what I can tell you, I will. When you sail from this place, the first obstacle will be two great rocks—dark blue and massive. On either side of a narrow strait they sway, always moving toward each other, then a little bit apart. Their clashing is always half-hidden in fog. No ship has ever passed through them. But you might—provided you release a dove just as you get close. If the bird flies through, hit the water hard with your oars and pull for your lives. If she is blocked, back water. You cannot go through. The gods do not wish it. If you try, the *Argo* will be crushed, even if her hull is made of iron."

If they survived that test, Phineus said, they should hold course for the river Rhebas. After that would come a series of exotic places: the island of Thynias, the lands of the Mariandynoi, Sinope, the Amazons, the Chalybes, Aretias. The peoples of the east were innumerable.

Their minds awhirl with the old man's directions, they tried to concentrate on the first ordeal to come, the Clashing Rocks. Soon enough, they reached a place of foaming sea and mist, heard the grinding of stone on stone. Euphemos stood ready at the prow with a quivering dove cupped in his hands. The ship rounded the spur of a jutting cliff—just in time for them to see daylight disappear as the two massive rocks facing them clashed together. All the same, Euphemos released the dove, which flew straight ahead. There was a crash of waves. A fountain of sea spray gushed higher than the *Argo*, and all was hidden in white water. When the mist cleared, they could no longer see the bird—only a tail feather fluttering down the rock face. She had made it through. With a shout, the rowers pulled hard at the oars. On the horizon they could make out the broad expanse of the sea beyond. Meanwhile, a gigantic wave was heading toward the ship. With a deft movement of the helm, Tiphys took it on the starboard quarter, letting the wave lift the *Argo* up and back. As the ship slid down the trough, and the heroes rowed for their lives, though the rocks were closing again, with one last mighty tug the ship shot forward, dashing through the rapidly narrowing open space ahead—but only halfway. With a thud the rocks closed in on either side of the stern, wedging it tight. When the next wave hit, they would be directly in its path, but pinned fast, unable to ride it like the last. The Argonauts would all be drowned. So the story would have ended had not Athena (who had been following at a discreet distance) shoved aside one cliff with her left hand, and with her right given the ship a push from behind—so powerful are the gods. The *Argo* squeezed through, with only the loss of a wood ornament from its stern. Athena, seeing that all were unscathed, flew back to Olympus. The dark Clashing Rocks stayed rooted to the spot, never to join again because one ship had finally managed to clear them.

Still, Jason was shaken. If only he had turned down this challenge! If only the pines to build this ship had never left their mountains! If only Herakles had stayed aboard . . . But such thoughts he kept to himself. He turned his face to the south and felt the warmth of the sun. Then he faced east and called to the companions. "Strike the sea, men. Beat it into gold." The crew gasped and strained, becoming one with their oars. Nothing in life would ever be as satisfying to them as this moment, but they could hardly be expected to know that.

For days they rowed, working like oxen yoked to a plow. They cut a furrow through the sea. One twilight, as they pulled into the island called Thynias, they had a smiling vision. Apollo passed in front of them, his golden hair streaming down, his silver bow and quiver gleaming at his back. He walked on, as if striding on the sea, and disappeared in the direction of his own people, the Hyperboreans, to the far north. The island trembled slightly from his divine steps. The men set up an altar in his honor, sacrificed a ram, poured wine, and sang Apollo's holy song, the *paian,* as they danced slowly in a ring around the smoking hearth.

The journey went on. Comrades began to drop away. Idmon, the soothsayer, was attacked and fatally wounded by a wild boar. The helmsman, Tiphys, died after a brief illness. Ankaios took his place steering.

The wind rose. The canvas bellied out, and the sheets grew taut. The sound of the wind whistling through the rigging banished the clatter and groan of oars. Twelve days passed and they arrived at Sinope, the harbor town named for a nymph who once succeeded in outwitting Zeus. (He had wanted her, and went so far as to promise her whatever she desired. "My virginity," she replied. And so he had been stymied.)

Here, the Argonauts took on board the sons of Deimakhos, who had been stranded ever since they split off from Herakles on his earlier expedition to the east. They were coasting past the country of the Amazons now, where the warrior women lived in tribes. But the young heroes did not stop to wage war.

Ares brought war to them, in another form, when they reached his island one evening. The wind dropped and birds with a wingspan longer than a man's height swooped down like lightning—they inhabited the war god's sacred home.

These hawklike birds could shoot their feathers like arrows. One pierced Oileus in the shoulder and he screamed in pain, dropping his oar. Before his companions realized what was happening, another bird attacked, and then another. Feathers rained down. Klytios tried to pick one up and use it like an arrow on his bow, but though he hit one huge black bird, the feather weapon glanced off its body. Real arrows were just as useless. Then one crew member recalled hearing about the famous deed of Herakles and the Stymphalian birds. A plan was devised: half the crew rowed, while the other men, their bronze helmets gleaming, roofed over the *Argo* by holding aloft their shields and spears, closely packed and impenetrable. They shouted and struck their weapons together. Launching one final wave of deadly feathers, the war birds gave up and flew away. But the Argonauts had to wonder why Phineus had told them to anchor there.

## 40.   A PRIZE AND A PRINCESS

They reached the limits of the great inland sea. By night they came to the river Phasis—the territory of the Kolkhians, the resting place of the Fleece. Beyond were the mountains of the Caucasus range. They heard (or perhaps imagined) the wild screams of Prometheus as the eagle ripped his liver in punishment, somewhere on those high peaks. It only added to the sense of mystery and dread they had begun to feel. Gliding into the shallows, they loosed the stays, unstepped the mast, stowed sail and rigging, and disembarked. Jason took a golden cup in his hands, filled it with wine and drops of honey, then addressed Earth and the souls of heroes past. "Be our protectors, we beseech you," he prayed, while he poured out a libation at the river's mouth. "How we are going to protect ourselves is the problem," said Ankaios when the ritual had ended. "Should we attack? Or can we find some other way, through cunning and intelligence, to defeat Aiêtês and return with the prize?" Jason, deep in thought, did not answer.

While the Argonauts were making themselves inconspicuous at their landing, the goddesses Hera and Athena were also puzzling out a plan. They decided to ask Aphrodite to make her son Eros shoot the king's daughter, Medea, with those arrows that produce in their victim a passionate love. "If she longs for Jason, the mission will succeed," said Hera. "That's the only way to get the Fleece." So they went to the house of the goddess of love, a beautiful golden dwelling that her husband Hephaestus had made for her when they first wed. There they found her alone, combing out her fragrant hair with a golden comb so that it streamed down over her white shoulders. The goddesses explained the situation, each stressing her affection for Jason and hatred of Pelias.

"I'd be glad to help," replied Aphrodite. "But I am not so sure I can get that boy to cooperate. Maybe he'll have more respect for you. He just laughs at me, or else he goes around complaining that I restrict him too much. He never wants to stay at home, and certainly doesn't care about learning his father's craft. He says *he'll* never be a sooty old blacksmith. Right now he's off somewhere with his friends, or out shooting his arrows recklessly about." She spread out her hands and shrugged in desperation. Hera and Athena smiled at one another. Aphrodite, not wanting to appear completely incompetent, continued: "Since it is so important, I'll try to persuade him—that is, if I can manage to locate him." And she went off to find Eros.

His mother discovered the boy in the vineyard, playing dice with Ganymede, the beautiful youth whom Zeus had loved and taken up from Troy to Olympus to be his cupbearer. Eros stood with his knuckle-bone dice cupped in one hand, shaking them in a professional manner. Ganymede, crouched on the ground, was losing. Just as Aphrodite came up, Eros rolled a winning pair and let out a loud laugh. This only made Ganymede more disgusted, and he stalked off. "You shameless little cheat, how could you rook that innocent boy?" cried the goddess as she grabbed Eros by the ear. "Do you want to win something bigger? Go and set on fire the heart of Medea, the princess of Kolkhis, and I'll give you a special prize—the toy that Zeus himself played with when he was a boy, living in the Idaean cave. It's a golden ball, with dark blue swirls, that lights up like a star when you throw it in the air. Even Hephaestus can't make the likes of it." Eros was still enough of a child to be interested. So he dumped his dice in his mother's lap, grabbed his quiver and bow, and set off for earth, far below.

Back in Kolkhis, Jason had concluded a council of the young heroes, where it was decided to try persuasion first. Taking three companions, he set off for the palace. They passed through the swampy ground near the encampment onto slightly higher land, where willow trees grew—a lovely sight at first, until they drew close. From each tree hung a leather bag, tied with rope, containing a corpse. It was a Kolkhian custom, since they thought it an insult to earth or fire to bury or burn their dead.

Thanks to Hera, who had shrouded the group of men in mist, they came undetected to the front gate of the house of Aiêtês. They marveled at the flowering trees; the four separate fountains gushing with wine, water, milk, and oil; the many chambers wrought out of gold and crystal. All these Hephaestus had made as a favor for the king's father, Helios, who had once come to his aid, after the Battle of the Giants. What they did not see was the other gifts of the smith god—two enormous, fire-breathing, bronze-footed bulls and an adamantine plow. But Jason would learn of these soon enough.

When the mist lifted, the crowd of Kolkhians were amazed to find among them these handsome Greek youths. The king and queen came to welcome them. Meanwhile, Eros, who had flown over farmland and sea, passed unseen through the crowd and targeted the king's daughter, Medea, just as she emerged from her chamber to see what all the commotion was. His magic arrow pierced her to the core. Immediately, she burned with love, her heart flaring up just like a fire that a working woman feeds with tinder before dawn when she gets up early to work, and keeps blazing in her hearth as she spins her wool. Medea felt bittersweet pain as she stared at the newcomer, the man who had introduced himself as Jason. He was telling her father of his mission, the journey for the Fleece. "But we will not take it without recompense," he said. "I and my crew are ready to fight for your kingdom against whatever enemies you have."

Aiêtês was at first inclined to kill the Greeks on the spot. It was his kingdom they wanted, of that he was sure. But he thought of a better plan. "It is not right for a brave man like me to give his treasure to just any old pretender. So we'll see how brave you are. There's a deed I can do, and let's see if you can as well. I yoke my bronze-hoofed bulls in the morning and all day long plow the field, and then sow it, but not with seed. Athena gave me half the dragon's teeth that Kadmos once put down in Thebes. Just like his, these cause armed men to spring up. They look like skeletons—except they're tougher than men in armor. I cut them down with my sword before they can get me, and that's my day's work. You must attempt this—or else you'll have to die." Jason was speechless for a long minute. But he recovered his voice and said, "I will," even though he already pictured himself being trampled by those bulls. He signaled to his companions, and they left.

Medea left as well and went back to her chamber, where she lay on her bed, her mind filled by this beautiful man—how he talked, and moved, and looked. When she thought of the way he was bound to die, it hurt her more than the thought of herself being overpowered by the bulls. She prayed for Jason's safety to Hecate, goddess of night, magic, and the crossroads, whom she served as priestess in her temple.

At the very time, one of the Kolkhians, a man whom Jason had found at sea a few days before and transported home, was advising him to seek Medea's help. "She knows all manner of herbs and spells," said this man, who happened to be the young woman's nephew. "She can stop flame and wind. Hecate has taught her how to make the moon stand still." When Jason reached the rest of the crew and told them of his plight, and how Medea might help, there was resistance. "Did we come all the way here to depend on women, instead of war?" shouted Idas. But a sign appeared from the gods: a dove, being chased by a hawk, flew down and fell straight into Jason's lap. The hawk, desperately swerving in his plunge, ran head-on into the stern of the ship

and dropped down dead. "Look how the bird of Aphrodite has survived. So we, too, should take the gentler way," concluded Mopsos,
the seer, as he interpreted this sudden drama. "Ask Medea for her aid."

As it turned out, Medea herself had come up with an excuse already. Shortly after her sister's son, sent by the Argonauts, had visited
his mother Khalkiope, Medea also came to her sister's house. She had
spent a sleepless night, filled with terror over Jason's fate. But she pretended it was for her nephews' sake that she was worried. And, indeed,
Aiêtês was already plotting to burn the *Argo* (once Jason was safely
dead) and then turn against his own grandchildren, as he had heard an
oracle once declare: "You will die by your offspring." Besides, they
were of the blood of Phrixos, the Greek who long ago had imported
the Fleece—what a nuisance *that* had turned out to be.

With her sister's approval, Medea resolved to help the handsome
stranger, even if it meant undermining her own father. Back in her
chamber, she took out her store of potions, selecting a vial of
"Prometheus' charm." Anyone who makes a sacrifice at night to
Hecate, and then anoints himself with this charm, becomes invulner-
able. Neither fire nor bronze can wound him. Once, when the eagle
was returning from his torture of Prometheus, there dripped from his
beak some drops of the *ikhor* of the god (for gods do not have blood).
From this there grew a flower, like a crocus in color, with a dark,
fleshy root. Medea, clothed in black, had squeezed out the juice of this
plant in the dark of night, after bathing in seven rivers and calling on
Hecate, queen of the dead. When she cut the root, the earth itself
groaned, and Prometheus on his crag felt a stab of pain. This was the
gift Medea would bring the stranger.

At the break of day, she bathed and dressed in a shining, fragrant
gown, put on her veil, and went with her serving maids to the shrine
of Hecate at the edge of the city. Word was secretly sent to Jason, who
came at once to find her. Love blazed between them like a comet when
they met. She could hardly speak. Jason, meanwhile, used all his charm
to beg Medea for help, even citing mythic precedent—how Theseus
once was saved by Ariadne. "In the same way will I spread your name
throughout Hellas," the young hero swore.

By now she had melted under his sweet gaze. Shyly, she drew from
her gown the precious vial and revealed to him its secret. She told him
how to use the charm. After bathing in a stream at midnight, he
should dig a pit. Once he had sacrificed a whole ewe for Hecate, he
should pour out honey—and not fear the footsteps he would hear, or

the baying of dogs. He was to mix the potion with water, rub it on himself, then sprinkle his sword, shield, and spear. That way, neither the bulls' fire nor the weapons of the Sown Men would harm him. Her instructions ended, she grew bolder, because she knew how much she was risking. "You say you will remember me—although I have no idea about your Ariadne. If not, and you forget, I will pray for a wind to sweep me away to Iolkos—wherever that is—so I can reproach you face-to-face." Jason had never encountered a woman like this before. He stared for a while, then replied, "You will not need any wind. You will come back with me. The people of my city will worship you as a goddess, seeing that you and you alone saved their menfolk. And you will be my bride." His words pleased Medea deeply, but even as she blushed with joy, she felt a chill of fear, sensing the pain she knew would come.

They parted. Night fell, and Jason carried out the magic rites. The chaos that followed—screams of wood nymphs, the angry barking of hellhounds, sights of serpents and a thousand torches—he steeled himself against them all, and when he had finished the sacrifice, he used the potion on himself and his weapons. Jason could feel the strange new strength in his arms and legs, the divine power throughout his body. In a few hours, he led his crew to the plain of Ares. Medea's father had arrived, glorious as Poseidon, beaming like the Sun. But the confident smile on the face of Aiêtês clouded over when he saw what happened next.

His bulls rushed out of their cave, right for Jason. The Greek, however, held out his shield. When they belched forth fire, nothing burned. Instead, Jason took first one, then the other, by the horn, wrestled them to the ground, and dragged them to the yoke. They raced the length of the field, again and again, throwing up thick clods of earth from a neatly sliced furrow. Onto the new-cut earth Jason scattered the dragon's teeth he had been given. For a time all was quiet. He took a drink of water. He spoke with his men. Then, glancing back at the field (the bulls had been unyoked and driven off), they saw nothing less than an army headed their way, with still more shadowy soldiers swarming up out of the furrows where the teeth had fallen. The field was all agleam, as if the sun were setting, its last rays falling on the corn. But the light came from the armor of the hollow-eyed Sown Ones.

Now Jason's first feat seemed trivial. Even with invincible arms, how could he advance and defeat so many? Then he recalled the last part of Medea's warning—he had dismissed it, it seemed so absurd at the time. Taking a large stone, he threw it into the midst of the inhuman warriors. Like wolves around a kill, they began tearing at it, slamming and kicking and trampling one another in the process. Jason threw another stone. The same thing happened to another group. It had a sort of logic—for men born of teeth, rocks resembled meat. At least it seemed so. Without musing further, Jason took his crew and rushed through the horde of fighters who were bent on killing one another, hewing down as many as they could to help in the mutual slaughter.

## 41.   JASON AND MEDEA

Aiêtês was not about to keep his promise, even though Jason had completed the required tasks. Nor had Jason really expected to be rewarded so easily. The king drove his chariot furiously back to town, while the Argonauts retreated to their beach encampment. That night, Medea secretly left her home for good. Her father was aware that only the help of a sorceress could have given Jason such power, and she knew what the consequences of his rage would be. On reaching the Greek ship, she begged, in a panicked voice, to be taken aboard. They welcomed her, and set out at once for the grove, farther upriver, in which the Golden Fleece hung from an ancient oak. The ram's skin was as brilliant as the day that Phrixos first dedicated it, ruddy gold, like a western sun. But as Jason and Medea approached, they heard a tremendous hiss. A gargantuan snake loomed up between them and the object of the quest. Roll upon roll of its thick body uncoiled. His jaws opened wide enough to swallow a man whole. Now it was Jason's turn to panic. Medea, however, stared into the snake's yellow eyes and began to chant a spell and prayer to Sleep and Hecate. The snake began to sway. Its coils, which had been tensed to spring, relaxed. For good measure, Medea sprinkled him with a juniper potion. When the snake's head hit the ground in sleep, Jason sprang to the oak and yanked down the Fleece. Then they rushed back to the ship, Jason bearing aloft the golden prize that shone like a torch, illuminating his joyous face.

The next days passed in a blur. Trying to recall them later, Medea was not sure what she had done, or what was enacted by a divinity using her mind and body, or even where she began and Jason ended—

so welded to him did she seem at that time. With his flagship heading a fleet of Kolkhians, her father pursued the *Argo*. Across the sea they winged their way, helped by a breeze that Hera stirred up. They managed to lose half the enemy fleet by dodging into a narrow river passage, and then decided to follow this inland waterway. After all, Phineus had instructed them to return home by a different route from the way they came. But the other half, led by Apsyrtos, Medea's brother, discovered their plan and gave chase, blocking the river mouth. They could not go back even if they wanted.

The Argonauts took sanctuary at a shrine of Artemis. Most were for a compromise: they would keep the Fleece, but Medea would be left in safekeeping with the priestess here until some judgment could be made as to whether she must return home. Medea reacted with threats and curses. They would never abandon her, and if they did, they would never make it back. She would haunt them all her days. Then, harnessing her wrath, she proposed a plan to Jason. She would lure her brother to a grove where Jason and his men could cut him down. And so that night, while his sister occupied him with a story of abduction, Apsyrtos was butchered on an island in the river. His last act, when he fell beneath Jason's sword, was to smear Medea's veil and gown with his blood. This the Furies, who avenge kin murder, would remember.

Later, there were stories that Medea had diverted the pursuing ships by tossing from the *Argo* portions of her brother's corpse. But that was only to increase her blame. The fact is, Apsyrtos was buried on the spot by Jason, after he had separated the poor man's hands and legs—a precaution to ensure his angry ghost would never walk. All this seemed later like a nightmare to Medea, these ruthless acts that her passion had caused. After the murder of Apsyrtos, the rest of the Kolkhians gave up and scattered.

The voyage became hard after that. Wind and storm and heavy seas showed them the gods' displeasure at their deed. After days of tempestuous weather, the prophetic oak in the *Argo*'s stern spoke out, telling them to seek Circe's island. Only she—Medea's aunt—could purify them.

They made their way up another river, the Eridanos. A foul burning smell was everywhere, and at night, the shrill cries of the daughters of Helios surrounded them. For this was where Phaethon had fallen—Phaethon, who once in his folly tried to drive his father's chariot. While living with his mother, Klymene, he was insulted by other

boys who said, "The Sun is not really your father. You're a bastard."
So he went off to prove his identity, journeying through Ethiopians
and Indians until he came to the palace of Helios. His father promised
anything he wanted, but regretted it when Phaethon made his choice.
Nevertheless, he taught the boy to drive, telling him not to fear the
dizzying heights or the beasts he would encounter in the sky—Bear
and Scorpion, Lion and Bull. Phaethon was supremely happy. He
mounted the gem-studded chariot and flicked his whip on the backs
of its four shining horses, Aithon, Eous, Pyroeis, and Phlegon. But the
steeds of the Sun ran off as though no driver ruled them; they felt no
weight in the car they pulled. Careening through the sky, Phaethon
froze in terror and lost control. The burning bright chariot of the Sun
plunged close to earth. Mountains and cities were set ablaze, rivers
and seas dried up, the earth cracked open. Gaia called on Zeus for relief. His only solution was to strike down Phaethon with a thunderbolt. The boy plummeted into the Eridanos. His sisters, weeping
continually after on the river's banks, were turned to poplars. Their
tears flowed out of the trunks and turned to amber. The story haunted
the somber landscape through which the Argonauts now were rowing.

North and west, day after day, they pushed on, one unmapped
river leading into another, until they were deep in the country of the
Celts. Then they took a sharp bend southward and after another week
they had reached the sea again, on the far side of Italy. Exhausted with
working the oars, they gladly spread sail. Soon they came to the island
of Aiaia. They found Circe purifying herself on the beach, for she had
dreamed during the past night of bloodred rooms and poison and
flame. Around her on the shore were flocks of creatures—they looked
like sheep, but something resembling a human look appeared in their
eyes. The famous nymph, the sister of Aiêtês, took them to her home.
She knew already who they were, for she had recognized Medea. All
descendants of Helios have eyes that flash like the sun. She also knew
why they had come. Holding a piglet over their heads, she cut its
throat and let the blood fall on the couple. She made the proper
prayers to Zeus the Purifier, with offerings of wine and cakes so that
the Fury might be appeased. With warning words, she saw them off.

With the help of Hera and Thetis, they passed Scylla and Charyb-
dis, and more wandering rocks. The Sirens posed a greater threat. A
Muse (Terpsikhore) had produced these divine singers after loving the
river god Akheloos. Once they had been the companions of Persephone, before her rape. Now, like beautiful seabirds, they inhabited

the rocks and lured sailors to their death with their sweet, delicate voices. As the *Argo* neared the spot where their music poured forth, the crew made ready to row in hard and beach the ship—even though landing was clearly impossible on the dangerous crags. Orpheus came to the rescue. He grabbed his lyre and struck up a loud, rapid tune, drowning out the Siren voices in the nick of time. He was too late, however, for one oarsman. Boutes, overcome and seduced by the women's sounds, had leapt from the ship and started swimming toward the rocks. His fellow Argonauts could not help him. (Later, it was said that Aphrodite plucked him from the waves. The Greeks never saw that and assumed he died.)

At the island of the Phaeacians, they were welcomed royally. Here Jason and Medea celebrated their wedding, spending their first night in a sacred cave, with nymph attendants, amid flowers, incense, and gold. From there it was a short way home. But fortune turned. A wild squall came up, accompanied by continuous north winds. The ship was driven for nine days, far past the land of Pelops, all the way to Libya and the deadly gulf of Syrtis, where the shoals and seaweed, the fly-infested standing water, doom whatever vessels wander in. The *Argo* ran aground, its hull wedged in the sand. There was no help for hundreds of miles; no water and little food. The crew began to lose hope, to resign themselves to a humid, slow death.

Jason, like the others, had wrapped his head in his cloak against the piercing sunlight. He felt a breeze, or a touch, and then a soothing voice. "Son of Aison, why this despair? We know all you suffered on the sea and on the land in your quest for the Fleece. You will not perish. We are the Heroines of Libya, her daughters." He threw off his cloak and looked around—there was no one. But the voice continued. "Poseidon's consort will release you. Then you must repay your mother, who carried you so long in her womb, in order that finally you may find your home." These last words were obscure, but the divinity fell silent.

Jason stood up and called like a madman for his men. He told them of the voice and the strange instruction. Before any could object that he was sunstruck or crazed, another marvel happened. Out of the sea a wonderful, golden-maned horse galloped toward them, halted, shook itself, and ran off to the west. Taking this as a sign of Poseidon's goodwill, Jason confidently turned his mind to the Heroines' riddle. Their "you" had been plural—yet he himself had no siblings. What was this "mother," then, if not the very ship in front of him, half-covered by sand, its halyards hanging limp, in whose insides they had spent the last four months? And so he ordered his men to "repay" the *Argo*; they would lift her, as she had borne them. For twelve days they panted and struggled through the desert, ship on shoulders. Only immortal heroes could have done it. They came to Lake Tritonis at last. Here they made an offering of the divinely made tripod, a gift from Apollo, that they had carried with them since before Kolkhis. In return, Triton, god of the place, showed them the exit to the sea that they had been seeking. Like a massive whale, he pushed their ship from beneath, speeding it on its way. They quickly came to the Aegean once again, and in two days' time they made landfall on Crete.

Or almost. For they could not come close enough to throw out stern lines. A giant bronze warrior held them off, heaving huge stones in the direction of the *Argo*. His name was Talos, and he was the last of the Race of Bronze. Zeus had given him as a present to his former lover, Europa, whom he had once brought to the big island. Talos was to guard Crete by running around its perimeter three times a day. He had a single more human characteristic—a solitary vein, running from neck to ankle, plugged at the bottom with a bronze nail. Medea made short work of him with her spells, so that he became disoriented, hit his foot on a rock, knocking the nail loose, which drained all the *ikhor* from his body. Talos swayed like a forest pine and crashed to the ground.

After a few days, they arrived at last in Iolkos. The joy that flooded Jason's heart on seeing once again the familiar harbor, with Mt. Pelion in the background, froze into grief when he landed. Word came to him that his parents had both died. Aison had been hunted down in the hills by the evil Pelias, who still feared that his half brother might gain the kingdom. The poor, aging man killed himself by drinking bull's blood rather than face slaughter. His wife hanged herself, after heaping curses on her enemy's head.

Now, at least, the curses would be fulfilled. Jason worked cautiously. With humble grace, he handed over to Pelias the Golden Fleece. Then he left Iolkos with his loyal crew and Medea, sailing to the Isthmus of Corinth, where they dedicated the *Argo* to the god of the sea—part thanks offering and part proud monument to display the heroic prowess of the Argonauts. On the way back north, he spoke often with Medea, plotting ways to destroy Pelias before the king had the chance to eliminate them first.

On their last evening away, the young woman told him: "I have

the solution. We'll need an old ram and a good-sized cauldron. Leave the rest to me." She smiled in that glinting sideways manner, her sun-blazing eyes flashing in the dusk. So it was that the great "rejuvena-tion" was staged. Medea, smart as she was, had already figured out that Pelias was afraid he would never get a male heir. Meanwhile, her own reputation for spells and enchantment had spread through town, as the story of Jason's journey and his new bride got around. "Yes, I know some tricks, but my magic cannot produce a son," she modestly told the king's daughters one day as they were passing the time. (Nei-ther side had made the last, fatal move. Pelias actually was letting Jason stay in the palace.) "One thing I *can* do is make people younger—in fact, maybe your father would appreciate that. You'd have to help, of course."

The daughters of Pelias thought that was a fine idea, so Medea gave them a demonstration. Taking the old ram that Jason had found, she slew it, cut it up into fist-sized bits, filled a cauldron and boiled water, and cooked the ram with some secret potions. She waited an hour, drained off the water, let the cauldron cool, and reached in, pulling out a live newborn lamb. "It's not too difficult, though he's still a bit warm to the touch," she explained, taking care to point out the telltale markings that the ram (now lamb) had on its ear and forehead. "You can see for yourself: it's the very same animal." All they had to do, Medea told the girls, was convince Pelias (or failing that, surprise him as he slept), slice him up just so, and carry out the rest of the recipe instructions. By the time the daughters did the deed, Medea and Jason were well out of town. Pelias, of course, never made it back out of the cooking pot.

For ten years Jason and his Kolkhian wife lived quietly in Corinth, raising two sons (their names were Mermeros and Pheres). At first people were curious about the hero and his foreign bride, but as the adventure story passed into myth, the real man, now approaching middle age, seemed forgotten. His sons listened to the *Argo* tale with less and less interest, being mainly concerned with their dogs and horses. Jason spent more and more time in the agora, discussing political news with other displaced aristocrats. Perhaps that is why he seemed like a good choice when Kreon, king of Corinth, was looking for someone to wed one of his younger daughters. Jason had the right pedigree. Besides, it would be wise to have him in the family rather than a potential source of disgruntled opposition. That he was already married seemed not to bother Kreon, nor for that matter, Jason, for whom the prospect of a royal match grew dazzlingly attractive. He accepted the betrothal, but neglected to tell Medea.

Of course, she found out soon enough. She had never been so insulted. For a long time she lay in her inmost chamber, moaning, seeing no one, inconsolable. But her eyes blazed fiercer than ever. Jason tried to rationalize the divorce. He only wanted to protect his sons, make sure they had the advantages of wealth and power. Medea pointed out—her rage barely restrained—that she, and no other, had been the one who enabled Jason to win the Fleece; that she had left her home and parents for him, and worse yet, helped to kill her own brother. Then there was the murder of Pelias—and worst of all, the oaths that Jason had sworn to cherish her always. Had the gods changed? Did oaths no longer count? Jason tried to argue still. After all, it was Aphrodite who really helped him. The goddess used Medea as a clever tool. And hadn't she, a foreigner, a barbarian, benefited from learning Greek ways, living in a civilized place? She was even famous, thanks to his expedition, and fame was worth more than all the money in the world. He would help her, give her letters of introduction to friends abroad. He wanted her to know, however, that she was not helping her case by making vague threats.

As it turned out, her threats were nothing compared to how the story ended. After Medea had persuaded Kreon to let her stay just one more night in Corinth (for he thought her dangerous, and wanted her to leave), she set to work. "Here is a present for the princess"—that is what, in a few hours, she told her sons. "Take it, and make sure she herself is the only one to receive it." Glauke, the king's daughter, was annoyed to see her rival's sons come to the palace, but delighted on opening the package and finding a fine-woven silk gown and golden diadem—a peace offering, she was told. She put them on right away. She took a turn around the room, smiling dreamily, checking her hem and hair. Then she fell, as if in a faint. A servant rushed to get the girl's father. An awful glow began to fill the room. It came from the diadem and the new silk gown, which gave forth a blue-white flame, like coals in a cooking fire. Glauke sprang up, shrieking in pain, frantic, grabbing at the crown and dress. But the more she pulled, the more they clung and burned. Flame and flesh melted together. Transfixed, no servant dared to touch her. Kreon, running into the room, embraced his dear daughter, calling her name and clawing at the poisoned gifts from the Kolkhian witch. He could not take them off her. Instead, they adhered to his skin as well, and like his daughter, he was annihilated, in the most horrible way, dissolving to mere bones.

Medea, hearing this reported, was pleased. "No one laughs at the granddaughter of the Sun," she exulted. Her next act was more painful. It is still unclear what drove her—whether she felt her sons would soon take the brunt of Corinth's revenge, or whether she wanted to cause Jason the ultimate wound. She killed the boys. Then, bearing their fresh corpses in her arms, she ascended into the skies in a chariot drawn by two dragons, supplied by her grandfather Helios. She fled to Athens, where she insinuated herself into the royal household of Aegeus.

As for Jason, an inglorious end awaited. He spent his last days revisiting the *Argo*, a rotting hulk now, still beached at the Isthmus where he and his fellows had pulled it ashore years ago. One afternoon, as he was dozing in the shade beneath the stern, half dreaming of Lemnos, and Libya, and the old days, a heavy chunk of wood broke off the boat, struck his head, and killed him—the "Healer," the former hero.

# BOOK EIGHT

## THE SAGA OF

## THEBES

TODAY, THEBES IS A SMALL, dusty town off the road between Athens and Delphi. It was an important palace site in Mycenaean times (circa 1500–1200 B.C.) and a leading power for many years later. But the ancient city of Thebes is best known for its reputation in the Greek mythic imagination, where it plays a key role as a place of conflict and confusion.

The paradoxical nature of the place can be seen in the extremes one meets there. It is the birthplace of Dionysus, the dangerous but attractive god of wine and the growth of vegetation. But it is also the place where Dionysus caused a mother to kill her own son. It is the spot where the world's most beautiful wedding took place, when Kadmos married a goddess, Harmonia. But the necklace given to the bride, passed down over generations, helped trigger the city's sufferings in a fratricidal war. Aside from these oppositions, there are odd repetitions of motif that seem to surface like repressed memories. The original inhabitants of Thebes were survivors of a battle among men who sprouted from the earth (for upper-class Thebans, like Athenians, claimed to be autochthonous). Later, the Seven against Thebes expedition entails another battle among men sprung from the same source. Kadmos, at the start of Theban mythic history, slays a dragon; at the end of his life, he turns into a serpent. The madness caused by Dionysus seems to come again in the recurrent madness of Herakles, the hero most associated with Thebes. Within one lifetime Teiresias is man, then woman, then man again.

The sense that there is psychological realism underlying many Theban stories has partly to do with their depictions of the way in which misfortune runs in families, ones that are often clearly dysfunctional. A prominent symptom seems to be the disordered relations between adults and children. Niobe unwittingly brings down destruction on her sons and daughters by boasting about them. Laios brings a curse on his entire house through his relation with another man's son. Because the mother of Teiresias happens to be a companion of Athena, the son stumbles onto the wrong scene and is blinded. And then, of course, there is Oedipus.

As the twentieth century dawned, the psychoanalyst Sigmund Freud began to mine the Oedipus myth for deeper truths in his *Interpretation of Dreams* (1900). As he elaborated the idea later on, Freud pinpointed the ages of three to five as the time at which young boys develop a desire to get rid of their father and "possess" their mother. (An analogous father-daughter relation he later named the Elektra complex, after the young woman who kills her mother Klytaimnestra in the myths of the house of Atreus.) The outright expression of this desire is short-lived and eventually repressed; the growth involved in dealing with the complex represents a key developmental step for the child's psyche. But for Freud the marks of this struggle remain in each person's unconscious.

Characteristically, Freud combined personal clinical experience with literary sophistication in citing as evidence for the underlying desire the (alleged) frequent occurrence of the motif of incest in patients' dreams, and the powerful effect that the ancient Greek tale of Oedipus has always had on audiences. Freud's reading of the Oedipus story—which he equated with one deservedly famous version of the tale, the drama by Sophocles (427? B.C.)—is profound, but also profoundly problematic. The drama, first of all, focuses not on the actual story of how Oedipus unknowingly killed his father and married his mother, but on the discovery of these painful events by Oedipus, now king of Thebes, years after they happened. If anything, the play is more like a psychoanalytic session, dredging up and purging the past, than it is an enactment of desire. Second, as Lowell Edmunds has pointed out, when compared with other ancient versions of the Oedipus tale, and worldwide folktale renditions of the same motifs (parricide and incest), the full story of Oedipus is not one of infamy, degradation, and revulsion so much as it is a paradoxical reflection on the way in which transgressing boundaries brings about a recognition of the need for limits. Oedipus, seen at his death (as in Sophocles' last play, *Oedipus at Colonus*), becomes a holy and heroic protector of the territory that entombs him. Freud thus has centered his interpretation on only part of the full tale. In his later career, he wove his own personal mythic version around the darkest side of the Oedipus tale, presenting in *Totem and Taboo* (1913) a theory about the origin of culture: a putative first parricide gave rise to feelings of remorse and guilt, shared by the horde of the sons of the father, and these feelings in turn, Freud speculated, produced all human moral sense, art, ethics, and religion.

In the mid-twentieth century, another interpreter saw in the wider story of Thebes a model for the way in which myth seeks to grapple with deep problems of culture. The French anthropologist Claude Lévi-Strauss (1908–94), a pioneer in the "structuralist" analysis of myth and society, pointed out in a 1955 article that most of the episodes in Theban mythic history can be arranged into a single signifying structure, like a code or analogy, based on central themes. "Overvaluation" of kin (as in Kadmos' search for his sister or Antigone's decision to die for burying her brother) is balanced by undervaluation (as in the tales of fratricide). In the same way, writes Lévi-Strauss, an origin from One (the earth, in autochthony) is juxtaposed in Thebes with problematic origins from Two (father and mother). The entire myth complex, in this view, attempts to transform an unsolvable problem (where do humans come from?) into a more tractable behavioral question (how should one treat kin?). The anthropologist's main focus was on contemporary cultures of the Amazon region, and on the ways in which myth functions as a cognitive tool. His single, rather densely argued incursion into the interpretation of Greek myth has nevertheless been highly influential.

## 42. Two Foundations

The city of Thebes and the stories that swirl around it have always been peculiar. What happened there, over the years, sometimes resembles the nightmares of the rest of Greece packed into one place. Even its beginnings are not easy to understand. Two stories are told, seeming to contradict each other—but, then again, Thebes has been built on contradictions.

According to some, Kadmos was the founder of the city. When his sister, Europa, was carried off by a bull while playing by the sea, their father was devastated. Not knowing that the bull was really Zeus and that he had headed to Crete, where Europa would produce a royal line, the king summoned his sons and ordered them to search the world to find the girl. "Don't come back until you do," he added. The sons went separate ways from Sidon. Phoinix and Kilix did not go far from home. After some time, when they had failed to discover their sister's whereabouts, both settled down and named regions for themselves: Phoenicia and Cilicia. Kadmos, on the other hand, who had a special affection for Europa, would not give up, and wandered all the way to Thrace. Perhaps it was because his mother, Telephassa, insisted. She traveled with him, also determined not to go back until successful. After years of scouting the new country, she grew weary and sick. On her death, Kadmos moved on.

At last he came to Delphi, center of the world. (The Greeks knew this because Zeus had once sent two eagles from the opposite edges of the earth, flying at equal speed, toward each other. Delphi is where they met, and the holy *omphalos* or "navel" stone marked the spot.) Kadmos, no longer the young man he was, but still unwilling to give up his search, asked the Pythia at Apollo's sacred shrine for news of his sister. As usual, the oracular reply was anything but clear: "End now your quest. Europa is safe in the land of the bull. Your line is from the cow. A cow you should follow." Part of this Kadmos could puzzle out. His great-great-grandmother was Io, whom Hera, in a fit of jealousy, had changed into a heifer long ago. But what was meant by finding a cow to track? Always obedient—and in this case more than a bit curious—he went off to see if he encountered a likely animal.

Before long he did, while still in the region of Delphi. She was standing by the path when Kadmos came hiking over a ridge, a ruddy cow with white markings like crescent moons on her flanks, and a gentle face. Could this be his sister? Stranger things had happened, at least in myths. With a flick of her tail, the cow began to trot off, pausing at a short distance to see if Kadmos was keeping up. So this was the one, clearly a guide. Kadmos took up his spear and hurried behind, and with him went a number of companions he had led from Thrace. The Pythia had said that he should establish a city on the spot where the cow lay down to rest. But this animal was choosy about where she lay. For days men and beast circled through Boeotia ("Cow-Land" as it came to be called) until at last, her tired legs wobbling, the cow sank down on a grassy spot in the plain.

"Now for a feast," said the leader to his men, "of cow. We'll make a fine sacrifice to Athena." He had abandoned as unlikely any thoughts of kinship with the annoying animal. While he prepared a makeshift altar, his companions went to a spring nearby to draw water for the ritual. But soon their screams, and the sound of clashing bronze, brought Kadmos running. He burst through the brush just in time to see a wicked-looking dragon, the size of a small hill, swallowing a man and swiping up another, while the remainder of the work detail stood by helplessly, paralyzed with fear. Without a second thought, Kadmos grabbed a spear from one of them. Running in close under the belly of the beast, he chose his spot and rammed home the bronze tip. It bent backward—not even a dent was made. Then he seized hold of a jagged rock lying at his feet. With one mighty hurl he drove it into the scaly gut that towered over him. Gore gushed out and after what seemed like an hour the monster howled and collapsed headfirst, nearly crushing them all. This must have been what Apollo once faced, the time he conquered Pytho and founded Delphi— but he was a god, and they were simply hungry, thirsty, frightened mortals.

Athena's sacrifice went on as planned. As happened in the old days, when the gods themselves on occasion came to join in human meals, Athena appeared to them. "You did well to overcome the great snake of the Spring of Ares," she told Kadmos. "Now, to complete the deed, you must take out the dragon's teeth. Give me half. Then scatter the rest on the earth, once you have made several shallow furrows. This will be Thebes' first crop." As you can imagine—since it was her half of these same teeth that Athena gave to Aiêtês—the crop that sprang up consisted of fierce armed warriors, an earth-born cohort of dangerous *Spartoi*—"Sown Men." Just as Jason was to do at a later time, Kadmos solved the problem of these instant enemies by tossing stones into their midst. One of the band, thinking himself under assault, turned on another, whoever he thought hit him with the rock, and slew him on the spot. Then another pair did the same, and another, until there was general chaos and slaughter and only five fighters left standing— all while Kadmos and his companions looked on in wonder.

Because he had slain a child of Ares—for that was the parentage of the great dead snake—Kadmos was forced to serve the god for an "eternal year," an old-fashioned period of punishment equaling eight of our own years. Meanwhile, the Spartoi became the founding fathers of Thebes, taking girls of the region for wives, and eventually every citizen of Thebes could trace his lineage to Earthling (*Khthonios*), Groundling (*Oudaios*), Snakish (*Ekhion*), Monster (*Pelor*), or Superman (*Hyperenor*)—the original five Sown Men. After his exile, Kadmos was rewarded by the very god for whom he slaved. Ares generously gave him the daughter he had fathered with Aphrodite. She was superb— a white-armed, long-haired beauty, with big eyes (like a gentle cow's, thought Kadmos). Her name itself was music to the ear: Harmonia. All the gods came to his wedding feast, each bringing the bride a special gift. They celebrated in the house of Kadmos (which the later Thebans preserve to this day). The Muses, in their golden chaplets, sang hymns praising the handsome couple. Kadmos presented Harmonia with a thin gold necklace that he had obtained from the craftsman Hephaestus. No one could foresee—except perhaps the gods—that this stunning piece of jewelry would one day bring destruction to the newlyweds' city.

That is the first account. Perhaps the second story of the founding of Thebes complements it rather than contradicts it. For it, too, involves music and initial harmonies. Like many tales, it starts with a river. In this case, it was Asopos, the father of three famous nymphs. Aigina was loved by Zeus, who took her to an island (named after her) where their lovemaking was to produce the royal line of Peleus and his doomed son Achilles. Her twin sister was Thebe, who lent her name to the new city. And the third girl was called Antiope. Zeus was taken with a passion for this sister also. When it was discovered she was pregnant, she fled in shame to Sicyon, near Corinth, with a mortal, Epopeus, who had fallen in love with her. The family could not tolerate this. A man named Lykos was sent to retrieve her, by any means possible. He took his job seriously. After sacking Sicyon, he took away Antiope in chains. The journey back was complicated by the fact that the runaway girl was in her final stage of pregnancy and could move only with difficulty. Within a few days of taking to the road, she felt labor pains. At a spot called Eleutherai, in Boeotia, she gave birth to twins. The cruel Lykos immediately took them to a hilltop to expose them. He assumed they were by Epopeus (whom he had recently killed) and was not taking any chances of starting a future vendetta. He gave scarce credence to Antiope's story, that these were twin sons of almighty Zeus—all guilty girls made the same claim. He had the grace to wait one day, then packed her up, took her home, and with his wife, Dirke, kept her imprisoned (as there seemed to be a dispute about the payment for his services).

You hear only about the exposed children who survived. Sadly, there were many who never did. It is difficult to imagine the scope of loss—what would-be heroes and heroines, athletes and poetesses, perished in the wild, cast out for being inconveniently born. The twin sons of Antiope were among the fortunate. A cowherd, on the track of a lost heifer, crossed the very hill where Lykos had hastily, an hour before, disposed of the baby boys. He took them back to his cottage, and the twins grew up to be fine men. Zethus took after his father—he was a born cattleman. Amphion, on the other hand, encountered that tricky cattle rustler Hermes early one morning, and got from him a lyre. All his days were taken up with making music, to his brother's disgust. "What good will that ever do?" he would say. "You'll starve if you don't work. Here, help me with this manure."

Antiope, meanwhile, passed her miserable days as a slave of Lykos. People began to forget why she was even there. The owners kept her locked up at night without really remembering what her offense had been. They just knew they had never been paid, and the debtor family had died off or moved away, and they needed a servant. Then one night, as Antiope was on the verge of falling asleep, as if by some unseen hand, her chains were gently removed. They dropped to the floor. Realizing this was her chance to escape, she made her way out of the house. In a dream, or trance, she trusted a deep, unspoken voice that fixed her direction—straight for Eleutherai, where sixteen years earlier her boys had been abandoned. One evening thereafter, the young men heard a knock at the door of the farmhouse, and when they went to answer, they found a tired-looking woman asking for a place to stay. They took her in. After the meal she related her story—which at first struck the twins as bizarre. But as the night wore on, the old cowherd, who still lived with them, began to pay more attention. The details about the sack of Sicyon, the mysterious birth—it all began to fit. He glanced more frequently, in the half-light from the fire, from this stranger to his sons and back again. The cheekbones, noses, even the slight outthrust of the chin, all corresponded. There were no tokens of identity, a scar or such, to prove it. But, without question, his boys were hers.

After their tears of celebration, Amphion and Zethus decided to go back with their mother to punish Lykos and his wife. The man they killed outright, but his wife, Dirke, the jealous mistress who had tormented Antiope, they tied to the horns of a bull. Then they goaded the animal with sticks until it ran wild, dragging Dirke to her death. The body was thrown into a hidden spring of water, the one the Thebans call by her name. A killing near fresh water was followed by a foundation—just as the story of Kadmos told. The young sons of Zeus began to build the city. Zethus grunted and strained at lifting rocks that no one nowadays could carry, moving armfuls that looked higher than hills. But that was nothing compared to Amphion's contribution. He played on his lyre and the rocks followed. A cliff here, a quarry there—all it took was a few tunes to make them move. So music erected the walls of Thebes, the only city ever built by art.

## 43.   Family Misfortunes

You have heard of Pentheus, how he was torn apart by the wild women of Dionysus, and of Aktaion, shred to bits by his own hunting dogs, of Ino and her mad leap into the sea. Disasters befell these daughters and grandchildren of Kadmos. Perhaps as compensation, or because his wife was divine, Kadmos came to a better end, although somewhat strange. After Dionysus punished Thebes, the aging king and his consort went into exile in Illyria, far over the mountains to the northwest. There they became the leaders of a warlike people, the Enkheleis. Under their rule, the warriors raided city after city, even threatening at one point the oracle of Delphi, a fight they would surely have lost. Before the assault, as it turned out, Ares took his daughter and her husband away to the Isles of the Blessed, where Zeus turned them both into ordinary snakes. If you believe that is odd, the alternative is odder: Kadmos and Harmonia shrank into serpent form even before they led a new nation, and that their loyal Enkheleis (the "Eel People") tramped about following an ox cart on which the honored snake couple rode. That's an interesting end for the hero who slew Ares' dragon.

After this followed another case of grief leading to transformation in Thebes—or perhaps before it, Theban time being so different from the norm. Zethus had married Thebe and named the newly constructed city after her. Their marriage was happy and uneventful. His brother, Amphion, took for wife a woman named Niobe. This had a graver outcome. She was the daughter of Tantalos, who would end up as a model of wrongdoing, punished in the underworld. At that time he was living in western Asia, among the Lydians. Somehow Amphion heard of the girl's great beauty and sent for her to wed. The couple flourished; they had many children. People lost count. Seven boys and seven girls, most say, but others tell of numbers from five to twenty. At any rate, they were not fated to live long. Niobe, in her pride and joy, once boasted, "Even Lêto could not match this family, and she is a goddess! Look at her, with only a set of twins!" Niobe and Lêto were actually friends, for in those days it was not uncommon for Olympians to visit humans. Her own father, Tantalos, got in trouble precisely because the gods often treated him to divine meals. But this boast of Niobe's overstepped the boundary between mortal and divine. Hearing about it, Lêto was livid. She went to find her children, Artemis and Apollo, and told them of the insult, goading them to uphold her honor: "If she wants to be famous for producing like a rabbit, let's see how she likes a hunt." Grimly, the twins undertook the ugly mission, for they feared a mother's power. Apollo ambushed the seven sons while they were out with their hunting dogs on Mt. Kithairon. All died by his arrows. Then the god went to help his sister. She had found the seven daughters in their home at Thebes, the young ones playing, the older girls doing chores. Before their mother's eyes, she shot them down one by one. Apollo saw the last girl cowering behind a pillar and helpfully pointed her out to Artemis. Cruelest of all, they spared Niobe, in order that she be driven crazy by her grief. Either that, or they ignored her feelings, since gods never have to die and sometimes cannot fathom human suffering. Niobe left Thebes to go back home, where her father took her in. Every day she would wander in the hills, in complete distraction, out of her wits. Every day she prayed to Zeus to end her grieving until one morning, as she sat on a ridge of Mt. Sipylos, pouring forth her laments, the father of gods took pity and answered her prayers, changing her to granite. The shape of the crying woman can still be seen in the rock, pouring forth water like hot tears from the cold stone.

After Amphion died, a lonely, childless man, the kingship of Thebes reverted to another, from an ancient bloodline: Laios, son of Labdakos, son of Nykteus, son of Khthonios. The lineage traced back to the soil of the place. His father seems to have died in the disturbances surrounding the destruction of Pentheus, and the son was exiled for a time in a region to the southwest, in Elis at the court of Pelops, another child of Tantalos. Pelops entrusted his own son, Khrysippos, to the care of the Theban. Laios was an expert chariot driver, and could teach the boy the skills needed for racing a four-horse rig. But Laios became infatuated with his pupil. The lessons grew longer and longer. He could not stand to be apart from the boy. One day, as they were on the way to the games near Corinth, where Khrysippos was to compete, his tutor took over the reins. He kept driving, past the road that led to the festival. He kidnapped his student, taking him off to a secret lair. There was no mention of demands for ransom. What happened later no one knows for sure. Some say Khrysippos died from shame. His father, Pelops, called on all the gods in anger, solemnly cursing Laios, so that he and his descendants would pay by their suffering. That was the start of the worst period of woes for the people of Thebes.

When the curse began to work, it was another Theban who saw in events the hand of the god. The seer, Teiresias, traced his ancestry back to Oudaios of the Sown Men. He was blind, but had the gift of inner sight, by which he could tell events yet to come. There are two accounts of how he came to lose his sight—like most stories about the city of Thebes. One version says that his mother, a nymph named Khariklo, used to be a friend of Athena. While his mother spent time out in the country with the goddess (which was itself unusual, since Athena prefers cultivated places), the young Teiresias stayed close, nosing about in the hills with his dog. Then mother and son would meet up at the end of day and go back to town. It was a pleasant arrangement. One day, after playing hide-and-seek with his pet, climbing trees, shooting arrows, and aimlessly amusing himself in general, Teiresias came to a spring—it was called Hippocrene ("Horse Fount")—and stopped to drink. He bent down, scooped up handfuls of water, and quenched his thirst. Only then did he look around. There, not a hundred feet away, was Athena, and she was nude. The goddess and her companions had been cooling off in the waters that pooled out from the source where the boy had paused. He knew one must never gaze on a goddess, yet as he was about to flee, Athena spotted him. With the palm of her hand she struck the water and threw it, in one swift gesture, into his face. Instantly, his sight left him, everything went black.

"No!" shouted Khariklo, close by Athena. But the goddess told her, "No one can see immortals unless we wish it. Your son will never see again. But I can promise this boon. He will be the most renowned diviner, a prophet and interpreter, and when he dies, an aged man, only he among the dead will retain his consciousness, so god-struck is his mind." She added that Artemis, her sister, would have been more cruel, as her encounter with Aktaion would soon show. As a mark of his status, Teiresias was given a cornel-wood staff, with which he managed to walk as easily as one with perfect vision.

The alternate story starts with a staff. Teiresias was not blind until, walking on Mt. Kyllene in Arcadia, he met up with two snakes mating on a path. He took his walking staff and struck them. Instantly, he became a woman. Seven years passed—or perhaps seven life spans. Time does not matter after you learn to tell the future. One day the female Teiresias, walking in the same place, saw the same snakes mating again, and acted in the same way, striking out with her staff. Why was she so insistent? That part the stories do not relate. But the repetition of the gesture transformed the woman back into a man.

Until this point Teiresias was still without the gift. He might have remained an ordinary man had not Zeus and Hera gotten into a fight. It began as a casual discussion and turned into an argument: who enjoys lovemaking more, man or woman? Zeus claimed women obtained more pleasure. Only Teiresias could resolve the dispute, since only he had been of both sexes and lived to tell. His judgment was for Zeus: "Divide Delight in ten, and men get one-tenth; women, the whole." Indignant at this answer, Hera blinded him. As a consolation Zeus gave Teiresias prophetic powers, with the additional gift of long life. And so would he experience all the troubles of his native land that he had himself foreseen.

## 44. SAVIOR AND DESTROYER: OEDIPUS THE KING

Laios, the king of Thebes, married Jokasta, daughter of Menoikeus, a local noble. After several years they still remained childless. So Laios, worried about producing an heir, went up into the mountains to Apollo's oracle at Delphi to find out what he must do. He returned in shock. The Pythia had made a harrowing prediction—that any son of his would grow up to kill him. It was best never to have a child; or if one was born, to let it die at once.

Within a year after his visit to the shrine, a child was born, a boy. Now Laios had to choose whether to disbelieve the oracle or expose the child, to save himself. Moreover, if he saved himself, the kingdom would thereby pass from his line. He might even be driven out before his time, with no sons to defend him, should another usurp the throne. His predicament seemed hopeless, yet Laios chose. Three days after the baby arrived, he asked Jokasta to give it up. She agreed. She wrapped the infant in swaddling bands, knowing these would be its tiny shroud. Before handing the basket with the baby to a shepherd, who was to leave it far out in the hills, Jokasta took one further step. Through the newborn's ankles she threaded a small iron pin, taking it from an old brooch of hers that had come apart. Perhaps she wanted to make it look as if the baby was born maimed, so there was a cause to let him die.

The shepherd did as he was instructed. He carried the basket to the boundaries of Thebes. On the borderlands, pasturage was common to all comers. Men even came from Corinth, driving their flocks up north for the summer grazing. They lived in huts on the mountain-side, spending most of their days drinking, joking, making up tall tales, and making fun of people who lived in towns. Over the years, the Theban shepherd had become friendly with a few of the older for-eigners, so it was natural that he stopped by to chat. When his Corinthian companion asked about the basket, the Theban (whose name has been forgotten) had the good sense to keep his mouth shut concerning the queen, but said merely he was doing someone a favor. "Well, why not do me a favor?" the Corinthian replied. "My master and his wife have been pining for a child. They can't have one. Now I can make them happy—and who knows, I may get a reward." To the Theban's great relief, he took the baby and carried it off with him back to his own country.

As the man had guessed, Polybos and Merope—king and queen of Corinth—were overjoyed with their servant's find. He never told them exactly how he came by the baby, and they never dared to ask for more details. They took the child into their house as their own crown prince, and gave him a name—"Oedipus." It was an odd one, based on the baby's most curious feature, his swollen feet (for that is what the name signified), still puffed up and sore from being pinned. The injury never affected his walking, although Oedipus had two barely noticeable scars. He grew up like any other royal son, proud and a bit arrogant, bold and eager to make a name. And so he would.

Time passed. Laios never had another child. More and more, he wondered what had become of the boy he abandoned. He had doubts about whether he had made the right decision. Oedipus never had doubts, being young—about eighteen—and healthy and a prince of high blood. He was supremely confident until one evening, after a festival, as the nobles sat around drinking and listening to the flute girls play, he started to lecture one man about kingly duties. "Just look at my father—" he began, but was cut off. "Your father?" said a man on the next banqueting couch. "And who would that be?" He snickered, along with a few of the others who were already too drunk to keep a prudent silence. "Not Polybos, I assure you."

Though inflamed, Oedipus resisted the impulse to hit the man. Instead, the next day, he went to his parents to learn the truth—where did he come from? Merope and her husband reassured him. They had the nobles in question disgraced. But his doubts grew. Oedipus had to know. One morning, therefore, he set out to Delphi. He did not learn his parentage, though, even when it seemed the Pythia was on the verge of telling. Something worse was uttered by Apollo's prophetess. "Your father, you will slay. Your mother, you will wed." In horror Oedipus fled from the temple, determined never to return to Corinth, and thus avoid the unspeakable crimes that were foretold.

He set out in the opposite direction, walking in the hot sun when everyone else was slumbering, deep inside their cool houses or under the shade of olive trees in the fields. Suddenly, the sound of clattering hooves roused him from his dark thoughts. A wagon appeared on the road, coming toward him, carrying someone important, to judge by the equipage. Two men rode forward, two behind, and a herald strode officiously ahead in the middle of the road. "Out of the way, peasant," the herald shouted at Oedipus as they came together at a spot where three roads met. But the young man would not stand to be insulted. When the herald shoved him, he shoved back. By now the wagon caught up with the brawling pair, entwined like wrestlers or snakes. From the middle seat a distinguished-looking man leaned out, took aim, and rapped Oedipus hard with his goad. But Oedipus was fast enough to grab the long wooden stick. He leaned on it with all his strength and flipped the old man backward out of his seat, and he fell headfirst onto the rocky road. "He's killed him," shouted one of the guards. The four men and herald lunged at Oedipus, who drew his sword and slew them all, except for one who ran off in the direction the wagon had come.

For months Oedipus wandered from town to town. His life in Corinth was over, and no other place felt like home. It was at this time that he heard about the Sphinx. With the body and breasts of a lioness, wings like a bird's, and a woman's face, this creature had terrorized Thebes for several years by carrying off young men whenever the citizens failed to answer the riddle that she posed. At times she flew right into the assembly and perched on a pillar. Other days, she stayed in her rocky lair outside town to snatch up unwary passersby. Some people said it was a punishment for the long-ago crime of Laios, the abduction of the boy being paid back now in kind, relentlessly. The riddle (which the Muses had taught the Sphinx) went like this:

*Two-foot, three-foot, one time four,*
*Four in the morning, two at noon;*
*Eve's three-foot creature, then no more:*
*What am I?*

The Thebans tried all kinds of answers from a broken wagon to a salamander. They discussed the riddle endlessly. But no one got it right, and the Sphinx kept devouring the young of the city, snatching them up and flying off with them to her haunts. Kreon, the new king, had become so desperate that he promised his sister, Laios' widow, to the man who could rid Thebes of this monster. Not only the queen, but the whole kingdom besides.

One bright autumn day, Oedipus came to Thebes to try his luck at solving the mystery. He listened as the Sphinx sang out her lines from her perch atop the palace. He scratched his chin; he squinted and stared at the ground. Then Oedipus spoke, just one word: "Man." The crowd was silent, waiting for him to add something more, something difficult and obscure. How could such a simple answer be correct? "A baby crawls; a grown man walks; and an old man uses a stick: four-foot, two-foot, three," explained Oedipus. With that, a terrifying shriek split the air and echoed from the mountain. The Sphinx flew up, without snatching her prey, then dived straight for the rough ground beyond the square. She had been beaten and could no longer live.

Oedipus married his prize. At last he had a home, with no danger of being forced back to Corinth by poverty or loneliness. He had two sons by Jokasta, named Eteokles and Polyneikes, and two daughters, Ismene and Antigone. His life was full; the people were at peace, confident in their king, proud of his intelligence. Two decades meandered by. Then, one day, just as suddenly as the Sphinx had arrived, another plague descended on the city. Crops withered, flocks died, women became barren, and scorching fever decimated the Thebans. Each day saw more pyres flame against the sky. Oedipus one morning found priests and supplicants, wool-laced branches in hand, massed at his palace doors. If anyone knew how to end this curse, it was their brilliant king—that's what was said.

Oedipus was a step ahead of them. He had already sent Kreon to Delphi for help. Even as the crowds were begging him, the queen's brother returned from his mission. "Miasma comes upon us," reported Kreon, "because we shelter a murderer in our midst." Laios had perished on his way to Delphi, seeking to know if somewhere his son was still alive. The killer (or killers) of the former king had never been found. Now the god had revealed that the guilty party was living among them. Oedipus, his mind racing, thought only of the future, not his past. "Whoever did this deed, we will find out. I make myself an ally of Apollo and Justice. If anyone knows his whereabouts and does not tell, then let that person, too, be cursed, and never share our sacrifices, prayers, not even conversation and our common life. Whoever keeps this secret—even if it be someone in my own household— let him be spurned, reviled, driven out. I shall fight for justice for the sake of the dead king, as if I fought on behalf of my own father."

Oedipus, out of concern for his city, also summoned its famous seer, Teiresias. But the old man was reluctant to say anything. Telling unpleasant truths had never helped him, and this time, he knew, it would mean catastrophe. Yet, given the character of Oedipus—his touchy anger, his passion for investigation, the pride in his own intelligence—Teiresias knew the truth would come out anyway. He endured the threats and insults of the king, the accusations of bribery, of working secretly for Kreon to usurp the throne. He gave only dark hints: that Oedipus "consorts most shamelessly with the most dear," that "even with sight, you cannot see." But the hints were enough.

A tyrant's paranoia grafted itself to Oedipus; he began to see conspiracy everywhere. They were framing him. The political—the fate of Thebes—merged with the personal, and the king's cool wits began to melt under his rage. Jokasta tried to calm him by pointing out that the so-called mantic art of Teiresias could not be trusted. "After all, an oracle once foretold that my late husband would be killed by his own son. And look what happened. He was murdered instead by some brigands at a crossroads. As for our son—yes, we had one once—but he only lived three days. He was put out on the mountain, feet bound, in a trackless place. So much for oracular utterances."

These words, supposed to calm Oedipus, launched him into a dizzying whirl. A crossroads? That had not come up before. Exactly where? he asked. Toward Delphi, where the road from Daulia comes in. When was the murder? Not long before Oedipus showed up in Thebes. The king's appearance, the five-man guard, one of whom ran away—the puzzle pieces began to fall into place as Oedipus listened in horror and fascination. But one detail was wrong. Jokasta had mentioned "brigands," more than one. There was still an eyewitness to be called, the former soldier who had escaped the slaughter that day, and who had turned to shepherding, on his return to Thebes—in fact, had asked to be sent off far from town.

While Oedipus waited for the man to be found and brought to the palace, another oracle was proven to be wrong (or so it seemed). A messenger from Corinth brought word that Polybos had died of natural causes: Oedipus was innocent. Apollo's prediction had been wrong. There was still the question of his mother, though. "What fear do you have of Merope?" asked the messenger. "That is, if the oracle can be known." "Apollo said that I would sleep with her," said Oedipus. Already, the words seemed absurd as he spoke them. "So that is why you left our city? I can put your mind at rest, and you can come back to be our king. Merope is not your real mother. Didn't they tell you? You were a foundling. In fact, I brought you to them myself. I'll prove it: I know why there are scars on your ankles."

Oedipus reeled. After this, the full unraveling did not take long. The Theban herdsman who had years ago received the baby from Jokasta was threatened with torture and confessed. The former soldier, the sole eyewitness to the murder, never came. But Oedipus had already convicted himself. Jokasta, meanwhile, after trying to stem the flood of revelations, rushed off to her chamber. They found her later, where she hanged herself. Her son, and husband, reached up to touch her gown and hug her still warm body. Then he put out his eyes by plunging into them the sharp iron point of his mother's brooch.

## 45.  FRATERNAL WAR

Thebes began, if you believe in the Sown Men, with brothers killing brothers. Warriors sown in the selfsame field extirpated one another until an odd number remained. In this land, imbalance offered the only stability. When the sides were even, or when generations collapsed, as with Oedipus, exposed as his own offspring's half brother, the strain was too great, and disaster ensued. So it was after he was driven out of Thebes, into the exile he had brought on by his own curse.

Led by the hand of his young daughter Antigone, blind and despised, the brilliant king took to the roads. Neither of his sons would accompany or help him, something Oedipus never forgave. For several years they wandered. The girl would beg for food, never letting the villagers know the identity of her aging companion. People already knew the story everywhere. If anyone found out who they were, or guessed, the pair were angrily driven out to the edge of the territory, like the sacrificial scapegoats in Apollo's rituals. Eventually, they came to Athens. Here, too, in a place called Kolonos, just outside the city proper, the people harassed them. But Oedipus secluded himself in a sacred grove, a shady green spot overgrown with ivy, bay laurel, and grape vines, where nightingales sang. The holy spot did not seem to match the character of the Dread Ones to whom it was dedicated, the Furies, fierce daughters of Earth and Darkness. People called them Eumenides ("The Kindly")—a euphemism to avoid insulting them. Of all the divinities in the world, these were the last you would ever want to encounter. They pursued murderers of kin; they carried out curses. Like rabid dogs, they chased and destroyed the guilty, ruined his fields and family, blasted his life. In their sanctuary Oedipus was safe.

Apollo had revealed to him that blessings would come to the city that welcomed Oedipus. Curses would fall on those who drove him away. The other secrets that he bore with him Oedipus could share only with the king of the country, who at that time was Theseus. As he waited in the grove for messengers to notify their king, Oedipus heard footsteps and voices drawing near. "Father?" someone said. He recognized Ismene's hesitant tone—the shy one of his two daughters, the opposite of Antigone. She had journeyed from Thebes with news. Her brothers, Eteokles and Polyneikes, had quarreled. They had made a pact at first to rule their father's city alternately, each every other year. But balance was never to be had in Thebes. Eteokles had driven out his older brother, seizing the realm all for himself, setting up a tyranny. Polyneikes, in turn, had gone in exile down to Argos, married into the royal house, and managed to raise an avenging army, who were even now on the verge of attacking his ancestral country.

"Why do you imagine I can help?" her father sighed, after a long silence. "I may not have cursed those boys outright. But if thoughts can count, they were already doubly damned. Which one of them raised a hand to help me when Kreon was all for annihilating me?"

"There have been oracles . . ." began Ismene. Oedipus dropped his head in despair. The gods had sent word (no doubt by Teiresias) that having Oedipus return to Thebes would save the city—even if it meant merely his corpse, buried at the border, as an invisible, magic defense. "A delegation is already on its way," his daughter concluded. "Thebes wants you back."

Next, Theseus arrived from nearby Athens. He knew all about Oedipus, but was not deterred. A hero himself, he recalled the many times that exile or need had left him at the mercy of another. He, too, had been a supplicant once. Theseus promised never to evict the aged, broken man, or give him up to enemies. Oedipus responded with frightening words: "Perhaps I could give Thebes salvation. But all that is pleasant turns bitter; change comes, just as night erases day. They will learn that, and so will you. Athens now has good relations with my homeland. That too will change. Buried in your soil, one day I will drink the Thebans' blood. I am the gods' gift to all of you."

When Kreon showed up to take him back, Oedipus adamantly refused. Never would he return to Thebes. In response, Kreon pushed harder; he had his men drag off Antigone and Ismene. Theseus, who had gone to attend a sacrifice, rushed back to Kolonos and intervened. Kreon was sent off, muttering threats. The Thebans were intercepted at the border, and the kidnapped daughters of Oedipus were handed back. And then the marvel occurred. Thunder rumbled and the sky darkened. Oedipus, hearing the sound, told Theseus that the right time had come. The blind man led the king and his daughters to a secret spot. Knowledge of the place, he said, would always be a mystery to all but the Athenian royal house. As long as this lore was passed down, the city would never fall.

As it was reported later, Theseus and Oedipus came to the place where the Athenian had dedicated a wine bowl that once held the oath-libation, poured out when Peirithoos pledged his eternal friendship. Then Oedipus sent his girls to fetch clean water from a spring, to wash him. They did so crying. When they were finished, they clung to his knees as he spoke softly, telling them that no one would ever love them as much as he had. Following another thunderclap, they heard a voice that made their hair stand on end: "Oedipus, Oedipus, why do we delay?" Getting up slowly from the rock where he was sitting, Oedipus said farewell to his daughters. He made Theseus swear to take care of them. He told them to stand apart—only Theseus could see the end. Going off a few yards with the king, he left them. It was over in a minute. By the time they turned around, the daughters and the king's messenger saw only Theseus, standing alone, his hand shielding his eyes as though he had seen a blinding flash of light, or something dreadful. They saw him bend and kiss the ground, heard him call on the Olympians. Whether Oedipus vanished in wind and fire, or walked into the open earth, we will never know. The man who knew the answer to the riddle, who found that he himself was the answer (four-foot, two-foot, finally three), had become the ultimate enigma.

Not long after the sisters Antigone and Ismene had returned to their homeland, the tide of war broke over Thebes. Polyneikes had been successful in recruiting an attack force, helped by his new father-in-law, the king of Argos. That connection had come about largely by accident. The night that Polyneikes arrived in Argos, wearing a rough animal hide against the frost and cold, he met another refugee huddled on the porch of the palace—Tydeus, who had to flee Kalydon after he killed a man. Both were looking for sanctuary. But since the serving maids provided only one blanket (to discourage those seeking shelter), a fight soon broke out. "What is all this infernal racket?" roared a voice from inside, and the king, Adrastos, stalked out onto the porch. It looked like beasts fighting. All he could see was a boar's skin, tusk still attached to the headpiece, lunging at a lion skin, the head and glaring eyes tossing every which way, as strange, barely human, growls and grunts emerged from the fracas. He was about to separate the two by his sword when a smile washed over his face, and Adrastos began to laugh in delight. That unexpected sound was enough to make Tydeus and Polyneikes stop brawling. What was so funny? "The oracle," said Adrastos. "It worked. I was supposed to marry my daughters to animals. The god has made some odd predictions, but that topped them all. Girls wedding beasts! And now I understand. You two are to be my sons-in-law—a lion and a boar, just as Apollo foresaw. He neither hides nor tells the truth. He just gives signs, and this fight of yours was the sign, for me to interpret."

The new arrivals were well pleased. Immediately Adrastos pledged to help Polyneikes regain his place in Thebes, and Tydeus, too, volunteered for the expedition. A pair of Argives, Kapaneus and Hippomedon, joined up. Finally, two other warriors stepped forth to round out the number of the famous Seven who marched against Thebes. One of these was Amphiaraos, the brother-in-law of the king. He had refused to go at first, because he was a gifted seer, and so foresaw the disaster that would befall the Argive army. But once before he had a terrible quarrel with Adrastos, and Eriphyle, the woman who bound them (as one's wife, the other's sister), resolved it. Consequently, both men promised that if a dispute arose ever again, they would defer to her. Whether Polyneikes knew this or simply made a lucky guess is not clear. But he managed to bribe Eriphyle to get her husband's support, and so put a stop to the ominous warnings. It would be bad for morale if an army knew they were going off to die. To buy the wife's aid, Polyneikes gave her the golden necklace of Harmonia, an heirloom that had passed for generations through the royal house of Thebes. Thus did this god-given emblem of bliss become the catalyst for fatal strife.

The other warrior was named Parthenopaios, which means "Girlish." The name was a wry joke, since his mother, anything but "girlish," was Atalanta, the famous huntress who had helped Meleager hunt the boar of Kalydon and even sailed on the *Argo* with Jason. To her consternation, this Atalanta was always being mixed up with a girl from Boeotia (she herself came from Arcadia), a silly creature (to her mind) who disliked suitors and so arranged a test to kill them off. That other Atalanta would race against any man who dared. If he won, he was to be awarded the girl herself as his wife. If he lost (and they all did), he was put to death. One day a young man, Hippomenes, dared to undertake the trial. He had seen how beautiful she was and was ready to risk his life. Hippomenes prayed to Aphrodite, who took pity on him and gave him three Golden Apples. After the footrace began, Atalanta got off to a fast start, but Hippomenes, rounding the turn-post, tossed the first of his apples just ahead of her and to the left. Charmed by the golden sphere, Atalanta veered off to pick it up. She hardly broke stride, but the move slowed her enough to put them neck and neck. After another ten yards, Hippomenes let go the second apple, this time a bit farther off the track. Atalanta again swerved off, but again made up her lost seconds with a burst of speed. Finally, Hippomenes threw the third apple, this time lofting it almost to the spectators' benches. As Atalanta bounded off to retrieve the fruit he pulled ahead, and before she could regain ground, her husband-to-be passed the finish line. Little good it did him. The couple began the journey to their new home, but, overcome by desire for one another, stopped to make love in a cave that served as a rustic shrine of the Great Mother, Kybele, immortal queen from the east. Shocked and angry at their sacrilege, she turned them into lions. No longer do they run free.

Tightly reined, they draw the chariot of the goddess. So that is the tale of the *other* Atalanta. Parthenopaios was the son of the more sober warrior. Even so, despite his courageous bloodline, he was to lose his most important fight.

The Argive army set out. Early on, the omens looked bad. At a place called Phlious, not far from Corinth, they stopped to find water. Amphiaraos came upon a nursemaid with a child. She had a royal bearing; she did not seem to be a slave. While she guided him and his companions to a spring, the woman told her name and story. She was none other than Jason's first love, Hypsipyle, queen of the women of Lemnos. After they had discovered that she alone never took part in their infamous manslaughter, that she had smuggled her father off the island rather than slay him with the other males, they locked her up, then sold her to a slave trader. She ended up doing menial jobs on the mainland, unknown and uncared for. Maybe it was the weight of her thoughts, or the distraction of visitors that day that brought about the accident. Hypsipyle left her master's baby, the infant prince Opheltes, on a bed of soft grass not far from the spring. After helping the chieftains, she discovered that a venomous snake had crept up and bitten the child. Amphiaraos, the reluctant seer, saw all too clearly the disaster that the event portended. They renamed the boy Arkhemoros—"Doom-starter"—buried him, and treated him like a hero who had died young, even founding athletic games in his honor. You can still see the stadium built on the spot, at Nemea.

After a few more days of hard marches they reached the borders of Theban territory. "I'll give them one more chance," said Polyneikes that night as they sat around their fire. "But if I go, I am sure they'll capture me. Someone else should make the offer." He looked in the direction of Tydeus. By now they had become loyal companions. "All right, but I don't trust these Thebans any more than you," he said. He took only a spear—no armor, no sword—to show his was a peaceful mission. At Thebes, Tydeus found the nobles feasting, all gathered in the palace of Eteokles. They did not know who he was. Hearing his proposal for a truce and for negotiations with Polyneikes, they laughed. "What if we don't agree?" said one. "All together, you and your seven commanders and all their armies have as much chance of beating us as you alone do, single-handed." Tydeus thought this was too good a chance to let pass. "Why don't we see?" he said, and challenged each of them to a contest on the spot, letting them choose their event. He defeated every one of them. This put the Thebans in a truly foul mood. "We'll get revenge, don't worry," promised Eteokles once Tydeus had left to report to his companions. Fifty men were chosen to ambush him before he could make it back to the border. But Tydeus turned to face them and killed all except one.

Battle lines were drawn. The Argive leaders made a vow to take the city or die in trying. They sealed their solemn oath by slicing open the throat of a bull, pouring the black blood into a shield, into which they plunged their hands. They came to Thebes, ringed by a thick wall with seven gates. To each gate an attacker was assigned. Meanwhile, inside the walls, defenders were found to match. Tydeus, carrying the moon and stars shining on his shield, faced "Black Horse" Melanippos. Kapaneus was paired against Polyphontes ("Killer of Many"), who would demolish the boast made by the design on that attacker's shield (a torch-wielding man with the words "I shall take the town"). Kreon's son, Megareus, was a defender, as was Hyperbios. At the gate by the tomb of Amphion, smooth-faced young Parthenopaios held forth his shield like an insult to Thebes, with a Sphinx painted on it, devouring its victim. Aktor, the Driver, was sent to meet him in battle. To the sixth gate came the prophet Amphiaraos, his bronze shield blank, his manner grim. Greater than his distaste for war was his scorn for Polyneikes, "Man of Many Quarrels," who had shamelessly maneuvered him into this fight. He knew they would both die in the attack. Lasthenes was chosen to resist him. Last of all, the seventh hero, Polyneikes, posted himself at the seventh gate. His shield, too, bore a design: the goddess Justice, with the words above her head: "This man I shall restore." Only one Theban could rightly be sent against him— his brother named Eteokles—"True Renown."

Now there was no feasting and laughter. The people were panicked; left on their own, they might have surrendered. Eteokles had to announce that anyone, man or woman, who disobeyed him would be publicly stoned. The warriors on either side of the walls set up a mighty shouting and clashing of spears on shield, bronze against bronze. Ugly talk, insults, and threats flew like shots from slings. Mounting a ladder at the wall, Kapaneus boasted as he reached the top that nothing could stop him now. Zeus hated such arrogance and blasted him dead with a thunderbolt. Melanippos wounded Tydeus with a sword stroke in the gut. As he lay dying, Athena came, intending to make him immortal with a divine potion. But Amphiaraos had his revenge. He had detested Tydeus ever since the refugee had roused up the Argives to accompany Polyneikes on this doomed mission. Taking the head of Melanippos, who had been slain, he gave it to his hated companion. When Athena arrived, she saw Tydeus, with his last strength, lapping up his Theban enemy's brains from the split skull. Disgusted, she let Tydeus die where he lay. Zeus, meanwhile, caused Amphiaraos to be swallowed up by the earth, along with his charioteer, as he fled from the city. Underground, he still gives prophecies. The battle proceeded like a fatal dance. The paired heroes clashed and stabbed and fell back as if led by some ancient tune, the music long ago trapped in the walls. At every gate Thebes won, except one. The sons of Oedipus died at each other's hands.

## 46.  THE FINAL SACRIFICE

So the inheritors of Thebes had ended with their equal portions. Each got a share of death. And yet there was still imbalance, a teetering inequity that would crash down in catastrophe when someone tried to make things even.

Kreon, brother of the former queen Jokasta, became king. Thebes was out of danger, but the ship of state had been battered by discordant gales. He intended to keep it sailing true, run a tight ship, keep a hard grip on the tiller. Insubordination could never be allowed. In his policies Kreon continued the wartime edict of Eteokles—disobedience meant death.

"A man of true honor, our beloved Eteokles, by the command of the Council is to be given full burial honors." So read the decree the morning after the war had ended. "The man of endless wrangles, Polyneikes, his brother, is to be cast out. Let dogs and birds diminish his flesh. Let him be cursed. If anyone shall attempt to bury him, let that person also be ritually accursed."

Antigone soon heard of the royal decision, and she told Ismene of her determination to violate it. Her sister advised caution and compliance, at least for the present. But she might as well have advised a rock or tree. Although Kreon had taken the precaution of posting guards over the unburied corpses (Polyneikes was left among the other attackers), Antigone nevertheless found a way to scatter a few handfuls of dirt on his body—enough of a burial to let his soul enter Hades. Later, she went out to finish the task. But this time the guards were watching. She was caught and dragged before her uncle, the ultimate power in the state.

She acknowledged the deed. "It was not Zeus who made the decree, or Justice. Your proclamations have not the strength of those unwritten laws. Yours are mortal, while those others live forever. I feared to face the gods, having neglected their ordinance to care for my dead kin." Just like her father, thought Kreon, the same unbridled will, the same arrogance. He stood for the city, embodied it in himself, and here his niece was talking about "family"—a quaint concept when wars were being fought for the nation's survival. Ismene came ready to defend her, but Antigone was too proud to share her martyr's death. "Go ahead, kill me. Haven't you got your criminal?" she taunted Kreon. But he was uneasy in his mind. His son, Haimon, was engaged to this passionate rebel standing defiantly before him. Haimon pleaded for his fiancée. Did not the trees that bent with wind and flood survive, while the unyielding were torn up root and branch? What would Kreon lose by showing mercy? This only inflamed the tyrant more. His own son was arguing for the subversive wretch. As a woman, she should know her place. As a daughter of Oedipus, she posed a danger to him. Kreon made up his mind to entomb her alive. She gave herself up to the ordeal and lamented:

> *"You look on me, women of my father's land,*
> *Going the last road; the freshest light*
> *Sees me, the sunlight—but never again.*
> *Hades, who puts all to bed, takes me alive*
> *To Akheron's bank. No wedding hymn*
> *Accompanies me at evening, no bridal song.*
>
> *Once I heard of Tantalos' daughter.*
> *Ivy clings to her, tendrils on a rock.*
> *Wind and rain and snow wear away*
> *Her face and neck. Always in tears*
> *She remains forever. A god grant me*
> *Such repose!"*

You will be famous, she was told. You'll die without blemish, without disease, unwounded, a law unto yourself. But Antigone was beyond such facile talk. Her thoughts went deeper. It seemed her father's marriage bound itself to her fate, never to wed. Why should she pay for his mistake? Had not even Oedipus, at the end, proclaimed his innocence? If this was simply working out some divine whim, where

was her will? Or his? Or anyone's? At least she had the comfort of having chosen, even if it came to choosing her execution. Maybe that was
why Oedipus had put out his eyes. At least that act was his own, improvised, not fated. And now, yes, she wanted them to cry for her.

Kreon's soldiers hauled Antigone away to the rocky underground
room in which she would be sealed. No sooner had they departed than
Teiresias, who had witnessed all the misery of Thebes, came to the
palace. He told Kreon that sitting in his usual spot for receiving signs
he had heard ominous sounds. The birds screeched and fought, their
wings beating and talons ripping feathers. When he had gone to test
the sacrifices, the fire merely sputtered. The altars were fouled with
pieces of carrion dropped by birds and roaming dogs. The unburied
were infecting the realm of gods. It was not too late to back down, to
forgive Antigone and bury her brother. But Kreon lashed out at the
seer, accusing him of lying for the sake of gain. Only when the old
blind man had left, with a warning of impending ruin, did Kreon reconsider. He went himself to the plain and saw to the rites for
Polyneikes. Then he hurried to the underground chamber. As Kreon
came near, he heard moans and wild sobbing. It was his son Haimon,
clinging to the body of Antigone, who had hanged herself with the
silk cord of her gown. Kreon, becoming frantic, called for him to
come out. But Haimon glared with maddened eyes and spat at him in
answer. Before anyone could reach his hand, he pulled his sword and
drove it deep between his ribs, collapsing against the body of
Antigone. The spurt of his blood spattered on her white cheek. So the
couple lay married in death.

Thebes fell in the next generation. The Epigonoi ("After-Born"),
as they called themselves, took it and razed it to the ground. They
were the sons of the original Seven, and marched with fewer men,
though with better omens. Diomedes, Sthenelos, and their companions in this venture were of the last great generation of heroes. They
cut their teeth on this short war against fellow Greeks. The longest
siege, their ultimate triumph, was still to come, in the distant east.

# BOOK NINE

## THE WAR

## AT TROY

THE LAST GREAT EPISODE IN Greek myth shades into legend. Thucydides, the Athenian historian of the late fifth century B.C., accepted the Trojan War as fact, as did most other writers in ancient times. But only since the end of the nineteenth century has evidence come to light that the siege of a great city on the east coast of the Aegean Sea at the end of the heroic age might actually have happened. Heinrich Schliemann was a successful merchant and adventurer who turned to archaeology in middle age. An incurable romantic with a penchant for fictionalizing his own experiences, he once claimed that from the age of ten he had been inspired to locate the legendary city described in Homer's *Iliad*. As he was later to write, a visit to the hill of Hisarlik near the Hellespont in modern Turkey convinced him immediately that this was where the great war occurred. In actuality, it appears Schliemann was directed to the spot by an English antiquarian long resident in the area, Frank Calvert. While Calvert tried in vain to interest the British Museum in excavations, Schliemann used his private funds to begin digging in 1870. In a remarkably short time he found the remains of several pre-Classical cities. Over the next twenty years nine successive layers of habitation were uncovered, reaching back to the early Bronze Age (3000 B.C.). Though no single piece of evidence yet confirms the identification of the site, Schliemann's discovery clearly represents a large, ancient city that underwent destruction by fire just at the period that Greek tradition pinpointed for the Trojan War, around 1200 B.C. Spectacular finds of gold jewelry, bronze weapons, gold and silver drinking vessels, and impressive fortifications all seem to tally with the Homeric picture of a flourishing high urban culture that fell suddenly to invaders.

In the years after Schliemann, archaeologists found further evidence in Greece that supports the poetic accounts of Homer and the ancient myth tellers. At Mycenae, in the Peloponnese, a rich palace complex was discovered, matching the fabled realm of Agamemnon. A smaller palace excavated at Pylos in the far west of Greece corresponds to the seat of Nestor's kingdom. Dozens of other "Mycenaean" age sites (1600–1200 B.C.) lend credence to the idea that a sophisticated, aristocratic culture based on military might existed centuries before recorded Greek history, one capable of mounting a huge expeditionary force to conquer a foreign rival—or retrieve an abducted queen. Further compelling information about this culture emerged when Arthur Evans began his excavations in 1900 on Crete. At the site of a vast pre-Greek palace complex in Knossos, thousands of baked clay tablets were dug up, inscribed with a series of non-alphabetic signs. In 1952, a young English architect and amateur code breaker, Michael Ventris, succeeded in deciphering the signs as an archaic form of Greek. In other words, the "Mycenaeans" were already speaking the language of Homer five hundred years before the poetry attributed to him. A number of words previously found only in Homeric texts also appeared on these so-called Linear B tablets, as did names familiar from legend: "Hector," for example, and "Achilles" (though these seem to designate ordinary individuals of the time). The newly found writing contained official records from an efficient palace bureaucracy, meticulous listings of weapons, armor, food, personnel, and supplies.

After the decline of Mycenaean civilization, shortly after the fall of Troy, this early form of writing was lost. The verses of Homer, commemorating the great battle from the distant past, depends instead on a long *oral* poetic tradition, which can be detected in the intricate and systematic formulaic style of the epics. Even when the Greeks adopted the alphabet (probably around 900 B.C., most likely from the Phoenicians), there was no immediate need to write down heroic epics, as this art form flourished in live performances, in which a bard sang fresh versions while using traditional building blocks (phrases, motifs, and plots). Such composition-in-performance of heroic poetry can be witnessed even today in a number of traditional cultures, from Egypt to Mongolia.

The tales that follow occur in some of the most prominent pieces of Greek literature—the Homeric epics and Greek tragedies. Despite the varying emphases of individual poets over several centuries, a number of key themes unite the episodes within the broad-ranging Trojan material. One is the conflict between the demands of the male-controlled city-state, with its fighting men, and the female-centered extended family. Agamemnon, faced with the choice of sacrificing his daughter or abandoning the expedition to retrieve his brother's wife, experiences the dilemma that Antigone, in a different saga, expressed. Does one choose the state, male solidarity, community values, and the publicly acknowledged "right"? Or does one place primary value on the claims of the household and its members, living and dead, the extended family, women and children, the "unwritten" instinctual law of the heart? The *Iliad* further elaborates on the clash, in a slightly different way, as Achilles pits his individual honor and sense of loss against the values of his commander, Agamemnon. The *Odyssey* offers a portrait of a loner and trickster who gravitates away from group affiliations and toward his individual home and faithful wife. For the modern world, the *Odyssey* has proven to be the more popular, perhaps because it seems to express more clearly a universal longing within its specifically Greek context. Our concept of an adventurous journey—an "odyssey"—owes its very name to the wily hero from an ancient myth.

## 47. THE COSMIC STRUGGLE

When did the Trojan War begin? You might as easily ask: when did the world take its present shape? The genesis goes back to eternal forces, to Gaia, the Earth, and her favorite grandson, Zeus.

Without the advice of his primeval grandmother, Zeus would not have been hidden away in Crete, saved from his cruel and voracious father. He would never have released the Hundred-Handers to fight his battles, nor swallowed Mêtis and thus encapsulated cunning. In short, he owed his continuing reign on Olympus to this (usually) kindly being. Therefore, when she had a complaint, he listened to her. Secure now in his kingship, he could afford to do favors. And besides, it was good policy.

"All these humans," she sighed one day when Zeus was visiting, "swarming all over, so many of them I feel crushed. It's like there's a weight always on my heart. And that's not all. You Olympians receive homage—which you should—but who sacrifices to Gaia these days? Instead, they're off digging holes in me, mining, quarrying, plowing, felling trees." By the way she looked at Zeus when she said that, he knew he had better act quickly. There was no telling what monsters Gaia would cook up deep in her insides.

"A war might relieve the burden," he suggested tentatively. "Or we could try another flood." On second thought, maybe that wasn't such a good idea. Humans had boats now and skilled sailors—witness the Argonauts. "Yes, a worldwide war. That should help," he concluded, and set off decisively to put things in motion. As it happened, some pieces were already in play. A gorgeous woman here. An upright hero there. Over at this side of the Aegean, a kingly line with some overdue curses in the family. On the other side, an excellent city, one that had already supplied the gods with a youthful cupbearer and a mortal lover—and fortunately, or not, had also ruffled various divine tempers. Like a chess master, he foresaw all possibilities. One decision could start the chain of events.

The decision was this: marry off Thetis to an unsuspecting man. Long ago, when the world was new and Zeus had not yet discovered delightful mortal women, he had his eye on this particular sea nymph, one of the fifty daughters of Nereus. She was beautiful and powerful, but she would have nothing to do with Zeus. She preferred her independence, under the waves. Living on a mountaintop was unimaginable to her. Whatever his attitude toward human women, Zeus respected divinities. He would never force her to marry him or do his will. There was a further complication. Once, when he was flirting with the idea of winning her over, he was warned (either by his grandmother, who knew such things, or by Blame) that a marriage with Thetis would produce a son stronger than the father. That was the reason he'd had to swallow Mêtis. Still, the knowledge that Thetis had rejected him, and the threat that she might pair up with one of his brothers, either Hades or Poseidon, annoyed and worried him. A son stronger than either one of those fathers would cause real trouble. He would defuse the problem now through an arranged marriage.

Peleus, like many another earlier hero, was living in exile because he had once killed a man. The victim was his half brother, Seal (Phokos), the son that Aiakos had with a nymph named Sandy (Psamathê). Aiakos himself was an interesting character. His father was Zeus, and his mother Aigina, daughter of a river (with relatives in Thebes). When he was a young man, a plague had wiped out the population of his home island. Aiakos prayed as he sat near a great oak tree sacred to his father, and Zeus took pity. The many ants that were busily marching over the tree's bark he turned into humans. "Myrmidons" became their name (after *murmex*, the word for "ant"). In later years, Aiakos became a sort of judge and wise man. Gods came to him to resolve disputes. Mortals came to have him pray for rain (because his father was the sky god). When Poseidon and Apollo were constructing the walls of Troy, Aiakos lent a hand. Resting, after they finished the initial foundation, the three builders noticed three gray-eyed snakes trying to crawl onto the stones where Aiakos had been doing his share of the labor. Two failed, but the third slithered up and over. "That is the spot, made by human hands, that will bring this wall down and the city with it," proclaimed the prophetic god. "Aiakos, it is your descendants who will wreck it."

To get back to the murder: why it was committed is obscure. Peleus and his brother Telamon may have been jealous that Phokos was such a good athlete (especially at swimming). Their mother, too, may have disliked this older stepson and hinted that he would not be missed, at least by her. At any event, the two made it look like an accident, a discus throw that went wrong. Aiakos found out, though, and he banished them both. Telamon moved to a nearby island, Salamis. Peleus traveled farther, up north to the court of Akastos in Iolkos (Jason's hometown), seeking to be purified of the pollution of kin murder. Yet he found only more trouble. After Jason and Medea returned, and disposed of the wicked Pelias by cooking him, the dead king's son Akastos held funeral games, at which Peleus competed. There the wife of the new king became infatuated with him. Every day she sent urgent messages, declarations of her passion. But Peleus was an honorable man. He would never repay his host and deliverer by sleeping with his wife. As the woman persisted, she became desperate, and angry at being spurned. Finally, she invented a story to get revenge. "Akastos, that murderer, the one from Aigina, do you know what he did? I'm blushing even as I tell of it. He made advances to me. He attempted to seduce me." And Akastos was deceived.

"Let's go hunting on the mountain," he said to Peleus one morning. "I can show you the best places for cover. We'll enjoy ourselves, just the two of us." Peleus was flattered and glad for the guidance. He had no experience of Mt. Pelion, although he had heard alarming stories—men kicked to death by Centaurs, hunters who simply disappeared.

Working their way deep into the woods, they had some success—mostly small game—ate lunch, and lay down for a nap. At least, Peleus slept, while Akastos only pretended to do so. When he was sure the other man was sound asleep, Akastos took away his sword and abandoned him. It would have been easier to kill him outright, and possibly more humane. But the king was afraid of the religious pollution that results from murdering a guest-friend.

After two hours, Peleus woke up to hear twigs crackling and what sounded like galloping horses. He reached for his weapon, his special sword made by Hephaestus, but found nothing. He called in vain for help. Centaurs were closing in. They had sniffed out human flesh and, even more keenly, the wine that Akastos had so generously brought along. Peleus clambered up a tree just as the horse-men came into the clearing. It would not have taken the beasts long to shake him out. They had hands as well as hooves, and they could brandish long branches. But the gods could not bear to watch an innocent man meet this ugly end. They ensured that Cheiron, the just Centaur, discovered Peleus in the nick of time. Together the two chased off Cheiron's dangerous fellow creatures.

Not only was Peleus saved, but he won a bride as a reward. By command of Zeus, Thetis was betrothed to him, without her having any say in the matter. Of course, if she had rejected Zeus as a lover, then you might expect that she would not be content with a mere mortal. When Peleus went to meet his future wife, he found he had to earn her affection or, more precisely, gain her attention. In fact, he had to pin her down, literally. She kept changing shape—now a lion, a panther, a snake. She was, after all, a sea goddess, changeable as the sea's surface. Her favorite trick was to become a fish. Yet Peleus hung on, and she finally gave in. The most splendid wedding ever held was soon arranged, a feast that put the marriage of Kadmos and Harmonia completely in the shade. As the guests rode to Mt. Pelion, Iris led the way, a rainbow of color announcing the divine procession. Hestia came, the hearth goddess who hardly ever leaves the house. Demeter and Dionysus, divinities of good food and drink, came as well. Royal couples rode in a row: Zeus and Hera, Poseidon and his consort Amphitritê, Ares and his incomparable bedmate Aphrodite. Nereus rose out of the sea to watch his daughter marry a mortal. Even Okeanos, the cosmic river, came. Cheiron brought them as a wedding gift an ash-tree branch (a significant item for a Centaur). Later, Peleus had this trimmed and fitted out as a spear.

For a time the couple lived happily on Mt. Pelion, a short distance from Cheiron's cave. But Thetis, true to her nature, pined for the sea. She could catch glimpses of it when she walked on the mountainside. If the sky was clear, she could gaze all the way out to the islands, where she remembered she used to sun herself between long swims. There was another weight on her mind as well. Would their children be mortal or immortal? If she had twins, would one be divine and the other not? She had heard of Herakles and the test his father had devised in such a case to see which child was what. Was there something less dangerous she could do?

The question was moot until she found herself with child. When he was born, Achilles certainly looked like an infant god. His fair hair and skin nearly radiated. He could have been the baby Apollo. But was he mortal? Thetis decided not to take any chances. Every day she washed him and rubbed on his skin a gentle ointment meant to protect him. Every night, while Peleus slept, she took the boy and held him over the fire in the hearth. If he was not immortal, this treatment would make him so, or at least that is what Thetis thought. Her experience with fire was limited, since she had never had it growing up under the sea. Some will tell you that Thetis took her child to the river Styx and dipped him in it to accomplish the same protection, and that the place where she held him, by the heel, was thus vulnerable, never having been immersed. That seems less likely. Why would she go that far? Besides, gods and goddesses shudder at the very mention of the infernal river in the realm of the dead. Whichever was true, one night the sea nymph got caught at her work. Despite her arguments, Peleus could not see how incinerating his son (so he called it) was ever going to make him immortal. Thetis in anger stormed from the house and never came back. She ran down the mountain and plunged into her native element. Later on, she would visit Achilles when he walked by the sea and called on her.

The boy grew up to be adventurous, handsome, strong—all that you might expect, given his ancestry. When he was seven, his father brought him to train with Cheiron, the molder of heroes. The wise old Centaur fed him lion innards, the guts of boars, and marrow of bear so that he would take on the strength of those aggressive animals. A few years later, before his beard began to sprout, rumors of the war for Helen reached the countryside. There was a prophecy that said Troy would fall only if Achilles engaged in the fight. Yet his mother, Thetis, knew that if he joined the expedition, he would not return. A long life without glory, or a short life with eternal fame—that was his destiny, for he was not wholly immortal. To forestall his death, she sent word that Achilles should go to an island named Skyros to the court of Lykomedes. She gave him girl's clothing. He was to hide there, in isolation, among the maidservants of the king. It was not the perfect solution, but it worked for a time. Meanwhile, from west to east, the clouds of battle were growing darker.

## 48.  Judgment and Reward

The wedding of Peleus and Thetis had seen two unusual incidents, each of which had an aftereffect. First, Apollo himself had played his lyre and sung at the feast. He composed a song honoring the couple, in which he prophesied many fine things concerning their child. Thetis would never forget that moment. The second was the squabble that broke out when Strife (Eris), who had not been invited, threw an apple. Tossing fruit is part of weddings, of course, but this was a special case. The apple was the finest, most luscious the gods had ever seen, and it bore an inscription: *Kallistêi,* "to the fairest woman." Even before Eris had stalked off, three goddesses claimed the apple as their own: Hera, Athena, and Aphrodite. Admittedly, all three were beautiful. But who was going to pick the winner in such a contest? It would be folly for a god to judge and then win the ire of the losing two. Thetis and Peleus hardly noticed the fuss amid the festivity—besides, gods were always quarreling. To prevent a full-scale fight, Zeus quickly arranged for an arbitrator among humans. Some innocent mortal could take the fall. And who would know more about beauty than the most handsome man? The father of gods sent for Hermes. "Take these three down to the hills outside Troy. Let Paris the shepherd give his ruling. Make sure he gets a good look at each one. And no funny business." For he knew the habits of his trickster son.

Troy traced its founding back to another son of Zeus, named Dardanos. From the start, it was a good country for horses. At one time the son of Dardanos owned three thousand mares. The North Wind,

Boreas, covered some of these, and a remarkable foaling was the result—a dozen wind-swift colts that could race even across the tops of waves. Tros was the grandson of Dardanos (hence *Troy*) and had a son Ilos (hence *Ilion*—another name for the town), as also Ganymede, so good-looking that Zeus took him up to Olympus to be his cupbearer. (Zeus contributed more fine horses as compensation.) Ilos had Laomedon, who fathered Priam and four other sons. Priam went on to produce fifty sons, nineteen of them by his wife Hekabe. One of them was the eventual key to his ruin: Paris.

When she was pregnant with him, Hekabe dreamed she bore a burning torch with serpents coiled around its base. Fiery sparks shot forth from it, and Mt. Ida's forests and the plain of Troy were soon aflame. Shaken, she told the royal dream interpreters, who advised the king and queen to abandon the infant when it was born—clearly, trouble would come through him. Of course, exposing him did not work. The child was found and raised by shepherds on the hills outside the city, which is where Hermes found him one fine summer afternoon. Paris was half dozing when he felt the light touch of the messenger's wand on his shoulder, and opened his eyes. "I must be dreaming," he thought. But it was no fantasy. Before him stood the three most desirable women he had ever seen. He had no doubt they were immortal. His first reaction was fear. Even though he had not heard about his father's cousin Anchises, terrified by Aphrodite after sleeping with her on this very mountain (for Anchises kept his promise and never told), Paris knew enough not to make any forward remarks. Hermes explained the situation, then let the goddesses parade before Paris.

"It is so hard to decide," murmured the shepherd after each had passed silently in review. So Hermes thought up a second event: each contestant would get the chance to say a few words—what she thought she might contribute to Paris' well-being. Athena stepped up first. Even without her helmet, she was an imposing figure, statuesque with keen gray eyes. "My craft is War," she said. "With me, you will win any fight you choose." Paris looked dubious. In his hillside occupation, there did not seem much use for that kind of ability. Let's hear the other options, he suggested. "Kingship," promised Hera, looking slightly bored. "Who do you think keeps Zeus himself in power? With me, you will rule any place on earth." That was marginally more appealing, thought Paris, but not as a good in itself, rather as a means to other ends—like excellent food and days of idle pleasure. Finally,

Aphrodite approached, standing noticeably closer to him than the others. Paris could smell her intriguing perfume. "Do you like girls, Paris? I have the right one for you." This was a language the young man understood. Now he was ready to give a verdict.

Hera and Athena were enraged by the personal affront they were handed that afternoon. Even before Aphrodite finished telling Paris about his reward, the two goddesses hurried back to Olympus. It was no good trying to kill Paris. He was under that tramp Aphrodite's protection now. But together they began to plot how the country of Paris could be destroyed.

Soon thereafter, Paris learned that Troy was indeed his country, and not simply by reason of his shepherding in its hills. He was a royal prince. The revelation occurred one day when several officials came from town and demanded from the herders their best stock. "There is a big celebration in the city tonight, the twentieth-year feast for the hero-baby, Alexandros." They proceeded to select a ram and some fat ewes. Paris was outraged. His demands for a fair price were laughed off with a shouted "Tell it to the king" from the officials, already on their way down the slope. He followed them, though at a distance. Inside the walls of Troy, altars had been garlanded and prepared for the evening's rites. Crowds were gathering, though not so much for the solemn commemoration. After all, it was in honor of an infant they never knew, "saving the city" only because he'd been left out to die two decades ago. What the people wanted to see were the athletes who would compete during the rituals.

Paris joined in the mob pushing toward the playing field. Strutting, long-haired aristocrats were doing warm-up exercises, testing javelin points and discus throw weights, strapping on boxing thongs, oiling their perfect limbs. Only the well-bred participated in such contests. What workingman of the people could afford the hours of training? Then again, part of the appeal for the crowd was watching their masters get trounced by one another. That gave a certain vicarious thrill. As Paris watched them wrestle, box, broadjump, spear-cast, and run, his resentment grew. These were the ones who grew fat from his animals. They ate his rich flocks while he existed on rough bread and cheese, water and olives. No wonder they were strong. He decided he would show them. He pushed himself forward and issued a general challenge.

As you might expect, he beat every man who faced him. Defenders of the games will tell you it was because Paris was of royal birth—

an actual commoner could never win. Whether that is true or not, his performance nearly brought about his death. The competitors were horrified that this peasant, in his smelly goatskin, took the prize. More than winning the games was at stake. Such a performance could give ordinary folk dangerous ideas. The games were meant to display one's inherent excellence and, therefore, right to power. How dare this clodhopper show them up! The only solution was to slay him.

While he was basking in the glow of his triumph, all of Priam's sons closed in on Paris, swords drawn. Just as they were readying for the slaughter, the prophetess Kassandra let out a shriek. "Kill not kin! Alexandros returns! Honor him." They would have dismissed the words as her usual crazy ravings, for it was her fate never to be believed, ever since she spurned the love of her inspirer, Apollo. But Priam, who was seated nearby, heard his daughter's proclamation and realized in an instant that the lost sheep had wandered home, despite his attempt to abandon it. "She's right—this is my son, whom we supposed to have rescued Troy." What he did not say was that Paris' failure to die meant, for the city, imminent disaster. He could almost hear it coming, like a boulder rumbling down a hill.

## 49.   On Pelops' Island

Paris, Achilles. One would kill the other and be slain in turn. But that came later, when Troy was already tottering, in her final year. One other part of the scheme remained to slip into place before the war began in earnest. Her name was Helen—Paris' reward.

On the side of her mortal father, Tyndareos, she came from an old Spartan family, one that (like Paris' Trojan line) traced its ancestry back to an encounter between Zeus and a girl of the Pleiades, the shining daughters of mountainous Atlas. Her mother was the lovely Leda, as you have heard, the woman whom Zeus visited in the disguise of a swan. After her unusual birth from an egg, she spent a happy, uneventful girlhood (except for the excitement when Theseus abducted her). By the time she was of marriageable age, everyone in Greece knew of her beauty. She had suitors from every corner of the land. Now, having dozens of young men gathered in one place, with one object, and itching to show off, more often than not led to violence. Cleverly, Tyndareos arranged for Helen's suitors, instead of coming in person, to send gifts. Marvelous items poured in: bronze tripods, serving girls, sewing baskets on little wheels, lyres, daggers, bolts of woven and oiled cloth, horse bits, saddle blankets, wheel spokes, silver tiaras, shield straps, perfume bottles, purple dye, sheep and cattle, pet weasels, wine mixing bowls, ivory combs, and a hunting dog. Odysseus was the only man who did not send a gift, for he was sure who the winner would be, and it was not him. He did, however, make a suggestion to Helen's father. He should hold all the suitors to an oath, that if anything ever happened (i.e., another abduction) they would rally to recover Helen, wherever she was. Tyndareos thought this an excellent idea. At the Tomb of the Horse (as we call it now), on the road out of town, he sacrificed a stallion and solemnly sealed the defense pact in blood. For his help, Odysseus was in turn aided by Tyndareos, who interceded with his niece, bearing a marriage proposal on the Ithacan king's behalf. She was a fine girl from the countryside, Helen's first cousin, named Penelope.

Helen was allowed to choose her own husband. Two factors may have influenced her. First, her sister Klytaimnestra was already married to Agamemnon, who had a brother not yet wed. Second, this brother happened to be the richest suitor. And so, as Odysseus had cynically foreseen, Helen picked Menelaos, and everyone approved. In retrospect, perhaps she should have paid more attention to family background and less to wealth. While the sons of Atreus were both handsome and well off, lords of hilltop fortresses and masters of thousands, their lineage was haunted by a curse, which ironically arose out of a marriage.

That story began back in Lydia, in western Asia, with the infamous Tantalos. Then the gods liked his company. He socialized with them on a number of occasions. He knew the taste of nectar and ambrosia (although the Olympians made sure he never had more than a taste). He began looking forward to being immortal. Overconfident, he decided to break the strictest taboo and share divine food with his friends in the town where he lived. For this he was eventually punished in Hades—the food and drink just within his grasp would maddeningly move away whenever he went to grab them. To add to his humiliation, his son, Pelops, was cast out of Olympus, where Poseidon had once brought him in a passion over the boy. Tantalos had been inordinately proud that his child had achieved such an important position, and the ejection of his son depressed him even more than losing eternal life. The final insult was that rumors spread concerning the boy's whereabouts. Some said that Tantalos had given the gods a feast of his son's own flesh. Demeter had even unthinkingly bitten into a shoulder (in grief over her daughter, she had not noticed what she was eating). The other gods discovered the horrid secret of the meal right away, and for this reason Tantalos lost their favor. Even when Pelops reappeared, the rumor irrationally kept going the rounds, and some claimed that the young man had an artificial ivory shoulder.

What proves the version about Poseidon to be correct is this: when Pelops had come to the age for finding a wife, he heard of a suitable woman and got divine aid by calling on the sea god. Their earlier bond led Poseidon to grant him a golden chariot and winged horses just when Pelops needed them for courting Hippodameia. That is because the father of this splendid young woman had presented an obstacle to any potential suitor. Before any man could take away his daughter, Oinomaos demanded that he join in a chariot race, all the way across the land from Elis to the Isthmus, in which the king was the only other competitor. Losers of the race lost their lives. Thirteen victims had already been claimed, and their skulls decorated the palace walls. The king was simply too swift and too brutal. Although Pelops had the better horses, when he came to the contest he decided to ensure his victory. He made the acquaintance of the king's charioteer, a fellow named Myrtilos, a son of Hermes. After a few casual meetings, Pelops made him an offer. If he would remove the linchpin that fastened the wheel of the king's chariot, half of the kingdom would be his. At last Myrtilos agreed.

The day for the "abduction" race arrived. (This was how the king devised it. Suitors had to pretend that they were running off with the bride in an old ritual known as "Centaur marriage," at which point Oinomaos, good father that he was, would "rescue" his own daughter and of course spear the unfortunate contestant.) Pelops got the usual head start. He drove up to the prescribed mark, grabbed Hippodameia, placed her in the chariot box, whipped his horses, and headed east at full speed. Then the father began to chase.

Anyone watching from a hill along the road would have seen the distance between them steadily decrease. Soon Oinomaos was standing with his spear ready, waiting to get close enough to drive it straight through Pelops. His horses were proving a match for Poseidon's—or maybe the god's were just warming up. Also warming up, however, was the wheel of the king's vehicle. It had stayed on thus far because Myrtilos had substituted a wax linchpin for the real one. But friction did its job; the wax melted and the wheel began to wobble. Myrtilos, seeing this, jumped off, not a moment too soon. The crash that followed killed the king instantly.

Pelops, now master of all the lands of central Greece, first named the whole territory west of the Isthmus "Pelops' island" (Peloponnese). Next, he embarked on a royal progress around his new realm. Myrtilos went along as driver. Whether the charioteer had misinterpreted the bargain made before the fatal race, or (as a trickster's son might do) was taking his chances and pushing his luck, at one point in the journey, when they had stopped for rest at a spot overlooking the sea, he tried to force himself on Hippodameia. She screamed; Pelops came running, seized his former conspirator, and hurled him off the cliff. As he plummeted down, Myrtilos cursed the house of Pelops unto the fourth generation. Or so some said. Darker rumors circulated later—for instance, that Myrtilos had not attempted rape at all. Instead Pelops simply reneged on his offer. Once he saw how rich his kingdom was, he could not bear to part with half.

This was the house that Helen married into. Even worse stories circulated about the intervening generations. It is well known that one son of Pelops, the boy Khrysippos, was indirectly the cause of a curse on the Theban kings. Pelops had two other sons, Atreus and Thyestes, who brought to fruition their own family's doom. After Pelops was dead and buried (at Olympus, where his ivory shoulder bone is still displayed), his heirs disputed the kingship of Mycenae, finest of his many cities. Atreus had the first claim (so he said). He rightfully held the scepter, the symbol of power that Zeus himself had bestowed on Pelops. Furthermore, a golden-fleeced lamb had been found in his flocks, an obvious indication of the gods' enduring favor. (Actually, Hermes had planted the animal, wanting to cause a furor and get revenge on the family that killed his son.) Thyestes found a way to hurt Atreus and get the kingdom in the process. He seduced Aeropê, his brother's wife. Then he proposed before an assembly of Mycenaeans that they should confirm as rightful king the possessor of the famous golden lamb. Atreus should have suspected something. But, confident that the animal was in a storage box where he had left it (after choking its life out, lest it wander off), he readily agreed. "Fetch the box," he ordered one of his servants. It was produced, was opened—and was empty. Aeropê had secretly transferred the lamb to her lover, Thyestes, who now became the king.

The dispute was not over yet. Atreus knew he had been cuckolded and tricked. At the coronation, he made an extravagant toast, which could also, by legalistic minds, be taken as an agreement: "To my brother Thyestes—may he be king forever, from now until the sun sets in the east!" To show there were no hard feelings, he even invited his brother to a feast. The wines were superb; the music enchanting; the food well flavored and carefully prepared. "Now that we have finished, brother, and made up in such an excellent way," said Thyestes when he had eaten his fill, "I'd like to bring in my children, so that they can see how good their uncle is. Where are they, by the way?" Atreus said, "They're already here. That is, the parts of them that are not inside you." With that he tossed at his brother three little boys' heads.

In disgust and horror at this deed, Helios, the Sun, who sees all, wheeled his chariot around. That day he did not finish his daily course. Of all the crimes he had witnessed since the beginning of the world, this fiendish banquet was the most awful. In shock he returned to his home in the east and sank into his bed. The condition thus was met. Time and cosmos were reversed. Thyestes gave up the throne and left the city, a broken man.

## 50.  PRELUDE TO WAR

Once installed in the royal palace, Paris had the means and leisure to carry out his plan to find the woman Aphrodite had promised him. He had a ship built for himself and rounded up a crew. Taking along his cousin Aeneas, he sailed for the Peloponnese. They landed on the south coast, near Gythion. On the way north to Sparta, the Trojans found a hospitable welcome with Kastor and Polydeukes, the twin brothers of Helen. At the palace of Menelaos and Helen a few days later, Paris dazzled the king and his wife with rich gifts from the east—silks and dyes, jewelry and dinnerware of the type the land-locked country gentry never saw. The adventurers had been in Sparta only a short time when Menelaos was called away by a death in the family. He would have to see to his cousin's affairs on Crete, he said, and he would be back in a fortnight. Meanwhile, Helen was to "give our Trojan guests anything they want."

Aphrodite appeared the night the king sailed for the south. Wine and torchlight, the sirocco and late-night walks, smoothed the way. Helen at last was in the arms of Paris. He planned their "escape" and went into action immediately. Helen, intoxicated by the power of Aphrodite, seemed to have only a moment of hesitation, in her parting with Hermione, her nine-year-old girl. After that, everything happened in a blur. She remembered later taking all the precious goods they could carry out of the palace and piling them onto a wagon and driving madly by moonlight for the coast. Even the storm that Hera sent, their forced landing in Phoenicia, the gaudy wedding, meeting all those new relatives at Troy, all seemed to take place in one breathless, timeless day.

Not long after their departure, Helen's brothers met their end, as the result of cattle rustling. The sons of Aphareus, who was the aggrieved party, pursued the Dioskouroi and attacked them on their way back home from Messenê. They had once all been crewmates on the *Argo,* and so Helen's brothers should have realized they could not hide. Lynkeus, one of the sons of the man they robbed, had the ability to see through solid objects. All he had to do was stand atop Mt. Taugetos and scan the woods below. He spotted Kastor and his brother hiding in a great hollow oak. Silently creeping down to the place, he plunged his spear straight through the tree bark and into Kastor's body. Polydeukes, the immortal twin, leapt out and killed both Lynkeus and his brother Idas with a sword. Then, in his grief at surviving, he begged his father Zeus to let him die so that his brother might have life. That would have been outside the bounds of what was allowed, so Zeus compromised. He gave the twins an alternating life. One of them breathed and saw the light on Olympus one day, while the other slept beneath the ground (at Therapnai near their boyhood home). The next day they would switch.

Menelaos got the double dose of bad news simultaneously: Helen gone, and her brothers (her rescuers in the past) no longer available. He hastened to Mycenae to consult with his brother Agamemnon. Clearly, the time for their sworn alliance had come. But this was not a course to enter lightly. Together, they made a trip to Pylos to see Nestor, wisest of counsellors, a man who had outlived two generations and was lasting out his third. They had to endure his old-fashioned storytelling, filled with mythic precedents and endless obscure details. He talked to them about Epopeus, Oedipus, the madness of Herakles, and how Theseus had abandoned Ariadne. If there was a point to all this, it escaped the brothers, but they were reassured that Law and Tradition (in the person of this aged warrior) were on their side. Not to mention Zeus—had not this been a violation of *xenia,* the universal custom of guest friendship, under the protection of the king of the gods?

With Nestor to lend authority, they then proceeded to gather war chieftains. The former suitors came willingly and swiftly—most of them. An exception was Odysseus, who had been a halfhearted suitor anyway. Penelope, the wife of Odysseus, had just borne a son—their first child—and the proud father was reluctant to leave Ithaca to go chasing after a rich man's flighty wife. When he heard that the recruiting party was approaching, he put on a fur cap, although it was summer, and yoked an ox and horse to his plow (an impossible combination for real fieldwork—besides, it was the wrong season). Agamemnon and the others found him sowing salt in the one furrow he had managed to dig. While they watched, he went back to the plow and started another row. "The man's mad," said Nestor, and his companions agreed. They were shaking their heads, preparing to go, when one of the group, Palamedes, stopped them. "Wait a moment," he said. Snatching Telemakhos, the infant son of Odysseus, from his nurse's arms, he ran down the row and placed the baby in the dirt two feet in front of the plow. Odysseus veered sharply to avoid running through his child. "See?" Palamedes turned to the other chieftains. "It's all an act." So the ruse of Odysseus failed, yet he never forgot the man who had exposed him.

On Skyros, where Achilles had been hidden, it was Odysseus who smoked him out. Together with Nestor, he had gone first to Phthia to visit Peleus, for an oracle had said that Troy would fall only with the help of that just king's son. "He is not here," the father said. It took some pressure and Nestor's vast powers of persuasion to extract from Peleus even the vaguest hints of where the young hero was. Odysseus, meanwhile, questioned the help, who were usually privy to palace secrets. After some time, he and Nestor focused on the right island. But when they landed at the place they saw no sign of a youthful warrior. A court, a king, a bevy of young ladies—that was all. It made Odysseus suspicious. He thought up a plan. Under the pretense of offering the women of the place suitable gifts, he and Nestor spread before them a selection of articles—belts and ribbons, baubles, beads, knucklebone dice, silk scarves. Also, scattered here and there were some less suitable items—a slender sword, a bronze spearhead, a polished hunting horn. These latter gifts the ladies ignored, while they busied themselves with handling the stylish accessories. But one girl, Odysseus noticed, kept eyeing the sword, even going so far as to run her finger along the blade when she thought the visitors were looking the other way. Their fish was about to take the bait. But no, she backed off, feigning interest in a perfume jar. Odysseus left the room. A short time passed, and then a tremendous trumpet blast sounded. Attack! The city was being invaded! The women screamed and scattered—all except one, who tossed off her veil and lunged for the sword, ready to run to the city wall to defend Skyros. "We found you," said Odysseus, reentering the room. That was his first acquaintance with Achilles, who never forgot the man who had exposed *his* ruse.

Next they had to take care of provisions. A team sailed to Delos, Apollo's island, where they arranged for the services of three remarkable maidens, the daughters of Anios—Seed, Olive, and Winette (*Spermô, Elais, Oinô*), whose special powers enabled them effortlessly to produce the foods and drink for which they had been named. When the warriors were ready to sail, they gathered at a place called Aulis. As they were sacrificing, an omen appeared. A speckled snake slithered out from a rock next to the altar. There was a nest of sparrows nearby, in a bush not far off the ground. The snake leapt, seized the nestlings (eight in all), gulped them down, and then devoured their mother. Immediately, he was turned into stone by the power of Zeus. "So it will be with us," said Kalkhas, the army's seer. "After nine years, we will seize Troy." What he did not say was why the Greeks should be represented by a snake in the grass, or what the serpent's petrification might imply.

They sailed the next morning. It was not an experienced crew. Perhaps if one of the old Argonauts had gone along, they would not have ended up missing their objective, since the *Argo* had sailed this way long ago. But Jason, Orpheus, Kastor and Polydeukes, Laertes, Herakles—all were dead, immortalized, or simply too old to join this, the greatest of the Greek expeditions. With only a vague knowledge of the coast of Asia, the army landed in fog and night miles away at Mysia.

The inhabitants rallied to defend their land. Achilles wounded one, the king of the place, called Telephos, who in the first wave of attack had killed Thersander, son of the ill-fated Theban Polyneikes. All the blood and confusion, cursing and screams of pain—this had not been Achilles' notion of war. It was a shock to discover the underside of glory. The Greeks were forced to retreat in disorder to the ships. Before they could find where they were supposed to go, a summer storm came up and scattered the fleet far and wide.

They went back to Greece to regroup and mobilize once more. Achilles arrived later. His ship had been blown off course, but came to land at Skyros, the very island he had hid on as a "girl" not long before. Now he came as a man, and immediately he married Deidameia, the king's eldest daughter, though he could only stay briefly. Soon after he rejoined the others at Aulis, Telephos arrived in much pain. An oracle had told him that he must find the one who wounded him in order to be healed. Achilles proudly admitted to the deed, "but I am no doctor," he said. "In my case how can 'the wounder heal'?" (That was the phrase of the oracle.) "This way," said Odysseus. From Achilles' long ash spear he scraped some flecks of rust, mixed them in water, and applied it to the wound. Telephos was cured. In return, he promised to guide the Greek fleet to Troy.

The ships and men were ready; the horses and provisions had been stowed. But now the breezes that would bear them east had died. Instead, a gale-force wind blew steadily, relentlessly opposing them. Kalkhas was called on to uncover the inscrutable workings of the gods. He tested the sacrificial signs, noted the position of the tail as the carcass burned, the marks on the liver, and concluded, "Artemis is offended." Agamemnon, it emerged, had shot a deer, the sacred animal of the goddess, in her sanctuary grove. To make matters worse, he had boasted of his shot: "As good as the Huntress, aren't I?" Others said later that it was not so much what the king had done, but what he was about to do: rip children from their mothers in Troy, raze a city, and destroy a nation. All those young were what the goddess had in mind; the pregnant doe, struck down, was just a harbinger. By this logic, the punishment therefore fit the crime. How would Agamemnon feel to lose his own fawn? That was what Artemis commanded. For the winds to drop and the fleet to sail, the chieftain's daughter Iphigeneia must be sacrificed on the altar of Artemis of the Golden Arrows.

Now his neck was in the noose. He could either ignore one divinity or the other—but which? To allow Helen's abductor and all his tainted city to go free, those who had trodden on Zeus' *xenia*, to disband the alliance of the warrior kings? Or to destroy his family by upholding Law? Agamemnon, groaning deeply, bowed to the cruel yoke of necessity. "Odysseus will go," he told the council. "Tell her mother Iphigeneia is to be a bride." And so Klytaimnestra heard from the wiliest Greek that Achilles, the world's most desirable son-in-law, was eagerly waiting at Aulis to wed her daughter. Iphigeneia bid farewell and set off from Mycenae with her dowry, her mother waving until the chariot passed from view. Every marriage, she thought, was like a death, with children handed over to a strange man far away. Later, when she heard how they had hoisted her like a beast and carried her to the altar, her young flower, clothed in a saffron gown, how she offered meekly her tender neck, Klytaimnestra lost all her will to live. She would keep going only long enough to take her revenge.

The winds subsided once blood had been shed. On the way to Troy, only one incident detained them. They put in at Tenedos for the night and were preparing their meals when Philoktetes was bitten by a water snake. The wound immediately began to fester, and the men complained of the foul smell. Worse, they thought this would pollute their rituals, offending the gods with its uncleanness. So they abandoned him with a few supplies and his famous bow (the gift of Herakles) on the island of Lemnos, not far from their final destination.

Their landing at Troy provoked a fight right away. Protesilaos died on the Greek side; Achilles killed a son of Poseidon named Swan (after his white hair). An embassy was sent to formally demand Helen and the stolen possessions, but the Trojans refused. Menelaos and Odysseus, the heads of the mission, barely escaped the city with their lives, so angry were the Trojans over the assault. Realizing that the omens of a long siege were probably right, the Greeks drew up the ships onto the beach and settled down to build their own defensive wall.

Occasionally, raiding parties were sent out to harass cities along the coast allied to the Trojans. At Lyrnessos, after Achilles slew the king and a number of fighters, he was awarded the widow of one man as his war prize. Her name was Briseis. At Thêbê, they sacked the city. Eetion was killed along with his seven sons. Later, his daughter Andromache would recall, amid all the horror, one honorable act: Achilles did not strip her father's corpse but burned it, in full armor, and he gave him the proper burial rites. Mountain nymphs planted slender elms around the tomb mound. Her mother had been spared and sold back for ransom, at Troy, where the daughter lived as wife of Hector, Priam's gentle son. From the same city, Thêbê, another prize of war came, the priest's daughter, Khryseis, won by Agamemnon as a mark of honor. She would one day set in motion the events that would kill Hector and in turn Achilles.

## 51.  THE WRATH OF ACHILLES

For nine years the siege and the raids continued. The Trojans, when they ventured out, could never reach the ships to burn them, or drive the Greeks into the sea. The Greek forces, meanwhile, although they included the men of a thousand ships or more, never could mount the walls of the citadel. It was a stalemate. Cables and halyards rotted on the beach. Camp followers moved in. The occupying force became a little city in itself. And like a city, it bred the plague. The dogs were the first to be stricken, then the mules. In humans the symptoms were all too plain—a rash, then a raging fever, accompanied by a desperate thirst; in the later stages, hallucinations, numbness, and death. It was as though Apollo had descended from Olympus with his quiver full of fatal arrows and was picking off the troops one by one. Every night the pyres blazed.

Kalkhas, the seer, knew the reason for the plague. But he was afraid to reveal the bad news until Achilles promised to defend him, no matter who was named as the cause of their ills. "Agamemnon," came the answer. "He has dishonored the priest of Apollo who came to pay ransom for his captive daughter. Because his prayers to the god were answered, we are paying with our tears, and shall pay until all is put right." The remedy was obvious: he had to return Khryseis. But Agamemnon was highly insulted at this turn of events. The loss of status, his war prize gone, the thought he was responsible for the deaths of his own men—it was too much. He lashed back. "I will release her, but let the Greeks give me another. Or if they don't, I'll just come and take any girl I want. Maybe yours, Odysseus. Maybe yours, Ajax. Or maybe Achilles' own. I cannot be without a mark of honor." This made Achilles furious. "Honor? We slave for you, and you take all of it. Nobody stole my cows or took my wife. I volunteered for this expedition to retrieve your Helen. And now you are carting off your own fighters' women!" He would have chopped down Agamemnon on the spot had not Athena restrained him, promising that his enemy would soon regret his hubris. In protest, Achilles quit the fighting. He retired to his tent with a threat: "One day you'll miss Achilles, when dozens die at Hector's hands. Then you'll gnaw at the very heart within you, seeing that you dishonored the best of the Greeks."

Still, the men of the chief took Briseis, Achilles' war prize. Afterward, the hero walked by the gray sea and prayed to Thetis. His mother emerged from the waves, asking why her son was so sad. Achilles recounted the story, imploring her to use her influence with Zeus. "Beg him to help the Trojans. Let the Greeks be pinned down and slaughtered against their ships. They'll learn what a good king is when they see what destruction Agamemnon has brought them." Hearing this terrible request, Thetis remained silent for a moment. Then she replied quietly, "When he returns from the Aithiopians, where the gods have gone to share a sacrifice—I will." When she did, Zeus consented. The tide of battle turned against the Greeks.

At first the goddesses who hated Troy—Athena and Hera—had helped their favorites prevail. But then, after Zeus banned the Olympians from entering the battle, Hector soon pushed the invaders to the edge of the plain. The next day would surely bring about their destruction. With Achilles not taking part, Troy would be saved.

The other leaders of the Greeks knew that Agamemnon had to give in. Reluctantly, he agreed. As if negotiating with a foreign power, an embassy came to Achilles' tent with the warlord's promises. Briseis would be returned—Agamemnon had never touched her, he swore by the gods. In addition, Achilles would be given seven tripods, ten talents of gold, twenty bronze cauldrons, twelve prizewinning horses, seven women (all of them knowing handicrafts) from Lesbos, where the girls are prettiest. If the Greeks should win, Achilles would also be given twenty Trojan women. Upon their return to Greece, he could choose whichever daughter of Agamemnon caught his eye and marry her. A list of the cities he might administer followed.

"Only have pity on us—that is all we ask," concluded Odysseus. Perhaps he was the wrong man for the mission, for Achilles not only despised him for his ruses, but saw through the offer right away. If he accepted the gifts, he would be obligated to fight. Besides, he had moved beyond such considerations. "One fate awaits us, whether you fight or not. We are dead men all, no matter how hard we strive. I risked my life day after day, spent sleepless nights, killing for a man's wife, and what does he do? Sit back and rake in all the booty, and take my personal prize as well. Let him have her. Do you think the Atreids are the only ones who love their mates? I'm leaving. Tomorrow, look out to sea. That will be me, in my ship, sailing home to Phthia. Tripods and cattle and horses abound. Plenty of them, all there for the taking. But once a man's spirit flies out his mouth, you can't recover it, can't steal it back. I have a choice: either stay and die at Troy winning glory, or go home—without glory, but a long, good life. So tell Agamemnon to concoct a better plan."

His other comrades tried to soften his stance. Phoinix, the old man who had been sent by Peleus to be his mentor and adviser, related the story of Meleager, Herakles' brother-in-law. This version was slightly different from the versions Achilles knew. Instead of dying at his mother's hands, when the log that signified his life was placed in the hearth, Meleager was cursed by her. She summoned a Fury to haunt him, because her son had killed his maternal uncle in a squabble after the Hunt of the Boar. Hurt and angry, in the midst of the war that followed, Meleager hid himself away. No one could persuade him to put aside his wrath and come out to defend the town—not the old men, the priests, his father, or his sisters, rattle the door and beg as they might. They offered gifts of the richest land. He refused. His companions tried. He turned them away. Then, when the enemy was at the gates, setting fire to the town, his wife entreated Meleager, telling him of all the sorrows that befall women and young children captured in war. Hearing this, he was moved to don his armor and wage battle. He saved the town, but the victory was harder won than if he had emerged from seclusion earlier. And furthermore, by that time the precious gifts once offered had been withdrawn. "So you, too," concluded Phoinix, "should fight before it is too late. It will be harder when the ships are all aflame. And the gifts are still here for you—take them now."

Achilles had just rejected those very gifts, but he knew Phoinix was too clever to be repeating the offer of Odysseus. A message was hidden in his words, something to do, he thought, with the odd detail about Meleager's wife—a new character, surely, in the familiar story. Kleopatra meant "glory of the fathers." Her name was like an ancestral memory and a call to action. "Stay the night," Achilles answered. "We'll decide about this matter in the morning."

The next day began as one of unrelieved disaster. In quick succession the leading fighters were disabled: Agamemnon, Idomeneus, Odysseus, all limped off the field. From his tent Achilles caught a glimpse of old Nestor madly driving another wounded soldier from the front line in his chariot and taking him to his tent. He suspected it was the doctor-hero Makhaon. Without the healer they surely would be doomed. He sent Patroklos to confirm who it was.

That is when Nestor hatched his latest plan. With Achilles' dearest companion still standing at the door, the old raconteur told of his own glory days. How he had gone to war at sixteen without his father's permission. Long-forgotten cattle raids, blood feuds, ambushes. Nestor the hero, Nestor honored like a god. "That was *aretê*, real manly virtue. But that Achilles of yours, he's throwing away his chance."

He shifted into a new key, reminding Patroklos of his father's instructions when he left for war (Nestor had been there, and remembered all the details). Patroklos was the older, wiser companion, Nestor pointed out. He should be the one to persuade his tent mate to join the fight. If Achilles still refused, then maybe he should let Patroklos put on his armor and be "a saving beacon to the Greeks" in his stead. At least this masquerade would give the embattled fighters some relief.

Nestor's words sank in deep. Patroklos entreated Achilles, but the wrathful warrior would not budge. A vow was a vow. He would stay put until fire reached the ships. But he did relent when Patroklos asked if he could take his place. "Carve out some space on the battle-field for our men. Show yourself to the enemy. They'll think you are me and run off. But don't pursue them or try to take Troy on your own. You'll deprive me of the honor." He made it seem like self-regard, but in his heart what prompted the last words was the fear his companion might not return.

That was precisely what happened. Pushing forward in the fury of the battle, Patroklos came right to the city walls. Apollo warned him: three times the god pushed him off. The fourth time, with one mighty whack of his hand, the god knocked all the armor of Achilles off his companion's body. (All that he left behind was Achilles' ash spear, too heavy for any but the hero to handle.) Naked to his enemy, Patroklos was stabbed by one Trojan and finished off by Hector with a slash of the sword.

After the hardest fighting yet, the body was finally recovered and brought to Achilles. He poured dust over his head, rocking back and forth in mourning. "I sent my dearest friend in my place, and so now I must perish." Thetis held Achilles' head, as if he had already died, while her Nereid sisters keened a lament. Then she went to request a new set from the divine craftsman Hephaestus, immortal armor for the final duel.

## 52.   THE END OF TROY

The wrath of Achilles turned outward, toward the enemy. The feud was settled in his own camp. He took Briseis back. "Even Zeus was once overtaken by Destruction," Agamemnon said as he presided over the little ceremony of return. The excuse did not impress Achilles. His mind was fixed only on finding the man who had killed his friend, and on venting his grief and rage on him in turn.

He refused to eat. Silently, he marshaled the Myrmidons. Then, taking the splendid immortal armor that Thetis had brought from Olympus, he plunged into battle. Light like flames blazed from his helmet and shield. Seeing him, the Trojans shrank back in pure terror.

Zeus now permitted all the Olympians to take sides and battle shoulder to shoulder with Greeks and Trojans. Achilles cut down the enemy like so many sheep. He herded them into the river, stabbing and wounding, drowning those who had not died by his spear. The river Skamandros was choked off with corpses. It rose up in anger and chased Achilles down the plain, a flood tide rolling behind him, cresting and rushing like a mad bull. The Greek hero would have been overwhelmed and drowned had not Hera sought out Hephaestus. "Rouse yourself, my child. Cast your fire at Xanthos" (this was the gods' name for the river). The lame smith aimed his burning blasts at the banks. Cypresses and elms on the riverside shriveled up. In its watercourse the bodies were incinerated. Eels and fish flapped wildly as the waters boiled. The whole plain became scorched. Still he poured on flames until at last the river called out, "Enough! I swear never again to aid the Trojans."

Meanwhile, the gods were battling one another. Athena struck Ares with a boulder. Poseidon and Apollo met to clash, but Apollo yielded, which enraged his twin sister. She tried to shame him into fighting with abusive words. Hera, however, yelled right back, "Go hunt deer in the mountains, you shameless bitch," then boxed her ears and took away her bow and arrows.

The Trojans fled toward the city walls. But Apollo, the main antagonist of Achilles, had taken human disguise to lure him apart from the fighting, making him give chase. He revealed himself at last, when many of his favored people had made it safely back. "It is not fated for you to take me." To which Achilles replied, "If I had the strength, I would."

He rushed toward the walls. He was like a baleful star that plummets through the dark sky, warning of pestilence. Priam, watching from above, and Hekabe, his wife, begged their son Hector to come inside, to save himself, but they could not persuade him. He waited, briefly wondering what would happen if he put aside his weapons and bargained with Achilles. If Helen, her possessions, and all the wealth of Troy went to the Greeks, the city could be saved. Then he snapped back into reality. "This is no place for friendly bartering. We'll fight to see which side the Olympians favor."

Yet when the final onslaught came, he ran. Achilles chased him three times around Troy. The fourth time Zeus held his scales of battle, and the life of Hector dipped low. Athena took a position at Achilles' side, assuring him that Hector's hour had come. Then she disguised herself as the Trojan's brother. Hector, overjoyed to see that he had help, took courage and challenged Achilles. The Greek's spear was cast but missed. Hector cast and also missed. He turned around to get a second spear from his brother Deiphobos—and saw that he had vanished. At that moment Hector realized that the gods had tricked him and were summoning him to his death.

Achilles felt an eerie sensation as he cut the Trojan down, since Hector was wearing Achilles' own armor (taken from Patroklos). And yet, in one way, it was a proper omen. Destroying his enemy would seal his own fate.

Then he was filled with rage exceeding all bounds. Berserk, he dragged the stiffened body of Hector through the dust around Troy every day for a week, tied to the back of his chariot by a belt looped through the ankles. With the gods' aid (for this horrified them as well) Priam personally visited Achilles and begged him to give his son back, offering a ransom. Looking at the aged king, he was reminded of his own father, Peleus, back in Phthia. Soon enough he too would mourn for a lost son. So that was the secret, he thought: the glory of ancestors lay in the sorrow of fathers. Achilles let his wrath go and returned the corpse.

After a truce for the funeral of Hector, the war entered its final stage. Two waves of allies came to support the city. First, the Amazons arrived, led by Penthesileia, their queen. She fought like a man and died like one, at Achilles' hands. It was respect for this opponent that enraged him when Thersites—ugliest soldier among the Greeks, a hunchbacked, squint-eyed, bowlegged little runt—mocked Achilles as he carried the Amazon's body. "Now you embrace your beloved," shouted Thersites. "I bet she's a beauty without the armor." He would have gone on in this disgusting vein had not Achilles knocked him dead with one punch. The next opponent was the most handsome warrior to join the fight: Memnon, son of Dawn, an ally from the east. He killed Nestor's beloved son, Antilokhos, after the young man had rushed into the fray to rescue his father, whose chariot horse had been wounded. Achilles slew him to avenge that deed. Then Memnon's mother, with the permission of Zeus, gently lifted him from the plain and brought him to the Isles of the Blessed, where he became immortal, just as the Dawn herself is deathless and unaging.

Achilles had known for some time not only that he would soon die, but where and how. Hector, with his last breath, had foretold that. "Paris and Phoibos Apollo will bring you down, noble as you are, at the Skaian Gates." Even the horse of Achilles (a divine one, Poseidon's wedding gift to his parents) spoke in prophecy before his entry to the fateful battle. "It was not our fault that Patroklos lost his life. You, too, are fated to perish at the hands of a god and a man."

As with most momentous events, it happened one otherwise ordinary afternoon. Achilles and a few select companions (Ajax was one) pursued the Trojans once more to the walls. They arrived at the Skaian Gates (the main entry, always a spot of fierce fighting) when Paris somehow got behind the Greeks and shot an arrow into Achilles' ankle. It was his one vulnerable spot, and how Paris knew this is not hard to guess, for even as he shot, say some who saw it happening, another, larger, helmeted figure guided his hand: Achilles' nemesis, Apollo. At last the god was satisfied. No mere mortal hero would ever be as dangerous as he was.

As Odysseus provided cover, Ajax brought his cousin back, Achilles' corpse slung over his shoulder, with the helmet off and the dead man's long blond hair hanging down. The Muses themselves gathered at the pyre to sing the lament for the most glorious of the Greeks. Thetis and the daughters of Nereus came from the sea, with a sound like rushing waves. At the moment when Agamemnon's torch was about to ignite the piled logs, as the ululations of the women were reaching their loudest peak, the sea nymph sprang up and plucked her son away. She carried him through the sea to the White Island, where he lives still, although his burial mound is pointed out today on the shore near Troy, the city he never lived to see conquered. At least, that is the pleasant version. More hard-bitten elders will tell you that the pyre burned for days on end, and then they carefully collected the white bones, put them in a golden urn—the same one that contained the bones of Patroklos—and buried Achilles with his beloved companion, as he had wanted. The usual games followed—men celebrating life by the pulse of their blood, as if to think away the darkness. Then the question of the divine armor arose. Who should be given it now that Achilles had passed on? Agamemnon said, "Let's take a vote. We have plenty of Trojan prisoners here—we'll ask them which did their side most harm, Ajax or Odysseus."

Of course, the Greek leaders—Agamemnon and his brother—tallied the results. "Odysseus," they announced. Ajax thought the voting had been fixed (as it may have been), and now it was his turn to withdraw in anger. In his quarters, he smoldered with resentment all that evening. He was the best, not that sneaking Odysseus. He would show those pompous oafs, the Atreids, and their lapdog from Ithaca, bastard son of Sisyphus. With these and similar thoughts, Athena stoked him into madness. Yet when he seized a sword, intending to kill Agamemnon and every other chieftain he could find, it was Athena who deflected him. She turned his wrath against a pen full of captured animals. Ajax slashed and cursed as he slaughtered them in blind delusion. Then, still believing he was exacting vengeance on his filthy enemies, he strung up a dead ram and tortured it inside his hut. This scene Athena revealed to Odysseus the next dawn, thinking he would enjoy the sight. Even the Ithacan, however, was revolted; sometimes mortals have more decency than gods. Ajax slowly came out of his trance. Ashamed of his actions, and regretting his loss, he went off to a spot by the river, stuck his sword upright in the sand, and threw himself onto its point. Odysseus, at least, showed mercy toward him. When the Atreids demanded that this lunatic who wanted their blood be left to rot, he intervened humanely, pointing out that "all of us are just images and empty shade." The right to burial was granted.

With Achilles gone, the possibility of taking Troy by storm was slipping rapidly away. As it happened, a captured Trojan prophet—Helenos, one of Hector's brothers—supplied a clue that would lead to victory. "You'll never take our city," the man told them, "not until the bow of Herakles himself shoots down our captain." At first the Greeks despaired: Herakles was long dead (or taken up to Olympus). He had once attacked Troy, in his vigorous youth, after Laomedon had cheated him out of the payment that was due him for subduing a sea monster. The father of Ajax, Telamon, had accompanied Herakles on that expedition. But that was in the past.

Odysseus came up with the solution to the dilemma. "The bow of Herakles—not the man. Just as the rust of Achilles' spear cured Telephos—not the man." He was always good at thinking logically. "And I know where that weapon lies, because I myself put it on the beach in Lemnos, with its owner. Do you remember Philoktetes?" Most of them did not, at first. Ten years had passed and still the Thessalian archer was confined to the offshore island, suffering from his festering wound. Odysseus volunteered to get the bow.

How he did it is disputed. Most likely, he used a disguise (another specialty of his). According to some accounts, he assumed the role of his own victim: that is, he managed to convince Philoktetes that he was a disenchanted soldier who had been a friend of Palamedes. Odysseus, earlier in the war, had framed the man (who had tricked him into joining the expedition). He made it look like he had accepted Trojan bribes as a spy, and Palamedes had been stoned to death. The friend of Palamedes later became suspicious, so Odysseus had him driven out of the camp. This extended lie so much appealed to Philoktetes that he befriended the "soldier" as a fellow enemy of Odysseus. Once he had gained the wounded man's trust, Odysseus snatched the bow (his only life support) and left. A kinder version says that Odysseus worked through an emissary—Neoptolemos, Achilles' young son—and obtained the needed bow by even more elaborate deceptions. At least in that telling, Philoktetes was cured. When he came to Troy with his weapon, he was healed by Makhaon.

By the arrows from the unerring bow of the old-time hero, Paris was shot down. With her second husband dead, Helen was married to the dead man's brother (as was the custom), the older Deiphobos. He was the one who accompanied her one night to view a marvel that had just been taken into Troy—a huge and beautiful horse, crafted entirely from wood, forty feet tall, with a tail that moved and realistic eyes. The Trojans had to take down a portion of the wall in order to get the horse into the city, where they dragged it up to the citadel. It was to be a dedication to Athena, whose statue stood on the heights of Troy. A huge celebration and days of festivity were planned, for now the Greeks had gone. The day before, the Trojans had seen huge fires at the end of the plain. The Greeks had burned their camp and taken to their ships, leaving only this strange object on the shore.

The Trojans had approached it cautiously. "Burn it," yelled some. "Toss it from a cliff," others insisted. "It can't bode well." Kassandra, the prophetess, nervously made warnings, but as usual no one heeded her. As they were debating, a bedraggled man, calling himself Sinon, came up the beach and signaled to the Trojans. They learned that he had been left behind because he hated the other Greeks—the ones who had killed his friend Palamedes. To get revenge, he was willing to betray them. He would tell the secret of this massive wooden horse. "It is an offering," he whispered. "They want to placate Athena so they can sail back to Greece without disaster befalling them. It's made so big because the Greeks wanted to make sure it would stay in place here. The city that encloses it will be impossible to conquer."

Laokoon, a priest of Apollo, was still not convinced. He even went so far as to toss a spear against the belly of the contraption. Some swore they heard a hollow thud. But before anyone could investigate, two giant serpents sailed in from the bay, slithered up the beach, and coiled themselves around Laokoon. His sons ran to save him, but they too were entangled. Helplessly, the Trojans watched as the family was squeezed to death. That was an omen, they thought. This was a gift for the gods, and anyone who questioned it was clearly wicked.

What they could not know was that Poseidon had sent the serpents to trick his enemies, that Sinon's little story was a well-rehearsed deception, and that Athena had inspired the Greeks to construct this horse. The Greek camp carpenter, Epeios, had built it according to her instructions. Small horse statues were frequently used in dedication, so the Trojans were not wrong to treat this giant one as a great boon. The reason it was so large, of course, was that the horse enclosed twelve handpicked Greeks. The rest had indeed sailed off—but only as far as Tenedos, just out of sight from the coast. Once Sinon made his way into the city—now trusted as a friend—he would light a beacon and signal the ships to return. Then he was to open the trapdoor of the horse, and let the heroes pour out. The crack team of fighters would assassinate the Trojan commanders, while the gates would be flung open for the rest of the Greeks to enter.

All was going to plan. But Helen, for some reason that to this day cannot quite be explained, walked around the horse that night before the final battle, and imitated the voices of the wives of every one of the heroes within. The men panicked. Had the Trojans somehow captured their women? Or were they dreaming about their deaths and already hearing their wives' laments? At least one man, Antiklos, tried to get out to see for himself, but Odysseus clapped his hand upon the warrior's throat and said he'd strangle him if he moved another inch. At last the painful mimicry ended. Helen walked away. What

Odysseus never understood was why she seemed to switch allegiance. Once, not long before, he had gone on a nighttime spying mission, creeping into the city by way of a sewer, and had come to Helen in her room. She bathed him, told him about the location of the holy statue called Palladion, and never gave him away. Disguised as a beggar, he was able to return the next night with Diomedes and steal the statue (a model of Pallas Athena, fallen from heaven, without which Troy would fall). Now had Helen taken on her captors' way of looking at the war?

When the trapdoor was opened, Ekhion in his eagerness leapt out, straight to his death. The others slid down by a rope. In pairs, they hurried through the city, straight to the commanders' beds, killing them before they woke. By dawn, the others had come up from the sea. Towers were set aflame. The city began to burn.

53.  THE RETURNS OF THE HEROES

The scenes of horror that day in Troy are difficult to understand, even when you consider the cruel war, ten years long, that both sides had endured. The gods saw these excesses and were offended. The repercussions would affect the Greeks for years to come.

Priam, the old Trojan king, who had seen so many of his sons die in battle, took refuge at the altar of Zeus in the courtyard of his palace. Neoptolemos, the young son of Achilles, a boy as fearsome as his father but without his strain of mercy, found Priam and put him to death as he knelt before the god's shrine. Priam's daughter, the unfortunate prophetess Kassandra, also sought safety with the gods. She clung to the ancient wooden statue of Athena that the Trojans kept in their citadel. That is where Ajax the Lesser discovered her and raped her—a brutal, unspeakable deed. Even the statue turned its eyes away. Deiphobos, the latest husband of Helen, was slain by her first husband—Menelaos, at last able to play the conqueror.

At the door of the house of Deiphobos, the moment that the Greeks and Trojans had fought for, in a war that had decimated and hardened both sides, finally arrived. Menelaos faced the woman he had married, she who had made him, for a time, the happiest man in Greece. He drew his sword. Without a word, he advanced toward her. He would have killed Helen then and there, had she not found a way to pacify him. Unclasping her red robe, she let it drop below one breast and stood there, calm and proud, still sure of the power of Aphrodite. Stunned, Menelaos immediately dropped his weapon. He took her by the wrist—just as he had on that day he took her from the house of her father—and led her off to the waiting ships.

Here and there were glimmers of justice. Antenor, the Trojan who had, at the war's start, welcomed the peace embassy to the city, was spared by the men he hosted back then, Odysseus and Menelaos. He had insisted—to no avail—that the guilty party return Helen and the stolen goods from Sparta. In thanks, the Greeks spared his house and family, hanging a leopard skin at the door, as a sign to warn away the attackers. After the sack of the city, Antenor and his family wandered far in exile to the head of the Adriatic Sea, where a colony was founded—the place we now call Venice.

Another Trojan, known for his righteousness and piety toward the gods, also escaped the destruction. With his aged father Ankhises clinging to his back, and his child holding his left hand, Aeneas made his way out of the smoking rubble. After years of wandering, in Asia, Crete, northern Greece, and North Africa, he settled in the promised land of Italy. His descendants moved to a place with seven hills, where long before Herakles had passed in his travels. There they founded the city named Rome. The story is a long one and the Romans still proudly tell it, making sure to give credit for success to Aphrodite—*Venus genetrix*, in their language—mother of the nation's hero.

Nonetheless, brutality ruled overall. The Greeks held a council, as if they had been gathered in a peaceful assembly at home. Their blood was still boiling, however. It showed in their decision to erase the future of Troy by murdering Astyanax. He was the baby boy that Hector had cherished, a child who gurgled and wriggled in his mother's arms when he saw his bloodstained father coming home from battle. Sometimes they met on the city wall, and Hector would have to remove his helmet, with its towering horsehair crest, because it scared the child. From that same wall, by the solemn decree of the Greeks, Astyanax was hurled to death.

The chieftains divided the spoils of Troy. Neoptolemos, the young man "new to war" (as his name showed), won Andromache, the widow of Hector, one of the hundreds his father had killed. Agamemnon, commander in chief, won Kassandra, though neither one would have long to live. Odysseus was given, as prize of war, Hector's mother, Hekabe. He hardly wanted her—certainly not for his bed—and he never had to worry about how to use her since before she even left Troy she turned into a rabid black dog. He left her there.

Other nightmares were to follow. Just as when they had set out on this endless expedition, contrary winds rose as they were about to sail. One night, above the tomb of Achilles, which they had built on the headland near the city, a wavering dim light, ten feet high, appeared to hover. It was the hero's ghost. He spoke, demanding a wife to accompany him in the world hereafter. "Polyxena," he specified. So the Greeks found that daughter of Priam, and Neoptolemos carried out the sacrifice. The winds dropped—yet they were delayed further. Kalkhas announced, "I feel Athena's anger." The seer knew the cause—Ajax the Lesser's brutal rape in the very precinct of the goddess within Troy. The Greeks were all for stoning their companion. They picked up the rocks and started to give chase, but Ajax, the coward, ran to an altar for sanctuary. His comrades knew better than to commit another sacrilege and they let him be.

Athena, however, might still be angry, reasoned Agamemnon, who wanted to remain until the proper rituals had been done to placate the goddess. His brother, Menelaos, wanted to leave immediately. They had a quarrel, after which Menelaos put to sea without a sacrifice. Nestor and Diomedes went with him in their own ships. Those two made it home in good time, with no fatalities. Menelaos, however, for all his haste, ran into a howling three-day storm. All but five of his boats went down. The rest were blown as far south as Egypt. There they were becalmed until a sea nymph told the king how to wrest the secret of homecoming from her father, Proteus. She led him and a few of his companions to a hidden beach. "Here, put these on," she said, handing him sealskins and a bottle of perfume (to keep off the seal stench). "Then wait." Sure enough, at the time she had said, Proteus, the sage, came out of the sea in the form of a sleek, old whiskered seal—lord of his flock. After what seemed like endless grunts and barks, with much flopping around the sand, he settled down to sleep, at which point Menelaos jumped up, threw off the skin, and seized him. Proteus went into his transformations—lion, fire, water, bird. Menelaos, who hardly knew what to expect next, gritted his teeth and held on. Finally, Proteus settled into human form and told him what he wanted to know. Sacrifices to Athena and Poseidon had to be made. Then the winds would be favorable. What awaited him could only be hinted darkly.

That, strange as it is, represents the more reasonable story. The odder version would make a mockery of the whole war, of the Greeks and their enemies, and all who died. According to some, when Menelaos landed at Egypt, confused and discouraged, he found a woman at a well. She told him her name was Helen—in fact, *his* Helen. She had never run away. Ten years before, Hera had lifted her up bodily in a great wind and whisked her off to Egypt. The one they had engaged in mortal combat to retrieve was no woman—only a cloudlike phantom, a divine deception. When Menelaos went to prove that the "real" Helen was in fact aboard his ship at that very moment, he looked up and saw the hard-won "woman" rise into the sky and vanish, like mist off the sea. Then he set about stealing back his own wife (who had become the object of the local king's desires). They hoodwinked the lustful Egyptian and returned to mainland Greece without further incident. So the other story goes.

Others never made it back. The prophet Kalkhas had been forewarned that he would die when he met a seer who was better at his craft. While journeying home on land with several other chieftains, he was welcomed at Kolophon by a local wise man named Mopsos. This diviner had an impressive parentage. Apollo was his father, and his mother was Manto, the daughter of the old seer Teiresias; the Argives had dedicated her for service at Apollo's great shrine after their final victory over Thebes. "So you are a seer," he said heartily to Kalkhas after dinner one evening. "Let's see what you can do—and then I'll show you a few little tricks of my own." "Well," replied Kalkhas, "I'm pretty fair at counting the innumerable." He demonstrated with some nearby blades of grass, coming closer to the actual number than you would think possible. Now it was Mopsos' turn. "See that fig tree? Let me tell you how many figs it bears." He took a moment: "One bushel—with one left over." He was exactly right. This was a power to be reckoned with.

"Now try this," Mopsos challenged Kalkhas. "That sow is pregnant." "Yes," said the older man, "with eight young in her womb." Mopsos smiled. "Actually, there are nine. They're male. And they will be farrowed at the sixth hour tomorrow—wait and see." All came to pass exactly as Mopsos predicted, at which point Kalkhas lost heart and died.

Of those chieftains who made it home, Agamemnon was the most unlucky. His first brush with disaster came shortly after they had set out, after making all the proper sacrifices to Athena. His ship was close by when Ajax the Lesser had his boat blasted out from under him by a thunderbolt wielded by Athena. She was determined to get revenge for his final sacrilege at Troy. Yet even then Ajax survived, clinging to a rock, and still had the strength to boast, "Nothing can prevent my return home in glory." This was too much. Poseidon, in sympathy with Pallas Athena, made sure he did not get away. Striking the rock with his trident, he sent Ajax hurtling into the sea. His body washed up later on the island of Mykonos, where Thetis buried him. You would think he would be forgotten, as an impious disgrace. But heroes always have their followers, and in Lokris they mourn him still with a sacrifice at sea, a ship laden with precious goods, which they fit out with a black sail, set on fire, and push out, unmanned, onto the deep water.

Shaken by this loss, Agamemnon nevertheless pressed on for home. The second hazard came as he neared Euboia. It was a moonless night, and a squall had scattered the fleet. But a few boats that had clustered together saw a beacon on shore, a friendly light to guide them to harbor. Or so they thought. Making their way toward it, they were wrecked on the rocks to which the shining fire had falsely led them. It was a shameless deception arranged by Nauplios, the father of Palamedes. He had learned all about the treachery of Odysseus— how his son was stoned to death because the wily Ithacan had framed him. Agamemnon, or so he heard, had gone along with the murder, trying to keep Odysseus on his side. To Nauplios it did not matter who was killed. Many men drowned that night to satisfy his vengeance on the Greeks. According to some, he had a hand in further nasty business. Even though Agamemnon escaped shipwreck on the jagged rocks, Nauplios was to exact his due. Some say that after the father tried to get compensation for the death of Palamedes earlier in the war years and was turned away, he set about visiting the heroes' wives, to corrupt them. Somehow—whether through persuasion or sly suggestions—he succeeded in bringing together Klytaimnestra, the wife of Agamemnon, with a new man, and he supplied at least four other wives with ready lovers.

Klytaimnestra resisted for a long time the urge to punish her husband while he was at war. Yet every day she wondered how she could ever abide living again with the man who had killed their daughter, luring her to Aulis with his lying promise of a magnificent marriage. Agamemnon had left his wife under the protection of a singer of tales. He figured this would ensure her fidelity, since a man of song could easily compose blame poetry that would shame her among the people if she tried anything improper. He miscalculated, though. The curse on the house of Atreus came back to subvert his plan. His uncle, Thyestes, had lost the kingship of Mycenae on that day he lost his own young sons, when the Sun turned backward at the sight. In exile, however, he soon fathered another child. This child's name was Aigisthos. He grew up deep in the country, forever resentful and angry at the clan who now ruled over Mycenae. Since he had not been among those pledged to defend Helen's honor, he was conveniently available when Agamemnon went off to war. Aigisthos soon made short work of the singer, sending him off to a deserted island. Then he set about seducing Klytaimnestra, and after a while she gave in. When at long last word came of the victory at Troy, through beacons flashing from mountain peak to peak, the couple was ready.

Agamemnon returned to a splendid triumphal procession. His wife feigned joy at his homecoming. She had a royal carpet stretched halfway down the hill to meet him, the sort of extravagance shown only by eastern potentates or gods. The king reluctantly trod on its lush crimson pile and wearily entered the home he left long ago. Even Kassandra, his prize of war, was welcomed into the courtyard, twittering all the while in her strange foreign tongue like a frantic bird. She, at least, knew what was to come. A bath was prepared. When Agamemnon finished soaking his tired body in the welcome hot water and called for a robe, his wife came personally to help him dress. She had woven a special garment for the occasion, one with sleeves sewn closed and no opening for the head. Completely unaware, the king donned the tunic, and while he struggled in it, like a boar in a hunter's net, Klytaimnestra split his head open with an axe. Aigisthos was there, too, to finish off his rival with a sword. Kassandra, who had foreseen all, also met her end in Mycenae that day.

So much blood had been shed, but it was not enough to wash away the curse. A child, a husband, and finally a mother in the doomed house of Atreus died violently. After her father's murder, his remaining daughter, Elektra, could not endure living in the palace. She married a peasant—mainly to spite her mother—and lived on his farm some distance from the town. Before leaving, she had taken the precaution of taking away Orestes, her younger brother, and entrusting him to an old and loyal retainer. Consequently, this only son was raised in the mountains of Phokis, while the rest of the household was told he had met with an accident. Every day Elektra prayed he would keep safe. As the years passed, her hope of revenge against her mother grew dimmer. But one day, when she had gone to offer poured sacrifices at the tomb of her father, she found curious signs that someone else had been there—a snipped lock of hair left as a dedication, and a footprint. A handsome young man emerged from the woods nearby, accompanied by an old fellow and a second youth. Her brother was back.

Together, they plotted revenge. The plan was to lure Klytaimnestra to the country. Up to now she had always refused, turning up her nose at her daughter's humble surroundings, and making snide comments about "that laborer." Now, however, she was drawn by a prospect that was impossible to resist: a first grandchild. Elektra had given birth (it was announced). Mother and child were well, but Klytaimnestra's help was needed. So the queen came, with servants and food, determined to take charge. Before she could see the newborn, she had to fulfill a vow to the gods. It was at this offering of thanks that the attack was made.

Orestes was emboldened by the word of Apollo himself, who, through his oracle, had permitted the matricide: "Blood for blood, in payment for the father." He approached the deed as he would a sacrifice. Yet Klytaimnestra nearly broke his will. She sobbed pitifully, even bared her breast and cried out how she had nursed him as an infant. But Pylades, his companion, steadied him and the sword was thrust home. When Elektra heard of their success, she was more jubilant than if she had borne two sons.

As had been arranged, Orestes returned to Delphi to seek Apollo's purification, and the rite was carried out (a piglet's blood sprinkled on the head). But then his persecution began. The Furies had sniffed him out. Like hunting dogs, they tracked Orestes and began to pursue him all over Greece. To those who did not know the cause, he appeared raving mad, talking with trembling voice about the hideous woman hounds on his trail, always in motion, fleeing from one town to the next. At last he came to Athens, the city famous for giving sanctuary. Oedipus, another notorious killer, had found refuge there, and peace. Maybe he could as well. In true Athenian fashion (since they are the most litigious sort) a trial was held. The Furies, defending a mother's rights, argued against Apollo, who spoke for the male prerogative. Harsh arguments, allegations, every rhetorical trick, came out—how women were merely receptacles, how it was the man who really generated life. The votes were counted, and a tie resulted. Athena cast the deciding ballot, in defense of the son's vengeance for Agamemnon, and in favor of the primacy of fathers everywhere. (This was natural, given her own birth. To her Zeus played both parents from the start.) Lest the Furies stir up trouble, she managed to placate them with a gift of land close by the Areopagos, the hill of the murder court.

Orestes entrusted his sister and her family to Pylades, son of his foster father. Then he departed on the last task that would complete his absolution of the kin murder's guilt. He sailed, at Apollo's command, to the Taurians, the "bull" people living near the distant Scythians. These natives had an unusual custom. There was a fire that spurted right up from Hades, hissing out of a rock within their sacred grove. Into this fire they threw all strangers. Orestes was to go there, take the wooden statute of Artemis from them, and return with it to Attica. Whether he had heard of the customary greeting for intruders like himself is not known, but it seems he did not. He was caught and hauled before the king of the place, along with Pylades. The king in turn remanded them to the priestess of Artemis, who would carry out the execution. To their surprise, the priestess spoke good Greek, not the *bar-bar-bar* of the locals. (That is what all non-Greek tongues sounded like to Hellenes, which is why they call foreigners *barbaroi*.) The reason was, she said, she had come from Greece, years before, when she was about to be married, and a horrible deceit was practiced on her. For the Greeks, she told them, she was a memory—the girl slain so they could go to war. No one in her native land ever knew what really happened after she went up to the hill altar of the goddess. Artemis had substituted a deer and taken the girl far off to the land she lived in now. Her name was Iphigeneia. Orestes had heard the tale, but he had been too young to recall her clearly. So now he was able to return with the statue and his long-lost sister to Greece.

## 54.  ODYSSEUS, LAST HERO HOME

Odysseus, no matter what else he might be called, was a survivor. His instinct and wits rivaled those of Athena, and she had protected him as long as she could. But her anger at the theft of the Palladion, and then the foul deed of Ajax the Lesser, turned her against all the Greek warriors, her favorite included. That was why his small fleet wandered from the start, immediately after leaving Troy. A city allied with the Trojans was their first port of call: Ismaros, land of the Kikones. Even after the wealth of Troy, the Ithacan and his men were bent on plunder, greedy for more. They sacked the city, but had to pull out quickly when a large number of horsemen arrived from a nearby settlement. In the fighting six men from each ship were lost.

They rowed for three days, until they reached a paradise. At least, it seemed that way to the war-weary crew. The exploration party that Odysseus sent out from the beach was greeted not by armed natives, but instead given a special welcome. The men were offered the fruit of the lotus to refresh them. The sun grew warmer, the sky more intensely azure. Entranced, the men forgot all about their shipmates. They left behind all thought of home, occupied only with their present bliss. Odysseus, too, might have chosen to taste the fruit, but he was a hard man, always practical and tough. The afflicted rowers tried to put up a fight (not a big one, since the lotus lulled them so much), but their captain dragged them back to the ships. Then they left the land of Lotus-Eaters in a hurry.

From eating the wrong substance to being eaten: that was the trajectory they made. With his twelve ships Odysseus arrived at a promising small island. It had good pastureland for sheep and goats, shade trees and fresh water, a small but well-protected harbor. If he had wanted to start a colony, thought Odysseus, this would be ideal. From the top of a hill he saw a neighboring island and he decided to visit it (even though his men groaned). Despite all the horrors of war he had seen, he retained the urge to explore, to know the minds of many peoples—perhaps there were some who were still just. He took one ship. They made their way up from the waterline toward a windy hill, and found there a spacious cave—inhabited, it seemed, although the owner was not home. He must be a dairyman, thought Odysseus, seeing the cheese baskets, goat pens, and rennet jars. Knowing that Zeus smiles on the stranger, Odysseus and his crew helped themselves to several wheels of cheese and a goat kid or two and waited for their host.

He—or it—was not long in coming. A huge creature appeared, like a man but ten times the height, and with one distinguishing feature: a single wheellike eye, topped by a bushy brow, in the middle of his face. He methodically penned the goats he had herded in from the field, rolled a boulder to stop up the cave opening, and sat down to supper. It would have been milk and curds, like every other evening, but tonight the Cyclops—his name was Polyphemos—caught a new scent in his cave, and paused. He noticed Odysseus and his crew cowering in a corner. "Are you pirates?" roared the creature. Even if they were, of course, Odysseus was not about to tell. "Let's say we are travelers. We come to you as guest-friends. We have been many years abroad, at Troy—" He did not have time to get to the story, for Polyphemos simply leaned over, grabbed a handful of men (two fit in one fist), smashed them on the floor, and swallowed them.

Odysseus thought that cannibalism had ended with Kronos— something the old gods did and, now and then, some unsuspecting humans. But this was so casual he guessed it might be the norm hereabouts. "So, you are my guests, eh?" continued the Cyclops, as if nothing untoward had interrupted him. "I have a special gift for you—what was your name, by the way?" "Nobody," said Odysseus. "Okay, Nobody—here's the gift: *you* I will save and not eat until last."

"That is very gracious of you," said Odysseus, without a trace of irony. "And I have a gift for you, right now." Saying this, he pulled from the corner a large skin of Ismaric wine. It had been a gift from Maro, the priest of Apollo whom they had spared during the sack of the Kikones' city. Deep red in color, with a scent of honey and hints of apple and oak—it was the finest vintage Odysseus had ever tasted. Like all Greeks, he diluted his wine with water, but he handed a huge cup to Polyphemos uncut—the better to dull his mind. The wine appealed to the Cyclops, and he had some more. After one more cup, though, the beast grew groggy. His head, and then his whole body, sagged to the floor.

All had gone exactly as planned. Now was the time to kill him. Odysseus still had his sword and it would be quick work. But on second thought, realizing that he and his crew could never budge the rock that sealed the cave, he decided to blind Polyphemos. They sharpened a long pole of olive wood, like shipwrights crafting a new mast. They plunged the tip into the fire and waited until it grew redhot. Then, with Odysseus quietly directing his men, they rammed the rod into the eyelid of the ugly Cyclops, searing his huge eye. He screamed in pain. He stomped around and howled. And he yelled for his fellow Cyclopes in the hills, who heard the ruckus and came running to the cave. "What is it?" they asked. "What's all the trouble?" "Nobody is hurting me," he moaned. "Really?" the nearest neighbor replied. "All right, then. If nobody is hurting you, just go to sleep. You'll feel better in the morning. And pray to your father."

The father of Polyphemos was Poseidon. Later, he did pray to him—and that would make all the difference. But for now he sank down in his cave and slept, whimpering occasionally because his sore eye pained him. In the morning, the ewes woke him with their bleating. They were waiting to be milked. The rams, too, were anxious to be out roaming the rocks and uplands. Polyphemos rolled away the boulder from the mouth of the cave. He stood at the exit as the oversized animals passed through, and he patted each on the back, making sure they weren't men. Yet the Cyclops was fooled. What he did not feel was the crew members clinging for dear life to their undersides, fingers gripping the thick wool. In that way all of the men escaped. Finally came a large ram to which the captain, Odysseus, had attached himself. The Cyclops stroked his favorite and addressed him: "My dear little ram, why are you the last one today? You are always first to crop the tender grasses, first to reach the river for a drink. You come home first, too, striding back to our cave. Now you're the last of all. Is it because you miss your poor master'e eye, the one that awful Nobody poked out with a stick, after he ruined me with his damnable wine?" (By now Odysseus was sweating, afraid he was going to lose his grip beneath the ram and slide right into the monster's lap.) "If only you could talk," continued his victim, "we'd find that crafty fiend and bash his brains out on the cave floor—yes, that would make me feel much better." He let the ram go, and it dashed for the hills. Odysseus was safe.

With his faithful men, Odysseus drove the Cyclops' sheep—that had been their salvation—to his own ship. They rowed offshore as far as a man can be heard when he shouts. Then Odysseus did something he came to regret. He could not resist revealing his identity. "Cyclops," he yelled, "did you think you could eat a man's companions as if he were a puny nobody?" The crew grew nervous. They tried to silence Odysseus, warning him that Polyphemos would locate them for sure now. But the warrior had to boast. "Cyclops! If anyone ever asks you about that ugly scar where your eye used to be, tell them who did it—Odysseus the City Sacker, son of Laertes, he whose palace is in Ithaca." That gave the creature all he needed to know, for now and time to come. He broke off a piece of a cliff and lobbed it in the men's direction. It overshot the stern but caused a wave that would have driven them back ashore had not Odysseus shoved off the rocks with the boat hook and ordered them to row hard. Then Polyphemos groaned aloud: "So it all came true—what Têlemos the prophet told me long ago! He said some Odysseus would take away my sight. But I expected a big man, encased in strength, not some pipsqueak. Lord Poseidon, earth holder, raven-haired! If I am truly your son, let

Odysseus the City Sacker return home only on these conditions: that first he loses all his men, ends up a passenger on another's ship, and once he arrives, finds pain and trouble in the heart of his own house." Odysseus heard the curse and shivered. Those rash words of his had gained him a much more dangerous divine enemy. Under a hail of rocks, the ship moved off.

The small fleet under his command had no way to orient themselves, sailing farther into a no-man's-land never before described, even in old sailors' tales. Soon they came to the island of the winds. Aiolos ruled there, his small kingdom enclosed by a sleek bronze wall built atop smooth rocks. Everything was in motion, even the island itself, which floated about on the sea. Only the king's family remained stable, in a bizarre way. No women were exchanged with other families, in the usual system that knits together the cities and clans of Greeks. Instead, the king's six daughters had married his six sons. In that way, they all stayed in their father's palace.

Aiolos was extremely kind. After a month's refreshment, when Odysseus and his crew were ready to depart, he gave Odysseus a leather bag in which he had bound up all the contrary winds. Zephyros alone he allowed out, to waft them onward (for Zeus had made him steward of the winds). So they sailed pleasantly for nine full days. But on the tenth—when they were within sight of their own home island, when they could even see the smoke rising from its hearths— Odysseus, who had constantly manned the tiller, fell asleep. Cunning as always, the captain had not revealed to his men the contents of the leather sack—or they had not believed him. "Now's our chance," whispered the crew members to one another. "He's got more gold in there than we ever took from Troy. Boon companion of Aiolos, everybody's friend—he's got all the luck. Let's have a look in there for ourselves." They untied the silver binding cord. Out rushed the winds in a terrifying howl. They formed a squall that instantly carried the ships far out to sea.

When Odysseus awoke, his first instinct was to throw himself into the waves and end it all. But he endured this latest catastrophe, as he had all the others. Eventually, they were blown back to the winds' home. Odysseus entreated Aiolos to help them once more. The king, however—his disposition as shifting as his breezes—this time had not a hint of sympathy. "Leave here immediately. The gods must hate you. It is not right to give you aid."

So they traveled on. The Laistrygonians was the next landfall.

They were giants and savages, fierce as the Cyclopes. At first, though, all seemed innocent enough. The harbor was a sort of fjord, calm, deep, and secure. The exploration party came upon a normal girl at a well, who took them home to meet her parents—who turned out to be as big as mountains. The man of the house ate two men before the others could take flight. The Laistrygonians pursued them and rained down rocks on the Greek boats. It was like spearing fish in a barrel. All the ships were lost, with their doomed crews. Only Odysseus, who had taken the precaution of tying his stern lines to a boulder outside the harbor, escaped unharmed, with his dwindling band. Once more they rowed away lamenting, the tears falling fast as they bent to the oars.

The name of the next island was itself like a fatal cry: "Aiaia." Again, all began pleasantly. They found a good anchorage, with fresh water and small game near the shore. On the third day, Odysseus, scouting around, saw smoke from a hearthfire somewhere inland. After that night's meal, he told his companions. They were afraid, for their captain's spying had led them into tragedy twice already. But in the end, he was their commander. They split up—twenty-two men went with Eurylokhos to reconnoiter; the other half of the crew stayed at the ship. As Eurylokhos told it later, when he returned alone to the beach, they found a beautiful woman, Circe, singing in her house in the woods as she worked her loom. Little did they realize, but this was the sister of Aiêtês, a child of the Sun, she who once had purified Jason and Medea. Lions and wolves roamed by the doorway, but they were like tame dogs, wagging their tails as if they expected to be fed. That should have warned the Greeks. Yet when Circe heard them and invited them in, they all entered her house, and all ate her fine bread, cheese, and wild honey. All except their leader—he, for once, exercised his captain's caution and so did not become a pig. For that was what Circe did to the others. After drugging their wine, she touched them with her wand, gave them snouts and bristles and hooves and grunts, and threw them acorns to munch while she drove them into pens. They still had human consciousness, but in every other respect they were swine.

Odysseus was determined to rescue his transformed men, even though those with him begged him to flee. Sometimes, the gods help those who dare. Alone, on his way to the witch's lair, he met Hermes, disguised as a young man. The god gave him *moly*, a magic root for his protection, and told him how to handle the goddess. The result was that when she touched Odysseus with her wand, he stayed unchanged. Then, at sword point, he made her swear an oath never to harm him, and forced Circe to turn his crew back into human form.

Though a sorceress, she was irresistibly beautiful. They became lovers. A year passed, in which they feasted every night. It seemed as though Odysseus had finally forgotten his home. Though he avoided being changed into a pig, he ended up living only for the day, in a kind of dumb animal contentment. It was his crew who brought him back to reality. Some of them were men he had dragged bodily from the Lotus-Eaters. Now they returned the favor.

"Wily Odysseus, man of many machinations, no longer stay if you are so unwilling," replied Circe, when he raised the topic before they slept next evening. "But first know the road you have to take. You must travel to the house of Hades, the dread realm of Persephone, and consult the spirit of Theban Teiresias. He will tell you the way to get home."

Odysseus broke down in tears. Sitting there in her splendid bed, he had no wish to live anymore. Was this Circe's revenge for being abandoned? Why not just kill himself and go to Hades' kingdom quicker? After a long time, he roused what little energy he had and managed to answer her. "Who is going to guide us? No one has ever gone to hell in a black boat."

She ignored his bitterness and provided the details. To his surprise, it did not involve descending through dark underground passages. Boreas, the North Wind, would fill their sail. Go to the stream of Okeanos, she said, the cosmic river. Watch for a grove of poplars and tall cypress trees. Find the spot where three rivers flow together—Akheron the river of sighs; Puriphlegethon, the fire-blazing; Kokutos, full of laments, a branch of the hateful Styx. Beach the ship and dig a pit, long as your arm and just as wide. Pour honeyed wine into it, with water and barley groats. Promise to dedicate cows and sheep to the dead when you return to Ithaca. Then slaughter a black ram at the pit, pour out the blood, and wait for the strengthless shades to appear, eager to drink and talk.

The companions set out, all but Elpenor, who had gone to sleep the night before on Circe's roof (he was heavy with wine and wanted air). When he heard the din below, he woke up with a start and forgot to take the ladder down; he broke his neck in the fall. The rest of the crew never realized he was gone, so distracted were they by grief and fear after hearing their captain reveal their next destination. They sailed with a fresh and constant wind to the edge of the world, a land of mist and night. Finding the exact spot Circe had mentioned, Odysseus carried out her instructions. Immediately, the dead swarmed about the pit, like flies at a milk pail in the springtime. He saw maidens who had gone to Hades unmarried; old, worn men; warriors, with their wounds still visible. They flittered here and there with ungodly shrieks, like bats in a cave. To their surprise, Elpenor approached first. His soul had traveled faster than any ship. Odysseus promised that they would return to Circe's island to give his body a proper sailor's burial. Then came the shade of Antikleia, the mother whom Odysseus had left at Ithaca years before. Desperate as she was to come near her son, though, he held her off with the sword from the pit of blood, until he could question Teiresias.

The Theban seer knelt and had his sip of ram's blood, which gave him strength and voice. "Renowned Odysseus," he began, first weakly, then with increasing volume. "You seek a homecoming as sweet as honey, but you must forget that for now. The god will make your way harsh. Poseidon is still furious at the blinding of his son. However, you may make it home unharmed provided you remember what I say. When you pass by the island of the Sun, and find his cattle there, grazing in the grass, leave them alone. If you harm them, your men will die. Even if you escape alive, you still must worry about Ithaca. Suitors have taken over your house, eating your flocks and cattle, courting your wife. They assume you have died, though she denies it and resists. One way or another, you will pay them back. But after you do, remember to do this one final act. Take an oar on your shoulder and travel inland, so far from the sea that the natives come up and ask you, 'What's that winnowing fan you carry on your shoulder?' When that happens, stop and build a shrine, fixing the oar in the earth atop a mound. Sacrifice a bull and a boar to Poseidon. You will be finally reconciled with the god. Gentle death will come to you later, as you govern your fortunate people, out of the sea at last."

So Odysseus learned his fate. He noticed the prophet had not given him directions about where to sail—he would have to ask Circe on his return. Then he turned to ask questions of his dead mother. She told him how she had died from grief, missing her only son. His own son, said Antikleia, was nearly grown now, Telemakhos, whom he had left an infant. His father, Laertes, was deeply depressed, living like a poverty-stricken peasant outside the town, sleeping on the ground, clothed in dirty rags. As for Penelope, his lovely, thoughtful wife, she missed him every day, and pined away the nights in tears. She still waited for his return. Odysseus, awash in a tide of emotions, reached out to cling to his mother, but like a shadow or a dream, each time he tried (three times in all) she receded. That was the way once one's body perished. No human touch would ever reach the dead.

He saw the past parade before him. Famous women approached Odysseus, one by one. Tyro, who loved Poseidon and bore him twins, Pelias and Neleus. She was old Nestor's grandmother. Antiope, whose sons had built up Thebes. Alkmene, who lay with Zeus and gave birth to immortal Herakles. The ill-fated mother of Oedipus. There was Pero, daughter of Neleus, who was won for marriage at the price of many cows. Leda, mother of Helen. Phaidra, Prokris, Ariadne, Maira, Klymene, Eriphyle. Each had her story, how she had loved, married, and died. Here was the other side of heroism, the heroines who made men and mourned them.

After that, the warriors who followed seemed less grand. Odysseus met his old companion, Agamemnon, who narrated the whole ugly story of his murder—a cautionary tale, a warning not to trust one's wife. He met Achilles and could not resist a barbed remark: "So lucky, my friend—a hero at Troy and now a great power among the dead!" to which Achilles answered, "Don't talk to me of death. I'd rather be a tenant farmer back on earth, owning nothing, the lowest of the low, than be king over all these corpses." That softened Odysseus a bit, and he was careful to answer with more warmth when Achilles asked about Neoptolemos, his son. When the dead warrior heard that his boy had been the bravest of all those who huddled inside the Trojan Horse, and had escaped the war unwounded, he bounded off in joy, filled with a father's pride in a triumphant son. What Odysseus did not know was that Neoptolemos had taken Orestes' wife after Orestes was driven mad by Furies. So Agamemnon's son killed Achilles' son at Delphi. Another report, just as awful, said that Neoptolemos had gone to Delphi to sack it, because Apollo shot his father. When he had stolen the dedicatory offerings and set fire to the temple, a priest of Apollo, Knife son of Divider, stabbed him to death. They buried him under the temple threshold.

The last warrior whom Odysseus noticed was standing apart from the other dead. It was Ajax, his old enemy, still stung because he had lost Achilles' armor to the cunning of the Ithacan. Odysseus tried to make amends, saying how the other Greeks had mourned him as much as they had Achilles. But Ajax merely turned away, stonily silent, and angry forever.

The whole spectacle of Hell unfolded. Minos, judging all the dead. The famous transgressors—the hunter Orion; Tityus who had assaulted Lêto; Sisyphus (whom some insisted was Odysseus' real father); the cursed Tantalos. Many more would he have seen had he not feared that Persephone would send forth the Gorgon's head and turn them all to stone. He retreated to the ship, and they all sailed back to Circe's island.

They buried Elpenor and planted his oar atop his mound. Then the goddess took Odysseus aside and sketched out their coming voyage: the Sirens, who could lure ships with their unearthly songs, and wreck them; doglike Skylla and the whirlpool Kharybdis, appalling twin dangers to squeeze between; and last of all, Thrinakiê, where Helios pastured his herds and flocks.

As they sailed off, Odysseus prepared them for the first stage of the voyage. He ordered his men to bind him to the mast, then to block their own ears with waxen plugs. In that way they rowed safely past the Sirens. Their ineffably sweet song drove Odysseus crazy with desire to be near them, to land at their flowery meadow in the sea and listen to them forever (even though the rotting bones of those who had done so lay in piles on the island of the two divine singers). But his pleading and begging were, as he planned, ignored by the crew. Thus Odysseus became the first to learn the Siren song and live.

About the next threat Odysseus was more vague with his men. He knew the choice, and that some of them would die, no matter what. The helmsman steered away from monstrous Kharybdis, a hole in the sea that was like a mouth, sucking down water, then spewing it back in waves. The crew watched, fascinated, as the whirlpool opened up. They could even see the sand at the sea's bottom. Meanwhile, the threat from the other side, Skylla, did her evil work. This six-headed, twelve-footed giant sea creature oozed out of her cave at the scent of passing mammals—whales or humans were her favorite prey. In each mouth were three rows of close-set sharp teeth. She yelped like a puppy and tore flesh like a wolf. As the ship coasted close to her, avoiding the whirlpool, Skylla reached into the ship and plucked out six men, flipping them up onto her rocky shelf like gasping fish. They cried aloud for Odysseus—their last words. In the middle of their screams, she devoured them.

The final test arrived. Odysseus ordered his crew to row past the Sun's isle without stopping. They soon heard the moos and bleats of the god's select animals. The men were exhausted, tired of the endless dangers with their relentless captain. Mutiny was brewing. Odysseus knew that he could not stand against so many. So he gave in to their demand and landed, after making them swear they would not touch any of the herd.

A whole month passed, with the southeast winds blowing hard, blocking any attempt to put to sea. Supplies ran out. They fished and hunted, with little success. One day, when Odysseus had walked far inland to find a proper place to make his prayer to the gods, he fell asleep. While he was gone, Eurylokhos persuaded the men back on the beach to slaughter several cows: "We can honor Helios later, once we return, with offerings and cattle, even build a temple. But now I don't care if the gods get angry and strike us down, I'd rather perish quickly at sea than starve slowly on a deserted island." The others agreed, though they did perform a makeshift sacrifice.

Odysseus knew what they'd done only when he was returning and caught the scent of roasting meat. But there was no help for it. The cows were dead. Soon enough the gods hinted at the catastrophe to befall them, by making the meat that was spitted on the skewers bellow and groan as though the animals still were alive.

Zeus carried out the will of Helios, who had threatened to desert the sky if his honor and his rights were not upheld. Within hours after they had left the island, the ship of Odysseus was struck by lightning. All its men, except for him, went to the bottom.

All night Odysseus clung to a spar from the wreck. The tenth day brought him to yet another island, Ogygia, home of the nymph Calypso. She took him in and there he stayed seven long years. At first he was glad just to be rescued from the deep. And it was a pleasure, of course, to be a gorgeous nymph's partner. He knew the dangers, however, of his position. Myths were full of stories that told about the consequences of divine love.

## 55. A RETURN TO ITHACA

Just about the time that Odysseus was discovered by Calypso shivering and naked on her island's shore, the suitors of his wife, Penelope, discovered the trick that she had used to hold them off for the past three years. Once the young men of Ithaca and the nearby islands learned that Troy had fallen, they waited to see if Odysseus would come home. When he failed to appear, they grew bolder. With the king missing, his wife and the kingdom that went with her were up for grabs. One hundred and eight hopeful, reckless men moved in uninvited, taking over the palace, eating the absent king's meat and drinking his wine as they vied with one another for Penelope's hand. "Wait until I finish this shroud for old Laertes, my father-in-law," the queen promised. "Then I shall decide which one of you to marry." Each day she wove. But at night, unknown to the suitors, she would unravel the previous day's work. Then a serving girl, one of the many whom they had corrupted, gave away her secret. The suitors, angry at being misled, began to badger Penelope. She came up with a new delaying tactic: "I want to wait until Telemakhos is grown." But after another seven years, that time too was fast approaching.

Twenty years in all had passed since Odysseus sailed for Troy. His son was old enough to assume the kingship. But for him to do so would mean acknowledging that his father was dead, while he still dreamed, like a young boy, of the day of his return. Becoming king would also mean having to give his mother away to one of the suitors. Only then would the arrogant mob leave the palace. In other words, Telemakhos would have to lose both parents. There was already friction with his mother; he rebuked her in public when she tried to stop the court poet, Phemios, from singing about the Greeks' return from the war. But he also depended on her. If she suddenly decided on her own to remarry, he might be shoved aside. All these thoughts he shared only with his one friend, the old pig herder Eumaios.

Something had to give way. The time was ripe. The goddess Athena set in motion the finale. Perhaps Odysseus had proved himself worthy of her attention once more. Or she could not resist his cunning ability, his combination of wiles, caution, and curiosity—he could be her mortal double. In any event, while Odysseus languished on Calypso's shores, pining to see the smoke from his own hearth, Athena brought his case to Zeus. "My heart is torn for him," she said, "the unlucky man. There he is, trapped in a wooded island at the navel of the sea. The daughter of Atlas keeps him by her side, seducing him with soft words, making him forget his home. What did he ever do to wrong you, Father? Why not let him go?"

Zeus agreed that Odysseus had always been ready with sacrifices, a good man, clever beyond all others. "It was my brother Poseidon, angry still for his son's blinding, that drove Odysseus off again and again from Ithaca. Now the sea god will give up his wrath. He cannot stand against us all."

Together, father and daughter devised a plan. Poseidon was away, enjoying the meat offerings of the Aithiopians, at the world's edge. With him distracted, Hermes would dash down to Ogygia and relay Zeus' orders, enabling Odysseus to leave Calypso. Athena, meanwhile, would take the disguise of an old warrior, a family friend, and visit Ithaca to put some courage into Telemakhos.

Calypso resisted at first. "You jealous gods!" she cried. "Always ripping away our mortal lovers! Look at Dawn when she got herself Orion. What happens next? Artemis ambushes him and takes him down. And then there's Demeter, who lost her lover Iasion—Zeus saw their lovemaking in the thrice-plowed field and burned him up with lightning. Now this. A fine man blown here by wind and wave, one I fancied I would make immortal!" Still, there was no resisting the son of Kronos, and she surrendered. She went off to find her bronze tools so that Odysseus could build himself a raft. As he was crafting it, planing the pine trees he felled and fitting them tightly together (for he was a master carpenter, another gift from Athena), miles and miles away his son was already putting to sea.

Athena had carried out her role in Ithaca. As the grizzled Mentor ("The Strengthener") she appeared one noon at the palace gate and had a private talk with Telemakhos while the suitors caroused. "They are disgusting! Your father would teach them a lesson," grumbled the goddess-in-disguise. "Just let him show up, helm and spears in hand, the way I knew him when he came up our place once. Looking for poison to smear his arrows, he was. Couldn't get it elsewhere, but my father let him have it. Loved him like a brother. I'd like to see him here right now!" Mentor advised his friend's son to send the suitors home (at least for now), then secretly sail to find any news he could about Odysseus from Nestor and Menelaos, the last ones to return from Troy. "If they say he died, then build the empty tomb and decide how to deal with these louts—by trick or force. Look at Orestes, what a brave lad he turned out to be. He came back and killed his father's murderer. You're a strong boy, seems to me—people will say good things about you, too." Telemakhos thanked him kindly, and Mentor strode off—only a few steps, though, before he turned into a bird and flew out the smoke hole, which the young man could not help but notice. He knew now it was Athena who had put him in mind of his father, and planted in him a memory so compelling he had to find him. The next day he called the assembly (the first since Odysseus had left the island), and publicly denounced the gang of suitors who were destroying his inheritance. That night he shipped out with a crew he trusted.

They made Pylos the next morning. A huge feast of Poseidon was going on—scores of bulls, hundreds of citizens lined up on the beach, and the grand ancient hero Nestor himself presiding. After Telemakhos and his men had their fill of tender meat and wine, the talk turned to their mission. Nestor knew only what had happened up to the time of their parting, after the quarrels between the Atreid brothers. "From what I hear," he added, "Philoktetes made it home, Idomeneus also. Agamemnon you know about. It's a good thing he left a son behind to avenge him." Another hint like the advice from Mentor. Nestor went on to tell the whole sad story as he had learned it, the killing and its aftermath, and how Menelaos arrived the very day Orestes was giving a funeral feast after having slain his mother and her murderous lover. "He's the one to see now," the old warrior concluded. "He won't lie to you. Take my son with you and go."

The two young men went by chariot inland to Sparta, where they came upon another feast, this time for a double marriage. The daughter of the house—Hermione, Helen's only child—was being sent to wed in Phthia. Also, the daughter of a rich man in the region had come to the palace to wed the king's son, Megapenthes ("Great Grief"—fathered by Menelaos with a slave girl after Helen had left him—hence the young man's name). Despite the bustle of the celebration, Menelaos gave the visitors his full attention. He told them of his own wanderings after Troy, intent on getting as many trade objects as he could, through Cyprus, Egypt, Phoenicia, and Libya, "where the ewes drop three times a year and no one goes without milk." Yet he could not be happy, even with these riches, for he thought every day of all the men the war had taken. Odysseus, the best of them, was the one he missed most. He had heard news of him, yes—but long ago, when he wrestled with Proteus in Egypt and forced from him the story of his comrades. At that time, the old sea god said he had seen Odysseus confined on Calypso's island, without companions or a ship to bring him back.

Telemakhos did not know what to think. This was the first glimmer of real hope he'd had. Yet Menelaos seemed to dismiss it even as he talked, rushing on to say how Proteus had promised that he and Helen would live forever in Elysium, since he was the son-in-law of Zeus. He ended with a magnanimous offer of a chariot and team to Telemakhos, but the son of Odysseus politely declined: "There is not much room on the rough ground of Ithaca for horse racing." Instead, he accepted a gift of a silver mixing bowl, with gold chasing, plus the Spartan king's offer to stay for a few days.

While his son was traveling in search of word of him, Odysseus took his leave of Calypso and put to sea in the raft he had built. As the goddess had instructed him, he navigated by keeping his gaze on the Pleiades, the seven shining sisters in the sky. Orion once long ago had pursued the girls, and they escaped the lusty hunter by appealing to Zeus, who changed them into stars. He still chases after them, for he, too, is fixed in the sky, never reaching his goal, while yet another constellation, Kallisto the Bear, keeps an eye on the hunter, lest he mistreat these maidens devoted to her patroness, Artemis. Looking on them, Odysseus thought there was a message hidden there, concerning women, desire, and self-control.

For seventeen days he sailed with the Pleiades on his port side. When the eighteenth morning dawned, he was within sight of land, a low slice of rock that looked like an ox-hide shield riding on the misty sea. A fine protected place—but not yet his port of call. Or so he imagined. Poseidon, however, had other plans. He was returning from the festivities among the Aithiopians when he caught sight of the raft and Odysseus, the puny human who had blinded his Cyclops son. He was so angry he yelled out, to no one in particular: "So! The other gods have changed their minds? Letting him get away, traipsing homeward bound! Now he's already close to Phaeacia, where the islanders will help him further. Still, I think he's not done paying for what he did. I have more to put him through!" With that, the sea god took his trident and stirred the sea, as though it were a deep cooking cauldron. He drew together the clouds and whipped up the winds. Wave tumbled over wave and the sky grew black. Odysseus felt his knees go weak. "So I am to endure more pain before I get back home. My companions who died at Troy were three times better off getting themselves killed in Agamemnon's war. I should have perished that day the Trojans nearly speared me through, when I was battling to recover Achilles' corpse. They would have buried me with full honors and spread my fame abroad. Now I come to this end, a nameless drowning." As such thoughts raced through his head, a huge wave, driven by Poseidon, smashed the raft to pieces and sent Odysseus headlong into the brine.

The new clothes Calypso had given him weighed him down. He could not get his head above the surface. At last he managed to struggle upward and gulp in a breath. A plank of wood was floating near him, and he succeeded in climbing on top. Odysseus did not realize he was being watched, but Leukothea—the White Goddess—had noticed him and, taking pity, came to his aid. She knew what it was like to feel divine hatred. Once she was called Ino, the daughter of Kadmos. Maddened by Hera, she had leapt into the sea and was transformed long ago into a deathless one, with all the honor and power of the divine. Now, in the form of a seabird, she alighted on the end of the wooden beam that Odysseus was straddling. "Here, take my immortal veil," she said when she had changed herself into human shape. "Wrap it around yourself—you'll stay alive that way. When you reach the land, toss it back into the waves." As she finished speaking, she immediately dove back into the sea. Odysseus hesitated. Was this some new plan meant to destroy him? But one more monstrous wave impelled by Poseidon washed over him, and that convinced him. Stripping off his waterlogged clothing, he fastened around his waist the veil of Leukothea, plunged into the sea, and started swimming toward the land he had seen on the horizon.

It took two days to get there, and even then he had to struggle to cut across the riptide near the island's shore. Exhausted, he finally collapsed on the beach near a river's mouth. Deep sleep held Odysseus in its grip for nearly a day. The sound of girls' laughter woke him. From the spot where he was resting, in dense undergrowth, the battered hero emerged, holding an olive branch before him to cover his nakedness. Three maidens, who had been playing with a ball on the beach, shrieked and ran when they saw this person, like a hairy beast, coming out of the woods. But the fourth—their mistress, the princess Nausicaa, a tall, slender beauty—stood her ground. Athena gave her the courage to stay. In fact, it was Athena who had inspired Nausicaa to come today to this very spot, to do the washing with her handmaidens. And it was Athena who emboldened Odysseus to make supplication, in his old smooth way. "My lady, are you a goddess? If so, you are surely Artemis—you have her height and grace. If not, your mortal parents are immensely blessed. How happy they must be to see such a daughter enter the dancing. And how happy the man to whom (no doubt) you are engaged!" In this mode, he continued with his delicate flattery, comparing her to a palm tree he had once seen on Delos, when he was sailing with his troops to Troy, and ending with a request for some clothes and directions into town.

The young woman handled the encounter deftly, so as to avoid gossip among the islanders, while still seeing to it that the stranger was welcomed. She had them arrive separately at the palace. Odysseus, following her instructions, managed to make his way inside to see her parents, with some help from Athena, who kept him hidden in a divine mist until the time was right. With a mix of astonishment, awe, and eager goodwill, the king and queen bade him stay and saw to his needs.

The royal couple ruled over the Phaeacians—a people with no cares in the world. They dwelt far from other humans, living in peaceful comfort, enjoying good food, fine clothes, sports, and steaming baths. The story went that they had a distant kin relationship with the gods, and their lifestyle, at least, reflected the connection. Until the arrival of Odysseus, it is not clear they had ever suffered. Nor did he intend pain for them, although that day would come. After a day of feasting, songs, and games (he won the discus throw), Odysseus, his hosts, and their noble guests sat in the hall. The king's blind bard, who was called Demodocus, began a song about the Trojan Horse. It was a new tale, just making the rounds, full of adventure and heroic names unfamiliar to the audience, for they had heard only secondhand about the war. Demodocus, staring with blank eyes, became enlightened by the Muses, goddesses of his art. He plucked the lyre and sang the story just as though he had himself been present at the city's fall and had seen everything. Vivid recollections flooded through Odysseus like a shock. He melted into tears. Only now did he reveal to the Phaeacians that he was a character out of the very tale they were so intently listening to, the warrior who had plotted the destruction of Troy. For the rest of the night, until Dawn rose from her bed, Odysseus, like a bard himself, held the Phaeacians spellbound with the long, thrilling story of his travels and his woes.

The next day, a fair wind was blowing, although it didn't matter. The Phaeacians had magic ships that could take any passenger anywhere, skimming along at the speed of birds. A select young crew took Odysseus, and all the many gifts the nobles had given him, straight to Ithaca. While he slumbered, they gently lifted him and his possessions onto the shore, and sped back.

That is when their kindness for Odysseus brought them pain. Poseidon waited until the returning ship was in sight of the Phaeacians' harbor, and then struck it with his trident, turning ship and crew into solid rock. The Phaeacians, watching their sons and brothers from the beach, were overwhelmed with horror and grief. No longer would they escort strangers, or live at ease. You can still see the boat-shaped small island near the old landing place that the Phaeacians abandoned when they moved away not long thereafter. Or so the sailors will tell you, the ones who claim to have traveled that far.

## 56.   END OF AN ERA

Now the net of destruction for the suitors was being drawn closed by the will of the gods. Odysseus, transformed to look like an old beggar, was guided by Athena to take shelter with his old swineherd, Eumaios, while he devised a way to get into the palace and assess the situation. Without revealing his identity, he listened carefully as Eumaios told how the unruly young men were taking away his fattest pigs and dining every day on pork in the palace of his absent master, never even offering proper sacrifice as they feasted. Odysseus kept silent, but in his heart he was already plotting to bring revenge down on their heads. As the aged servant continued, it was obvious he had remained loyal to Odysseus—or at least to the memory of the king, as the swineherd imagined he had long ago perished.

"He is dead and gone now. He treated me kindly, like an older brother. I choke up every time I think about him. I still miss him. So does his wife and father and son," said Eumaios. "You should see the boy—fine and tall, just like his father was when he was younger. But now some god has driven him crazy. He got a notion to head off to Pylos, just like that, and now those suitors are getting ready to ambush him. They want to snuff out the master's line on this island. Enough of this, though. Tell me, old man, what brings you to Ithaca?" Odysseus thought quickly and invented a plausible story about being a hard-luck Cretan rover. He even mentioned having heard Odysseus was alive and on his way home. All the time, though, his heart was wrenched with the thought that his boy Telemakhos was in danger.

Meanwhile, Athena had been busy. She went to Sparta and appeared late at night to Telemakhos, who was a guest still in the palace of Menelaos. "Head home quickly, before it's too late," she urged him, "and know this: the suitors have laid a trap for you. Sail in under the cover of darkness, and make sure to avoid the strait between Ithaca and Samê." So the young man roused his companion, Nestor's son, and they took their leave early next morning, but not before accepting fine gifts from Helen and her husband—a silver bowl for mixing wine and a beautiful robe for whichever woman he would marry. "When I get home, I wish I could tell my father Odysseus how well you have treated us," said Telemakhos. As he finished speaking, an omen appeared. An eagle, seemingly out of nowhere, flashed down and snatched a white goose from the palace courtyard, then flew away. It was Helen who interpreted the sign. "Just as this fat goose was seized, so suddenly Odysseus will come home and seize the suitors for their hubris. Mark my words." Encouraged by her prophecy, the young men mounted a chariot and headed back to Pylos by the sea.

A day later, Telemakhos cast off and set sail for home from Nestor's land. They made good time, sailing by the stars, with a fresh wind from the southeast. As Athena had warned him, he avoided the strait that led to the harbor closer to town, and instead put in at a little-used cove on the far side of Ithaca. The crew made their way home over the hill while Telemakhos, wishing to lie low for a day, headed to the hut of his friend, the swineherd. The old man was having his breakfast with his new acquaintance, the beggar. He leapt up in amazement when he saw Telemakhos at the door, and wept tears of joy, just like a father whose son has been away a long time. The first thing the young man wanted to know was whether his mother had remained steadfast. Eumaios reassured him that no suitor had taken her away. Then, while they all sat down and ate together, Telemakhos told the stranger about his dilemma. Odysseus reacted with anger against the arrogant interlopers, although he had to pretend he had no personal stake in the crisis. Afterward, Telemakhos dispatched Eumaios to the palace, to let Penelope know that her son had returned. As soon as the swineherd left, Athena appeared to Odysseus just outside the open door behind his son's back. Excusing himself, he went out to meet with her. With a touch of her golden wand, she made him younger and taller, restored the blue-black sheen to his beard and hair, and clothed him in a clean tunic. Telemakhos was terrified when Odysseus reentered the hut. He averted his eyes, in case this divine apparition might blind him, and cried out, "Have mercy on me. Surely you are one of the gods!" The hero replied, "I am no god—why liken me to them? It's me, your father. Because of me you have been suffering." He kissed his son, at last allowing himself to cry. Telemakhos, however, could not believe him. Some god was deceiving him, just to make his life more bitter. Only after Odysseus explained how Athena had transformed him did he embrace his father, and the two wept for a long time, keening like hawks robbed of their nestlings.

The final act began. Together, father and son made a plan. Telemakhos was to mingle with the suitors, then casually remove all the shields and weapons from the great hall, saying he was concerned the smoke from the hearth would damage them, or that there was a danger they might get drunk and start a fight. Only two spears and two swords would be left, for their own use. Odysseus, meanwhile, would resume his disguise, begging throughout the crowd of feasting men. At his signal, they would attack. With Athena's help, victory would be theirs. For now no one else was to know that Odysseus was home—not even his wife.

Inside the palace, the suitors had learned that Telemakhos had safely escaped their ambush, and they suspected that he had enlisted allies abroad. Some talked of killing him openly, right away. Others urged restraint, at least until they could determine the gods' will. With a mother's intuition, Penelope felt the danger, and she dis-

tracted the suitors by appearing before them and berating the ring-
leader, Antinoos.

Accompanied by Eumaios, Odysseus approached the palace. No
one recognized him, for Athena had made him look like an old man
once more. But as they came near the great hall, an old dog, scruffy
and flea-bitten, noticed the beggar. His tail started wagging, and his
ears stood up. Only he was too old and sick from neglect to move even
a little way from the dung heap where he was lying. It was Argos,
whom Odysseus had been training as a puppy when he was called to
Troy. This was his first sight of his master in twenty years, and his last.
Odysseus did not dare to greet his old hound, lest someone see. So he
moved past, and that moment Argos passed away.

As he had expected, Odysseus was abused by the crowd in his own
house. He put up with the taunts, the cow hooves and stools that were
hurled at him. The disrespect helped him pinpoint the worst among
this lawless bunch. So unruly were they, however, that he avoided
Penelope in their presence. She had heard from Eumaios about the
beggar's stories, including his news about Odysseus, and she wanted
to meet him.

That night, when all had gone to sleep, they sat together by the
hearth. The torches flickered on the walls. Half in shadow, Odysseus
spoke first, praising the queen, for her fidelity, he said, was famous.
Penelope answered in desperation: she did not know how long she
could hold out, with her husband gone so long, and suitors clamoring
for her to wed. She was running out of tactics to delay them. She questioned the beggar further about his claim to have seen Odysseus. He
replied with complete accuracy about the clothes that Odysseus had
been wearing that day long ago, even down to the details of his decorated tunic clasp. Whether this gave her a sign or not, Penelope felt a
growing closeness with this strange old man, and she told him of her
recent dream—that Odysseus, in the form of an eagle, had attacked
her pet geese and made her sad. "That was a good omen," replied the
beggar. "Your husband is very near."

The serving woman Eurykleia was called to wash his feet. As she
bathed him, she recognized the mark of her master's identity, a long
scar from a wound he had received at age fourteen when he was visiting his maternal grandfather, Autolykos. This man, Real Wolf,
was the one who had given him the name "Odysseus" as an infant.
So it was right that he later presided over Odysseus' initiation into
the world of manhood, his first boar hunt, on Mt. Parnassus. The

boar had gashed the boy's leg so deeply that the scar stayed with him for life. This was what the old nurse saw, but before she could cry out, Odysseus clamped her mouth shut and pressed his stout hand over it. "Not yet," he hoarsely whispered. Penelope never noticed the minor disturbance, for Athena diverted her attention just at that moment.

The next day, Penelope put into action the plan that Athena had inspired her to carry out. She had already told the beggar about this contest of skill the night before. Whoever succeeded in stringing the great curved bow of Odysseus (the one he had left behind when he went to war) and shooting through the shaft holes of twelve iron axe-heads would be the man Penelope would marry. Sad but determined, she carried the polished bow out of a cedar-fragrant storeroom. Eumaios shed a tear on seeing it. Telemakhos made the announcement of the contest and added, "I will try it first, just to see if I can match my father." He struggled three times to bend the curved bow and place the twisted string around its tips. The fourth time he might have done it had not Odysseus signaled him with a movement of his head to let go. Next Lêodês, the man who acted as augur for the suitors, gave it a try and failed, as did some of the younger men. Eurymakhos and Antinoos, the leaders, were about to make their attempts, when they thought better of it. "Tomorrow is a feast of Apollo the Bowman," said Antinoos. "We'll sacrifice the best goats to him, make our prayers, and then he may give one of us the strength to string this."

At that moment Odysseus chose to interject, "Let me try." Gales of laughter burst around him. "It is not enough that we let you stay and enjoy our company, you dirty old beggar. Now you want to join in our fun!" said one. Another added, "The wine must have gone to your head. Watch out! You know what it did to the Centaurs." Antinoos slipped in a threat as well: "Careful, or we'll ship you down to old King Ekhetos. Nobody comes back from his place." But Penelope, who had been watching the proceedings, spoke up. "It's not fitting to mock a guest in our house. Do you really think this man would marry me, even if he strings the bow? I'm sure he hardly wants that." And so she shamed the suitors into giving Odysseus a chance.

As the suitors joked and made snide remarks, they did not notice that the swineherd and other servants, whom Odysseus had finally let in on his secret, quietly were locking the doors of the great hall. The hero inspected his bow with care, every inch of it, which only caused the suitors to laugh more. "A connoisseur of weapons, this vagabond!" someone shouted. Then, standing at his full height, with the bow locked in position by his leg, Odysseus easily strung it. Like a musician, he plucked it, and it gave out a clear note, like a swallow's. In the distance, Zeus rumbled with his thunder, an ominous sign that made the suitors turn pale. In one swift movement the beggar notched an arrow, crouched by a nearby stool, and shot straight through the course of axe-heads, lined up in a row. "My strength is still with me," he observed coolly, and before anyone in the crowd could manage to speak, he said to Telemakhos. "It's time to cook these suitors their supper." Leaping to the doorsill, his cloak thrown aside, Odysseus shouted out, "Now for another target!" He took aim and shot Antinoos, the meanest suitor, clean through the throat, as he was taking a drink from a golden wine cup. The others were more angry than alarmed, for they still thought it had been an accident, that the old man meant to hit something else. They soon realized it was not. "Dogs, you thought I'd never return! You ruin my house and court my wife, and all the while I was alive," Odysseus said in a low growl. "Death has come for you now—all of you."

By the time the slaughter had ended, all one hundred and eight suitors lay dead. Telemakhos proved himself a warrior in that fight, his first battle. The faithful servants bravely joined in. Athena, too, did her part, in the guise of Mentor, Odysseus' old friend. Holding high her *aigis*, the magical device that strikes fear into all who see it, she caused the suitors to stampede like maddened cattle.

While the great hall was put in order and purified, Eurykleia, the old nurse of Odysseus, hurried off to tell Penelope the news, how her husband had come home and taken his revenge. The long-suffering wife of the hero did not believe her. She insisted it had been some god who, finally fed up with the suitors' hubris, had visited the palace to punish them all.

Penelope wanted to test him. If this was truly her husband, not some impostor, there was one secret only he would know. She came to the hall and sat opposite the stranger, staying silent so long that Telemakhos, who was standing nearby, exploded in exasperation, "What other woman among the Greeks would act like this?" But she took her time. Odysseus, meanwhile, gave orders for the servants to make it seem as if a wedding feast were taking place, with music inside the house, lest the kin of the suitors learn too soon what had happened and begin the inevitable vendetta. So it was to a background of marriage songs that Penelope finally spoke. "Yes, and once the master is bathed and clothed, see to it, Eurykleia, that his bed is made, the covers spread, and blankets put on it—that one just outside the bedroom, the bed he crafted himself."

Odysseus was taken off guard. "Move my bed? Who did it? Not even a god could budge it. You know very well our marriage bed is built from living wood. I made it so the main support was an ancient olive trunk, growing up like a thick column inside the bedchamber. To move that bed, you'd have to cut the tree right at the base. Who did it?"

At this her knees gave way. Only Odysseus could have known this detail. "I'm sorry. So many have come, and I was afraid. We have suffered so much, being apart for twenty years. I thought maybe a god had come to cause more trouble. But now you have persuaded me." Wife and husband embraced, as welcome to each other as land is to the sailor who lands safely from the churning sea. That night Athena held back the horses of the Dawn, to prolong the couple's talk and lovemaking, as they deserved.

Odysseus told his wife of all his adventures, not omitting the parts about Circe and Calypso. He let her know, even now, that he would one day make a final journey, as Teiresias had ordered, to a place farthest from the sea. He would have to walk inland with an oar carried over his shoulder, until he reached a spot where the inhabitants, not knowing about boats, asked, "Why do you bear a winnowing fan?" There he would build a shrine to the god Poseidon, his long-standing enemy. After that, he'd come home and grow old peacefully among his people and die a peaceful death free of the waves. But that was far off. Now there were more pressing needs.

The next day, he went into the countryside to find his aged father. Laertes was overjoyed to see him home, even though Odysseus rather cruelly kept up the pretense that he was in fact somebody else when he first came upon the poor old man. Soon after that, Odysseus had to face the families of the men he killed. It was the proudest moment of Laertes' life. He saw his son and grandson, at the height of their war strength, ranged against their enemies—his bloodline in full flower. Only the intervention of Athena, sent at the last minute by command of Zeus, kept the feud from blowing up into a full-scale war. Both sides ultimately went away in peace. And as their spirits descended to the underworld that same day, the suitors could tell all the generation of heroes gathered there—Achilles, Ajax, and the rest—how the wily king of Ithaca had returned to his steadfast wife. "Lucky Odysseus," sighed the ghost of Agamemnon. "You were remembered well in your own home. The gods gave you—not me—an excellent woman. Now the immortals will remember you both in a splendid song for the rest of time." And that was how it all turned out.

# FURTHER READING

The primary texts of the ancient writers mentioned in the Introduction are available in Penguin Classics (translation only) or in the Loeb Classical Library of Harvard University Press (Greek or Latin text plus translation). In addition, the following modern anthologies and interpretations of Greek myth are recommended:

Bonnefoy, Y., ed., *Mythologies* (Chicago, 1991).

Bremmer, J., *Interpretations of Greek Mythology* (London, 1987).

Brown, N., *Hermes the Thief* (New York, 1969).

Burkert, W., *Greek Religion,* trans. J. Raffan (Cambridge, Mass., 1985).

Buxton, R., *Imaginary Greece: The Contexts of Mythology* (Cambridge, 1994).

Detienne, M., *The Creation of Greek Mythology,* trans. M. Cook (Chicago, 1986).

————, and J.-P. Vernant, *Cunning Intelligence in Greek Culture and Society* (Sussex, 1978).

Dowden, K., *The Uses of Greek Mythology* (London, 1992).

Edmunds, L., *Myth in Homer: A Handbook,* 2nd ed. (Highland Park, N. J., 1993).

————, ed., *Approaches to Greek Myth* (Baltimore, 1990).

Gantz, T., *Early Greek Myth: A Guide to Literary and Artistic Sources* (Baltimore, 1993).

Graf, F., *Greek Mythology: An Introduction,* trans. T. Marier (Baltimore, 1993).

Harrison, J., *Prolegomena to the Study of Greek Religion,* 3rd ed. (Cambridge, 1922; repr. Princeton, 1991).

Kirk, G., *The Nature of Greek Myths* (Harmondsworth, 1974).

Leach, M., and J. Fried, *Funk and Wagnall's Standard Dictionary of Folklore, Mythology, and Legend* (New York, 1949; repr. San Francisco, 1984).

Littleton, C., *The New Comparative Mythology: An Anthropological Assessment of the Theories of Georges Dumézil*, 3rd ed. (Berkeley, 1982).

March, J., *Cassell Dictionary of Classical Mythology* (London, 1998).

Martin, R., *The Language of Heroes: Speech and Performance in the Iliad* (Ithaca, N.Y., 1989).

————, ed., *Bulfinch's Mythology* (New York, 1991).

Nagy, G., *The Best of the Achaeans: Concepts of the Hero in Archaic Greek Poetry*, 2nd ed. (Baltimore, 1999).

————, *Greek Mythology and Poetics* (Ithaca, N.Y., 1990).

Parada, C., *Genealogical Guide to Greek Mythology* (Jonsered, 1993).

Powell, B., *Classical Myth*, 2nd ed. (New York, 1994).

Puhvel, J., *Comparative Mythology* (Baltimore, 1987).

Reid, J., *The Oxford Guide to Classical Mythology in the Arts: 1300–1990* (Oxford, 1993).

Rose, H., *Handbook of Greek Mythology* (New York, 1959).

Shapiro, H., *Myth Into Art: Poet and Painter in Classical Greece* (London, 1994).

Sourvinou-Inwood, C., *'Reading' Greek Culture: Texts and Images, Rituals and Myths* (Oxford, 1991).

Stoneman, R., *Greek Mythology: An Encyclopedia of Myth and Legend* (London, 1991).

Tyrrell, W., and F. Brown, *Athenian Myths and Institutions: Words in Action* (Oxford, 1991).

Vernant, J.-P., *Myth and Society in Ancient Greece*, trans J. Lloyd (Atlantic Highlands, N.J., 1980).

Veyne, P., *Did the Greeks Believe in Their Myths?*, trans. P. Wissing (Chicago, 1988).

Woodford, S., *The Trojan War in Ancient Art* (Ithaca, N.Y., 1993).

# ABOUT THE AUTHOR

**Richard P. Martin** teaches Greek and Latin Literature at Stanford University, where he holds the Antony and Isabelle Raubitschek Chair in Classics. A native of Boston, he received his B.A. (in classics and Celtic literature), M.A., and Ph.D. (in classical philology) from Harvard University. He worked for several years as a general assignment reporter for the *Boston Globe*. Before taking up his current position in California, he taught for eighteen years at Princeton University.

Professor Martin is the author of *Healing, Sacrifice, and Battle: Amechania and Related Concepts in Early Greek Poetry* and *The Language of Heroes: Speech and Performance in* The Iliad. In addition, he has edited *Bulfinch's Mythology,* published numerous articles on Greek poetry and myth, and with a team at Stanford produced an Internet version of Homer's *Odyssey.* His scholarly interests include ancient and modern poetry and poetics, Irish language and literature, modern Greek culture, and the study of oral epic traditions worldwide. He has traveled extensively in Greece to see firsthand the places associated with the myths that he retells here.